THE GOSPEL OF ELIANA

Mayet Ligad Yuhico

For Bons,
Bodi, Eric, Mathew, David
Lily, Natalie, Paolo and Anna

uthor's Notes

The Gospel of Eliana is a novel of history and imagination. It is not an actual gospel, nor does it belong to a religious canon or seek to define doctrine. While the events and characters are imagined, they are inspired by real histories, enduring questions, and the hopes of people navigating faith, doubt, and the enduring power of love in a world both distant and familiar – from the first century to our own.

Contents

Chapter 1

E liana

Memphis, Egypt

In the third year of Gaius Claudius (AD 43)

His towering presence made the Bedouins cower. Lips and elbows pressed into the sand, they dared not move, dared not breathe. Would they be trapped like this until death? Was this the day it would come?

"The One," they whispered, and bowed lower.

They called him The One, a figure already legendary around Giza. Blue-eyed, light-skinned, taller than most Egyptians, he spoke Greek without the faintest trace of an accent. No one would guess he was Judean.

"Eliana."

His gaze fixed on her, his voice cutting through the desert air.

If Yeshua were alive, he would have been amused at the absurd drama. Thaddeus—once the meekest, kindest of the Apostles—had changed. Now the Bedouins called him The One. His presence fit the name. All of them had changed since Yeshua's death.

"Yes, Apostle Thaddeus," she said, rising.

"Bring the scrolls. See if they are yours."

The desert tribes—the Bedouin, as the townspeople called them—brought sheaves of parchment to her feet.

She knelt and slipped a reed stalk from her robe. It was her favorite tool—uninked, sharpened to a fine point. With it, she lifted the brittle sheets, separating the first two leaves. One glance was enough. On the top page, the word Eliana—

was clear, with three tiny teardrops marked in the upper corner.

"They are mine," she whispered.

"Nabil," Thaddeus said. "Bring the men closer."

"*I*—yes." Nabil stepped forward, his voice as firm as the Apostle's. He moved with composed, confident grace, his Egyptian heritage evident in the calm strength of his bearing. "*Na erthei pio konta*—come, stand before Apostle Thaddeus."

She never stopped marveling that Greek ruled even here, centuries after Alexander.

"Who ordered you to hide these in the pyramids?" Nabil's hand slid to his sword. Steel rasped as he drew it, the sound scraping across her nerves.

The men crumpled to the ground, their shoulders shaking.

"Two men from Yehudi," one sobbed. "From Judea."

Her breath caught. The scrolls had been stolen from her home in Kfar Nahum only a moon ago. Who in her village could have betrayed her? She had written those pages to keep memory alive—to record the wonders of Yeshua's final years. They were never meant for other eyes. Who else had read them now?

Her stomach twisted. Acid rose to her throat. She forced herself to look away, toward the vast tombs looming against the desert sky. Whispers called them cursed, haunted. No one ventured near these magnificent tombs. A perfect place to hide her writings.

A scream pulled her back. Thaddeus's sword pressed to the throat of a kneeling man.

"Speak of this to no one," he said in Greek.

Then he turned to Nabil. "Call the guards who keep the tombs."

Nabil strode off, returning moments later with two older men. Their sand-stained robes marked them as caretakers. One felt faintly familiar. Had she glimpsed him once, long ago, at the edge of a crowd when Yeshua taught in Judea?

"*Eirēnē soi, adelphe Pamenche*—peace be with you, brother Pamenche," Thaddeus greeted.

"*Eirēnē soi, apostole*—peace be with you, Apostle," the man replied.

"You once saved Maryam and Yusef," Thaddeus said softly. "They trusted you with their lives. Thank you for warning us."

"It is an honor, The One," Pamenche added. "We saw the Bedouins hide the scrolls. We kept them safe and never let them out of our sight."

"Thank you. You have done well." Thaddeus placed his hand on their heads, then traced a small cross on each forehead. To each, he whispered words too soft for her to hear. Was he murmuring a prayer meant only for them?

The guards bowed and withdrew toward the pyramids. Thaddeus's eyes found hers.

"Come, Eliana. I would like to speak with you. Follow me."

He strode ahead, his robe flashing against the sand. Eliana hurried after him, her gaze catching on the stitchery at his hem: a vertical and horizontal line intersecting, two twigs bound as one, like the beams of a cross. She had seen others wear the symbol—stitched on robes or hung as pendants—in many places they had visited the day before.

But where was he leading her?

To the animals.

Camels rested in the sand, and he gently patted one, feeding it dried leaves.

She smiled faintly. Even Yeshua, when seeking counsel, would find Thaddeus among animals. The Apostle and his beasts—always at peace together.

He turned as she approached. "Biti Eliana, the hour is short. One of your scrolls must reach Maryam of Magdala. She is here in Egypt. Nabil will guide you."

She leaned close, whispering in Hebrew. "Ger. He's a stranger, Dod Yudah."

When they were alone, formality fell away. In his eyes, she was still the child of yesterday—Biti Eliana—and he remained Dod Yudah, her father's beloved friend.

His eyes softened. "Not a stranger. He traveled with us from Kfar Nahum, thirty days beside us. He was there in Judea with Yeshua. You were too young to remember. But I trust him with my life—and so would your father."

"But what of you? You will be alone, if anything should happen—"

He laid his roughened hands upon her shoulders and bent to kiss her brow. "Yeshua will protect us. Go with Nabil before the sun sets. I will meet you in the Nabataean Kingdom. He knows where."

He clapped sharply. One of the camels raised its head. He mounted, and with another clap, it rose to its full height.

"My eyes shall find you again, my child," he said, and with a wave, rode into the swirling sand.

Her protest died on her lips. Nabil stood beside her, already gathering the scrolls from her arms.

"It is time," he said.

She turned reluctantly to her own camel. Its great eyes watched her with calm expectation.

"Oh, Samuel," she murmured. "Have you eaten?"

"Yes. The Bedouin fed them. Now we must go." Nabil placed the scrolls back into her arms.

She slipped the papyri into her pera, a leather satchel slung across her shoulders.

The wind picked up, whirling sand around her. She turned, hoping for one last glimpse, but he was gone.

"The khamseen wind brings fierce storms. We must hurry," Nabil urged.

She nodded. The sun burned low, its white fire softening into orange. She shivered beneath her robe. Time to leave this haunted place.

The guards had vanished into the tombs, the trembling Bedouins with them. She whispered a prayer that their lives were spared.

Would her writings bring danger to those who carried them? The thought gnawed at her. But it was better to trust them to faithful hands than risk defilement.

What would Yeshua say? Likely, he would tease her compulsion to write his words. A tear slid down her cheek. He had been gone ten years, and still the world reeled from his death.

Her scrolls were her testament. Her gift. The only way she knew to keep his voice alive.

Chapter 2

S imone

The Maignon Building, New York City

Tuesday, October 17—7 p.m.

Even the air felt cooler at this height, thinner, purer.

Simone balanced in fourth position—one foot angled ahead, one arm lifted, the other poised upright. Then she leapt from the parapet, landing neatly on the ledge. Years of ballet training had not abandoned her.

She patted the dust from her pants and leaned against the stone, gazing down. Cars rushed past, sirens wailed, and the food trucks below were still busy with late-night diners. Delancey Street had become a mecca for North African food—a city of cuisines stacked corner to corner. She imagined cumin and coriander rising through the night air, sharpened by the scent of mint and cilantro.

Her mind drifted. Falafel with her father in Jerusalem—the crunch of chickpeas fried golden, eaten off a dingy street cart. She sighed. She missed them.

"Oh yes, before I forget," she murmured. Dropping to her knees, she drew a plate from beside her. "Here you are. Happy birthday, Pops."

Baklava, his favorite.

"I made this from scratch," she whispered. "And yes, I cut the dough into a dozen little pieces before baking."

She placed a candle in the center, lit it, and hummed softly. A year had passed before she could admit it: her parents would never sing to her again. She blew out the flame and watched the smoke curl upward.

The pastry tasted sweet, but not enough to lift her spirits. Lights from the Empire State Building blinked red, pink, yellow, and green—confetti colors her mother adored, though her father always called them tacky. "But who cares what they think, right? They're not here," she shouted into the wind.

She tossed the plate into a trash can. No one would condemn her for it.

Being an orphan was unbearable—yet freeing. She no longer carried the weight of their fame, ambitions, follies, and secrets. But there were nights, like this one, when she wanted to step from the ledge and take those secrets with her.

Her father had warned her often: the truths they kept, if revealed, could tear the world apart—pit father against son, brother against sister, topple long-held beliefs into dust. Was it wisdom that made him say it, or ego? Did he believe himself one of the keepers of civilization?

Her parents were flawed, but they had passed down one certainty: never back down. They had fought for their secrets until the end.

But was it her fight? The world was moving faster, changing beyond their methods, their age.

She stepped down from the ledge, steady now. A year without them had passed—long enough. It was time. Time to uncover what had been hidden for two thousand years.

The elevator doors opened, carrying her to the floor below. Her father had unlocked it for her every birthday, and since his death, she held the key herself.

She slipped it into the door and entered. Paintings her father, grandfather, and ancestors had gathered lined the room, resting on centuries-old easels.

Da Vinci. Van Gogh. Warhol. Each year her favorites changed, but one truth never did—the masters struck her like a force of nature. Silence stole her breath, colors exploded behind her eyes, her chest tightened, and she could not move.

Tonight, she stood before her favorite: a Da Vinci study of the Mona Lisa. Not the whole painting—just the face, repeated five times. The eyes caught her. Da Vinci had shifted the light, adjusted the tones, searching, never satisfied. She loved it for that—proof of his struggle, his humanity.

When her pulse steadied, she reached behind the frame. From its back she drew out a sheaf of rolled papers, copies made to match the originals her father had guarded.

She unrolled them. Dried papyrus leaves stared back, the English translations clipped alongside. At the top, in the Syriac-Estrangela language stood the word Eliana—

ܐܠܝܐ

Her name. From her earliest memory, she had known the documents as the Gospel of Eliana.

Three teardrops marked the corner. Then beside it, a single letter—

ꝏ

No scholar had ever explained them, so she had accepted them as the writer's mark, the equivalent of S in the Latin alphabet.

Her father had read from these pages every birthday. Tonight, she did the same.

Aila, Nabataean Kingdom

In the third year of Gaius Caesar (AD 40)

I remember that night.

It was my duty to wash the feet of the Apostles. But Yeshua took the basin from me and said he would do it.

I let him.

I wanted to serve food from the house of Yosef of Arimathea, our host. But Yeshua insisted on simpler fare—stewed lamb, unleavened bread, olives, wine.

For once, all the Apostles were gathered. Wine was poured, stories told, laughter shared. His smile always lightened the room.

Two days later, we faced death—Yeshua's and Yudah's. The earth shook daily, and the skies stayed dark. Roman soldiers fled. We Judeans were left to grieve alone.

I was only fifteen, far from home in Yerushalayim. I longed for Kfar Nahum, for our house near the waters of Yam Kinneret.

But my father, Shimon, ordered me to prepare the herbs for Yudah's burial. I could not look at him, knowing of the betrayal.

"What about Yeshua?" I asked. "Who will care for him?"

"Yudah has no one," he said.

I obeyed, though my heart rebelled. Even if heaven itself should fall, I vowed—I will see Yeshua.

Did Eliana ever imagine her words, meant for her eyes alone, scattered through centuries for others to gather?

A vibration at Simone's collar startled her. Nic. She ignored the first nine calls, but on the tenth, she blinked twice, activating her neuro-lenses. His face hovered before her.

"Hey, Simone," Nic said. "Aren't you coming? You said you were returning—deliveries are piling up."

"Oh, okay, Nic. I'll be there soon."

"You sure you're okay?" His voice softened.

"See you," she said, blinking the image away. The birthday celebration was over. It was time to return to Harper Art Institute.

The elevator was slow. "Come on," she whispered, tapping her foot. When the doors opened at last, she found Filigree—the doorman, Eliziano Filigroso—still at his post.

"Ms. Harper, need me to call a cab?"

"It's fine, Mr. Filigree." She smiled, warmed by his presence. She reminded herself to bring him cookies soon.

"I guess that's your ride," he said, nodding to the curb.

"Thanks for being here," she told him, and his smile followed her into the car.

The driver greeted her as she buckled in. She groaned inwardly—she'd ordered a driverless ride. Another human she didn't need. But she stayed quiet, leaning back.

Crowds surged in the streets. She counted absently—two hundred, then stopped.

"Gallery Week," the driver muttered.

"Aaaaah." She nodded. Always parties in the nearby studios, spilling into the night. Frenetic, unstoppable. She closed her eyes, drifting into darkness until a jolt woke her—revellers thumping against the car's sides.

"Drunkards," the driver cursed.

She exhaled and glanced up. "Take me to Basement 3, please."

The subterranean passageway stirred her pulse. Darkness never frightened her—it thrilled her. This was where treasures arrived.

Two unfamiliar vans were parked near the entrance. She leaned forward. "Stop here."

The basement had been her father's obsession. He had unloaded crates himself, directing traffic, eyes alight as each new painting was revealed. She could still see him pacing the rows, calling colleagues, debating late into the night—a man obsessed with the art pieces he guarded.

Now the air was still. She froze as a figure stepped from one of the vans. Broad shoulders wrapped in tailored fabric. Black hair, gleaming under the lights. A voice, low and unmistakable.

Her breath caught.

Was that Xavier?

Chapter 3

X avier
Harper Art Institute, New York City
Tuesday, October 17—8 p.m.

He checked his wristwatch, its subtle glow the only light in an underground loading bay that felt more like a tomb than a garage.

"Stop here," he said.

The van rolled to a halt. Xavier stepped out and walked towards the entrance.

A US postal truck idled in front of the steel doors. Two men were hauling packages from its cargo bay—fast, efficient, almost military in their rhythm.

Then came the alarm, a deafening sound reverberating off the concrete walls.

"New protocols," a security officer barked. "Step away from the doors. Place all deliveries on the side."

The postal workers froze, exchanged a glance, then roughly dropped the parcels onto the floor.

"Your security sucks," one of them shouted from the van. "We don't have an hour to bring it to the side!"

"Man, really? You're just unloading them this way? Fuckers!" the security man yelled.

He chuckled. New Yorkers behaved in such funny ways. He walked towards the scattered packages and crouched to get them.

"Professor Jang, it's you!" a guard called out. "Santino here. Leave that to me. Are there any deliveries for Ms. Harper today?"

"Santino, you have a lot of work. I can bring the two packages to Simone myself."

"Oh, sorry, Professor Jang. New rules. Only we can bring deliveries to the twentieth floor. Everything has to go through here now."

"Wow, that's big. A new one?" Xavier asked.

"The Hubble," Santino said, rolling his eyes. "As ugly as that telescope. Makes our work harder, what with all these deliveries."

"Let me get my packages from the van then," he said.

He went to the back of the van, opened the door, and lowered two wooden crates to the ground. Each was as tall as his chest and wide enough to span his entire body.

As he turned back, another security guard stepped forward.

"Whoa, those are big boys!" Santino said. "Let me help you with that."

Together, they carried the wooden crates to the Hubble. When the boxes disappeared inside the machine, Xavier felt his shoulders ease; he felt his whole body relax.

"By the way, where've you been? Haven't seen you in a month. Oh, wait, hang on," Santino said, heading toward a wall of numbered lockers.

He stopped at one marked "OFFICIAL," rummaged through its contents, and retrieved an envelope. Jogging back, a little breathless, he handed it over.

"Here it is. Ms. Simone told me to give it to you if you ever dropped by," Santino said, his face red from the extra chore.

"Thank you, Santino," Xavier said softly. A letter, at last. For a year, most of his deliveries had gone unopened.

"I'm afraid I have to tell you to step away from the Hubble, Professor Jang," Santino added in a more formal tone. "Time for your packages to go through."

"Of course, and thanks for your help, Santino," he said, distracted by the letter.

He turned the envelope over in his hands, tracing Simone's distinctive cursive—graceful, deliberate. A hopeful sign.

He watched the crates slide into the Hubble's inner chamber. How could Simone react when she saw what was inside? After a year of silence, he realized one truth—he knew nothing about Simone Harper.

His mission for this trip to New York was done. Or was it?

"*Sia fatta la tua volontà*—Thy Will Be Done."

He made the sign of the cross and walked into the darkness of the underground lot, the sound of the Hubble humming faintly behind him.

Chapter 4

Tarquin

Harper Art Institute, New York City

Tuesday, October 17—8:30 p.m.

Tarquin stepped deeper into the shadows of the parking garage and clicked on a small flashlight. He reached into his right pocket and pressed a button; total darkness was dispelled. He was safe at last.

He pulled out a narrow black box and flipped it open. Two tiny metallic insects were inside. He tapped them lightly, and their eyes glowed green.

From another pocket, he drew a pair of glasses and slid them to his face. One more tap on the insects' back, and they lifted from the box. A slow humming emanated from the flapping wings, indicating they were ready to fly. Tapping the left lens of his glasses turned the screen into a grid; with another tap, the insects flew higher.

He had spent a week in Rome shadowing Xavier Jang. As the head of the Vatican Museum, Xavier's activities were easily traceable. He was in his office from eight in the morning and would linger there all day, meeting with different people.

In just one week, he had dined twice with Pope Lucas and once with his brother Mathew, a Cardinal of the Vatican and the Pope's closest confidant.

When word reached Tarquin that Xavier was transporting several works belonging to Pope Lucas to New York, the directive was immediate: track them.

Now here he was, in the depths of the Harper Art Institute, following the trail to its end. Had he left the Vatican treasures in this basement? And why of all places did he deliver them to Simon Harper's address?

"Target set. Come on, boys, do your work," Tarquin said. The two tiny flying robots lifted off and glided toward the still-open doorway into which the packages had vanished. It mimicked real insects, and he shuddered at how disturbingly authentic they were.

Nano surveillance had been outlawed for a decade. He could go to prison for doing this, but the Obscurati reassured him that the insects were undetectable.

He touched his watch. 8:30 p.m. People worked late in this part of town.

It was the first time surveilling the Harper Art Institute. He scrolled through the names of the occupants until one name stopped him—Simone Harper.

A quick search brought up fragments of her public life: a video of Simone introducing the newest exhibition, another of her examining works of art in the Institute's restoration lab. Heir to Harper Industries, art world royalty turned recluse. A year ago, she had been a fixture at every charitable gala. Now there were no photos, no sightings of her. Why the silence?

He crouched down and adjusted the eyepiece over his right eye. Through the feed, the insects had perched on top of the wooden crates, undetected by the men carrying them. From their vantage point, he could clearly see what they saw.

He listened as Xavier exchanged a few casual words with the security guard, Santino, and then waved goodbye before disappearing into the shadows of the garage.

Why the friendly banter? Was Xavier a regular visitor to this building?

"Hey, Nic, packages for Simone. From Xavier Jang," Santino called out. "Okay, sir. Through the Hubble."

The men slid the crates into the massive scanner. No alerts sounded, and the next step of the journey was an elevator.

Tarquin waited for a beat, then tapped the sensors on his glasses. Instantly, the world shifted to the insects' point of view. The elevator's buttons glowed like small fireflies in the night. The crates were ascending—floor by floor.

Up, up, up. His pulse quickened. After weeks of pursuit, his hard work was about to pay off. What would the insects reveal this time?

Chapter 5

Simone

Harper Art Institute, New York City

Tuesday, October 17—8:30 p.m.

She stood frozen, watching Xavier walk back to the white van and drive away.

A year had passed since she had seen Xavier. She called it the 'Paris Debacle'—a fucking disaster.

Yet, there was something about seeing him that made her immobile, her pulse quickened, and a thousand colours burst behind her eyes.

The same electric surge—the one she felt when standing before a masterpiece.

Xavier Jang is a magnificent work of art.

He had lost weight, and even the finest Italian clothing couldn't hide it. The change only sharpened his tall, lean frame; his stride, once composed, now carried a restless edge.

Her gaze shifted—and caught another man observing Xavier. The stranger lifted a metallic receptacle, and insects flew around it.

She blinked twice. Her lenses activated, scanning the area. Faces flared into soft outlines across her vision. She focused on one—Nic's face.

A faint tone rang in her ear, then his voice.

"Simone?" he said, startled.

"Hey Nic," she replied, relief flooding her voice. "I'm in the basement. Check the security feeds—what's being delivered now?"

"Wait a sec..." Nic said.

"And look for the other guy, about fifty feet from the entrance. He's watching everything."

"I'm looking..." Nic said, his voice tightening.

"I'll head up there," Simone said. "Press Red Alert. Not sure if nanobots are in play. Send me the live feed, and I'll monitor too on my end."

She ran to the right side of the entrance toward a private elevator—one only her family could access. It was a security feature that her mother had insisted on installing years ago. It sparked many arguments. It was expensive, but now she was grateful for it.

An alarm began to wail through the building, echoing through the thick walls. Who was the stranger, and what did he want? Xavier? Or the Vatican packages he'd just delivered?

———◆———

She rushed to the twentieth floor, and when her elevator opened, two men greeted her.

"Ms. Harper!"

"Oh, hi, Santino. Why are you here? You said you'll be attending a rugby game for Dylan," she admonished.

"The coach had an accident, Miss Harper," Santino said. He lifted a square box that went up to his chest. "I don't know when all this became so complicated. Is it okay to put these big babies inside the Observation area? Looks like paintings. There's a letter with it," Santino said.

A plexiglass barrier was in the doorway. In its middle was a slot sized for letters and other packages.

"Can you please place the letter in the middle slot, Santino?" she said.

"Sure, Ms. Harper. I'll get back to the basement and deal with other clowns coming our way," Santino said.

There was a whoosh, and foam covered the envelope and the packages.

"Whoa," Santino said. "That always looks like a science experiment to me!"

"Hey guys, have dinner on me. I've disturbed you too much already," she said.

"Sure thing, Simone," Santino said, and waved as he walked back to the elevator.

Once Santino was gone, Simone pressed another button beside her console. The elevators to the twentieth floor sealed automatically—no one from outside could enter now.

Gone were the days when a delivery could simply be unwrapped. There were too many unknowns now—nanobots, coded worms, even microscopic eggs fused to the surfaces of the crates.

The Observatory stretched before her—a vast, white chamber where every new arrival was scanned, measured, and catalogued. Artwork and correspondence travelled through a transparent pneumatic tube, propelled by air until they reached the far end, where each piece hovered weightless, awaiting inspection by the Institute's analysts.

Footsteps echoed behind her. She turned. Nic was watching the process from a distance, his eyes following each motion with quiet fascination. Was he surveying the scene like a curator, picking up clues from what was presented in front of his eyes, and making sense of it all?

She took in his outfit and smiled. "Hard day at the office?"

Nic wore a sharply tailored business suit, clearly expensive, but his tousled hair and yellow-ombre glasses betrayed his bohemian, scholarly streak—a man balanced between art and analysis.

"I was talking with the gods at the Met," Nic said. "Submitted the loan requests for our next exhibit. Anyway, is this letter from ..." His voice faltered as he squinted at the envelope.

"Not sure who the recipient is, but Xavier Jang brought it from the Vatican," Simone replied. "Let's start with the letter. Looks clean to me. Let's turn on the wall screen."

The three walls around them were now transformed into massive displays.

"It's private correspondence, Simone. I don't have to read it," Nic protested.

"You know what," she said quietly. "I've decided—no more secrets. How long have I known you, Nic? If I can't trust you, then my life isn't worth a damn. Measure the dimensions of the envelope and the letter?"

Nic flicked a switch. A holographic grid appeared, showing the precise measurements of the letter.

"Nobody writes on stationery like this anymore," Nic murmured. "Geez, and what beautiful handwriting!"

"Note letter—five inches by five," Simone confirmed.

A mechanical arm slid from a console, unfolding the pages one by one. The soft click of digital shutters filled the room as each side was scanned and recorded.

She lifted her face and observed her assistant's expression. He was watching her instead of the screen.

"Why'd you come back?" he asked. "You didn't have to return, you know. Oh shoot, it's your father's birthday. Damn, I forgot."

"It's fine. You'll never know what people drop off at the Institute. I'm not letting you have all the fun around here." She pointed toward the glowing wall

The image was magnified until the letter filled the space, making it legible from a distance of twenty feet.

"Is that ..." Nic began.

"Yes," she said. "Pope Lucas. The current Pontiff."

"Oh wow!" he whispered.

"Let's begin," Simone said. She drew a breath and began to read.

⁓◦✢◦⁓

To Simone Harper, from Pope Lucas

They say whoever possesses a part of the Gospel of Eliana lives a cursed life, for they will never stop searching for the rest until it is complete. Yours was touched by the curse last year when we entered into your life.

But I'm dying. And all bets are off. They say the writer chooses her readers, and for millennia, this document has remained hidden. Was it the writer's intention? I think not. The time has come to reveal it.

The twenty pages came with the Mona Lisa study passed down in my family. Five pages from the Van Gogh are attached. I entrust them now to you and to Xavier.

Good luck—and Godspeed.

⸺❖⸺

"Okay, the letter is scanned and archived. Let's move to the crates," Simone said. "Let's see what Rome has sent. Unveiled, do your job."

Unveiled came to life—a machine made of millions of sand-like cells, flowing into form as its cameras aligned around the crates.

"Brown acid-free tissue paper covers both," Nic observed. "Let's separate them."

"We'll let Scissorhands handle that," Simone said.

A mechanical unit descended, two articulated tools whirring to life. They sliced through the acid-free layers with surgical precision. The paper peeled away, revealing two simple wooden boxes.

The hum of the cutters deepened as Scissorhands exposed museum-grade foam and climate buffers designed to protect the artwork as it crossed oceans from Rome to New York.

"Time to open it up, Scissorhands," Simone commanded.

The clamps fastened to the lids. With a hiss and lift—

Both of them screamed.

"Who... the Mona Lisa?" Nic whispered.

"A study, definitely," Simone replied, stepping closer.

"And that—Van Gogh?" Nic's voice trembled.

"A charcoal sketch of Café Terrace at Night. The original is in Kröller-Müller Museum in Otterlo," she said.

Simone caught Nic's awestruck expression and smiled faintly. "Please continue with your observations, Nic," she said.

"This Mona Lisa matches the Louvre version's dimensions," Nic said, already scanning. "Seventy-seven by fifty-three centimetres."

"And the weight is 8,164 grams. Exactly right," Simone added. "The panel's wooden. We'll run dendrochronology later to see if Da Vinci used oak or another type of wood."

"I can see faint sketch lines along the lower half," Nic said.

"But we could see the experimental colours here before Da Vinci did the final version in the main painting," Simone said. "He must have tested pigments before beginning the final version. Was this Da Vinci's primary board? Once the image was complete in his head, did he abandon this to work on the final piece we see at the Louvre?"

He nodded, reverent. "He worked on the Louvre painting for thirteen years. His students said he never finished it, and was still working on it till the day he died."

"The study, though, is alive," Simone said softly. "You can feel his thought process, every hesitation, and breath. He was thinking about how to complete it."

"At first glance, they look like replicas," Nic said. He stepped closer until his nose nearly brushed the wall display. "But see the differences? In Da Vinci's case—an artist notorious for leaving works unfinished—the background is not as defined as in the Louvre version. This might have been something he showed a patron before beginning the final piece. Or it could be a study from one of his students in Florence."

"And the Van Gogh?" she asked.

"He had no patron except his brother Theo," Nic said. "Van Gogh would sketch first like this, send the drawings with his letters to Theo, then paint them in oil later. This version has no patrons in the café, less silhouettes of the other buildings, the night sky in this painting is less pronounced too. There are two big stars that look like swirls?"

She turned back to the Da Vinci. She pulled a slim pen from her pocket, and a narrow beam of light fell on the model's hands. "The right thumb's hidden here," she said.

"Yeah. All fingers are visible in the Louvre portrait," Nic noted.

He stepped back two paces from the screen. Simone mirrored him, stopping midway between the two projected works. From this vantage point, she could view both studies. "But, what connects them?" she asked in a serious tone.

Nic hesitated, then cleared his throat. "Professor Harper," he said, formal and tense.

Simone grinned. "Got ya again, Nic. I was kidding—relax."

"I always get nervous when you use that professorial tone, Simone," he said, laughing, though uneasily. But his laughter did not reach his eyes. He was nervous for some reason.

Something in him had shifted. Nic was rarely rattled. She'd mentored him for years—an art historian with not only encyclopaedic knowledge about art but also a preternatural instinct for spotting fakes. They usually had the same conclusion on a work of art, but their methods differed, so she always questioned his observations.

"The front tells us half the story," Nic said. "Sometimes the back offers more clues than what is in front."

"Alright," Simone said. "Let's flip it."

In an instant, both studies were flipped, revealing the reverse sides of the studies.

"Holy Jesus," Nic said. "Are these ancient papyrus leaves?"

"Copies, definitely," she said. "We can ask Natalie from Manuscripts and Documents to verify later. But I'd bet my career it's a copy."

With deft fingers, she tapped the keys of the Unveiled and focused on the corner of the page. There were teardrops at the corner of the page. There was another distinct symbol beside the teardrops.

ܩ

"It's an ancient Syriac script," she said, tracing the character. "The letter —◻our letter M equivalent in the English language, isn't it?"

She was curious about .◻This was different from her father's collection marked with, the letter S equivalent.

"And the Van Gogh study?," she asked. "Another letter!"

܀

"I need the translation," Nic said. He returned to the console and tapped some keys. Translation boxes appeared on their wall.

"It's part of the Gospel of Eliana, given to followers of Jesus Christ," she said. "Thank God for brilliant translation tools," she sighed in relief.

"But I thought they were rumours only?" Nic asked.

"My father has been collecting works of Eliana his whole life, and this looks authentic, although we need to verify this first," she said.

(TEXT BEGINS IN TRANSLATION)

Kfar Nahum,

in the third year of Gaius Caesar (40 AD)

We were forbidden to go near his burial site. Roman soldiers stood on guard, on the orders of the Roman governor, Pontius Pilate.

By then, Pontius Pilate had washed his hands of the fate of the Judeans. He had retired to his mountaintop retreat in Masada, soaking in the Roman baths, and remained isolated for a week.

Our beloved Maryam of Nasrath told us to return to Galila. There was nothing we could do in Yerushalayim, a place of pain and betrayal for all of us.

I packed a few pieces of clothing into my satchel and slept, knowing that my father would wake me before we started for Galila.

When I opened my eyes, Maryam of Magdala stood before me, holding my cloak.

"What is it, Habibti Maryam? It's the dead of night," I said.

"Let us visit Yeshua one last time," Maryam said. "I had a dream that we should see him once more before we leave for Galila."

Women were not supposed to be seen at night, much less move about town unaccompanied by a male relative. But Maryam had a fierce temper and an unyielding character. She was as headstrong as my bull-headed father, Shimon. There was no stopping her once she had decided.

We avoided the open roads and stayed close to the houses. Darkness was our friend as we walked silently toward our destination.

Maryam stopped suddenly as we approached the tomb where Yeshua had been buried. I bumped into her and heard her sharp gasp.

Before us lay scores of Roman soldiers asleep on the ground. Still, she pressed ahead, and we proceeded toward the tomb in silence.

"Hurry," she whispered.

The great stone that blocked the entrance had been rolled aside. When we entered the tomb, there was light—but nothing to see.

"Alleluia," Maryam knelt before the empty tomb. "Yeshua has risen, just as he foretold. We must wake the Apostles. Our mission has not ended—it has only begun. He has not forgotten us. Alleluia!"

She turned to me. "Go and tell your father, Habibti Eliana. Be the first to bring him the good news."

"If Yeshua has risen, where is he?" I asked.

"He is with His Father, silly lamb," Maryam said.

"Is it not dangerous, with all the Roman soldiers nearby?" I asked.

"Yeshua will protect me," Maryam replied. "After you tell your father, go to Maryam of Nasrath and tell her the news."

"Yes," I said.

At early dawn, I ran to find my father. Knowing he was preparing for the journey back to Galila, I went to Yosef of Arimathea's shed. He was in the barn where the donkeys were kept.

"His body is not there!" I shouted. "I saw it with my own eyes—Yeshua's body is gone!"

My father stared at me in disbelief. "Then where is Yeshua's body?" he asked.

"He has risen," I said.

He dropped what he was doing and ran toward the burial place. The Roman soldiers were still asleep instead of standing guard. Maryam was waiting for us, openly weeping.

"I was crying," she said, "when a man I thought was a gardener spoke to me. He asked why I wept, and when I turned toward him, it was Yeshua."

Instead of rejoicing, my father turned on her.

"And why should I believe you?" he demanded.

"Because I saw Him," Maryam said. "He told me, Go to Galila, and I will reveal myself to you."

Just then, the Apostle Thaddeus appeared before us.

"You cannot stay here. The Roman centurions have placed a price on your heads for the soldiers injured near the tomb. Go to the place where we last shared supper with Yeshua. Go now. I will fetch Maryam, the mother of Yeshua, and meet you there," Thaddeus said.

My father took my hand, and Maryam followed close behind.

The Upper Room was one of the storerooms where servants kept pressed olive oil—the air thick with the scent of fruit and stone. It was also where the Apostles had shared their last meal with Yeshua. Few would think to search for us there.

We ran to it, seeking safety.

Soon, Maryam of Nasrath arrived with the Apostle Thaddeus. Her face bore deep grief, but her expression changed as *she entered the room. It was as though Yeshua Himself were waiting for us to gather again.*

The moment the door closed behind us, a great gust of wind rose from nowhere and sealed the room.

Then it came.

Tongues of fire appeared above our heads, and a brilliant beam of light shone down among us.

Voices burst forth—languages I had never heard before—yet I understood them all.

Through the storm of sound came a plea, not in words but in knowing. It was Yeshua, urging us to return to Galila, where he would appear next.

A new strength entered my heart. Fear fell away. I was no longer afraid of the Romans or of death. The others felt it too—I saw it in the way they lifted their faces to the light.

We did not flee from Yerushalayim like thieves in the night. We walked out openly, heads held high, leading our donkeys through the streets toward Galila. The soldiers watched us pass, but none raised a hand.

The fire had touched us.

I knew it would never leave.

The translated text faded from the screen. Simone leaned back, breath caught between centuries.

"Fascinating," Nic said.

"We can return it to the Pontiff when we're done," she said.

It felt almost providential that these studies had arrived at the Harper Art Institute on this day—her father's birthday.

Chapter 6

Eliana

Memphis, Egypt

In the third year of Gaius Claudius (AD 43)

The camel's steps had slowed as they approached Memphis. Ahead, rows of colourful, makeshift tents shimmered in the midday heat, lining up the street. Children thrust their wares toward her. She smiled at one or two of them.

"Off with you, little ones," Nabil said as he shooed the children blocking their path.

She and Nabil had been traveling for hours, and not a word had been exchanged between them.

She studied him from the corner of her eye—five years older, perhaps. Yeshua was older, too, but he was not as silent as this man. Nor as unsmiling.

She missed Yeshua and his listening ear. He was always curious about what she had to say. Even in his busiest moment, you knew he would stop, even if he was doing something.

There were times—random, piercing moments—when she felt his absence. She missed his voice, his patience, his laughter, his questions. She missed him.

Nabil's face remained stony. The silence was a welcome respite from the heat.

She turned her gaze outward. The desert gave way to the outskirts of Memphis, and they passed through a marketplace, where stalls were propped up by rough-hewn wood and shaded by cloth awnings to shelter the merchants and buyers from the blazing Egyptian sun.

She heard a jumble of languages as they passed by—Greek, Egyptian, a smattering of Aramaic or Hebrew from traveling Judeans, and Nabataean from traders. They hawked their wares, calling out to buyers—"Fresh dates, fine linen, papyrus leaves, spices!" The streets were buzzing with activity, and suddenly felt she was far, far away from her home in Kfar Nahum.

All she wanted to do was rest in her own bed. But rest had been elusive.

"Roman guards," Nabil hissed. She covered her face and bowed her head. To the Romans, she was his wife, his property—and not allowed to speak.

The uniforms were unlike those in Judea. After the defeat of Mark Antony and the pharaoh Cleopatra VII, Egypt was under Roman rule. These soldiers looked fiercer, their tempers darker and more volatile. She was used to their ways and knew she could never underestimate their cruelty.

Nabil was near a cluster of date trees at the edge of the marketplace, where the camels could rest in the shade. He helped her get down gently.

"It is near here," Nabil said. "Let us walk east, as Apostle Thaddeus instructed."

The sun was beating on her head; the fierce heat could melt stone. Her throat ached for water, but she stayed silent and followed Nabil.

At last, they reached a narrow doorway. Nabil knocked. No one answered, but they could hear voices inside.

"*Chaíre*—greetings," he called in Greek, knocking again. "Apostle Thaddeus has a message for you." The words weren't finished yet when the door opened.

"*Eirēnē soi*—peace be with you," said a woman's voice. Her eyes rested on Nabil, then lingered on Eliana. "I am Ammunet. Apostle Thaddeus sent word of your arrival. Come and enter the house of Yeshua, and may peace dwell with you."

"Is Maryam of Magdala here?" she asked.

"Come," Ammunet said softly. "She awaits you."

Chapter 7

Tarquin

Harper Art Institute Basement, New York City

Wednesday, October 18—5 a.m.

As soon as the nanorobots infiltrated the twentieth floor, the flying units dropped to the floor and reconfigured into ground crawlers. Ants could climb over walls, linger on curtain linings, and attach themselves anywhere. A thousand images streamed into his possession.

He left the Harper building and retreated to another basement in a nearby structure, where he could observe Simone and Nic as they examined the studies and papyrus copies that Xavier Jang had delivered.

Simone and Nic scrutinized every page of Eliana's writings. By five in the morning, they were spent. Simone read and reread the last sheet, then folded herself onto her office couch and fell asleep.

His insect cameras had caught the whole thing in detail.

He lingered on Simone's image. Extraordinary—a rare combination of East and West. Morena skin, brown-gold hair, almond eyes from her mother, Amara Nair Lim, the celebrated artist whose Malay and Chinese blood ran deep. The wide-set eyes and aquiline nose—those belonged to Christopher Harper, the father and founder of Harper Industries.

He adjusted the focus. She lay fast asleep. So near, yet impossibly far.

He tapped on some keys and the lens shifted to the studies and the papyrus copies of the Gospel of Eliana hanging on air. Safe in one of the most secure buildings in the world. Impenetrable. Until it can be breached.

It was time to move.

He whispered a single command. The insect spies stilled—and died.

Chapter 8

S imone

Harper Art Institute, New York City

Wednesday, October 18—8 a.m.

The sounds of rush hour traffic stirred her awake.

Her gaze turned to the window. Judging from the subdued hue of the reflected sunlight, it must be seven or eight in the morning. Three hours of sleep!

She was still wearing the clothes she had worn the night before. Nic lay splayed on the floor, a throw pillow wedged under his neck.

Fragments of the previous night surged back, and with them, the many reasons why she was at the Institute, instead of her home. During the night, they had copied the papyrus pages from Pope Lucas, and she was clutching them now to her chest.

The Gospel of Eliana.

On the wall before her glimmered hundreds of images, captured from the studies they had reviewed. She tapped a few keys, enlarging a photo of the original document sealed within its glass security bubble.

Good, good, good. The Da Vinci and Van Gogh studies were still there, and it was not a dream.

She checked the environmental readings: the temperature was steady, and the humidity was optimal. The chamber remained fire and bomb-proof, sealed against everything and everyone.

Nic stirred and, in a low, croaking voice, said, "Simone, you awake?"

"Just checking on the treasures. I'll make coffee," she said. "Then I'm taking a shower."

She slipped through the door, down the corridor, and opened another door to her own personal suite—a quiet sanctuary of wood, glass, and cool light.

Nic followed her and headed to the kitchen. Damn. He'd beat her to the coffee machine. She liked her coffee much darker, more bitter than he preferred.

"Now, I don't want to hear any complaints," Nic called. "My head's splitting as it is."

The crisp business suit of the night before was gone. This was the Nic she remembered—sleepy-eyed doctoral student in bedraggled clothes coming to class with a dour look on his face.

"Hey, no shoes in my room. And espresso, no milk," she said, and heard Nic groan.

"So sorry, Simone. Okay, okay," she heard Nic mutter, as he bent to take off his shoes. Some cursing followed. "Go to a coffee shop if you want full service. Jeez!"

"Hey, I can hear you, Nic Aishish," she shouted as she headed to the shower. Good thing she always kept a set of clean clothes at the office.

"Oh, of course, Professor Harper," Nic replied, pitching his voice theatrically. "I meant the coffee is now prepared according to your exact specifications."

She was halfway to the bathroom when the shrill ring of the landline froze her mid-step.

She glanced at Nic; his face showed that he too was wary of the call.

"When will you ever get rid of that antiquated device?" Nic asked.

"Answer the phone, will you?"

He was shaking his head. "It's your personal suite. And it's so early in the morning they might think we're playing footsies."

"Yuck. Fine," Simone said in a sharp tone, then grabbed the receiver. "Harper here."

It was Gabby Henry, the Chief Curator of the Whitney Museum and Simone's closest friend.

"Gabby?" she said in a softer voice. She pressed the speakerphone and motioned for Nic to listen in.

"I couldn't reach you. I was so worried about you." Gabby's voice sounded muffled. It was obvious she was crying. "My God, your office line still works. I sent you tons of messages, but you weren't answering. We have an emergency. The curatorial staff was up all night. Two of the paintings in the main exhibition have been declared fake, and the Whitney Museum's board has requested their removal today. The donors are furious. They've called in outside experts."

"The Homage to the Last Supper exhibit, you mean?" Simone asked.

"Yes," Gabriel said, near tears.

The Whitney's feature show was a collection of Last Supper paintings in homage to Da Vinci's work. It was one of the city's most anticipated art events of the year.

"Which paintings?" Simone asked, holding her breath.

"The Cosimo Rosselli on loan from the Rijksmuseum, and Warhol's," Gabby said in a tremulous tone. "But the donor insists they're genuine. It's chaos. And now, no one knows who the 'experts' are that the board brought in.

"This is Nic, by the way. I'm not playing footsies with the boss. Just some extended important work from last night."

"Oh, hi Nic," Gabby answered. "I've pulled an all-nighter too, with no end in sight. With regard to your question, no one knows yet which experts will appear this morning, which deepens the mystery. That is why I'm asking for another set of eyes."

"If so, Whitney is pretty serious with the charges," Simone said.

"Can you look at them, Simone? I don't think I'm wrong. We were taught too well by you and other professors," Gabby said, her voice clearly distraught.

Two experts in disagreement were bad news.

But there had to be a mistake if the Whitney thought the Rosselli and the Warhol pieces were not genuine.

"Can you visit when the museum opens? That way, there's less of a crowd," Gabby pleaded.

Simone hesitated. But Gabby's distress left no choice. If their roles were reversed, she'd do the same. And the Whitney was not far from the Institute.

"I'll be there once it opens," she said. "I'll message you when I'm almost there."

"Thanks, Simone. You're an angel, like always," Gabby whispered, relief breaking through her tears.

"Hush, my love. I'll be there soon," Simone said in a gentle tone.

When she hung up, Nic was shaking his head. "So, who's the Vatican expert? Xavier Jang? The art expert of art experts?"

She closed her eyes. She did not want to hear that name—not yet. But to meet him face to face? It was too soon for her.

"Or should that title belong to you, Professor Harper?" Nic teased, pouring coffee for himself and had one eyebrow raised as he questioned her.

"Are you questioning me or mocking me?" she shot back. "How about the Warhol specialist?"

"Maybe Professor Divali," he mused. "Both are dreamboats. I've got a crush on you, sweetie pie. All the day and night, hear me sigh," Nic broke into song, and waltzed around the room.

"Oh, shut up, Nic. Do I get tongue-tied in their presence? I do not," she said in exasperation.

"I'd still bet on Dr. Jang. Saranghaeyo," he said the words in a sultry voice, made a deep bow, stood upright and flashed a heart sign with his fingers.

"Naughty, naughty Nic." She wagged a finger at him. "Watch over the store while I'm gone, alright? I need a quick shower."

She paused at the doorway. "Let's hope there's no more trouble dropping by our door today."

❖

She stood outside the Harper Art Institute on 2nd Street, wavering between booking a ride and walking to the Whitney. Her good deed and good mood had already started to ebb. Of all days for Gabby to call for this favor.

The idea of two master artists' works dropping from the skies in Harper Art Institute last night was mind-boggling, not to mention the precious cargo in her purse, and that's all she wanted to focus on.

On impulse, she turned toward the entrance of the High Line, which was just a hundred steps from the Harper Art Institute, then climbed the stairs to the repurposed elevated rail line. When she reached Gansevoort Woodland, she turned toward a tiny nook that tourists were unaware of.

There was a wooden bench inside, hidden from the public. The gray birch and serviceberry trees covered it completely.

She liked to sit there where dwarf lady ferns and amethyst American wisteria bloomed in lush abandon. It was a favorite spot to get lost in—no one knew who she was, or what she did for a living.

The bench faced a fantastic view of the Meatpacking District. By force of habit, she rummaged around her purse for her cigarettes, then stopped herself. Yes, she had kicked that nasty habit. Good God.

The area in her view had been home to slaughterhouses in the 19th century and factories related to meat packing in the 20th.

By the 1980s, it had become a minefield of BDSM clubs and a part of the city unsafe to visit at night. But by the 1990s, a slew of high-end boutique stores started invading, and the art galleries followed suit. Now, one couldn't walk by this district without seeing a newly opened art gallery.

Great-grandfather Christopher Harper arrived at Ellis Island with ten dollars in his pocket, with nothing except his name and the experience of being a butcher from Sweden. The Harpers were dirt poor. They were nobodies in the town of Lund. At least, that's what he told people.

But Christopher's skills were of value to the newly opened slaughterhouses in the New World. Life was hard, but the slaughterhouses thrived.

What was lacking in the meatpacking community, however, was flavour.

Christopher's wife, great-grandmother Emilia, had apparently been a wizard at creating new flavours of sausages. But it was Christopher who smoked the cuts of the meat himself.

He knew he could not properly care for his family with his income from butchering.

On his days off, he sold sausages and homemade hams he spent cooking and smoking to the nearby farmer's market on Gansevoort Street.

Smoked meat proved a hit, and soon, the Harpers were selling premium meat to hundreds of customers. Demand grew so quickly that Christopher left his butcher's stall and became a manufacturer of fine meats.

At first, he built simple machinery to speed up processing; when profits came, he hired others to design more complicated machinery. The Harper fortune expanded. With his earnings, Christopher bought an entire row of buildings beside his slaughterhouse—investments that would later anchor the family's empire.

Or that's what Christopher always claimed.

His son, and her grandfather Liam, expanded the food business and never strayed from it. Under Liam's watch, Harper Foods became a household name.

Simone's father, Gordon, had other ideas.

When her father inherited the company, Harper Foods had already gone global. The new corporate headquarters rose in New Jersey. But his most passionate interests lay elsewhere.

He collected art, perhaps to rebel against his father, who wanted him to focus on the food manufacturing business.

"It was your great-grandfather Christopher's fault," her father used to say. "He pretended to be poor, but his family owned masterpieces of art centuries old. Was he really a butcher? A fugitive? A thief? He never gave a straight answer. One look at those treasures and I was hooked."

As a boy, her father had been allowed to view the paintings only on his birthday. He never forgot the unfairness of it all. He wanted to look at art every day.

Gordon devoted his life to art, expanding the secret collection he inherited—masterpieces known only to him, Simone, and her mother. His tastes leaned toward American painters in the 1920s, and over time his collections rivalled the Whitney's next door.

Always competitive, her father knew he could not compete with Gertrude Vanderbilt Whitney's collection. It angered him that art dealers always gave him the second-best pieces, many of which were forgeries.

Instead of hiring authenticators, her father founded his own school. A sanctuary for art experts, born from his conviction that knowledge was the only true provenance.

He hired the best teachers, and by its second decade, the Harper Art Institute ranked alongside the Courtauld Gallery in London.

Gordon also recognized the need to preserve art, not merely collect it. He was one of the first patrons to focus on the conservation of painting. Pretty soon, museums around the world were requesting authenticity examinations from the Institute—proof that her father's legacy had expanded beyond wealth to include reputation.

A message pinged. It was Gabby, looking for her.

As she stood up and headed toward the Whitney, she noticed a man walking behind her. She took a couple of quick, surreptitious glances to size him up. He was wearing rugged, beautifully cut boots from Europe. A hoodie from Andare, a known European retailer. And the expensive type of sunglasses usually worn by pilots flying the friendly skies.

She turned around for one more look, but he was gone.

—◆—

Her quiet break at the High Line took more time than expected. She messaged Gabby: On my way. Five minutes.

When she reached the Whitney, people were chattering loudly in the lobby and milling about the hotly anticipated 'Homage to the Last Supper' exhibit on the eighth floor.

"Simone, it's so good to see you," Gabby said and embraced her.

Gabby appeared wraith-like and pale. The board's decision to ask art experts to authenticate two works had clearly taken a toll on her health.

"The museum is packed," she murmured, eyes moving over the lines stretching in front of each painting.

"I know. One expert is here already," Gabby whispered.

"This early?" she asked. "Anyone I know?"

Gabby hesitated, eyes downcast. "The expert was out of my hands. I'm sorry, Simone. It's Xavier," Gabby said, and then hugged her. "Let's talk later. The staff told me that he arrived ten minutes ago. So let me go with you. Oh, wait." She fumbled for her phone. "You go ahead, Simone. You know where the exhibit is. I'll catch up as soon as I make this call. Here—take this."

She pressed a heavy exhibition catalogue into Simone's hands. Then Gabby turned away without waiting for an answer.

"But I... know already most of these pieces," she began, flipping through the glossy pages—Renaissance reinterpretations, postmodern echoes. Then she paused at a section of newer American works she hadn't studied. "Well... not everything then."

Loud sounds of chatter came from the stairway. The elevator doors opened. Simone got in and pressed the eighth floor where the Warhol exhibit was displayed. About twenty people entered the elevator with the same intention. Their cheerful excitement jarred against the tightening in her chest.

Anger. Check. Rage. Check.

The elevator doors slid open and the group spilled into the gallery like a wave of color and sound.

Warhol's "The Last Supper" was opposite the elevator doors.

And there he was.

Xavier Jang.

Head of the Vatican's vast archive—guardian of the largest repository of the Catholic Church's treasures spanning over two millennia—Xavier stood before the work of an artist known for his pop art featuring Campbell soup cans and lithographic print screens of Marilyn Monroe and Elvis Presley.

She got out of the elevator and crossed the polished floor toward the Warhol. Its sheer scale always shocked her. She took a deep breath, trying to calm her nerves.

For a moment, it felt as if the ground gave way beneath her. He was as arresting as ever—unmistakably magnetic. He did not have perfect features—his nose and jaw were too strong for symmetry, his eyes dark and unreadable, as though holding a thousand thoughts behind them. Yet, when he smiled, his eyes would twinkle, and the world felt safe again.

The exhibit program slipped from her grasp and landed with a thud at her feet.

He glanced at the book, then his gaze settled on her.

"Did you get Da Vinci and Van Gogh's works?" he asked quietly.

"Yes," she managed. "Thank you for bringing them all the way from Rome." She hesitated. "How is Pope Lucas?"

"Dying," Xavier said simply. "Depressed. Hopeful. Seeking atonement—from you. Same as me."

He sighed and shook his head. It was as if he wanted to say something more, but stopped himself. He turned his head and pointed at the Warhol work.

"Did you know Warhol was a deeply religious man?" he asked softly. "He went to church every day."

"Angels and demons, one couldn't really say from the outside," she said.

Xavier chuckled.

For a fleeting second, it was as though nothing—not distance, regret, or time—had ever stood between them.

"You should be looking at the Cosimo Rosselli painting, which is your expertise. Not Warhol's, right?" she asked.

"Art is art, in whatever century it is," Xavier replied. "So tell me, what do you think about this piece? Does it look fake to you? I'm drawn to his paintings, for some reason," he said. "Come here and see this." He pointed at one part of the painting.

As she stepped closer, she caught sight of a familiar figure three paintings away—the man she'd observed at the High Line. The same distinct jacket and footwear.

"What do you think?" Xavier asked.

She closed her eyes, gathering herself. When she opened them, instead of training them on the work at hand, she stepped back and let her gaze settle on a painting across the room. After a few seconds, she turned back to the questioned Warhol. She would need maximum objectivity.

The art world was littered with fake Warhols. This artist had always created several exclusive editions and trial runs in a form called proofs. The trial runs started only when Warhol was happy with the result. If it took a hundred copies of the trial run, then a hundred copies were left lying around, undocumented.

"Is this a trial proof or the artist's proof?" Xavier asked.

"If this is a forgery, it's perfect. Only Professor Divali can answer this question. Where is he?" Xavier asked, turning around to look for the modern art expert.

"Warhol signed it in the right space," she said. "But look at the colours surrounding it." She moved in for a better look.

It was then that she felt the slight tremor and heard a clap of thunder. A gunshot?

She turned toward the sound.

When a man with a gun walked in front of the Warhol painting, she froze and found herself staring straight into his eyes.

Without hesitation, the shooter fired a round at people next to her, then another toward the back of the room.

From the corner of her eye, she saw Gabby entering the space and running toward her.

The shooter turned to her, and before he could pull the trigger, someone tackled him. It was Xavier. He forced the gunman's arm over his head, and she heard another shot—but this one was discharged into the ceiling.

And that galvanised her into action.

The scream that tore through the room came from her own throat. For a moment, she thought this must be what it feels like when the body separates from the soul. The sound was blood-curdling.

Xavier had pinned the gunman's other hand over his head. She added her strength to his. And then others joined in. The crush of them all literally took her breath away.

But there was no way the gunman was going to shoot again.

"I've seen your faces. I'm going to kill you all," the gunman screamed.

She heard the sound of flesh connecting to bone. Someone punched the gunman in the face. Shouts replaced his words.

She was pushing so hard on the gunman's arm; her hands were turning white.

How long could she hold on?

Chapter 9

D etective Paolo Rodrigo

Outside the N line, New York City

Wednesday, October 18—10:30 a.m.

The air was crisp and dry; the clouds were white and dazzling. It was one of those days when it was nice to walk to the 10th precinct station after a jam-packed commute on the N line from his home in Astoria, Queens.

It was his ritual to stop at Billy's Bakery, a block away from the precinct, and get his usual coffee and chocolate mint bar.

He got in line and scanned the treats available for the day. He allowed himself this tiny window to eat whatever he wanted in the early morning. The rest of the day, he ate like a monk, subsisting on coffee and tea. Proteins and salad occasionally when he had the time.

The barista smiled at him. "How are you, Detective? The usual? Maybe a whoopie pie this morning?"

"You read my mind. I was eyeing it. But I'll get it tomorrow," Rodrigo said, casting a wistful look at the confection.

He took his food to the pink table by the window. He always sat facing the front door, a habit he couldn't shake after fifteen years as a cop.

As he stirred his coffee after adding milk and lots of sugar, he observed the faces of the customers waiting in line. This babble of conversation made him smile. Last week, another ordinance was introduced regarding the latest Danzhou variant of SARS-24 and masks required for indoor dining. He followed city ordinances and wore a mask. The discussions in the coffee shop about masking were lively and unrestrained.

Thank God. It was an ordinary day, he thought. And instantly regretted it.

Was he teasing the gods of chaos?

He took a sip of coffee and turned to look out the window. The hurried pace of the people outside comforted him. Many of them were well-dressed and walking quickly to work. The only people at a leisurely pace were pushing thousand-dollar strollers.

The Meatpacking District had become the place where nobs mixed with skints like him. Gone were the days when drag queens and sex workers ate their breakfast in greasy diners. If it weren't for the welcoming atmosphere in this bakery, he wouldn't step into this fancy schmaltzy establishment.

The chocolate mint cookie always put him in a good mood; anything sweet was his hard liquor for the day ahead.

A flashing message on his phone interrupted his morning reverie.

It was the highest alert for the NYPD. One glance at the screen, and he bolted from his seat.

"Active shooter. Whitney Museum," the text said.

The mint cookie fell to the floor. Three employees behind the counter stared at him as he picked up the cookie.

"Gotta go," he said and headed to the door. He paused outside to orient his location, then started running towards the Whitney.

It was a fifteen-minute walk on good days, but he made it to the entrance in five. An evacuation was underway. Staff at the museum were funneling people towards the main door.

"Put your hands up so the police can see that you're unarmed," one staffer cried in a panicked voice as she motioned for the crowd to hurry.

"Detective Rigo, over here," a police officer called him.

"Hey, Sam. Why are you here? Do we go in? Who else is here?" he asked one of the officers from his precinct.

"I had to bring my daughter Claire. It was uh, Museum Day. She's okay, and she's with her teacher. I'm afraid I have bad news. So far, it's just you and me, Detective," the officer said.

The statistics weren't good. Half of the law enforcement officials who engaged with a shooter were injured or shot.

They headed towards the emergency stairs. "I don't hear shooting," he said. He calculated the odds. Sixty percent of shootings ended before the police arrived, and forty percent of the incidents ended with the shooter committing suicide.

The shooter was either finished with the evil deed, heading towards them, or something else.

Terrified people were running past them.

A body lay splayed in the middle of the staircase, but they couldn't stop to help. Priority was to subdue the shooter.

They were on the sixth floor when they heard another shot, then there was silence.

They ran faster towards the eighth floor. When they opened the door, there was silence. There was a cluster of people at the far end of the gallery. Where was the shooter?

"I could see all your faces, motherfuckers," a voice deep within the bodies shouted.

He met Sam's eyes, and, with a quick signal, they both moved into the room.

A man in a beige coat punched someone at the center of the pile.

It was a brutal, almost mesmerizing sight.

"Police! Freeze!" Sam shouted, then they both ran towards the melee.

"Please help us," an exhausted female voice came from the pile of bodies.

"Son of a bitch! You won't catch me alive," the voice from the center of the pile shouted again. The shooter's arms had been wrenched over his head and were held there by multiple hands.

Another man boxed the talker's mouth. "Shut up, you fucker," the man said.

He reached towards the group of people straining to subdue the shooter, and then cuffed his hands. Sam helped secure his feet.

"Thank God," a female voice cried underneath the bodies. "I think I'm holding his neck."

Just then, the boots arrived. The SWAT armada surged in full force. He sighed in relief.

"No other shooter sighted, Detective Rodrigo," one of the troops shouted towards him.

"Let's call EMT," he said, and turned to the people who'd held the shooter.

He'd never seen anything like it at a crime scene. A small group of people who'd run toward danger instead of away from it. Two men and one woman were now standing and stretching aching limbs.

One of them had initiated the attack against the shooter. But who?

He observed two men. One was a tall and distinguished man, dressed in an expensive beige coat. The other man seemed to be a foreigner with his European jacket and shoes. French? Both were tall and athletic, and they carried the same fierce, determined bearing. Former army?

As the paramedics arrived, he noticed one person still crouched, unmoving. Another woman survivor was patting her shoulder. Were they friends?

The woman on the floor appeared shattered. He knew that vacant stare—shellshocked, dishevelled, her mind still trying to catch up with the horror around her.

"Miss... I'm Detective Rodrigo. What's your name?" he asked in a soft voice.

"Simone," she said, and began to shake.

"I'm Gabby. I work here in the Whitney. C'mon Simone, I'll help you stand," Gabby said.

"Hey Joannie, we need help," he called to one of the paramedics who was now at the scene.

One of the paramedics turned to him at the sound of her name and ran to his side.

"Hey, Detective Rigo? Sergeant Kolinsky needs you to go to the station," one of the SWAT team members called out to him.

"Now? But, we have an active crime scene here," he said, and wondered what was happening elsewhere.

"Hey Sam, good job, man," he called out to the officer who charged up the stairs with him. "Can you wait for the Lab team and help get this area closed and processed? I don't want this shooter to go scot-free because of fuckups in evidence."

"Sure, Detective," the officer nodded.

The paramedic helped Simone stand and tried to lead her past the scene of the carnage.

He wondered how she would fare from this tragedy. As well as the other survivors.

"Sam," he whispered again, as he tapped the sergeant's shoulder. "Get me the names of these survivors, and when I'm through here, I'll follow them to the triage area. If it's a hospital, message me which one."

He was curious about Simone and the other survivors. Something was not adding up.

Somehow, there was a connection among them. But how? Best to follow his instincts and investigate these further. His instincts had never led him astray.

Chapter 10

S imone

Whitney Museum, New York City

Wednesday, October 18—11:30 a.m.

The dead were everywhere, in various poses and contortions. As the paramedic helped Simone leave the gallery, her gaze landed on something bright amidst the chaos—a purse adorned with jewel colors. It seemed horrifically out of place.

Xavier was talking to another paramedic. He was safe. And so were the others who'd tackled the gunman.

She craned her neck and searched for Gabby, but couldn't see her.

The paramedic led her to the hallway. She made it only a few feet before she stopped.

"Let's walk to the entrance, shall we?" the paramedic said, giving her shoulder a gentle pat.

Simone pointed at her bare feet, and tears sprang to her eyes. What had happened to her shoes? How could she leave this horrible scene if she didn't have them?

"Okeedokee, that's not a problem. Let's try this," the paramedic pulled something from her medical bag. It was thin, disposable plastic boots of the kind used by the police and EMTs at a crime scene.

The boots were far too big, but at least they were better than nothing.

"Steady, steady, I'm holding your hand," the paramedic said. Her hand was a lifeline leading her through the slippery liquid she felt under her feet. Past artwork worth millions, past corridors she knew by heart.

As they descended the narrow stairs toward the main door of the Whitney Museum, vehicles of various shapes and sizes flashed their lights. There were ambulances, police cars, and fire trucks.

A crowd of policemen guarded the front door.

"Make room, make room," shouted the paramedic holding her hand as she pushed her away from the crowd of people.

"Who is she, Joannie?" She heard different voices ask the same question. Joannie had covered her face with a cloth.

"She helped bring down the gunman," Joannie said.

"I'm not wounded. Do I have to go to the triage area?" Simone asked.

"Protocol, ma'am. We have to go."

The bright lights and noise diminished as soon as she entered the tent. A woman with green eyes, her black hair speckled with warm honey streaks approached, as Joannie led her to a chair.

"I'm Dr. Pauline Lassiter. Are you feeling pain anywhere?" the doctor asked. Her warm, even, matter-of-fact tone eased Simone's galloping heartbeat.

"No, no pain anywhere, Dr. Pauline. Maybe a slight sprain here because I held the wacko down," she said and pointed to her arm.

"Wacko indeed. He's being processed as we speak, Dr. Pauline," Joannie said.

"Hmmmm..." the doctor said, nodding and taking in what they were saying. She touched her arm and tried exploratory pats on different parts of her body. But she didn't feel pain anywhere.

"No internal injuries. Ice those arms today, and the pain will ease. But we need to remove your footwear and clothes, and leave them with the police for evidence. Are you okay with a change of clothes?"

"Oh, yes please," she said, her voice catching in her throat.

A small, round tub appeared before her feet, and a nurse directed her to soak her feet in the warm water. The ugly plastic shoes were placed in a container and tagged as evidence.

As her feet were soaking, another nurse appeared and brushed her hair with a fine-toothed comb. Perhaps to look for more evidence? Seeing nothing, the nurse asked her to look up and close her eyes.

"We don't see any kind of foreign object in your hair or face. Is it okay for us to clean your face? There's a bit of blood on your forehead," Dr. Pauline said. "We have to tag it for evidence."

She nodded.

"It's all right, Simone. We're here for you," said the kind doctor. "You can open your eyes."

"Is it all right to change your clothes?" Joanie said. "We have some things here. Nothing fancy."

"I'm all right with whatever you have," Simone said, smiling faintly.

A standard dark blue shirt and pants were given to her, and a pair of white, plain sneakers. She walked to the corner of the room where no one could see her. She changed and folded the clothes she wore at the Whitney.

"I feel so much better already with the change of clothes. Thank you."

"Are you a size 8?" one of the nurses approached her, then held a cardboard shoe box with simple sneakers.

"Thank you so much," she said. And a tear slid out of one eye.

"You can wear it later, after triage," the nurse said, and gave a quick pat on her hand.

"Hey, Dr. Pauline, someone wants to see you," a nurse said as she stood outside the tent door.

"Who is it?" the doctor asked.

"It's me Detective Rigo, Dr. Pauline," a gruff voice answered. The man was wearing an all-purpose black jacket and a distinctive green Aero light t-shirt underneath. A baseball cap. She recognized the detective who asked her name on the eighth floor.

"Is it all right to get an interview, Dr. Pauline?" the detective asked.

"Let me call the EMHP first, Detective," Dr. Lassiter said.

The look that passed between Dr. Lassiter and the detective set off warning signals in Simone. She had seen enough power struggles in the art world to recognize one, and decided it was best to be proactive.

"Why don't we call the EMHP, and the person can be here while the detective interviews me. That way, no one's time is wasted," she said.

"Is Esperanza in this tent?" Dr. Lassiter asked one of the nurses. A woman appeared.

"I heard my name, Dr. Lassiter. Ms. Simone, I'm Doctor Esperanza, your assigned Emergency Mental Health Psychologist for today. I received your chart from the nurse who called me when you arrived. Any questions, just ask. Any questions you don't want to answer, you ask me," Dr. Esperanza said.

"I can be interviewed now," Simone said.

The Emergency Psychologist sat down in a chair beside the gurney on which Simone had settled.

"Okay detective, you may begin," the EP said, motioning for the detective to come forward.

"I'm so sorry, but I have to ask you some questions. I know it's a difficult time," the detective started, but she didn't want to hear any words of sympathy from anyone.

"Is the shooter in custody?" she asked.

"Yes, the shooter's in custody," the detective said.

The words relieved her, but there were so many questions.

"Why?" was all she was able to ask. "Why did he do this? And who is he?"

"We don't know who he is or his motives," the detective said.

"Have you seen Gabby? She's my friend. She works at the Whitney. She was in the same room when the shooter..." she couldn't continue.

"Simone, Gabby is fine. In fact, she also stopped the shooter," the detective said.

"How can that be?" she said. "She must have been on top of me."

She closed her eyes and exhaled for five seconds. She'd felt like she was holding her breath for an hour, but now, there was a measure of relief.

"How many people were shot?" she said. "Were any paintings destroyed? Thinking of bullets in the works of art deepened her emotional pain.

"Unfortunately, I don't have answers for you yet. But it's all under investigation," the detective said.

"How about the other people who tackled the gunman. Are they all right?" she asked.

"They are," Detective Rodrigo answered. "I would suggest that you talk to a professional about all this and ask Dr. Esperanza about referrals. We'll be here if you need anything."

As she nodded, the horror of it all washed over her again.

"You saved a lot of lives, you know," the detective said.

There was a knock on the door. Another nurse.

"My cue to leave. Would you like me to call anyone?" the detective asked.

"No. My office is nearby," Simone said.

The detective turned and touched his ear.

"What now?" she heard him mutter as he stepped out, eyes fixed somewhere far beyond. He listened, nodded, then turned toward her.

"What is it?" she asked, a sense of foreboding rising in her chest. She knew that expression, the same look that her parents had shared whenever something catastrophic had happened, and they were trying to keep it from her.

"Are you the CEO of Harper Institute?" the detective asked.

"Yes," she said in a tentative voice. Why was the detective's face looking so serious?

"I'm afraid it's bad news, Ms. Harper," the detective said with no preamble. "My chief just called to tell me there's been a major robbery there. A pair of Da Vinci and Van Gogh studies are involved."

She felt her heart stop. "Robbery?" she said. And then she turned to the doctors.

"I need to leave," she said.

"Let me accompany you. My precinct has jurisdiction there," the detective said.

All she could do was nod.

The Harper Art Institute had one of the most advanced security systems in the art world.

How were the paintings stolen? And why?

———··◆··———

A swarm of police cars lined the street in front of the Institute. Photographers crowded the sidewalk.

Light bulbs flashed in her face as she approached the gallery's front door.

Two cops approached Detective Rodrigo. As Simone entered through the lobby, Nic and her security team surged forward to meet her. Behind them, staffers were held back, straining to reach her through the cordon. Seeing her own people made her calmer, and she could breathe a little easier.

More staffers lined the hallway, waiting.

"Ms. Harper, what happened to you?" Santino asked. The question alone was enough to bring tears to her eyes.

"I'm okay, guys. You're the best," she said, waving to the other Harper Institute staffers gathered nearby. Then she turned to the detective, who had stayed close by. "Detective Rodrigo, meet the Deputy Director of Harper Art Institute, Nic Aishish."

Nic led the police team upstairs to the elevator. Twentieth floor. The ride up to the twentieth floor was wordless. Simone noticed Nic's glance slide to her outfit. She raised a finger to her lips—quiet.

Sim opened the door to the Observatory, and one look at the middle of the room, she knew. It was true. The studies were gone.

She felt faint, clutched at something, and missed.

Luckily, Detective Rodrigo caught her.

"Give her some air," "Let her sit," voices from various people called out as she staggered. When she was guided to a chair, she dropped her head onto the table in front of her.

"Jesus Christ," she said.

"Someone get tea for Simone," Nic said. A couple of staffers rushed out to get it.

Detective Rodrigo sat beside Simone, but soon stood up when he recognized a police technician who was trying to catch his eye.

"A word, Detective? During Code Red at the Whitney Museum, Tube-3 pressure dipped; checksum suppressed during lockdown," the technician whispered. Detective Rodrigo nodded. Simone heard the conversation and wondered if the details she heard from the technician led to the breach.

The detective turned and faced them. "May I ask how you got these paintings?" he asked, directing the question to her.

Nic answered. "They arrived yesterday."

"They're from Pope Lucas at the Vatican, sent here by Xavier Jang, Director of the Vatican Museum," she said without preamble.

"I can show you all the security footage, Detective. We can establish the timeline, and I will be happy to answer any questions you may have. Let's give Professor Harper some air right now," Nic said.

"Nic, how about Eliana..." she asked, standing suddenly.

All eyes turned towards her.

"Professor Harper was also given a document we spent the whole night verifying. It's part of the early writings of one of Jesus Christ's followers. Experts have called it part of the Gospel of Eliana. It's good we made a copy. But it's gone, just like the paintings," Nic said. "The bubble was breached—the papyrus leaves are missing."

The shock of it all made her swoon again. But this time, there was no one near enough to catch her.

Chapter 11

Eliana

Memphis, Egypt

In the third year of Gaius Claudius (AD 43)

"*Shlahma alaykh*, Maryam of Magdala," she said in Aramaic. "Peace be upon you."

Maryam stepped toward her and gathered her into her arms. "Eliana—I thought I'd never see you again," she whispered. "It was good that Apostle Thaddeus sent you here. Many are still searching for us."

Tall, with auburn hair reaching her knees, Maryam had always been striking, beautiful in a way that inspired devotion in her friends and envy among Yeshua's enemies.

Her father, Shimon, had always treated her with the same affection he gave his fellow apostles, a closeness that went beyond blood. Yet he had been wary of Maryam's closeness to Yeshua. To his quiet consternation, Yeshua regarded Maryam of Magdala as an equal among them.

No one, however, could question Maryam's sincerity. She was utterly devoted to Yeshua, and to his mother, Maryam of Nasrath.

The women who followed Yeshua had chosen their path with the same conviction. They walked where he walked, tended to those who gathered, and steadied the multitudes that pressed in whenever Yeshua appeared.

"Come, come inside. The direct rays of the sun will be hurting your precious skin, Eliana, talyti habibti, my dearest one," Maryam said.

Eliana smiled. The apostles had always called her habibti—my precious child. And somehow it became shortened to Biti. No matter how many years passed, she would always remain a child in their eyes.

Inside the cool confines of the home, she noticed several bundles tied in burlap stacked by the doorway.

"Are you leaving for somewhere, Maryam?" she asked softly.

Before Maryam could enter, a man entered. David of Beit Anya—cousin to Dodta Martha. His skin was bronzed from travel, his hair leonine. The last time she had seen him was a decade ago, when he was still a young follower of Yeshua.

"Eliana, is that truly you?" David asked, his voice rose higher in recognition. "How is your father, Shimon?"

"I'm meant to travel to Anatolia to see him, but I'm not certain where he is now," she said. "He moves from place to place..."

"As we all do, Eliana," David said in a soothing voice. "We are preparing to leave soon, to continue Yeshua's work."

She hesitated. "But where will you go?"

"Some of our kin have settled in Gaul," David said. "They've promised us safe passage there," David said.

"I understand that you have something for us to keep?" Maryam asked.

"It's my writings," Eliana said, her voice tentative. "I wrote about what I witnessed when Yeshua was with us."

"Hush, dearest Eliana," Maryam said. "David and I, we could not yet speak of those days after He left us. It's good that you were able to write of them."

Eliana drew a bundle of papyrus documents from her burlap bag. The faint rustle of the pages filled the small room.

"Oh, the beautiful papyrus pages you make!" Maryam said, smiling. "I remember visiting your home, and your father was so proud of your work."

Eliana laid twenty sheets on a table.

"I hear other writers who never saw the truth of those days writing down their own accounts," David said, his tone edged with anger. "Untruths! They may be good men, but I pray they do not speak falsehoods."

"I wrote it in a tongue that no one can speak," Eliana said. On that day when Yeshua appeared to them after his death, she and Maryam of Magdala had been given the gift of tongue, understanding languages they had never known.

"You were given these precious gifts for a purpose," David said gently.

"Perhaps if I read it, I will understand," Maryam said.

"Yes," Eliana replied. She didn't need to say more. The look that passed between them bridged what words could not.

"Do not fear about these pages. We will keep them safe," Maryam said.

"I must go. It is not safe to stay here a second longer. I wish you safe travels to Gaul," Eliana said.

Maryam of Magdala drew her into an embrace. Eliana held her tightly, unaware that it would be years before she would see her again.

Chapter 12

Tarquin

Grand Central Station, B-3, New York City

Wednesday, October 18—6 p.m.

A black van with covered license plates waited for him in the shadows when he pulled into the lowest level of the garage. The air surprised him—no exhaust, no stale fumes—just a vast, echoing emptiness that felt more like a bunker than a parking bay.

Two figures sat inside. The woman in the passenger seat wore a beret, mask, and dark glasses, her face turned away.

The driver stepped out wearing the same anonymous disguise. Without a word, he moved to the back, opened the trunk, and lifted out two long wooden packages. Thin but deceptively heavy—chest-high and shoulder-wide.

He handed them over.

Tarquin caught the weight easily and gave a brief nod. A silent, practiced exchange—one he had done many times before in his life, though never quite like this.

"Thanks," he said quietly.

The man acknowledged him with the smallest tilt of his head before slipping back behind the wheel. The van's taillights glowed, then faded as it ascended the ramp, leaving Tarquin alone with the crates and the clang of his pulse.

Only then did he realize he'd been holding his breath. He exhaled slowly, steadying himself the way he had been trained long ago—slow inhale, longer exhale. Control the breath, control the nerves.

Could he really do what he needed to do in an hour?

His phone buzzed again.

A message from Cassius Turbierri:

Dinner in your honor is confirmed.

Tarquin swallowed. His day had already nearly ended his life.

The shooting at the Whitney Museum replayed in jagged flashes—gunfire, screams, people collapsing. The metallic tang of blood and dust still clung to him. He had stayed to help with triage until the paramedics pushed him aside, telling him to go home.

Tarquin returned to his apartment exhausted, disheveled, barely holding together.

Ten minutes later, a courier knocked at his door.

A hand-delivered envelope. No return address.

Inside was a Metropolitan Transport Department ID with his photo, and a folded instruction slip:

Grand Central Station

Basement Level 3

6 p.m.

No signature. No emblem. No explanation. Just the sort of assignment that came without questions—assignments he had been quietly trained once upon a time, far from New York, under a banner few civilians ever thought of beyond ceremonial uniforms.

The van was gone now, leaving only a vast stretch of concrete that suddenly felt colder.

Tarquin carried the crates to the rental van and started the engine. The sound reverberated through the hollow chamber.

At the exit booth, a flickering monitor came to life. Tarquin tapped his MTA card. The barrier lifted, and he drove out into the night.

Whatever lay ahead, he had already stepped onto the tightrope.

And he had no choice but to run it.

Tarquin gripped the wheel.

He just prayed he wouldn't fall.

————···◆···———

St. Anthony the Divine, NYC

October 18—8 p.m.

The applause shot to a deafening crescendo.

The Da Vinci and Van Gogh studies from the family of Pope Lucas were displayed on one wall, surrounded by glass, and the buzz of jubilant voices was heard throughout the enormous room.

The papyrus pages were on another wall, and people were lined up to see them.

"Hear, hear." Cassius Turbierri's deep voice boomed across the chamber. "I'd like to thank Tarquin Vern—a descendant of Benjamin, one of the Sanhedrin bloodlines. Because of his work, there will be fewer sources to dilute the Gospel."

A murmur rippled through the crowd.

"The Council of Avenna," Turbierri went on, his gaze lifting to the fresco above the dais. "You ask when one Gospel—John—was chosen above all? It was here, in 580 AD, when Pope Silvano, another of our blood brothers, decreed that only one account should remain. The rest were not destroyed, merely sealed. Silenced. Forgotten by history, remembered only by us."

A few heads bowed in reverence.

"Judas became the betrayer, not we. And for thousands of years, we have lived unseen."

Tarquin turned slightly. The room had grown still, all attention pinned to the man on the dais. These were the descendants of that small circle of Temple authorities who had once convened in a hurried nighttime meeting—men who had argued for Jesus' arrest and execution in defiance of every rule of Second Temple law.

No proceedings at night.

No trials on Passover.

Nothing about that tribunal had ever made legal or moral sense.

Only John avoided the story entirely—no nocturnal Sanhedrin, no chamber of chief priests, elders, and scribes present, no interrogation before Caiaphas, no council chamber filled with mockery and blows. In John's account, Jesus was taken first to Annas, then, by early morning, to Pilate. There was no formal assembly. No verdict. Only silence where a trial should have been.

Rumors had long whispered of the fuller accounts preserved in Mark, Luke, and Matthew—stories now lost to time.

Two millennia of guilt had hardened into purpose. The Obscurati gathered whenever another scroll surfaced, bearing the names of their forefathers. By keeping those accounts hidden, they had reshaped history into their own design.

"Cheers to the New York branch. Cheers to you, my brother," another voice said. The crowd erupted in applause.

"Your Eminence," Turbierri said in greeting and turned around. Tarquin caught the flicker of surprise in his expression.

The cardinal stepped forward, embraced Turbierri, and kissed him on both cheeks.

The famous Turbierris. Cassius Turbierri was the leader of the worldwide organization, a tall, athletic, broad-shouldered man with a shock of pale-blonde hair. His features were refined, almost perfect, until one noticed his cold blue eyes and pale lips that thinned quickly to show displeasure or annoyance in an instant.

Iñaki Turbierri, Archbishop of Chicago and Cardinal-Priest of Sancti Verbi Domini in Rome. A Cardinal of the old guard, a scholar appointed by Pope Boniface. An older, greyer version of Cassius, and one of the most vocal critics of Pope Lucas.

The Obscurati New York branch didn't meet often, but when it happened, a huge turnout was guaranteed.

"This is impressive, Cassius. The renovation of this church has been outstanding. I remember saying Mass here as a young priest," the cardinal said, tipping his head to look at the ceiling. "Are you trying to rival the Sistine Chapel?"

"Oh no, no, Cardinal Iñaki—we could never rival the masterpieces of Michelangelo. Let me show you around," Turbierri said. "Tarquin, come with us."

He heard the command and nodded. Turbierri took a step back and caught his attention.

"How is the DNA collection of Simone Harper?" Turbierri asked.

"Haven't had the chance. I'll make sure I get it in a few days," he said.

St. Anthony's Chapel was a former cathedral, one of the many magnificent properties the Church sold in a fire sale to raise funds. Neo-Gothic in style, it was called the twin of St. Patrick's Cathedral. Built in the same year, 1858, construction stopped during the Civil War, and yet it eventually surpassed its twin in every aspect. Its spires rose higher than St. Patrick's, the northern towers held twenty bells, and the church housed three pipe organs. And yet, it ended up sold.

Tarquin wondered how the head of the Obscurati had managed to acquire such a prize.

Turbierri had refitted the space like a modern museum, complete with climate-controlled vitrines and the kind of equipment used for extensive collections of paintings or rare books.

"We still have work to do in finding the complete version of the writings by Eliana," Cardinal Iñaki said quietly to Turbierri.

"However, thanks to Tarquin, our collection has grown," Cassius said.

Tarquin inclined his head. "The insects were a great help."

"Come," Cassius Turbierri said. "Would you like to see where the other hidden writings have been kept over the years? Follow me."

He then led Tarquin and the other guests toward a side entrance with a vaulted ceiling. A bronze door stood at the end. When Turbierri pressed his hand to the sensor panel, the lock disengaged with a mechanical thrum, a continuous rhythmic sound pulsing as gears and locks slid free. A hidden passageway opened, revealing a hallway lined with glass cabinets. Rows upon rows of yellow-tinged papyrus filled them.

"These are the visitor favorites," Turbierri said. "The Gospel of Matthew, the Gospel of Mark, the Gospel of Luke. Which interests you today?"

"I'm more interested in the most recent one," Tarquin said. "Eliana. She's one of the youngest writers."

Turbierri nodded and guided him toward the vestibule where the gospels were displayed.

"And now... Eliana," Cardinal Iñaki whispered, gazing at the papyrus leaves with obvious pleasure.

Eliana's writings had been placed among fifty or more accounts—gospels written by followers of Jesus Christ in the last three years of his life. Most manuscripts were loosely bound, their ancient pages visible from where Tarquin stood. All had been discredited over the centuries, thanks to the Obscurati.

"And a daughter of Simon Peter, as Hegesippus, an early chronicler, says," Turbierri said with glee. "It will be easy to silence this one like the rest. Find the complete Gospel of Eliana, and the riches of the Obscurati are yours."

A soft buzz touched Tarquin's ear. His phone implant signaled an incoming call.

"Don't let me keep you. You are welcome here anytime," Turbierri said and turned toward the other guests.

It was Detective Paolo Rodrigo. Tarquin waited until Turbierri was out of earshot before answering.

"Tarquin, how are you? Detective Paolo Rodrigo here," the detective's voice seemed hesitant.

He exited through the bronze door into the corridor. "I'm fine, Detective Rodrigo. How may I help you?"

"There's a two-session support group for those who stopped the gunman yesterday. It's been arranged by the NYC Emergency Psychology Department."

"Yes, I got an invite from Dr. Pauline Lassiter," Tarquin said. "She treated me at the triage area. I'm thinking of attending."

"It's tomorrow. Please attend if you can. Free donuts," the detective said, half-laughing, then paused.

His first instinct was to refuse and disappear. But would avoidance raise suspicion?

"Alright," the detective said, filling the silence. "See you at 10 a.m. at Mount Tabor Hospital. Seventh Floor, Magnolia Terrace."

"Ok, Detective. See you there. I'll bring coffee for everyone," Tarquin said.

"Tarquin!" Cassius Turbierri's voice echoed from across the hall.

"I have to go, Detective," Tarquin said quickly. "Big event tomorrow."

From across the room, he caught sight of Turbierri, and a sudden rush of hatred rose in him. It was not the time to show anger or emotion. He turned away, avoiding the circle of guests around the Turbierris, now focused on the different gospels laid out before them.

For all their wealth, the Obscurati did not have the resources of major museums. They accepted the Da Vinci and Van Gogh studies like greedy dogs, making no apparent effort to authenticate the works. The same held true of Eliana's writings—now encased in glass, exhibited like trophies.

Tarquin's jaw tightened. He slipped from the room, disgust burning in his chest.

At the exit, he paused, glancing back at St. Anthony's. Shadows pooled at the base of the structure like judgment.

Then he stepped into the night, walking back toward Nakharin, the weight of everything pressing heavier with each step.

———⬥———

The kitchens were dark and silent. He switched on the lights, and everything was in order. No smell of gas, all burners off. He ran two fingers across the steel counter and stopped at the faint imprint of a glass.

Bodi, he thought. The new commis. He could almost see him, finishing his shift, taking a quick drink before going home.

He opened the lowboy fridge to cook eggs, but lingered, straightening the cartons until they were perfectly aligned.

When he stood, he noticed the chopping blocks were out of order. A tiny speck of red clung to the grain of one board. He brought it to the kitchen sink and scrubbed it until the red stain disappeared.

By the time he finished, his appetite had vanished. The red mark had bothered him more than it should have. Maybe because it was related to Turbierri's order to draw Simone's blood.

How was he supposed to do that? He had to find a way to meet with Simone again.

Detective Rodrigo had been right. He would attend the therapy sessions tomorrow. It was the perfect opportunity.

He had to complete the task and uncover Simone's bloodline.

Chapter 13

X avier

Mt. Tabor Hospital, New York City

Wednesday, October 18—8:30 p.m.

Doctors went in and out of Simone's room in the hospital, but he stayed rooted outside her door, unable to move where he was standing.

He had brought this upon her. The Da Vinci and Van Gogh studies and the writings of Eliana had painted a mark on Simone's back.

Two days ago, a summons early in the morning to the papal apartments was a message difficult to ignore. Xavier knew that ignoring such an invitation was not an option.

The Pope had been waiting for him, seated beside his brother, Cardinal Mathew, the air thick with tension.

"I have just met with the doctors," Pope Lucas began, his voice weary, "and the prognosis is not good. I have many faults, but it was to safeguard two-thousand-year-old secrets. Secrets that still shape the world today. I'm deeply sorry for letting you and Simone meet in Paris last year. It was I who prodded Julian from the Louvre to connect the two of you. I thought there would be a spark of connection between you—one that I could exploit. If you felt used, curse me. But here's a peace offering. It may yet heal the broken relationship between you and Simone. Take these to her."

The man who had taught him faith was confessing manipulation.

Xavier said nothing. His face was impassive, but the silence was a verdict in itself. When his gaze met his brother's, a flicker of sorrow crossed Mathew's eyes.

His gaze followed the line of sight of the Pontiff. He recognized the two thin wooden boxes the Vatican Museum used to transport works of art.

"It belongs to my family, Xavier," Pope Lucas said in a soft tone. He then slid two photographs into his hands. "The studies inside the wooden crates."

He was shocked and had no inkling about these two works of art that belonged to the Angelo family. The Pontiff had secrets upon secrets foisted on him. What a burden, he thought.

"I've chartered a plane for you. Please bring these to Simone today. At the back of the studies are copies of the papyrus pages written by Eliana two thousand years ago. I was not successful in gathering her work. Perhaps you'll have better luck with Simone. I hope we can still repair our relationship, Xavier."

It was the first time in a year that the three of them were in the same room, outside of work. When Xavier received a 112 text from Mathew, he knew what it meant: drop everything and come to see him. Whatever problems existed between them did not matter in this emergency. It was time for him to see his brother and Pope Lucas.

Once, they had shared regular Sunday dinners after Mass, a ritual of sharing food and laughter that had been a part of his childhood days.

But this was before Paris. Since then, their relationship had splintered, irreparably broken.

He hadn't stepped inside a church in nearly twelve months. His prayers had long since curdled by bitterness, his faith in God eroded by the maneuverings of two men he once revered—the master manipulator and his flunky, as he had come to call Pope Lucas and his brother Mathew in his darker moments.

He had even handed in his resignation twice as head of the Vatican Museum, but Pope Lucas refused to accept it.

He should have cut ties last year. Had the Pope's schemes set off the chain of events that brought a gunman to the Whitney Museum and left Simone in a hospital bed? He had seen Simone accidentally when Dr. Pauline Lassiter came out from her hospital room, and he had seen her asleep.

A burst of conversation interrupted his thoughts. Nic and Gabby had arrived, carrying paper bags of food. Still, he remained half-hidden behind the partition. He had messaged Nic and inquired about Simone. It was he who mentioned that she was confined in the hospital, and he didn't elaborate further.

"Why did she faint? Has she eaten anything since the all-nighter?" Gabby asked.

"We only had coffee," Nic said in a mournful tone.

"Great," Gabby said dryly. "Shooting, robbery, and caffeine for the day. Perfect recipe for collapse."

A nurse appeared. "Professor Jang, I've been looking for you. Time for your meds."

"Ok, thanks," he said softly, stepping away from his perch. His anxiety attacks over the past hours had been relentless—tight chest, trembling hands, nausea, the crippling sense that the walls were closing in. Dr. Pauline Lassiter, who had seen him in triage, insisted he be admitted for further tests in the hospital.

He turned once more toward Simone's room. Had something else happened after the Whitney shooting? A robbery?

He rushed back to his hospital room and switched on his phone—silent all day while he endured scans and bloodwork. A flood of alerts followed; a hundred messages poured in, all about the theft of studies owned by Pope Lucas.

He closed his eyes. For a moment, the cacophony of sounds reverberating in his brain stilled to a single, undeniable truth: there was nothing he could do about the robbery.

What he could do was see Simone—if she allowed it.

He took a breath and walked toward her room. The room was silent. Gabby and Nic were gone. Leaning against the doorframe, he whispered to no one in particular.

"Let it go where it will."

A nurse interrupted him mid-step. "I'm sorry, Professor Jang, it's past visiting hours. Visitors have been in and out. She needs a night of real rest. You can see her tomorrow."

"Can I just take a quick look? From the door?"

The nurse's smile softened.

"Of course."

For a brief moment, he saw Simone's face, bathed in the dim, forgiving light of the ward. No trace of sadness, disappointment, anger, or pain—emotions he had seen in his last meeting with her in Paris. There was only peace.

He hoped to see that sense of peace again, this time because of him, not in spite of him.

Right then, he made a promise. He would stay in New York until that smile returned—not for her alone, but to make peace with himself.

Chapter 14

S imone Harper

Mt. Tabor Hospital, New York City

Thursday, October 19—9 a.m.

It was that distinct smell of flowery disinfectant that woke her. The brightness of the fluorescent light confirmed her location. She covered her eyes against the glare and turned away.

The hospital. Why was she here?

The room felt familiar, especially the wall color, which reminded her of ripe buckthorn berries. She tried to sit up but felt faint. On her second attempt, she managed to swing her legs over the side of the bed. Her eyes landed on a utilitarian clock by her bedside.

Nine a.m.

It had been almost a day since she'd fainted. Jesus Christ.

She stood up to see if the world spun around her.

Good. No spinning axis. She began to inch toward the door, careful to include the line of dextrose attached to her arm.

She opened the door and peeked into the hallway. It was deserted.

Suddenly, she thought of the shooting incident, and pain flitted across her chest. What was happening to the world? Works of art were considered sacred, and museums were among the last spaces on earth where violent acts were committed. Why did the gunman choose the Whitney? What did it all mean?

In the hallway, she spotted a circular room with the nurses' station in the middle. She recognized the place now.

There was no evidence that the city was experiencing the Danzhou variant of SARS-24C in this bustling hospital. When she and her parents were confined here last year, doctors and nurses seemed to flee from patient to patient, all either dying or coding. She swore she'd never return to this hospital. But something about the familiar place now calmed her. She went back to rest.

A tap-tap-tap sound followed. A female doctor with green-speckled eyes opened the door and peered inside the room.

"Dr. Lassiter," she said in relief. It was the same emergency doctor who treated her yesterday after the shooting.

"I was following up on my cases from yesterday, and I heard you were here. I told the nurses to page me once you were awake. How are you feeling?" Dr. Lassiter inquired, looking at her face, perhaps trying to decode clues from every feature that would determine her health and recovery.

"May I?" the doctor asked, without waiting for her answer, as she pulled up a chair and sat down near the bed. "I learned from your records that you've been experiencing the long-term effects of the first Danzhou virus strain. Sleeplessness, restlessness, depression? But you were able to get past all these without incident. Did the incident yesterday add to your trauma? How are you feeling now?" Dr. Lassiter asked.

"Rested. I had a good night's sleep," she said.

"You fainted yesterday, and they said you were clutching your heart. I checked your tests. There's nothing wrong with your heart. It could be that the shooting at the Whitney and the incident at the Harper Art Institute affected you profoundly. It could be PTSD combined with panic attacks. You feel like you're having a heart attack when nothing of that sort is happening. Detective Rigo mentioned that Dr. Esperanza, the EP you met yesterday, had arranged a therapy session for the survivors of the Whitney shooting. I advise you to participate."

She turned away from Dr. Lassiter. Panic was rising again inside her throat, but she tried to calm herself.

"I'm sorry. Was that too soon? You are a survivor, Simone. I suggest you attend. These group therapy sessions will help you. It's just two sessions," Dr. Lassiter said.

"Where will they be held?" Simone asked.

"Here at Mt. Tabor, where two of the other survivors are being treated. I understand there's a meeting in an hour," Dr. Lassiter said, checking her watch.

"Who else is confined here? Would you know, Dr. Lassiter?" she asked. "Was Professor Xavier Jang hospitalized too?"

"I'm afraid I can't answer your questions, but Detective Rigo can," Dr. Lassiter said.

"Oh," she said in a faltering voice.

"Is there a problem?" Dr. Lassiter asked.

Her heart was beating fast and also hurting.

"Breathe, breathe, Simone," she heard Dr. Lassiter say. She didn't want to faint, but she wasn't sure she could stop herself.

"I guess this is another panic attack," she gasped.

"Breathe slowly. Try to sit up and focus your eyes on something," the doctor said. "Focus on the clock. Name five features that you see."

"It's an ugly ass clock, Dr. Lassiter. I'm sorry," then she chuckled. "Where do they buy this stuff? Okay, okay. The main body has pink neon colors. Apple green hour hand. Yellow minute hand. Red second hand. Gosh, the colors hurt my eyes."

And it worked. The chest ache slipped away, and she felt her heartbeat return to normal.

"It's interesting how I can view the symptoms with dispassion, and yet still be very aware of what I am experiencing," she said.

"You work as an art expert, right? Do you try to determine the authenticity of a work of art? Your profession requires you to observe and to check your feelings at the door. This skill will greatly enhance your healing progress, I can assure you. We can take out the dextrose right now," Dr. Lassiter said. She pressed a button, and a nurse came by for the new orders.

"I guess you do a lot of observational analysis too, Dr. Lassiter. Tell me, are you as self-critical as I am?" she asked.

Dr. Lassiter laughed. "Self-critical to a fault. But there are some things you really can't unsee, especially if it's violent. And that is why you need another observational eye to help you. Dr. Campo is the best. She will find a way to help you go past the panic," she said.

There was a knock at the door, and the balding head of the detective appeared in the doorway.

"Speak of the devil. Detective Rigo, Ms. Harper has a couple of questions for you," Dr. Lassiter said, checking her watch. "I'm afraid I have to look in on other patients."

"Thank you, Dr. Lassiter," Simone said. She grasped the doctor's hands. "I'm very grateful for your help yesterday."

"It's my honor, Ms. Harper," Dr. Lassiter said, as she pulled her hands free and fished for something in her pocket. She brought out her wallet and slid out a white card.

"Just in case you have a question, don't hesitate to call me, all right?" Dr. Lassiter said, and opened the door for the detective.

Detective Rigo was standing in the doorway. Was that hesitation? He was holding a box of some kind.

"Give me a minute while I change," she said, and hurried to the hospital cabinet, opening it. Nic or Gabby must have brought this for her, as she fished out a shirt and pants. She quickly found a comb and, with quick strokes, tried to untangle her hair. Then she brought her purse with her.

She turned around, and the detective was studying the painting in her room. She studied the detective's face. Why do cops look like thugs? she asked herself. Well, the detective could be classified in her mental file as a fashionable thug. She approved the distressed jacket and the light, stone-washed jeans, which were back in fashion. Maybe he'd had them from the last time they were popular. Perhaps the detective didn't follow fashion but inspired it.

Here she was again in her judgy way. Her observational eye never failed her.

He was an interesting-looking man. If she had a pencil and a piece of paper, she would draw his face—dark, ebony skin tone; brown, inquisitive, intelligent eyes; broad nose; full lips. He was fit, like he boxed on weekends and ran long distances on his off days. A short, cropped haircut from a barber. He was holding a bakery box in his hands. A rich, sweet smell filled the room.

"Donuts?" she said.

"I pass by Billy's Bakery every day. I thought you needed something sweet after the incidents yesterday," he said.

She smiled. It was the first time someone had given her donuts in a long time. In general, she hated sweets, but today seemed like a good day to have one.

"Would you like some coffee, Detective? I know there's a nook here somewhere near the terrace," she said and stood up. She needed to see sunshine.

She moved quickly in the hallway. "You seem to know the place very well," the detective said as he matched her pace.

"Yes, too well, I'm afraid. I thought I'd never return here, but I was wrong," Simone said. She waved as she passed by the nurses' station. They registered confusion at her gesture.

"Hahaha, they'll be scrambling to match my face to the names of the patients. Let's see how good they are."

She pushed open the door leading to the terrace and headed outside.

"Fantastic view, huh?"

The detective was looking at her, not at the view. Then he smiled.

"Let me ask, how was it that you were the first responder to the shooting?" she said, sitting on a metal chair that faced the East River.

"I was at Billy's when I got the call. It made sense that I was the first responder," the detective said as he sat down and opened the box.

"How long have you been with the police force, Detective?" she asked as she took one of the donuts. The neon pink donut was almost garish, but what the hell.

"Ten years in a few months," he said. "First shooting in a museum, though," then he shook his head.

"Are you from New York?" she asked.

"Queens," he said, smiling.

"Same here—I mean, I'm from around here," she said. A subtle eyebrow lift, a quick smile, as if her answer was full of bullshit. Well, she'd spent her life in the city, so she was from around here. Then he laughed softly.

"If you're from here, then I'm from outside there in New York," he said, in a deadpan voice.

"Very funny, detective," she said. "But may I ask who the shooter is?"

She was surprised to verbalize the question. Did she really want to know the answer?

"He's from London. And he has a history of violence and religious intolerance that's different from his faith, and—"

"You mean there's no relation to the artwork?" she asked, shocked.

"He was babbling some nonsense about demeaning his faith. Do you want some coffee?" he asked. In response, she stood up.

"Let's get the coffee together," she said.

She tried to catch the barista's eye, and when she was successful, the woman smiled and waved at her.

"Lily's still here. You just have to tell her your order," she instructed the detective, then blew a kiss to Lily, who blew a kiss back.

"How long were you in this hospital last year?" the detective asked.

"Two months? I was recovering from the long-term effects of Danzhou. But my parents didn't make it." Saying those words was painful.

"I'm really sorry," she heard the detective say, and she felt his sincerity. She patted his arm. "Lily's eyeing you. What's your order?"

They took the coffee back to their former spot.

"May I ask you about the paintings that were stolen?" the detective asked and took out a notebook from inside his jacket. "It's my case now. I'm trying to find out if the Whitney shooting and the robbery are related."

"We made a record of everything, so you can go to the Institute and confer with Nic, my deputy. We haven't told the press about this, though. I hope the contents of my purse are still intact after the fainting spell." She rummaged inside her bag and pulled out a pen. "Thank God, I still have it."

The pen had a logo from the Harper Art Institute. Should she give the detective a copy?

Her life until now was a maze of secrets, and she vowed on the terrace a few days ago not to live a life of subterfuge. Why not start with this detective? She was sure the police had copies of it from Nic, but it was still different to be given a copy for personal use. For some reason, she trusted him.

"You can have this digital file, Detective Rodrigo," she said.

She noticed the confusion on the detective's face. Was he shocked? Flustered? This detective kept his cards close to his chest.

"Call me Rigo," it was all the detective could say. "I'm beyond speechless. Thank you."

"All right, Detective Rigo," she said. "It's a copy of writings by Eliana, allegedly one of the daughters of Simon Peter, the apostle. For centuries, it's been called the Gospel of Eliana. And I don't really believe in coincidences, so here—you can have it."

"Is it related to the stolen paintings?" the detective asked.

"Yes, it's related. Technically, you can call it a painting. But both works of art are studies. The artist did not intend them to see the light of day. The papyrus pages in the digital file are copies that originated from the Mona Lisa study, which Pope Lucas owned. It had twenty pages hidden behind it, while the Van Gogh study has five pages."

"Very interesting. Two artists with Eliana material common to both," the detective mused. "Is there a possibility that other parts of the Gospel exist?"

Simone nodded. "Pope Lucas gave me these pages so I can find the others."

"I'm honored, Ms. Harper," the detective said. His voice had softened.

"Please confine this work to a small circle of your peers in the police force. It has stayed hidden for centuries for a reason," she said.

"The police will be looking for the thieves," the detective said. "But why Pope Lucas? Why did his family inherit the papyrus scrolls?"

She searched inside her purse again and pulled out some hard copies of the Eliana pages and placed them on the table.

"Your purse can store a ton of things," the detective teased.

"A teacher's habit. You just have to have everything inside, including the blackboard," she answered with a breath of laughter. "Anyway, see the markings on the corner? What do you see? Are they the same?"

"Three teardrops and another symbol," the detective said. "Perhaps it indicates ownership?"

"Very good, detective," she said. "The writings were entrusted to two people. This one with this symbol is equivalent to our Roman letter M. M is Mary Magdalene, the ancestor of Pope Lucas."

"And the other symbol, which is different?" the detective's eye zeroed in on the differences in the documents in a few seconds. She was impressed.

"The symbol in Syriac Estrangela is for Yod, similar to our Y," she explained.

"It could mean it was intended for Yaakov or Yohan?"

She had always trusted her gut, and she knew the detective fulfilled that role. Robbing the Institute was a brazen act, and she needed all the help she could get. It was time to reveal the secrets that had been kept for two millennia.

"Just message me if you have any questions," she said.

"Thank you. I'll keep this to a close circle of associates I trust. But I'll treasure this—thank you," the detective said. "Shall I accompany you to the therapy session?"

She would have said no yesterday. But a series of events had happened as soon as she decided upon her rooftop, standing on the ledge, to open up and say yes.

It brought her the studies, Xavier Jang, a shooting incident, a robbery, and this detective. A whole range of possibilities opened, and she was willing again to enter into the chaos her choices brought.

She was unmade up, her hair a mess, and she wouldn't be caught with this kind of casual wear outside her home.

She raised her hands and felt the warmth of the sun. A smile spread across her face. Then she glanced at the detective.

"Yes, I'm open to an hour of the therapy session. Why not?" Simone answered.

———…◆…———

The detective brought her to another part of the hospital. It was also on the rooftop, but the view now faced Long Island City and Queens. Before bidding goodbye, the detective bowed to her, and she bowed back playfully.

She turned, and Xavier was standing at a distance, his tall frame draped in the most expensive clothes money could buy. He did not dress this way last year. Now, his clothes reeked of formality, rigidity, and distance.

"Thank God you're safe," she heard a voice say. She turned, and it was Gabby walking toward her.

"Oh Gabby," she ran to embrace her. She brought both of her hands to cup Gabriel's face. "I heard that you, too, ran toward the shooter. Why did you do that?"

"You and Xavier were subduing the shooter, and thought I could help," Gabby said, a quick laugh escaping her. "Now, all my muscles are aching."

"Did you have a checkup in the hospital?" she asked.

"Yes, they insisted," Gabby said. "I was about to visit you, but Dr. Lassiter said that you'd be attending this session, so here I am."

The group settled into chairs arranged in a circle. Xavier sat beside Simone.

An older woman dressed in an elegant Galinco coat stepped forward. "I'm Patricia Campo, your therapist," she said. "Dr. Esperanza created this group, but I'm the one handling the session for now. Let's introduce ourselves, shall we? And please call me Patricia." Her voice was soft, with a sing-song pattern. It reminded Simone of gentle chirping birds near her parents' home in Sweden.

"Simone," Patricia said. "Why don't you start first with yourself?"

There was no getting out of it, so she plunged ahead. "I'm Simone Harper, I'm..." she faltered, then caught herself. "I work at Harper Art Institute. I was supposed to assist the Chief Curator at the Whitney in authenticating a painting at the museum when the shooting started. Thank you all for holding on to the attacker. I'm happy you are all safe, and I hope we can benefit from Dr. Campo's sessions."

She passed an invisible baton to Xavier.

"I'm Xavier Jang. Call me Xavier," he said. "I head the Vatican Museum, and I was at the Whitney yesterday to meet and confer with Professor Harper when the shooting started. I have never been in a situation like this, and I hope I never will again. Thanks to everyone's help. I don't think it would have been possible to subdue that guy without the group's collective effort."

There was a smattering of applause, and Xavier turned to his right.

Simone realized he was the man from the High Line, and she also saw him at the Last Supper exhibit. His style was so eclectic and strange, but somehow fashion-forward.

"I'm Tarquin Vern," he said, "the chef at The Nakharin next door. You can call me Tarquin. Nice to meet you all."

The battered black leather jacket he wore seemed destined for the trash heap. But that didn't fool Simone. She'd seen rapper Dd wearing one like it at the Met's opening. Its zigzagging zippers were dizzying, like a mad artist who had a silver sharpie and scribbled it all over the garment. His shoes were Yazlo, a shoe brand once gifted to her by a curator friend based in Berlin. This guy wanted to appear nondescript, but her discriminating eye told her a different tale.

Whereas Xavier's hair was immaculate and closely trimmed, Tarquin's was dyed blonde and appeared self-cut. His hands were red, calloused. Whoever he was, he did a lot of manual labor. But wasn't being a chef laborious work?

"You're all invited to my restaurant tomorrow. I heard Xavier is an MMA enthusiast. We can watch the Brazilian Jiu-Jitsu championship while I'm trying some new dishes," Tarquin said.

She'd been to Nakharin several times. She wondered if she had seen his face in the kitchen before. He had a distinct accent that she couldn't quite catch.

"Let's give the floor to Gabby," Patricia said.

"I'm Gabby Henry," she said. "I work at the Whitney and a friend of Simone's. We met when I was a student and a young mother with a restless child. I brought Ethan to the Harper Art Institute to view the paintings on display there. The paintings calmed him, which was not the case when I brought him to the Whitney."

Everyone around her laughed.

"I requested Simone to come to the Whitney, and I've been waking up with nightmares knowing that I could have been responsible for another person harming her. Because Professor Xavier led the charge, we're all safe," Gabby said as she blew him an imaginary kiss.

Xavier made a slight bow. And with that, the introductions were complete, and Dr. Campo got down to business.

"Anyone not sleeping well?" Dr. Campo asked, and there were nods all around. "Would you like to share experiences? You can talk about anything here."

Gabby went first. "It feels like a big chunk of coal is in my throat now. And any sound makes me jumpy," she said.

"I've been feeling the same, Gabby," Simone answered. The rest turned to her. "So, are these trauma symptoms, Dr. Campo?"

"It is trauma," the doctor confirmed. "I would like to offer some exercises, with your permission. Can you take off your shoes and sit in a circle in the middle of the room?" Patricia rolled out a round mat, and everyone joined her on the floor.

"Can we all hold hands?" Dr. Campo said once all were seated.

Simone was surprised when Xavier sat next to her and reached for her hand.

And then he closed his eyes. The warmth of his hand was incredibly soothing. Without any reason, Simone felt a tear escape her eye.

"What happened yesterday was not your fault," Patricia said. "We will never understand the motive of the shooter. That is his problem and not yours. Your brain may continue to try to focus on what happened. I want you to focus on what you can control. Focus on the hand holding on to you, focus on what you can hear, and focus on the clock ticking. This moment is the present, and that's the important part."

"What if my mind is focused on the blood trickling under my feet yesterday?" Simone asked.

"We will not bury the memory. Instead, focus on your breathing and what's happening before you. Can we do that?" Patricia said.

"I'm furious at the son of a bitch who shot innocent people," Gabby said.

"Alright, Gabby. Now, I will save you years of therapy," Dr.Campo said. "Think of the nerves as fractured, a broken leg. It needs to heal. There's nothing we can do with broken bones. Accept what you've been coping with for the past twenty-four hours, whether it's waking in the middle of the night, vomiting, or having heart palpitations. Your body has experienced trauma and is trying to cope with these conditions. These are your metaphorical broken bones."

"Do we wait for them to heal?" Gabby asked.

"If your heart feels like it's exploding, believe me, you are not having a heart attack. You are just being more sensitive to your heart beating. Studies have borne out this phenomenon. People who are having panic attacks have no rising beats per minute. It's normal. If you have the shakes, just accept them and let them ride out. And I'll teach you to float past it." Patricia stood and put her hands overhead in a diving stance.

"Float?" Gabby asked in an incredulous tone. "My son Ethan would love that."

Simone turned to look at Xavier. This exercise was a foreign concept to him, she bet. His face was impassive, although his mouth twitched a little.

"Here's a good way to help you," Dr.Campo said to Xavier. "Stand up and bring your hands forward."

With reluctance, Xavier did as she asked. Patricia pushed against his arms.

"Feel this pressure?" Dr. Campo asked Xavier. "Stop fighting, ignoring it, or putting up a stiff upper lip. You're trying to fight your nervous system," and she released her hands. "Accept these uncomfortable physical feelings and let time pass. Imagine that you're swimming, using any swimming stroke, and swim away from the feelings. Raise your hands and let's swim, float past it. The shaking continues, but you can leave it behind. If you're scared of water, think of floating past a cloud."

Simone copied Dr. Campo and raised her hands. And then she closed her eyes, stretched her hands out, and thought of swimming on a beach in Boracay a long time ago.

"Is it better?" she heard Dr. Campo's voice again. "Let's return to the present. Now I will confer with you individually and give you sedatives if you need to sleep tonight. Our session has ended. See you in two days for the next one."

As she got to her feet, Xavier stood in front of her.

"Would you like to have a cup of..." Xavier was about to finish his sentence when Tarquin's booming voice interrupted.

"Coffee, everyone? I've asked a good friend who's a doctor here if I could bring a small coffee machine from Nakharin. Step out that door, and we can have coffee in the mini garden," Tarquin said.

"Sounds good," she said and headed for the door.

Xavier walked with her. "Nic asked me to go to the Institute tomorrow to discuss the Mona Lisa and Van Gogh studies. Pope Lucas will join us," he said.

He seemed to find it easy to speak to her about their profession. There had never been awkwardness between them where art was concerned.

"Yes," she said, "I'd like to hear your thoughts on the robbery. Do you think it's related to the Whitney shooting?" As soon as she asked the question, a look of concern flashed in Xavier's face.

"I want to see Nic's documentation," he said after a pause. "Then we can start to piece out the mystery."

The smell of brewed coffee lured them into the gardens. A man with "Nakharin" engraved in a chic apron stood beside the coffee machine.

"Here's my man Carlos," Tarquin said. "He brought some Thai sweet dishes you might like to try."

Tarquin set the table for them and helped with everyone's orders. Dr. Campo took a seat in the corner to speak with anyone who wanted to talk to her privately.

The desserts were wrapped in colorful paper. Simone took one and sat in a chair, savoring the delicious dessert. It was the first time in two days she'd felt her muscles relax.

"Tarquin, this is a godsend," Gabby said, as she brought the coffee cup to her nose so she could savor the scent. "What coffee is this?" she asked.

"I didn't know what everyone liked, so I chose our best-seller, Tanzanian Peaberry," Tarquin said and sat next to Simone. He turned to the others. "Hey everyone, are you on for dinner at Nakharin tomorrow?"

"I'm in," Gabby said without hesitation. "Ethan is with my Mum for the whole week while I recover from this incident."

"I'm in, too," Xavier said. "I've deferred work for now."

"You'll enjoy it, Simone," Gabby said. "I think watching live sporting events makes us vicarious martial artists. Anyway, it's only because of you that I went charging in after that psycho. You were so brave, and I thought you needed help."

"I'd like to join you," she said, surprising herself.

"That's great. See you tomorrow night," Tarquin beamed.

"Simone," Xavier said. He had moved his chair close to hers.

She stood up. "I must go. Doctor's appointment. I'll see you tomorrow, everyone," she said. She didn't need to see Xavier's face to see the disappointment in his eyes. She felt it.

She promised the detective that she'd say yes for an hour. And she survived. But that's her limit for now.

Baby steps. It was so unlike her to be so impulsive, but the ground beneath her had disappeared after yesterday's events. Who knew what the next hour would bring?

She was ready to find out.

From the corner of her eye, a nurse waved at her.

"Ms. Harper, you still need to accomplish some additional tests before the hospital gives the all clear," the nurse said. "You left your room, and Dr. Lassiter mentioned it's for a therapy sessioCampo."

All eyes were on her, but she waved them away.

"I'll see you tomorrow morning, Xavier," she said.

"Bright and early. See you tomorrow," Xavier replied softly.

It was a productive therapy session, and she felt good about learning a few techniques. She hoped the panic attacks would go away in a few days. She needed to be in a good place to find the missing pieces in Eliana's work.

Chapter 15

Xavier

The Standard, New York City

Friday, October 20—8 a.m.

The meeting with the Pontiff and Simone was still an hour away. The Standard, a Brutalist muse of rectangular lines and glass, was too gray and modern for his Roman bones. He wanted some sunshine.

He walked out and stopped. Now, which way? He turned toward the Hudson River. Hmmm, sunshine and water. Perfecto.

The early morning meant the streets were now devoid of tourists. He crossed the street from 14th Street toward Pier 55. The memory of the deteriorating pier of olden times bothered him. As he approached the Hudson River, timber pilings were still visible from the waters, the only remnants of a once-bustling landing for transatlantic voyages.

A bloom of giant tulips on man-made cement stilts rose above the water. Above the tulips were a collection of trees, abloom in gold and red, heralding the glorious colours of fall.

A sign on the side—Little Island. He walked towards the entrance of the park, sat at a nearby bench, and saw an oasis of maple and dogwood trees surrounded by lush ornamental grasses.

His breathing slowed down amidst the greenery. It was the first time in his visit to this city that he was able to pause and just be still. The events of the past days had not fully registered yet, and the therapy helped to make him more aware of what was happening inside his body and mind.

He raised his hands and faced the sun, basking in its warmth. That felt so good.

There was a faint beeping on his wrist, and he opened his eyes. Enough of paradise. It was time to go back to reality. His meeting with Pope Lucas and Simone, with other art experts, was set in thirty minutes. It was time to walk toward Harper Art Institute, which was a seven-minute walk from this quiet spot.

He stood up and took a different route, this time opting for the walkway beside the peaceful, calm waters. He took a deep breath and turned towards the bustling 10th Avenue, where the corner hotdog stop was open, and he waved at the proprietor setting up shop, who waved back.

Other than that, it was a quiet walk towards the front doors of the Institute. A receptionist greeted him and led him to one of the conference rooms on the ground floor.

No one was around—*Calmo e silenzioso come una notte senza vento*—calm and silent like a windless night.

It was his first time visiting this part of the building. The Art Deco designs inside the room were extraordinary. He surmised that the finishes had stood intact since the 1930s, when Christopher Harper, Simone's great-grandfather, bought the building. The motif was modernized with butter-yellow walls, and the windows were widened to accommodate the light from outside.

His eye caught the furnishings, and he walked towards the conference table. He was drawn to the grain of wood on the conference table. He tapped on it. *Legno di noce*—walnut?

His Renaissance desk in his Vatican office was made of walnut. He glanced around and, seeing no one, knelt on the floor to look at the desk. Nordic furniture, characterized by its clean lines, was likely produced in the 1940s.

He stood up again and noticed the unique structural lines of the chair wrapped in sheepskin. *Pecora islandese*—Icelandic sheep? His thoughts were interrupted by a discreet cough.

"Professor Jang? I'm Nic Aishish, Simone's assistant. Welcome to Harper Institute," he heard a voice, and turned around to reach out and introduce himself.

"Xavier Jang," he introduced himself. "Boy, this redecoration is fantastic."

"This is all Simone's design choices," Nic said, his voice warm with pride. "But the desk is Gordon Harper's, Simone's father. He liked the clean, modernist ethos of his Nordic roots. He didn't like the Art Deco so much, but Simone insisted."

"Thank you for arranging this on short notice, Nic. Looks like the materials are nicely prepared," he said, and pointed towards the table where stacks of material were neatly arranged.

"Oh, you're welcome, Xavier. Thanks for arranging the breakfast spread," Nic said and pointed to a buffet table being set up for the meeting. "How about some coffee?"

He smiled. *"Ci vuole proprio un espresso. Grazie*—what we really need is an espresso. Thanks."

"One for the espresso. Here comes the cavalry," Nic said as he turned towards the door.

A group of voices was heard, and with a sigh of relief, he knew everyone he had invited was here. There was Rebecca Fournier, the New York representative for Hampton Institute, Pierre Ganouche from the Ganouche Galleries, and Sam Stewart from Cooper & Smith.

"*Buongiorno*—good morning, Xavier. Hey Nic, nice spread here," Pierre Ganouche said in enthusiasm, going straight to the buffet table and choosing the cannolo.

"Try the one dipped in chocolate or nuts, my friend," Xavier said.

Even with an invitation by the Pope, he knew everyone was busy with packed schedules, and it was a sacrifice for them to attend this meeting. As the representative of the Pontiff, Xavier wanted the guests to feel at ease. Yes, the buffet was more than generous for five guests. He would have to remind Nic to invite the staff of Harper Institute to partake of the pastries and coffee after the morning meeting.

"Impressive cast, huh, Xavier?" Nic whispered. "It is the greatest minds in the art world."

Just then, Simone walked in. Her expression was indecipherable, but Nic waved at her and she acknowledged his greeting with a nod.

"It's the least I can do, after the theft. How's Simone coping up?" he asked.

"Not so good," Nic said and made an up and down motion with his hands.

He turned and watched Simone. She was still pale, but she was listening with intensity to the conversation between Rebecca and Pierre. A pair of *pica picas*, those chattering birds he hated in parks in Rome. Time to cut the gabfest.

"Good morning, everyone. I am grateful that you could join us on short notice. Is the breakfast spread to your liking?" Xavier asked.

There were various sounds of approval heard around the room.

"Throw me a rye ciabatta anytime, X," Rebecca said. He chuckled.

Everyone in the conference room were his rivals and competitors, as well as his former students or teachers in academia. They were trusted colleagues as well. He knew they'd be the first to help him when he had a problem, like now.

"How is the Pontiff, Xavier?" Peter asked. The eating and bantering suddenly stopped. "How is he taking the robbery of family heirlooms?"

"Every conversation I've had in the past days starts with the fabulous collection of his family," Rebecca said. "Who could have taken it?"

"The Pontiff is not showing that he is affected," he replied. "I heard he brought another guest yesterday using a Gianni car, took the wheel, and drove it off somewhere after hearing the news."

Groans and laughter were heard around the room.

"Better to have some fun times after getting some bad news," Rebecca said.

"Was the Pontiff five when he started winning races?" Pierre asked.

Xavier nodded. Scion of the powerful Angelo family, founder of Gianni Motors, there was no vehicle the Pontiff wouldn't race. He was a raconteur, a bon vivant who lived life in the fast lane.

"Here are the works that were stolen," Nic interrupted the bantering and turned to the wall. The two stolen paintings were now in front of the assembled group.

"To hide this beauty in the family treasury was quite a mean thing to do, but sharing it with the world in the past days was quite generous," Rebecca said.

"Who knew Da Vinci did so many studies of the Mona Lisa?" Pierre said.

"You can say all of this to the Pontiff. Here he is," Xavier said. There was a collective gasp of surprise, and an image of Pope Lucas appeared on the big screen, in front of the conference table. He wasn't looking directly at the camera. He seemed to be observing the scene outside a window behind him, where a breathtaking view of hundreds of orange trees and workers busy with various tasks lay.

"Pope Lucas, *Buon pomeriggio*—good afternoon. It's four in the afternoon in Rome, but 10 in the morning here," Xavier said. There was a stark difference between the early morning jesting of the participants around the table and their solemn demeanors now.

Pope Lucas smiled when he realized he was on camera, and the mood inside the conference room brightened as well. Ah, the perils of a public life, Xavier thought. You had to act in certain ways even if your mind was somewhere else.

"Oh hello, Peter, Rebecca, and Pierre," said Pope Lucas. Then he turned towards Simone. "Simone. Thanks so much for meeting me this early morning."

Everyone present, except Simone, had acted as brokers when benefactors wanted to donate and add to the Vatican's treasures. On a personal level, most had acted as consultants for the masterpieces the Gianni family had wanted to buy over the years. Of course, they were all grateful, Xavier thought.

"Oh, hello, Pope Lucas," Rebecca said in a cheerful tone. "It's so good to see you. We have a lot of questions about the works of art, which were unfortunately stolen from here."

There was an awkward silence. Xavier was glad Simone didn't avert her eyes but instead met the Pontiff's gaze.

"Fire away, Rebecca," the Pontiff chuckled. "You always like your ducks lined up."

"Ready to shoot," Pierre said in a playful tone from the other side of the table. Simone's glance shot daggers. What a word to use in front of her. Then Pierre realized his mistake.

"Oops, my apologies, Simone, for my wrong choice of words. I've belatedly realised it's too soon to mention," Pierre said and clasped his hands together in supplication. There was no reaction from Simone, still affected by the robbery.

Rebecca wasn't interested in any drama in the room. "Alright, how did the studies get into your hands? I know some parts of the story, but not all of it," she said.

"When I was a young man, before entering the priesthood, I had an accident at Le Rise in Switzerland," the Pontiff said, "I became very despondent. I was eighteen, and I was just told I might not be able to walk. That was a death sentence. I stayed in my room and did not talk to anyone. My mother, bless her soul, did not fight against my mood. I mourned. And my mother did not lecture at all.

"She did not give me books to read, nor did she encourage me to see psychiatrists," the Pontiff said. "Instead, after a few months in a convalescence home in Switzerland, I went home to Italy. I started roaming around the halls, which were full of the paintings my forefathers collected over the centuries," the Pope said.

"I bet it's Aladdin's cave of treasures in there," Pierre said, and laughter burst from the room.

"You know, I was never aware of these works of art until the accident happened, and in those months I spent alone, my eyes popped open. Caravaggio paintings, Michelangelo sculptures, and other masterpieces. And then this, the Mona Lisa study by Da Vinci. It was just sitting in the corner of the drawing room, amidst other grander paintings.

"There was something compelling about the Mona Lisa study. I took it down and noticed the paper behind it was loose. I opened the painting's back, and voila, discovered a few pages from Eliana. To say that I was shocked was an understatement.

"And then, my mother gave me another morsel to chew on. She told me we were the descendants of Mary Magdalene," the Pontiff said.

"More like a bomb to chew on!" Pierre said.

The Pontiff laughed. "Good to hear your voice, Pierre. I thought you were going to charge me a thousand dollars for every word you uttered," he said.

"But how about Eliana? Is she related to Mary Magdalene?" Rebecca asked.

"If you read the pages, you'd know in a heartbeat who she is," the Pontiff said.

"Alright, fair answer. What is the original language of Eliana's writings?" Pierre asked.

"It's in Syriac—the Estrangela hand, a script so old that even the scholars in Eliana's time will have a difficult time understanding it. Thank God for our modern translation tools," Simone said.

"Your Holiness, did anyone from your family seek experts to study it?" Rebecca asked in a serious tone

"My family is based in Italy. We were pioneers in engineering, and in the 1800s, we were torchbearers for the barely understood sport of motor racing. We were considered vastly wealthy but intellectually inferior. The academics scorned us," the Pope laughed. "But yes, experts have seen it and there are translations as well, if you are interested."

"And besides, would you talk about this beauty outside the home?" Xavier said and pointed to a photograph of the painting on another screen.

"How true are the rumours that St. Peter is also one of your ancestors?" Rebecca asked.

"Actually," Pope Lucas paused, "We are not related at all. I hold in my heart a list of some of the descendants of the Apostles, but can't reveal it lest my enemies make their lives a living hell."

There were oohs and aahhs around the room.

"There were rumours that David, the eventual husband of Mary Magdalene, was also a follower of Jesus. But due to persecution, he and Mary fled to Gaul, modern-day France, and some ancestors eventually landed in Italy," the Pope said.

"Did you hear any stories about who possessed the complete works of Eliana?" Simone said.

"What I heard was that the complete writings were divided, and five trusted disciples were given a copy," the Pope said.

"Five Apostles from the original twelve, you mean?" Rebecca said.

"No. Four of the original twelve. The fifth is Joseph of Arimathea, said to be a blood relative of Mary, mother of Jesus," Pope Lucas said. "The Apostles were in contact one way or the other. But when Pope Gregory called Mary Magdalene a prostitute in 140 AD, all bets were off for our family. We knew that the descendants of the Apostles would be targeted. We didn't know if it was because the enemies knew who'd held the Gospel of Eliana over the centuries, or were trying to find out."

"How many pages of Eliana's work were hidden in the Mona Lisa painting?" Sam Stewart asked.

"Twenty pages. And just five pages in the Van Gogh study. As you all know, the Van Gogh is a recent piece. The original owner gave it to our family around twenty years ago.

"Mary of Magdala was a recipient of Eliana's writings. Who was the recipient of the pages in the Van Gogh study?" Pierre asked.

"Many have hidden their identities, but we are still trying to identify the owner of the Van Gogh study was. It arrived anonymously to my family," the Pontiff said.

"Can we start the Mona Lisa study?" Rebecca asked without preamble.

"Nic," Simone said, "can we have the images for the two Mona Lisas—the Louvre and the other, the study?" The screen shifted to show both images side by side.

Simone grabbed the pointer and clicked on its light. She pointed to the face of the Mona Lisa, which was magnified a hundred thousand times.

"I've compared this with the Louvre painting. We all know from experts that there were letters L or LV in Mona Lisa's right eye and S, B, or CB in her left eye. In the study owned by the Gianni family, only the right eye has the same letters," Simone said.

"The Roman numeral LV means 55," Pierre said. "A treasure trove of clues."

"The numbers were fascinating," Simone said. "But it was the hands of the Mona Lisa I was interested in. Luca Pacioli, a noted mathematician during Da Vinci's time, wrote 'Summa de arithmetica, geometria, proportioni et proportionalita' which assigned value to finger positions. May I show another image?"

"Of course," Xavier said.

"Here's a chart showing how to represent numbers using finger positions. And if we compare it to the Louvre Mona Lisa, her right hand seems relaxed with fingers together, while the left hand looks folded but not clenched," Simone said.

"It's equivalent to 3,000," Rebecca said.

"Which doesn't make sense at all," Pierre said.

"But if we look at the Gianni study, the left hand's index and middle fingers are shown while the right hand's thumb, index, and middle are seen," Simone said.

"Here's a chart showing how to represent numbers using finger positions. And if we compare it to the Louvre Mona Lisa, her right hand seems relaxed with fingers together, while the left hand looks folded but not clenched," Simone said.

"Cinquantasei. 56," he said.

"What does it mean?" Rebecca asked. "It must be related to the Van Gogh study in front of us."

The image in front of them changed to one of Van Gogh's works, "The Café in the Terrace at Night."

"With regard to this Van Gogh work, many in the art world know that it is a Symbolist Last Supper. See the 'waiter in white' in the middle of the restaurant with 12 patrons," Simone said. "And there are visible crosses too."

"It's thirteen, if you include the hooded figure," Rebecca said.

"Any idiot would know it's Jesus and his 12 Apostles," Sam said. "And I'm an atheist. Apologies, Pope Lucas."

"Apologies taken," Pope Lucas said and blessed him on screen.

"There's even a black figure near the doorway, which represents Judas the Betrayer," Nic said.

"Ah-huh. But notice the Gianni study, there are no patrons in the restaurant except the white and black figures," Simone said. "But who can see the similarities?"

"In the oil, I see a lot of 6 in the roof? But not in the drawing. My God," Rebecca said in a high-pitched voice.

"I see a number 5 in the drawing. Sneaky artists," Sam said and laughed. "You have your 55 or 56 here as well, Xavier."

"There are a lot more studies of Da Vinci's Mona Lisa at the Louvre," the Pontiff said.

"I have a few days off. I would like to go to the Louvre and see the magnification at its Research and Restoration Center," Simone said, and applause spontaneously burst around the room.

"Way to go, Simone." "You deserve a break!" She heard a lot of comments and did a semi-bow.

"I just need a break from shootings and robberies, thank you very much," Simone said.

"You will go to Paris? It's the first time I've heard of it," Nic said, raising his eyebrow.

" I need a break anyway," Simone said. "I'll be swinging by Arles too, where Café by the Terrace was painted."

"Arles. There could be something in that place, connected with the charcoal study, that might help reveal more Eliana pages from Café by the Terrace," Rebecca mused.

⸻ ◆ ⸺

Nakharin Restaurant, NYC

Friday, October 20 - 6 p.m.

The therapy group went to dinner in Nakharin to watch a World Brazilian Jiu-Jitsu fight. The fight was exciting, but his attention was divided equally among Simone, Gabby, and Tarquin.

Simone was distant and wary, all the while downing several glasses of wine, watching everyone's moves. Her eyes would move to the door, as if she was expecting another shooter to come to their midst.

Tarquin had a nervous, distracted energy, his furrowed brow more pronounced than it had been yesterday as he conferred with both his staff in the kitchen and the servers who brought food to the various tables. He was flitting from one table to another, their moves precise yet graceful like a perfectly choreographed ballet scene in Teatro dell'Opera in Rome.

He noticed that Gabby was distracted too. She watched the fight in intermittent moments, often standing up to walk outside and talk in private. Still solving problems with the Last Supper exhibit?

Perhaps everyone was still affected by the shooting two days ago.

"How about some dancing, huh? Let's just burn our nervous energy," Gabby suggested. "Ade Lane Club after dinner at Nakharin, anyone?"

"*Perfecto! Balliamo e scatenamoci!* - let's go dancing and let loose," Xavier agreed and stood up.

"Let me hand this circus to my sous chef then. I need a break," Tarquin said in relief.

There was a slight lift in Simone's mouth, a small smile. Does she like to dance? He had no idea at all.

They followed Gabby's lead and walked a block away. "C'mon, follow me." She turned and stepped into a noisy bar, pushing past the rowdy drinkers, until they reached the top of the stairs, where loud music pulsed from a floor below.

"I love dive bars. C'mon, Gabby, let's dance!" Simone said, catching both of Gabby's hands, dragging her down the steps where a dance floor appeared. People were dancing to the tune of Distract. She started clapping and began to swing her hips, raising her hands in the air.

And Gabby copied her moves. Tarquin followed them to the dance floor and joined in the dancing.

He secured a table in the jam-packed room and was about to follow them to the dance floor, but he stopped when he caught sight of Simone, Gabby, and Tarquin dancing.

The noise and the upbeat music changed the mood for everyone. He could stay here all night and observe Simone.

Xavier had never seen her this way.

Two days in Paris. That's all the time spent with her last year. He was still paying for its consequences till now.

But then, Simone waved her hands and motioned that she was returning to the table. Gabby and Tarquin followed.

"Four bottles of Birra Moretti and four shots of soju, please," Simone called her order to a server. "You have to try this!"

When the drinks were set at their table, Simone lined up the glasses, poured beer into a glass until it was halfway full, then dropped a shot of soju into each glass.

"In honor of your Italian and Korean roots, welcome to New York, Xavier. This drink is called somaek," Simone said, and drank the concoction till it was empty. "Cheers!"

"Hey Xavier, dance a little, would you? I'll save the table," Tarquin said.

"Alright," he said and stood. "But Tarquin, chef with nimble cooking hands, teach me some moves, will you?"

"You got all the moves, Xavier. Go, and enjoy," shooing him to the dance floor.

"How about I dance with you ladies. C'mon, Simone and Gabby," Xavier implored and stretched out his hands. Simone offered her hands, and he took them. Simone's moves were a bit hesitant, but when Gabby tapped her on the back, indicating that she'll join them, she started to dance in wild abandon to the music. They were both jumping up and down, in time with the beat.

Simone started to pirouette in fast spins. And faltered as she neared the edge of the dance floor. He walked towards her as she stumbled and fell into his arms.

The smell of freesias and pears. The same perfume Simone had used last year.

"Xavier," she said.

"Shhhh...shhhh... just stay in my arms till the alcohol wears off a bit," he said.

"You son of a bitch, you're a heartless monster. You are," Simone wagged a finger. "You're a ..." Then Simone placed her head in his chest. "I need to drink water," she said.

He led her to their table.

"I'm ok, I'm ok," Simone said as she sat down. Gabby had returned to their table too, and requested a glass of water to give to Simone. Tarquin had stopped dancing and sat down with the group.

Xavier started to relax. The dancing really helped. For a few minutes today, he forgot a little about what he had seen a few days ago. Memories of dead bodies vanished inside this club.

"Hey, what are your plans for the weekend?" Simone asked the group, her words a little slow, but clear.

"I'm leaving for Paris tomorrow. Two chefs I know based in France are celebrating their birthdays," Tarquin said.

"Paris in the weekend! I'm checking out some stuff at the Louvre," Simone said, then smiled as she turned to face Xavier. "Why don't you come with me Xavier? Tarquin, we're taking the same route. Come, join me. And hey, why don't you join us too, Gabby? You're on leave for two weeks. What do you say?"

"Simone, you're drunk, my friend. But the night is young," Gabby said. "Let's go dance!" Gabby stood and reached for Simone's hand.

"I'm serious," Simone said. "I'm using my father's private jet for the last time. I'm thinking of shuttering the gas guzzler behemoth. I'm inviting you to France - Xavier, Tarquin, and Gabby tomorrow. Let's go, let's go. Just for a day. We'll be back by nighttime. It's my treat. Tomorrow. Hangar 10, JFK. 8 a.m. Your company would be great. Please?" Simone asked and brought two hands together in a gesture of supplication.

"Why not? Paris, here I come," Gabby yelled. It was an ear-splitting sound.

The music picked up with a Japanese jazz beat that was currently all the rage. Simone stood up and ran to the dance floor, turned around five times, and dropped into a ballet split.

The crowd shrieked and clapped.

"Thank God for ballet lessons!" Simone shouted.

She wobbled a bit as she stood up, and Tarquin reached out to catch her elbow.

"Simone," Tarquin said. "Let's call it a night, huh?" He draped an arm on her shoulder.

"Ouch, your fingers pricked me," Simone said and wagged a finger at Tarquin. "Your chef hands are too sharp, Tarquin. Geez!"

He moved towards Simone.

"Let's call it a night, huh? We have to all wake up if we're going early to Paris tomorrow," Xavier said.

Simone patted his chest. "Xavier, when will you relax? Come on, man, you have to loosen it up. The night is young," she said as she leaned on his shoulder. She was dead drunk.

"Let me bring you home," he said in a firm voice.

"All right, all right. But I'd better see you tomorrow, okay?" Simone asked.

"I'll bring her home. Let's call it a night, shall we?" Gabby said as she stepped forward to support Simone's left arm. He stood and took the other arm.

They all started towards the exit. Xavier turned around and saw that Tarquin did not follow them to the door. Instead, he stayed at the table.

Xavier tapped Gabby and shifted Simone's weight to her.

"Can you watch Simone for a minute? I think I dropped my device," he said, pointing to his ear. He darted back towards the table, but instead of going straight to look for it, he held back and watched Tarquin.

Tarquin took off a ring and placed it inside his pocket.

Why did he do that? Was that the ring that scratched Simone when Tarquin placed an arm around her? Was he looking for someone's DNA from the group?"

He turned back and returned to Simone and Gabby, who were now outside the dive's door.

"Thanks for your help, Gabby," he said. "Let's bring Simone home, then I'll bring you home as well."

"I'll get the cab," Tarquin said, appearing beside them.

Deceitful bastard. No, you won't get in a cab with us and get our addresses, he thought.

"It's ok. I have a car and driver waiting for me. "*Molte grazie* – many thanks," he said.

"*Ci vediamo* – see you then," Tarquin answered. "I might take up Simone's offer tomorrow. Will you join us on a trip to Paris?"

There was no way in hell he was going to leave Simone and Gabby with this person.

"Yes, I'll join you. *A domani* – see you tomorrow," Xavier said.

"*A domani. Buona notte* – see you tomorrow. Goodnight," Tarquin said, and saluted the air as he walked away.

"Got you," he thought. He was wondering where the peculiar accent came from, given his perfect, unaccented English. Then he realized – Tarquin was French.

He waved him off and smiled. But Tarquin was not smiling back.

Chapter 16

S imone

The Maignon Building, New York City

Saturday, October 2—11 a.m.

A drunken fool. She had acted drunk while dancing the night away at Ade Lane.

But she was sober all the time.

Years of subterfuge had taught her to act one way and be another person.

She'd noticed Tarquin's every move at Ade Lane. There was something very odd about him.

She shooed Gabby and Xavier away when they reached her apartment. She signaled Mr. Filigree at the entrance of her building, and he opened the door. But she didn't enter at first.

"I'm serious. I'm ok," Simone said and walked back to the street curb where Xavier's black car and a driver were waiting. "See you later."

When they left, she waved to Mr. Filigree and hurried back to her apartment. As soon as she closed the door, she entered a small room and turned on the shower. Instead of water, a gooey, sticky liquid poured over her. It was primitive and decades old in technology. It showed traces of DNA elements from people who had touched her, whether accidentally or not. It also revealed traces of material she had touched.

The machine beeped, and red splotches of trace materials appeared.

She pressed another button, and pictures were taken of what was found. They were then filed and cross-referenced by the machine.

She opened the lights, and pictures of fingerprints, DNA, and their accompanying owners were now visible around the room.

"Uhmmm, interesting," she said. "Gotcha!"

Tarquin's face appeared, and she compared it with the others on her list. Sure enough, there he was, a descendant of Benjamin, one of the 71 members of the Sanhedrin. Benjamin was also a cousin of Yudah, Yaakov and Yohan of Kerioth. Interesting.

"Thank you, Amanda," she said, and patted the machine.

It had been built by Amanda Price, an inventor Gordon Harper had commissioned years ago to design a machine that could expand the collection of DNA he had accumulated over the years from people he had met. It was a pipe dream, a source of fights between her parents. But it was now paying off dividends.

Amanda observed that the DNA of the Apostles' descendants shared an identical anomaly: a delicate protein film coating each strand, bound to trace amounts of a rare compound called bonifacine.

Most people's DNA carried only histone proteins, easily stripped away with the standard extraction kits.

Without Amanda's sophisticated tools, a blood sample was the only way to get an accurate reading of the special bonifacine marker.

There was another new thread—Xavier's? It came back to her—he had touched her before they left the club. The DNA she tried to catch from him last year in Paris didn't survive the trip back to New York.

Xavier's DNA matched with someone who was in the circle of people who believed in Jesus Christ.

Her heart started pounding again.

"Give me contacts. Call Gabby," she whispered to the room around her.

"But of course, Simone," she heard her device say in a soft tone. A ringing sound, then Gabby answered.

"Gabby, you still around here?" Simone asked.

"Yes, in Stan's, just around the corner," Gabby said.

"Come on up. I'll let Mr. Filigree know you'll be here in a few minutes."

Chapter 17

G abby

Stan's Diner, New York City

Saturday, October 21—3:30 a.m.

Gabby gathered her things after Simone's call. The diner was still full, packed with people who had finished their Broadway shows at midnight.

Stan's Diner was an institution in New York City serving breakfast food all day—hash browns and eggs, corned beef and rye.

She eyed her coffee cup and was about to return it to the counter when she heard a voice from behind her.

"Leave it there, Gabby. I'll grab it," someone shouted at her.

"Thanks, Lucy, you're an angel," Gabby blew her a kiss and pointed to the bills on the table, mouthing to keep the change.

"See you around, Gabby," Lucy called, now busy with another customer.

She stepped out in the cold air and adjusted her scarf. She started walking quickly, eager to reach Simone's warm apartment.

Five years earlier, when Gabby had been a graduate student in NYU's MFA program for History of Art and Curatorial Studies, the heir to the Harper Institute had guest-lectured for four weeks. Something about Simone had immediately put her at ease.

On the final day, she hesitated and approached her after class.

"My family owns some masterpieces," Gabby confessed. "But I haven't asked anyone yet to authenticate them. Would you look at them? Just an hour? My family wants them to remain hidden," she began. "I don't know what I should think about it."

"Do you have any photos?" Simone asked.

She brought out her father's old phone. "Pretty antiquated, huh? I can't bear to get a new model. All my precious photos are here."

Simone glanced at the screen and froze. A flicker of disbelief crossed her face.

"I have another lecture in 30 minutes," she said quickly. "But instead of me going to your place, why don't we go to my apartment after the lecture? There's something I want to show you."

A chauffeured car whisked them off from NYU's 78th Street campus to Chelsea. When it stopped, Gabby looked up in awe.

"Oh my God, your family owns the Maignon Building."

"Formerly a meatpacking factory," Simone said with a small smile. "Yes. You're correct."

"I've always admired the bones of this building," Gabby said. "I was depressed for months, thinking the old factories would be torn down. Of course, many were eyesores. But what you did with it is just fabulous."

They stood together, taking in the front of the building with its original HARPER INDUSTRIES still etched into the brickwork.

It was her father who fought to preserve the structure's frontage, retaining its original roots as a meatpacking factory. The bricks were still the same stones from the original exterior of the first building her great-grandfather had bought, as he was establishing a name in the meat-smoking business.

Simone ushered her inside, bypassing the grand lobby for a quieter service entrance that opened into a gleaming minimalist kitchen. From a narrow window, Gabby caught the shimmer of the Hudson, and beyond it, the faint horizon in Jersey City.

"Let me change quickly," Simone said as she dashed inside one of the rooms and came out in soft athletic wear. "I have something to show you."

She set a kettle on and then poured water over the pale green tea leaves.

"Kusmi, amande verte. It's also my favorite," Simone said with a slight grin.

Gabby smiled back. "Mine too."

When they'd finished the tea, Simone led her up a circular entrance to the formal entrance. There, a sculpture of a mother and child greeted them—fluid bronze forms intertwined.

"Amara Nair Harper. Your mum? Amazing! I just connected it now," she said.

"I'm impressed, you know contemporary art, although your major is in the Renaissance period," Simone said.

At the end, there was an enormous door which she unlocked with a key.

"Remember the pictures you showed me? My great-grandfather had similar paintings—a Da Vinci and a Van Gogh," Simone said, and opened the door.

As they stepped in the door, right in front of them was a Da Vinci study of the Mona Lisa, along with a study of Dr. Gachet by Van Gogh.

"Oh my God, I don't believe it. Are our ancestors related?" she asked. She brought out her phone and placed the phones on the table side by side.

"Are we international thieves? Pirates? Goons?" Gabby asked.

"Do you belong to a religious organization?" Simone asked.

"Agnostic. No churches," Gabby said.

"Same here," Simone said. "Are there any documents behind the paper in the back of the paintings?"

"Yes, there are copies of ten pages in papyrus," Gabby said. "But I have never seen it. My parents forbid it."

"Perhaps for a reason," Simone murmured. Then, after a pause, "Come, I want you to meet Amanda. Touch here."

"Amanda?" she asked.

Simone led her to the side room with faint humming and blinking light. "She's a machine that records DNA I come into contact with," Simone said. "Perhaps we have common ancestors?"

Simone sprayed something, and a red glow appeared; a machine then started taking pictures.

"See, this will show you your genealogy. Do you have any inkling as to your ancestry?" Simone asked.

"My parents are mum about it," she said.

"Perhaps, it was to protect you," Simone said. "Okay, here it is."

A picture appeared before her. An ancient man.

"Who is that?" she asked.

Lines of light began to spiral on the screen, coalescing into an image.

"Jude, Apostle Thaddeus," Simone said in a surprised tone. "It's the first time I've seen this lineage. Your ancestors have done a wonderful job of hiding this."

"As in the Apostle?" she asked.

"I'm afraid so," Simone said. "Did your parents live a life of subterfuge? Concealment?"

"Yes," she said, feeling wobbly at hearing those words. "How did you know?"

"I lived the same way," Simone said softly. "Afraid of my own shadow until I rebelled in my teens. Here it is."

Gabby leaned forward.

"I think we're descended from the Apostles," Simone continued.

"The Apostles in the Bible?" Gabby heard herself say, incredulous.

"Yes," Simone said simply. "I've been searching for the complete writings of the author behind the papyrus documents hidden in my family's paintings. From what I've learned, our ancestors were hunted down and killed for protecting them."

Gabby's pulse quickened. "And who is your ancestor?"

"I'll tell you who I am," Simone said, "if you can ask your parents about the papyrus behind your paintings. Then we can compare notes. I believe your ancestor was close to the author of those writings—Eliana herself."

"Eliana?" Gabby repeated.

"Yes. Eliana."

Gabby blinked. "My middle name is Eli. And one of my aunts—a nun—is called Liana."

Simone's eyes lit with recognition. "Invite your parents here. Let's show them these collections. Are they free right now?"

"Let me call them."

Gabby reached for her father's old phone—its screen slightly cracked, its ringtone a relic from another decade—and pressed the numbers. "Dad, remember the guest lecturer at NYU? Professor Harper? She's inviting us to her apartment. She has paintings like ours. Please bring the papyrus documents from behind them." She ended the call before he could answer, her heart pounding.

Simone, meanwhile, had summoned her own parents from the floor below. Within half an hour, both families stood face-to-face.

Gabby wondered what her parents were feeling—shock, disbelief, maybe awe. True enough, they appeared flustered, slightly breathless, but their eyes shone with anticipation.

"Professor Harper, it's a pleasure," her father said, extending his hand. "Call me Sebastian. Meet my wife, Clara."

Simone smiled warmly. "Sebastian and Clara, meet my parents—Gordon and Isabel Harper."

They all began speaking at once, voices overlapping until laughter broke the tension. Simone led them into the living room, where sunlight from the Hudson spilled across a long marble table.

Gabby had never seen her parents so animated with strangers. There was an instant connection, a shared pulse of recognition that filled the air like static before a storm.

"I've kept this for years," Sebastian said, looking at his daughter. "Never knowing if I'd ever have the chance to show it to anyone outside the family. My parents told me I'd know when the right moment came."

Clara rose and placed a cylindrical container on the table. With practiced care, she opened it and unrolled a set of fragile documents. "These are copies, of course. The originals are secured in a private archival vault."

Six people leaned in, reverent. The papyrus leaves shimmered under the light, each bearing three teardrop marks and a single symbol—

ܬ

"Taw," Gordon said softly. "The last letter of the Syriac—Estrangela alphabet. It's the T equivalent in our Roman alphabet."

"Is Apostle Thaddeus your ancestor?" Simone asked, excitement threading her voice.

"Yes," Sebastian said. "Thaddeus is the Aramaic form of Taddai—it means 'a heart that is courageous.' His real name was Yehudah bar Ya'akov. But there were two Yehudahs among the Twelve."

"I know," Simone said. "Yehudah Ish-Qeriyot—Judas Iscariot—was one. He was also called Yudah. After Christ's death, Thaddeus stopped using the name Yehudah. And this," she said, pointing to a line of text, "mentions Humeima. That's forty-five kilometers from Petra."

"I've never shown it to anyone," Sebastian said, his voice catching. He reached for Gabby's hand. "So many have died protecting this—including your grandfather, Erik."

A heavy silence settled over the room. Six people, three families bound by time, stared at the ancient pages—each tear, each stroke of ink a whisper from two millennia past.

"I have something to show you too," Gordon said. "Like your family, only a few people have ever seen this."

He opened a narrow case and drew out several papyrus leaves, placing them beside the Thaddeus documents.

"Also a copy?" Sebastian asked.

"Right you are," Gordon replied with a small smile.

They all leaned closer. At the corner of the ancient sheets were the same three teardrop marks—but beside them, a different letter.

"That's not Tav," Clara exclaimed. "It's Shin! Not Samekh! How could that be?"

"There were two Apostles whose names began with Shin," Sebastian said, excitement rising in his voice. "Shim'on ha-Qan'an—Simon the Zealot—or Shim'on Kepha—Simon Peter. Who is your ancestor?"

His gaze moved from one face to another before settling on Simone. "You even share a first name."

Clara Henry spoke then, her tone measured but full of quiet pride. "My father-in-law, Erik, devoted his life to searching for descendants of the other Apostles. His search ended in Lund, Sweden." She stopped when she saw the look that crossed Gordon's face.

"Our ancestral home is in Lund," Gordon said softly. "What are the odds? My great-grandfather Christopher left there as a young man and settled in America."

Sebastian made the sign of the cross. "Then you are descended from Shim'on Kepha—Simon Peter—and his daughter Eliana." He smiled through misted eyes. "No one could trace your line after your great-grandfather left Lund. Well done. And now these papyri—at last—they've found a home in the Institute. I can rest my weary bones."

"But of course," Gordon said. "The Thaddeus papyri will be protected in the Institute, temporarily in our care."

"Have you found the rest of Eliana's writings?" Sebastian asked.

Gordon sighed. "Still the greatest frustration of my life—spending decades searching for her complete work and never finding it."

She heard the persistent honking of the horn beside her, and she was startled when a man slid his door window open. "Hey miss, are you going to take the ride or not?"

She quickly stepped into her ride and stopped in front of the Maignon Building. The present night air stung her cheeks as she stepped out. Eliziano, the loyal doorman, was already waiting.

"Mr. Eliziano, these hours aren't kind to you," she said gently.

"I can't sleep at home," he replied with a tired smile. "These old bones can't rest."

"I'll bring you chocolate cookies next time," she promised.

"Thank you in advance, Ms. Gabby. Ms. Simone has been waiting for you," he said, accompanying her toward the elevator that led up to the penthouse.

As the doors closed, Gabby thought back to that first night years ago—the meeting of their parents, the laughter and awe, the ancient pages spread across a marble table.

From that moment on, a friendship was born between two families bound by a shared past—by secrets guarded through centuries, and a burden no longer carried alone.

Simone was hunched over her desk, eyes narrowed at the glowing interface of Amanda, the sprawling machine humming softly beside her.

"Great balls of fire!" Gabby muttered. "Two new apostolic ancestors in one night? If you count Pope Lucas, that's three in a week. Is the world ending?"

Then she looked up. "Oh, Gabby—no cheesecake from Stan's?" Her tone was mournful, like a child deprived of dessert.

Gabby grinned. "The cheesecake ran out, but I brought divine brownies." She produced a familiar brown paper package from behind her back.

"Yes!" Simone clapped her hands in delight.

Gabby pulled out one giant brownie and, as always, split it cleanly in half. They each took a piece, savoring the first bite before turning to the holographic display.

"Okay," Gabby said, licking a crumb from her finger. "So, there's Pope Lucas—and as he revealed this week, he's a direct descendant of Mary Magdalene. But what about him?"

On the screen, a photograph of Xavier hovered, his lineage concealed beneath a strip of virtual parchment.

"Naughty, naughty," Gabby teased. "You covered it! I want to snatch it off and see his ancestor."

"It's more fun if you guess," Simone said. "Besides, I didn't have this big lug of a machine in Paris. I knew Xavier was acting strangely last year. I'm convinced my meeting with him was a setup by Pope Lucas—they wanted proof I was descended from one of the Apostles."

Gabby gestured toward another face on the display. "And Tarquin? Was that chance meeting at the Whitney shooting a setup too?"

Simone sighed. "Maybe. But let's not dwell on the evil. Ready for the big reveal?"

"You open Xavier's, I'll open Tarquin's."

"Ready... set... go!" Simone cried, and together they swept away the virtual parchment.

Gabby leaned closer. "I'll be darned," she whispered.

"Xavier is related to Joseph of Arimathea," Simone said softly.

Gabby exhaled, stunned. "In Arthurian legend, Joseph of Arimathea is said to be Mary's uncle—the one who gave his own tomb for Jesus's burial. That was an extraordinary act of generosity for his time."

"And Tarquin..." Simone trailed off, tracing glowing lines from Tarquin's name to two branching paths. "At first, Amanda linked him to Benjamin. But with the new biomarker update, the DNA trace now connects to Yaakov—the brother of Judas Iscariot." She frowned. "So is Tarquin descended from Yaakov… or from Judas himself?"

Silence hung between them, heavy and electric.

"Are they truly helping us complete The Gospel of Eliana?" Gabby asked quietly. "Or are they trying to destroy it?"

"The theft of Pope Lucas's papyri doesn't bode well," Simone said grimly. She rolled up her sleeve and showed a faint mark on her hand. "And Tarquin thought I didn't notice—but he scratched me. Took my blood."

Gabby groaned. "Ah, the old-fashioned method. They don't have Amanda." She patted the machine affectionately. "How's he going to store it?"

"Tarquin kept the ring inside his pocket," Simone said. "Perhaps he placed it inside a cooled vial case later on. Perfect for preserving DNA."

Gabby folded her arms. "Which group do you think he's with? Our families have dealt with so many enemies over the past two millennia."

Simone's expression hardened. "There's one way to find out. I hope Xavier and Tarquin join us in Paris tomorrow."

She turned and handed Gabby a small leather satchel. "Your day bag. Everything's inside—your toiletries, your favorite travel packets. As requested."

Gabby smiled faintly. "I'm ready for Paris. Honestly, I just want to leave New York behind."

"Me too, my friend," Simone said. "Let's see what Paris brings."

———◆———

Gabby stayed the night in Simone's penthouse. The extra bedroom had been prepared just as she liked it—fresh linen, a small reading lamp by the bed, a view of the Hudson lights.

But sleep eluded her.

Her son, Ethan, was with her parents, and that alone gave her comfort.

Simone looked peaceful for the first time in months, and Gabby didn't want to disturb that fragile calm with her own secrets.

Because she had one.

Just a week earlier, an emissary from the Vatican approached her—on behalf of Pope Lucas himself.

He told her the Pope knew she was a descendant of Jude Thaddeus and wished to speak with her directly.

She had two thoughts on this. How did Pope Lucas know? And,who could ignore a call from the Pope?

She thought of the years Pope Lucas had ruled the Catholic Church—his reach, his networks, his unrelenting curiosity had eyes and ears everywhere. Was there a secret he didn't know?

"Gabby, how are you!" His voice had been warm, almost paternal. He asked about her research and how she had discovered her lineage. Then his tone shifted.

"I'm calling because I'd like to know if you would take charge of the Gianni Family Collection," he said.

The Gianni holdings were legendary—some of the finest Renaissance works still in private hands.

"The family foundation plans to create a museum in the style of the Frick," the Pope continued. "You really need to lead your own institution at this stage of your career."

For a brief, dazzling moment, she imagined herself living in Europe with Ethan—art, freedom, a new beginning after the divorce from Stephan.

Then reality returned. This man was Pope Lucas.

Simone's and Xavier's experiences with him were cautionary tales. He never gave without expecting something in return.

She waited for the other shoe to drop.

"I'm dying, Gabby," he said quietly. "May I call you Gabby? I'm worried about the works of art my ancestors inherited—especially the writings of Eliana."

For the first time, she heard genuine vulnerability in his voice. The master strategist, facing his final checkmate.

"Alongside the Gianni collection, could you also safeguard the masterpieces handed down by my apostolic ancestors?" he asked.

Gabby hesitated. "Why not send them to Simone? The Harper Art Institute has better conservation and security facilities. I'll think about your offer handling the Gianni collection, if you let Xavier deliver the apostolic masterpieces to Simone—you owe them that much."

"That sounds reasonable," the Pope said, after a brief pause. "May I ask one more favor?"

The shoe dropped.

"What is it?"

"If I send the masterpieces to the Institute, my enemies will try to seize them. I've arranged for a staff member inside to create forgeries for the thieves, while the originals are secured."

"The Harper Institute is one of the most secure facilities in the world—more modern than the Whitney itself," Gabby replied. "How can that happen?"

"Let me worry about that," Pope Lucas said. "But be careful. They've always wanted to eliminate every descendant of the Twelve

Apostles. For Ethan's sake—and for your parents'—exercise caution. The Obscurati must be stopped."

The name of the enemy chilled her. Suddenly, the life of secrecy her parents had maintained made perfect sense. Did she wish Ethan to live in the same way as they?

"Anything I can do to help, let me know," she said quietly.

Her shoe had dropped, too.

Chapter 18

E liana

Hejav Desert, Northwestern Arabia

In the third year of Gaius Claudius (AD 43)

There was a thudding noise, and the sound of voices cursing. The caravan had stopped again.

The wooden beams of her howdah, a carriage mounted on top of her camel, gave a creaking sound. Curtains were wrapped around this delicate contraption, and she wondered if any more sudden stops would weaken the structure, and she would fall any day now, from the camel's back to the ground below. But the howdah remained as steady as ever.

The stop gave her a reason to move the curtains to peep at the scene outside.

There were around four hundred camels in the caravan, and half were carrying incense and other goods wrapped in leather saddlebags, which were then tied one on top of the other on the backs of the camels.

There were hundreds of people guarding the caravan, hired soldiers who had swords hanging from their sides, caravan leaders who were on foot to direct the camels' path, and men whose sole purpose was to walk the massive, muscular Molossian Hounds, dogs that the Romans prized for their deep barks and powerful jaws.

Eliana heard it first—the piercing cry of the shofar, a sound that tore through the desert air.

"Lēstai! Phyláxasthe!"

"Bandits! Thieves!"

In an instant, a hundred swords unsheathed from the side of the foot soldiers. Another movement, and they had brought the bows slung at their backs and prepared their arrows toward the enemy.

At the same time, without a second wasted, the drivers directed the camels with the most prized carriages to be pulled inward, with the rest of the caravans guarding the outside perimeter.

A hundred dogs began to bark—low, frantic, overlapping—melding with the shofar's piercing cry until the air itself seemed to vibrate with alarm.

Instinctively, she slid to the base of her howdah and unsheathed her knife. Her back pressed against the papyrus leaves she had been writing on. The touch jolted her memory. She gathered the pages with trembling hands and stuffed them beneath her garments, hiding her work against her chest.

Nabil, riding on another camel, had already halted. With a single command, his beast stepped backward until their carriages aligned side by side.

Eliana pulled back the curtain just enough to peer through.

Twenty horsemen circled the caravan in a slow, deliberate sweep. Their dark robes blended with the desert dusk; all but one kept their faces concealed.

"Keep still," Nabil leaned close, the words barely audible above the wind. "And don't say a word."

Her breath caught as she recognized the uncovered face of the leader.

"Isn't that Nicanor? Why is he here—in Humeima—with bandits?" she whispered.

"*Kyría Elianá*—Lady Eliana," Nabil said sharply, switching to the Greek formality that signaled danger. "Be silent."

The moments that followed stretched endlessly. Then, after a tense exchange among the riders, the bandit leader motioned his men forward. The horsemen turned away, deciding the caravan was not worth the risk.

Three short blasts from the shofar split the air—a coded signal: the threat had passed.

She breathed a sigh of relief. A man was approaching their howdahs. It was Eleazar, a family friend from Galila.

"The bandits are gone," Eleazar exclaimed.

She heard the Galilean accent, a distinct, softer tone that set them apart from those coming from Yerushalayim.

"I would have thought you said that the wine sellers are gone, my friend," Nabil teased Eleazar.

"*Lekh lekha, Miṣrī*—go on, Egyptian!" Eleazar bantered back.

A merchant of spices and oils, Eleazar had helped them cross into the Nabataean Kingdom by letting them pose as *Meturgeman*, highly prized translators needed when selling products in the incense route's trading network.

"Was that Nicanor? What is that lovesick *tipshā*—fool, doing so far from Judea?" Eleazar ranted. "I'd say, he's the person from Galila who stole your works, Biti Eliana. What have you done to make him so angry?"

She was about to answer when the shofar's horn sounded. It was time to resume the journey.

"Never mind, don't answer that. Twenty-five more days, and we will reach Petra! I will kiss Petra's soil when this journey ends. *Tityashar orkhakh u-tehein raglakh qashtin*—may your path be straight and your feet swift," Eleazar said.

Eliana bowed her head slightly. "Thank you, *Mari* Eleazar," she said, her voice warm with respect.

Eleazar gave her a small bow in return.

"Go in peace, old friend from Galila," Nabil said.

Eleazar waved them off and walked towards his howdah.

The shofar's horn blasted one final warning, and the caravan moved.

Seeing Nicanor in the flesh unnerved her.

It seemed so long ago.

She recalled Yeshua's insistence to her father that she accompany him to the shores of Tiberias in Judea to watch a Roman play. It was the only time she had heard Yeshua appeal to her father to use the fishing boat to travel three hours away from Kfar Nahum.

"Yeshua, I'm a fisherman from Galila," her father said. "The people from Yerushalayim laugh the moment I open my mouth. What more in Tiberias?"

"But it's for Eliana. She'll listen to a Greek play written by Terence, a Roman writer," Yeshua said. "She'll be fluent in many languages in no time."

"Anything for my dearest and beloved daughter," her father said and turned to her with a smile.

We left Kfar Nahum at mid-morning, and arrived at the harbour by noon. It was a small distance to get to the Roman Amphitheatre, and their party of three walked in the noontime sun.

People they met on the way to the theatre were looking at them, and she became conscious of the clothes she was wearing. Did it mark her too much as a child of a fisherman, as her father mentioned? She gazed up at Yeshua's face, and he was smiling. Clothes didn't matter to this man. She reached out to touch his hand, and he grasped it, looking at her with a warm smile.

From the harbour, one could feel the air, the buzz surrounding the dome, and the sense of undeniable anticipation. Even the Roman soldiers were not as strict and waved us to sit in the empty spaces.

People would stand and holler and stomp their feet as their favourite actors appeared on stage. She thought the dome would collapse from the weight of the spectators.

The stage was set for a play written called Adelphoe, a comedy about two brothers set in Athens, Greece.

Although she was still learning Greek and Latin, Yeshua knew all the lines, and in time, he would stomp his feet too when he was pleased with the acting.

The greatest applause was reserved for the moment when the play ended and the two actors who played the main leading roles as brothers took a bow on stage. They took off their masks, and the crowd erupted in applause.

People were chanting "Yudah" and "Nicanor," and their names reverberated around the amphitheatre.

She was surprised when her father stood up, standing and calling out their names. Actors from Rome or Caesarea usually played Tiberian plays. And it was rare for Judeans to perform.

Yeshua led the way, and after the play, her father and Yeshua approached the stage and waited to speak to the leading actors, who were surrounded by people with a manner of dress and speech that was distinctly different from ours. But one of the actors noticed our presence and waved for us to go nearer.

"I told you to be proud of being a Galilean," Yeshua said, and nudged her father to go near the actors.

"Peace upon you elders. I'm Yudah and my friend Nicanor," Yudah said, with a slight bow. She noticed Yudah's distinct, formal tone. A Galilean would be warmer and friendlier.

"Wonderful acting!" Yeshua exclaimed. "Are you from Yerushalayim?"

"Our parents were born in Kerioth. But we both studied in Athens as boys. How about you? Where are you from?" Nicanor asked in a direct way.

"Kfar Nahum, by boat," my father said. "It was worth the three-hour trip. I really loved the play."

While the adults were speaking, she observed Yudah and Nicanor. They were wearing short Greek tunics, emphasizing their height and leanness. They were the most handsome men she had met in her life.

"Eliana," her father prodded for me to speak, but she was tongue-tied.

"She is mute. This moment is rare indeed," her father said, and everyone laughed.

"I have never been to Kfar Nahum. I would love to visit you when we have a free day performing in the play. May I drop by your home?" Nicanor asked and then smiled at her.

"You are welcome to our home any time, Nicanor and Yudah," my father said.

It was time to go back home to Kfar Nahum, and her thoughts were on those two handsome men she had seen on stage.

She was daydreaming about Nicanor and Yudah when Yeshua said he wanted to stop by *Yardén*—the River Jordan, to see his cousin Yohanan, before returning to Kfar Nahum. She was tired and sleepy, but it was an extraordinary day, and Yeshua was so insistent on going on these trips. Yeshua did not request often, and her father thought the world of him.

Yam Kinneret—the Sea of Galila, was turning rough, but as soon as we entered the river, it had calmed down, and we were able to navigate and stay near the shore.

People were congregating on one side of the shore, so her father brought his fishing boat to the side as well.

A man was near the shore, wearing a coat of rough, camel hair, his hair a mass of grey-tangled wires flying in all directions, his face and arms burned from the sun.

"'*Yohanan Ma'amdanā*—John the Baptist!' That's the prophet from Jordan. He is here! He is here!" people were chatting in excitement.

Yōhanan was baptizing a person, submerging him in the river, and then bringing his face up to the sky. As if sensing our presence, he turned to us and pointed at us.

In a voice loud enough for people to hear, he shouted—

"Brothers and sisters, behold, this is the Lamb of God, who takes away the sin of the world," Yōhanan said.

Then Yōhanan rode a boat, and propelled his oar, and went straight near us.

"Hānā hu Bar'Alāhā—This is the Son of God!" he cried, and the people surrounding him looked about in confusion, unsure of what was happening. Others began steering their boats towards us. Fear gripped her, and she tried to hide behind her father.

As soon as he said those words, the clear sky turned dark, and lightning darted from the sky to the waters near them.

The women shrieked, and the children began to cry. The men stood like statues, unsure of what to do.

The clouds parted, and a white dove flew from the sky and landed on Yeshua's shoulder. The light was piercing and blinding, but the glow was warm, like a parent's warm pat on a cheek, while battling a fever.

The waters swirled, and chaos reigned. Her father clutched her as the boat bopped up and down, the waves lifting the tiny boat.

"There comes after me one who is mightier than I, the strap of whose sandals I am not worthy to stoop down and untie," Yōḥanan said, pointing at Yeshua.

Her limited brain could not comprehend what she had witnessed with her eyes.

Yeshua was human, a dear family friend, a fisherman from Kfar Nahum. But now he is the Son of God?

How could her life return to what she knew?

All thoughts of the handsome young men acting on stage a few hours ago disappeared. More important questions flooded her brain, begging for answers. Who was Yeshua? And is he the Son of God?

Chapter 19

Simone
Hangar 10–Teterboro Airport, New Jersey
Saturday, October 21—10 a.m.

Hangar 10—known to insiders as the Flying Vault's home—housed the Harper family jet, a constant source of debate between her parents.

She stood before the sleek Dassault Falcon, admiring the plane her mother had called a worthy investment, and her father had denounced as a colossal waste of his bloody money.

Her mother had refitted it to include a conference area, dining room, and private suite, plus a hidden humidity-controlled vault for transporting valuable works of art. Over time, the Falcon became an essential asset of the Harper Art Institute—clients trusted it to carry masterpieces under armed security and controlled lighting.

"Hi, Ms. Harper. James and I are reporting for duty," one of the pilots called from the lounge.

"Thanks, Rod. Hi, James," she replied.

"Wheels up in an hour," another voice chimed in.

"Oh, Stacy, you look stunning in uniform—" Simone didn't finish before Stacy enveloped her in a hug.

"I've been flying with you since you were this high," Stacy said, holding a hand at knee level. "You always remember to compliment me. A few grey hairs later and I still get to fly to France for the day—can't complain. I'll call you when it's time to board, all right?"

"Thanks, Stacy," she said, and hugged her.

Stacy laughed and returned to the plane.

There was no one around and she began pacing around the aircraft to burn off nervous energy. The click of her heels echoed across the hangar like a tap dance.

No one else was around.

So she spun doing ballet turns—one, two, three turns—then lost count after twenty.

Laughter carried across the concrete. Gabby and Tarquin Vern entered, Tarquin balancing a recyclable bag in one hand and coffee in the other.

"With clotted cream and strawberry jam? You're an angel, Tarquin," Gabby said.

They'd both slept after three in the morning. When Simone nudged her awake earlier, Gabby had simply waved her off.

"I'll see you at Teterboro, Sim. Don't worry," she'd mumbled before disappearing under the comforter.

Now, Simone studied Tarquin in daylight. There was something about those eyes—guarded, distant—and beneath the charm, an undertow of sadness.

"Hey, Tarquin, it's warm. You can take off your coat," she said gently.

He hesitated, sighed, then relaxed. "I hope you like the scones. Couldn't sleep, so I baked these instead."

He handed a Nakharin takeaway box to Gabby. "Care for one, Simone? I brought extra for the crew."

His long, loose kurta-style shirt hung past his knees, topped with a knitted vest of heavier weave—an echo of India or the Middle East. Simone caught herself staring too long; Tarquin's brow lifted slightly. She turned her gaze back to Gabby.

Gabby bit into a scone and moaned appreciatively. "Blueberry? I'm in heaven."

"Time to board, Ms. Harper," Stacy called from the jet's stairs.

"Still waiting for one passenger. Ten minutes," Simone replied.

Just then, Xavier appeared.

"Do I smell something delicious?" he asked.

Xavier's clothes would be the perfect backdrop to the deep reds and oranges of the autumn trees in Paris. He was wearing a charcoal grey coat past his knees, but he paired it with light blue jeans, and there was a hint of orange and mustard in his light sweater.

Tarquin brought out another box and gave it to him.

"Let's board and continue the conversation, shall we?" Simone told everyone.

No expense was spared to make the jet feel comfortable. Her Mum had decorated it like it was her own living quarters.

The buttercream yellow colors of the interiors felt like early morning sunlight in a hot, tropical paradise. A few steps from the entrance, instead of airline seats, there were comfortable sofa chairs scattered around. Modern paintings were hung on one wall.

"Make yourselves comfy, guys," she said.

Gabby headed straight to the massage chair located in the corner.

"Dibs on that," Gabby said in a weary tone. She plopped herself down and closed her eyes. She was asleep in seconds.

"Late night?" Tarquin asked, and directed the question to her. Before she could answer, Stacy came out with coffee for everyone. Tarquin gave her a box of scones, and she smiled in delight.

"Homemade scones! I can't wait to try it. Some coffee?" Stacy asked Tarquin.

"How about some light tea?" he asked.

"Sure. How about you, Ms. Harper?" Stacy approached her and set a cup in front of her. She poured coffee, and the aroma of freshly brewed coffee made her smile. "Here's the menu for the trip. You guys tell me what you want, and I'll get it for you, okay?"

She glanced at the menu. All her favourites were on the list, which were specially prepared and delivered to the Vault this morning. She observed her co-passengers.

Tarquin had not seated himself and instead walked towards Xavier who was in front of the wall of paintings that her Mum had carefully chosen for the Flying Vault.

"A Helms? This oil is one of his early works," Tarquin said, his voice confident in tone.

"1970s work," Xavier said and turned towards Tarquin. "You have a good eye."

"My father had a collection since Helms was a young unknown. Guess where this work was done, oh the art experts?" Tarquin asked in a joking tone.

"France," she and Xavier answered at the same time.

"Hey, we've got some Helms enthusiasts here. I'm impressed," Gabby said, who was now wide awake after a short nap. "Your Mum

Isabel would have loved to know the pieces she had picked for the plane were appreciated."

"Clear weather is forecasted all the way to France, folks. Let's buckle those seats and start our journey," the pilot's voice intoned from the cockpit.

As they were buckling up, she had a thought.

"Hey, I have a favor to ask," Simone said. "This document was left at the Institute a few days ago with studies of Da Vinci and Van Gogh. It could use another pair of eyes."

There was a long whistle from Tarquin.

"Awwww, I guess this isn't a free ride to Paris after all," he moaned in a false dejected tone. But then a smile appeared on his lips.

"Oh, you wish, Tarquin. I need your brains to make sense of these," she said as she nibbled on a scone.

Her father would have locked these documents away and shared them with no one.

But she was not her father.

All her life, Simone had trusted her instincts—they'd never failed her. And something in her gut told her that the people in front of her, even Xavier, who had once broken her heart, could be trusted now.

They were descendants of the Twelve Apostles. Whether their purpose was to protect or to destroy her, she couldn't yet tell. But some truths required a leap of faith.

She reached into her bag and brought out three ArqPads—thin, translucent devices she often used with her students when she wanted them to study ancient texts in an immersive format.

"I feel like a grad student again," Gabby said, grinning as she powered hers on.

Simone smiled faintly, then transmitted the encrypted manuscripts to each device.

A soft pulse of light rippled across their screens as the works of Eliana appeared—illuminated, fragile, alive.

One by one, they accepted the files in silence, handling the devices as though they were holding relics rather than code.

"Have a seat, gentlemen," Stacy said, ushering them toward their chosen spots.

The low rumble of the jet engines filled the cabin—a sound Simone had always found comforting. Since childhood, it had meant only one thing: adventure. Journeys with her parents to distant places, chasing art, mystery, and beauty. The promise of discovery.

What will she discover this time? she wondered.

Today, she was determined to set her worries aside. She looked at Xavier, Gabby, and Tarquin—each of them scarred by the chaos of recent days, each deserving of this brief peace between storms.

They sat in silence, absorbed in their own worlds, eyes fixed on the glowing ArqPads in their hands.

The cabin lights dimmed slightly, and the hum of the engines deepened. Outside, the clouds began to rise to meet them. Inside, the past—the lost words of Eliana—unfolded quietly before their eyes.

———◆———

The landing was smooth. As they exited the plane in a private hangar, a tall, elegant lady in a chic Dior vintage suit met them.

"Antonia, bonjour," she said, and kissed her on both cheeks.

"I love your suit as always," Simone whispered to her.

"From my mom's collection," Antonia whispered back.

"Everyone, this is Antonia DeMartin, Harper Institute's liaison in Paris."

"How are you, Professor Jang?" Antonia said, turning to Xavier. "I didn't know you were coming for this trip. Gabby, what a pleasure! What is this gathering? The Vatican Museum, Harper Art Institute, and the Whitney heads all in one square meter of real estate?"

"Well, we do want to see the studies of the Mona Lisa at the Louvre," Xavier started.

Antonia shook her head with a deep sigh. "Julien is not in a good mood this week. Messing with the public's schedule with the Mona Lisa today didn't put him in a good mood at all."

"We'll see about that," she said and winked at Antonia. "Tu as été vilaine — we are the villains here."

"Boss, you're always the troublemaker! Naughty, naughty," Antonia exclaimed in a teasing tone, but her eyes were directed at another person. "And who is this civilian with you?"

"Antonia, nice to meet you," Tarquin said and shook Antonia's hand.

"Welcome to Paris, and call me if you have any questions while you're in the Louvre today," Antonia said, and she led the way to Immigration.

As Simone expected, there were no issues with Immigration since none of them carried any luggage.

At the terminal exit, Simone turned to face the group. "Tarquin—Xavier, Gabby, and I are going to the Louvre for some business," she said to Tarquin. "You can come with us or jump from the Louvre to somewhere. We'll be having lunch at Le Café Marly. You're welcome to go off elsewhere."

"I'd like to see the Mona Lisa with you, if that's okay?" Tarquin asked.

"Of course. Come along for the ride," Simone said.

———◆———

They piled into the black SUV that was waiting for them at the curb. It was five in the afternoon back in New York, but it was ten in the morning in Paris, the morning air crisp and clear, the skies a perfect blue.

Gabby took pictures of people walking along the street with her phone. Simone noticed that Xavier and Tarquin had settled in seats far away from each other. Neither seemed talkative once they landed in France.

A motorcycle cut through, and the van stopped, jerking the passengers.

"*Merde, l'idiot s'est arrêté d'un coup*—the idiot just stopped!" Tarquin cursed.

She was surprised at Tarquin's language. He was clearly fluent in French. So, she was correct about her previous observations. English was not his first language.

As they neared the city centre, the sidewalk of the 19th arrondissement burst with raw and vibrant energy, the newly migrant population mixing with the modern apartment buildings and older neighbourhoods, bringing freshness and cultural diversity to the streets of Paris.

Sunlight bathed the old buildings as they neared the 1st Arrondissement, and the shadows cast in the early morning were softer and less harsh.

Famous songs had been written about Paris in the spring, but she loved the fall season there best. There was something about the temperature that invigorated her, the biting wind stirring up the city's energy. People huddled closer in coffee shops because of the cooler weather, as sunlight became more and more precious.

When the famous I. M. Pei structure appeared, Gabby brought her hands together in silent prayer. "Louvre, here I am again. Please surprise me with new insights."

Xavier turned to Gabby and said, "If you want new insights, try the Medici galleries. They brought out new works, I heard." Gabby nodded.

The vehicle stopped at the curb of the Carrousel du Louvre. A petite redhead dressed in a distinct, chic Delphine ash grey suit greeted them.

"Amelie, bonjour," Simone said as she hugged and double-kissed her. "Everyone, this is Amelie, head honcho of Antiquities in the Louvre. Amelie, you know Antonia of Harper Institute, Paris branch."

"Of course! Antonia, bonjour! How are you, Professor Jang? And oh my, Gabby," Amelie turned to Gabby and hugged her in a tight embrace.

"And so, is Julian in a good mood this morning?" Simone asked in a mock serious voice. "What should I watch out for this time? The anarchists, the objectivists?"

"Monsieur Julian is not in a good mood these days. He's waiting for you and Professor Jang near the Denon alley," Amelie said. "Let me lead the way."

"I'll be off now, and see you after lunch, Simone," Antonia said.

Simone nodded and blew her a kiss.

They followed Amelie into the massive museum through the Carousel Mall.

A man dressed in a bright, elegant Cifronelli suit approached. Julian Gautier was the head of the Louvre and an eco-warrior who had vowed never to buy any new clothing. His outfits were all vintage, of the finest materials of French tailoring.

"Simone and Gabby," Julian said, his voice catching, and hugged them like long-lost friends.

"*Cosa ti porta qui?* – what are you doing here?" Julian switched to Italian and directed his question to Xavier. "What a great surprise," he smiled tentatively, and then he turned to Simone and whispered. "What are you doing with him here?"

"What brings us here? We want to see the Mona Lisa with fresh eyes, analysed in your new Louvre Lab," Xavier said.

"I had to close the Mona Lisa for ten minutes to the ticket holders who have travelled far and wide to view this painting. Make every second count!" Julian said in a stern voice, then turned and walked towards the Salle des États room.

Crowds were waiting at the entrance of the Mona Lisa as staff blocked the lines so the group could view the painting in private.

They stepped into the Salle des États—the Room of the States, and Simone paused for a moment. The sheer size of it always caught her off guard, the lift of the ceilings, the sweep of the space, the way the distinct Parisian light filtered into the room. It was hard to imagine that this same hall hosted legislative sessions under Napoleon III.

One's eyes were always drawn to the "Wedding of Cana," the largest painting owned by the Louvre. The work of art took up the space of one wall, depicting the biblical story of Jesus turning water into wine.

A whistle came from Tarquin's lips.

"That was part of my thesis in grad school," Gabby said. "I had to study one hundred thirty people in that painting, all celebrating a wedding. But what I should have done was study the real treasure—the painting in front of this massive work of art."

Everyone turned and faced the Mona Lisa.

Julian was standing in front of it.

"The Mona Lisa. I'm always amazed by how tiny it is," Gabby said.

"Julian, I hope you read the notes I sent you. Does Summa's illustration make sense? What is the significance of these numbers? 56, 72?" asked Simone.

"Look at La Gioconda's hands. Luca Pacioli, Da Vinci's friend, who created the illustrations for Summa, gives meaning to the art of counting or expressing numbers with fingers. The study by Pope Lucas clearly indicated that the fingers entwined in the Mona Lisa represent 5 and 6. But not the final version in the Mona Lisa here," Julian said.

"56 or 72," Tarquin said. "Coordinates to a map?"

"Oh, how interesting," Julian said, nodding with approval. "It could be possible since Eratosthenes used coordinates in the 3rd century to convey the latitude and longitude of certain maps."

Tarquin took out his phone and tapped on the screen. "Edinburgh Castle in Scotland is at 56.49 N," Tarquin said.

"Tarquin, I'm using the same phone. Vintage, huh. I love using it too. Anyway, Stonehenge has 56 Aubrey holes," Gabby said. "They're chalk pits that circle inside Stonehenge. I visited it once."

"Bravo," Julian said.

"And I have 56 questions," Simone said.

"*Voilà, déjà dix minutes*—look at that, ten minutes already, Monsieur Julian," a docent called out at the ten-minute mark.

Julian waved back at the docent. "Look at that, ten minutes is up!" Julian said in surprise. "Let's allow the public access to the Mona Lisa. Now let's go to the Louvre Lab."

Julian moved with efficiency and walked at a hurried pace towards the nearest elevator. The rest of them scrambled to keep pace with his steps.

The Louvre Lab was a new addition, and the government of France contributed half of the cost to set up the newest Scanning Electron Microscopes, which magnify an artwork a million times.

"Voilà, everyone. I prepared the image of the Mona Lisa as you requested, Simone. So, here is the painting in the size you saw it five minutes ago. Now, close your eyes for three seconds. Ready—*Une, Deux, Trois,*" Julian said in a commanding voice. "Now, open your eyes!"

The image from the microscope refocused to a magnification of 100,000, followed by 500,000. And the last to 1,000,000.

"The letters L and V and I," Tarquin said in wonder.

"That's 56," Gabby said.

"Yes, I see it clearly now," Simone said. She had seen the studies on paper, but it was different to see it with her own eyes.

"There are other numbers you've mentioned, Simone. Now, let's also focus on the bridge in the background," Julian said. "Do you see that?"

"Brilliant. I can see 72 clearly. But why this number, what does it signify?" Xavier asked.

"There are 72 privately owned bridges in Venice," Tarquin mused. "Jesus Christ appointed 72 disciples, aside from the first 12. Latitude 72 is in the Arctic."

"Simone's friend, what is your name? You're Einstein," Julian said in a playful tone.

"Tarquin, Sir," Tarquin said.

"Petit génie. Little genius," Julian chuckled. "You're the first person to spout the 72 facts."

"Maybe 56 and 72 can show us the way to the other writings of Eliana," Simone said.

Julian didn't answer. He just stared at the Mona Lisa painting.

"How about the Café by the Terrace painting by Van Gogh, any thoughts on that?" she asked.

"I have a surprise for you. Come, let me show you," Julian told them.

Outside the Louvre Lab, there was a small anteroom, and Julian pointed them towards the entrance.

"I arranged with the Graphic Department at the Louvre to lend five drawings of Van Gogh for your visit," Julian said. "He left 1,000 drawings, and most of them were preparatory works before he created them in oil. Here are five of them, all done in pencil and ink."

In front of them was a climate-controlled cabinet, and Simone glanced at the markings on the side. The temperature at 20°C, the humidity level at 50%. She nodded in approval. The drawings were protected and could only be viewed by peeking through the glass-topped viewing drawers.

Everyone congregated around the cabinet.

"I've never seen these drawings by Van Gogh of Café by the Terrace," Gabby said, her tone sombre.

"What an unbelievable gift for you to arrange this, Julian. *C'est magnifique*—it's magnificent!" Simone said in awe.

"I prepared a slide of the final version of Café by the Terrace, which is now housed in the Kröller-Müller Museum in Otterlo, Netherlands, and also the Van Gogh study owned by Pope Lucas," Julian clicked on a device and another screen appeared on another wall of Van Gogh's work.

"Okay, let me see if I can make sense of this, if I may, Julian," Simone said, and at the same time took the clicker device from him. "Guys, the image of the Kröller-Müller is on the left. It has all the elements that you can see in the five drawings that the Louvre has kindly lent us, namely the twelve apostles as patrons seated at different tables. Plus one hooded image, 'Jesus' as the server in the middle of the café, with a big cross at his back. 'Judas' is a shadowy figure who was not facing the café at all. The edifices are all in the background. What's interesting is that if you add all the patrons, it adds to 13, not 12."

"While the Pope Lucas study, which we see on the right, has no twelve Apostles or patrons at any of the tables and 'Judas' is facing the café," Xavier said.

"Plus, there's no food on top of the tables. What gives?" Tarquin wondered.

"But the Pope Lucas charcoal study had an abundance of curves on the wall and floor that can indicate the numbers 5 and 6, and on the ceiling of the café. It is more marked in charcoal than in the oil painting," Gabby said.

"And look at the buildings to the right of the café. Why isn't it in the Pope Lucas studies?" Tarquin asked.

"It's like playing a game called 'Spot the Difference' in Sunday newspapers," she said.

"Trova le differenze—Spot the Difference in our Sunday Italian newspapers," Xavier said.

"I miss your father all the more today. If he was here, he would urge you to go to Arles, ma chérie, if you want to solve this. Van Gogh was every inch like Da Vinci, hiding symbols in his works of art," Julian said. "That said, I can give you another ten minutes before the Graphics Department whisks away the works."

"Since we're here, why don't we make a quick stop to Arles, site of Café Terrace at Night?" Simone asked everyone in the room. The whoop of joy from Gabby was enough of an answer for her. "But let's take a quick lunch first at Le Café Marly?"

There were faint nods from the three, and it was enough for her. She walked towards Julian.

"Julian, merci beaucoup—thank you so much," Simone said. Then she hugged him in a tight embrace. "Here's a gift I've given to a few people. Let me know what you think. I've decided it was time," she said and handed Julian a pen.

"A digital file? *Mon Dieu*—my God... I've heard rumours, but never knew if it was true," Julian's voice was tinged with joy. "I will treasure this," he said, and he peppered her with a triple kiss. "I'll look at the Mona Lisa again and let you know if I get new insights."

"Ton rendez-vous de midi t'attend, Julian—our 11:30 appointment is here," a voice piped in from the door.

"*Simone, le taf, ça finit jamais... comme ton boulot à l'Institut Harper*—the work never ends, like your job at the Institute," Julian said.

"*Mais si, je comprends*—yes, of course, I understand," she said.

Julian held her elbow and whispered, "Méfie-toi un peu pour ton cœur avec cette personne. *L'année dernière, c'était la catastrophe*—be a little careful with your heart with that person. Last year was a catastrophe. Your father told me before he died."

"I didn't know that he knew," she whispered back.

"Gordon had the instincts of a bloodhound. Au revoir à tous, je vous souhaite le meilleur—goodbye everyone, I wish you all the best." Julian turned to Xavier, Tarquin, and Gabby, and left at a run, his green Cifronelli suit disappearing in the crowd.

"Alors!" she said. "Please take your time and roam around. We can meet in thirty minutes at Le Café Marly, off the side of the Louvre. Anyone interested in lunch?" she asked.

"I'm off to see my friends. I'll try to catch up with you at Café Marly. See you soon," Tarquin said, and turned around without waiting for an answer to exit the door.

"I have a brief meeting with Anna at the Musée d'Orsay, Simone. Let me catch up with you in an hour," Gabby said and sent her an air kiss, as she followed quickly behind Tarquin.

"I have some errands as well. See you at Marly in half an hour," said Xavier, and bolted off without waiting for her reply.

She was left alone with the valuable Van Gogh drawings. The staffer from the Graphics Department appeared and waited discreetly at the side, allowing her to finish viewing the works.

There were so many clues in the artwork Julian showed them. Would she be able to decipher them? Would they lead her to more of Eliana's writings?

Chapter 20

X avier

Outside the Louvre Museum, Paris

Saturday, October 21—11:30 a.m.

He kept his distance as he followed Tarquin weaving through the crowds outside the Louvre. Ever since he'd seen him bump into Simone, and then slid something into his pocket, Xavier had wanted to shadow him all the way home. But concern for Simone had pulled him back. He'd needed to make sure she went home safely.

He had never seen her inebriated before. Seeing her in that state unsettled him.

Tarquin walked towards the Grand Couvert, where hundreds of trees provided cover from the slight rays of the sun. He strolled casually, his pace unhurried and natural.

Was Tarquin meeting someone?

The lush foliage served a double purpose: it protected him from being seen and also concealed the identity of whoever Tarquin was meeting.

And then he heard a voice.

It was a distinct voice, the tone a kind of growl, unlike any he had encountered.

Turbierri. His shock of white hair and his tall frame were unmistakable. He was known as "*Fenicottera*—the Flamingo" in Vatican circles. His family, based in North America, was one of the most significant contributors to the Vatican Museum. What was he doing here, talking to Tarquin?

He couldn't hear what they were talking about.

They walked near a huge tree, their heads bent together in conversation. Would they notice him on the other side of the tree, listening to their conversation? It was worth a try.

"Thank you for swiping Harper's blood," Turbierri said. "She is descended from Apostle Simon Peter. Direct descendants have an unusual molecular shield around the DNA that can only be extracted the old-fashioned way. Try to find out if their family had hidden paintings related to the Gospel of Eliana material inside them. Then find a way so she's out of the scene."

Were they talking about Simone? What did being out of the scene mean? Silence? Kill her?

"The incident at Whitney was a colossal flop. Let's try to find another time, shall we?" Turbierri said.

"The biggest traitor of them all—Judas. Have all the descendants been killed?" Tarquin asked.

"Like flies, in a vehicular accident," Turbierri answered. "The only living descendant is one I couldn't find. Maybe Pope Lucas had hidden him."

Mass shooting. Murder. What unspeakable crimes have they committed in the name of their organization?

The Harper Art Institute robbery had exposed the link between Pope Lucas and his ownership of the Mona Lisa and Van Gogh works. Donating the works to Simone had placed a clear target on her back.

He stopped, a wave of faintness washing over him. Guilt pressed on his chest—shame, too—for having brought the studies to Simone, for painting the target himself.

Did Turbierri mean they were going to find another chance to kill Simone?

He clutched his heart. He felt his heart beat harder. Was this a panic attack? He tried to remember Dr. Pat Campo's swimming imagery. He closed his eyes and tried to imagine swimming on Jeju Island in summer when he was a young child with his parents. They spent a lot of time on the gentle, shallow shores in Woljeongri Beach, and just thinking of those wonderful moments slowed down the beating of his heart.

He turned to look at Tarquin and Turbierri, but they were gone.

He started back toward the Louvre, his mind racing.

Were Turbierri and Tarquin behind the robbery at the Institute? And was the Whitney shooting part of the same plan? How far would they go to stop the recovery of Eliana's writings?

A chill ran through him. He was in danger too—he could feel it.

But his fear sharpened when Simone's face flashed in his mind. Whatever happened to him no longer mattered. If this was the last thing he ever did, he would use every breath, every second to protect her.

Chapter 21

"Gotcha," Rigo murmured, snapping a burst of shots of Turbierri and Tarquin Vern meeting in the Tuileries Garden.

He turned to Andrea Tatin, the FBI liaison in Paris. She flashed a quick thumbs-up toward the Police Judiciaire team stationed nearby. Two PJ detectives were already photographing the exchange between Turbierri and Vern, while a surveillance van across the boulevard captured video of the entire conversation.

"The U.S. Ambassador had to jump through a lot of hoops to get this set up," Agent Tatin said with mock horror. "He's going to owe the PJ director big-time."

Rigo leaned back against the tall, manicured hedge and closed his eyes for a second. The flight to Paris hadn't been a waste after all. The past few days had been pure madness.

Back in New York, the NYPD Chief of Detectives had authorized a multi-precinct task force comprising twenty-five to thirty investigators, eighteen from the NYPD and twelve from the FBI, to investigate two linked cases: the Harper Art Institute robbery of the Da Vinci and Van Gogh studies, and the Whitney Museum shooting.

A lead captain commanded the NYPD contingent; Rigo was one of three senior detectives dividing the caseload—half on the art theft, half on the homicide. Under him, twelve detectives had been split into three-person teams: one for the crime scenes, one for witness interviews, and one for suspect tracing.

His assignment had been the Whitney shooter.

Sirio McAuley, a British national, first-class lunatic. He'd ranted about "interlopers of the faith" but had no ties to any religious group. A hired gun, nothing more. His weapon and ammunition had turned up no prints, no markings, no trail.

He was a ghost, if ever there was one.

He had spent days poring over hundreds of security feeds, tracking Sirio McAuley's movements across New York. Another detective finally caught a lead: McAuley had been spotted smoking outside a de-consecrated church—St. Anthony the Divine.

Rigo pulled the property file. The former church had been purchased from the Archdiocese years earlier and folded into a single-purpose LLC called Synaxis Properties. The corporation existed for one reason only: to hold that single building.

Was McAuley there to meet someone?

Rigo queued every available camera within a ten-block radius. For hours, he scanned the grainy footage until the figures seemed to drift through his dreams—black-and-white ghosts slipping in and out of the same doorway.

There had been a private event at St. Anthony's the night of the Whitney shooting. When he ran the footage through facial recognition, the hits came one after another.

Tarquin Vern—the same man who had tackled the gunman at the Whitney—emerged from the church around 9 p.m.

Other matches followed, but one name stopped him cold: Cassius Turbierri.

Turbierri—brother to the Archbishop of Chicago and Cardinal-Priest of Rome. A lawyer, head of the Turbierri dynasty. Old money, older influence.

Rigo pulled the family file.

The first patriarch, Benedetto Turbierri, had left Navarra, Spain, during the 1880s steel boom. In Chicago, he rose from immigrant foreman to factory owner, commanding the Basque-Irish strike-breaker crews that policed the steel mills. By the turn of the century, he had controlled his own steelworks in St. Louis and had speculated in rail land that later became part of the Great Northern Railway, his fortune secured.

For generations, the Turbierris had bankrolled the Church, including conservative seminaries, diocesan projects, and even papal pilgrimages. They had fought Vatican II tooth and nail, opposing ecumenism and modern reform. By the 1970s, they were whispered about as the money behind the Catholic Church. Some believed the current Cardinal was a contender for the papacy itself.

But what was Cassius Turbierri doing in New York? Why was he quietly buying up abandoned churches under shell companies?

A repository for stolen treasures? A training ground for the ultra-traditionalist clergy?

A shadow Church?

Rigo didn't know. What he did know was that Simone Harper had asked him to keep a particular document off record—a fragment linked to the Harper Art Institute robbery.

He couldn't. It was evidence.

At One Police Plaza, the NYPD's South Annex, the eighth floor had been converted into the task force war room. Rows of detectives hunched over monitors, sifting through the mounting data: stolen art, missing manuscripts, and shell companies.

He called for a meeting and spread the images of the papyrus documents which Simone had given him across the table for the Lead Captain and the two senior detectives on the task force. The scent of coffee and sugar filled the small conference room as they took their seats, cups and donuts in hand.

"Oh man, that's motive if I've ever seen it," Captain Grey said, leaning back in his chair.

"A letter from the Pope to Ms. Harper, and a copy of ancient papyri written by one of Christ's followers show up—and the next day they're stolen." Detective Alaine Rivers, one of Rigo's long-time partners, shook her head. "That's too many coincidences."

"Aren't those two Vatican faction rivals?" another detective asked.

Rigo nodded toward Senior Detective Santiago Fuentes. "Your ears are glued to the ground, my friend."

Fuentes smirked. "Like yours, Rigo. Nothing a couple of good Catholic boys wouldn't know. Pope Lucas is left of left—open to women's roles in the Church, big on inclusion. Cardinal Turbierri? Right of right. Translation: screw you if you're different."

"If Pope Lucas dies," Rivers added, "his nemesis takes over—and the conservatives run the Church for another century."

"The feud feels older than just politics," Captain Grey said, tapping the table. "Check whether it goes back more than a hundred years."

"Will do, Captain," Rigo replied. "Ms. Harper asked that the contents of these documents stay within a small circle."

Grey nodded slowly. "I'll need to loop in the FBI supervisor anyway. Secrets this old have a way of clawing their way back to daylight." He looked around. "Everyone clear on tasks?"

"I'll keep digging into the robbery," Fuentes said.

"Rigo," Grey continued, "you focus on Cassius Turbierri and Tarquin Vern. Their proximity to the shooter is no coincidence."

Rigo's assignments were clear. He had just settled in at home, ready for a few hours of sleep, when a message from Grey buzzed in:

"FBI task-force head reports Turbierri and Vern flying to France tomorrow.

Your tickets are ready—commercial flight, early morning. Meet the FBI liaison at the U.S. Embassy in Paris."

He groaned aloud. Sleep could wait; he'd rest when he was dead.

By the time his flight touched down at Charles de Gaulle, exhaustion clung to him like a second coat. Agent Andrea Tatin, the FBI liaison in Paris, met him at the arrivals area.

"Welcome to Paris, Detective Rigo. The surveillance team is already in place. Turbierri landed an hour ago—he's under watch."

He nodded, fighting a yawn. "Good. Maybe after this I can get a decent beef bourguignon—or at least a baguette sandwich."

Tatin smiled faintly. "Maybe later. Right now, our intel says Turbierri's meeting with Tarquin Vern at the Tuileries Gardens. We can grab a bench nearby."

A ring was heard within the vehicle, and Tatin pressed the button of her car device to answer it.

Tatin listened and nodded. "Reçu. À tout de suite au Louvre," she answered.

"Any news?" he asked.

"Turbierri is heading toward the Tuileries Gardens," Tatin reported. "We can still record Turbierri meeting with another person."

His captain's words came back to him—the ancient rivalries, the power struggle within the Church. Maybe everyone here was connected somehow, he thought. Maybe the bloodlines and betrayals reached all the way back to the time of Christ.

It was only a hunch—his gut talking again, but his gut had never been wrong.

+++"Gotcha," Rigo murmured, snapping a burst of shots of Turbierri and Tarquin Vern meeting in the Tuileries Garden.

He turned to Andrea Tatin, the FBI liaison in Paris. She flashed a quick thumbs-up toward the Police Judiciaire team stationed nearby. Two PJ detectives were already photographing the exchange between Tubierri and Vern, while a surveillance van across the boulevard captured video of the entire conversation.

"The U.S. Ambassador had to jump through a lot of hoops to get this set up," Agent Tatin said with mock horror. "He's going to owe the PJ director big-time."

Rigo leaned back against the tall, manicured hedge and closed his eyes for a second. The flight to Paris hadn't been a waste after all. The past few days had been pure madness.

Back in New York, the NYPD Chief of Detectives had authorized a multi-precinct task force comprising twenty-five to thirty investigators, eighteen from the NYPD and twelve from the FBI, to investigate two linked cases: the Harper Art Institute robbery of the Da Vinci and Van Gogh studies, and the Whitney Museum shooting.

A lead captain commanded the NYPD contingent; Rigo was one of three senior detectives dividing the caseload—half on the art theft, half on the homicide. Under him, twelve detectives had been split into three-person teams: one for the crime scenes, one for witness interviews, and one for suspect tracing.

His assignment had been the Whitney shooter.

Sirio McAuley, a British national, first-class lunatic. He'd ranted about "interlopers of the faith" but had no ties to any religious group. A hired gun, nothing more. His weapon and ammunition had turned up no prints, no markings, no trail.

He was a ghost, if ever there was one.

He had spent days poring over hundreds of security feeds, tracking Sirio McAuley's movements across New York. Another detective finally caught a lead: McAuley had been spotted smoking outside a de-consecrated church—St. Anthony the Divine.

Rigo pulled the property file. The former church had been purchased from the Archdiocese years earlier and folded into a single-purpose LLC called Synaxis Properties. The corporation existed for one reason only: to hold that single building.

Was McAuley there to meet someone?

Rigo queued every available camera within a ten-block radius. For hours, he scanned the grainy footage until the figures seemed to drift through his dreams—black-and-white ghosts slipping in and out of the same doorway.

There had been a private event at St. Anthony's the night of the Whitney shooting. When he ran the footage through facial recognition, the hits came one after another.

Tarquin Vern—the same man who had tackled the gunman at the Whitney—emerged from the church around 9 p.m.

Other matches followed, but one name stopped him cold: Cassius Turbierri.

Turbierri—brother to the Archbishop of Chicago, and Cardinal-Priest of Rome. A lawyer, head of the Turbierri dynasty. Old money, older influence.

Rigo pulled the family file.

The first patriarch, Benedetto Turbierri, had left Navarra, Spain, during the 1880s steel boom. In Chicago, he rose from immigrant foreman to factory owner, commanding the Basque-Irish strike-breaker crews that policed the steel mills. By the turn of the century, he had controlled his own steelworks in St. Louis and had speculated in rail land that later became part of the Great Northern Railway, his fortune secured.

For generations, the Turbierris had bankrolled the Church, including conservative seminaries, diocesan projects, and even papal pilgrimages. They had fought Vatican II tooth and nail, opposing ecumenism and modern reform. By the 1970s, they were whispered about as the money behind the Catholic Church. Some believed the current Cardinal was a contender for the papacy itself.

But what was Cassius Turbierri doing in New York? Why was he quietly buying up abandoned churches under shell companies?

A repository for stolen treasures? A training ground for the ultra-traditionalist clergy?

A shadow Church?

Rigo didn't know. What he did know was that Simone Harper had asked him to keep a particular document off record—a fragment linked to the Harper Art Institute robbery.

He couldn't. It was evidence.

At One Police Plaza, the NYPD's South Annex, the eighth floor had been converted into the task force war room. Rows of detectives hunched over monitors, sifting through the mounting data: stolen art, missing manuscripts, and shell companies.

He called for a meeting and spread the images of the papyrus documents which Simone had given him across the table for the Lead Captain and the two senior detectives on the task force. The scent of coffee and sugar filled the small conference room as they took their seats, cups and donuts in hand.

"Oh man, that's motive if I've ever seen it," Captain Grey said, leaning back in his chair.

"A letter from the Pope to Ms. Harper, and a copy of ancient papyri written by one of Christ's followers show up—and the next day they're stolen." Detective Alaine Rivers, one of Rigo's long-time partners, shook her head. "That's too many coincidences."

"Aren't those two Vatican faction rivals?" another detective asked.

Rigo nodded toward Senior Detective Santiago Fuentes. "Your ears are glued to the ground, my friend."

Fuentes smirked. "Like yours, Rigo. Nothing a couple of good Catholic boys wouldn't know. Pope Lucas is left of left—open to women's roles in the Church, big on inclusion. Cardinal Turbierri? Right of right. Translation: screw you if you're different."

"If Pope Lucas dies," Rivers added, "his nemesis takes over—and the conservatives run the Church for another century."

"The feud feels older than just politics," Captain Grey said, tapping the table. "Check whether it goes back more than a hundred years."

"Will do, Captain," Rigo replied. "Ms. Harper asked that the contents of these documents stay within a small circle."

Grey nodded slowly. "I'll need to loop in the FBI supervisor anyway. Secrets this old have a way of clawing their way back to daylight." He looked around. "Everyone clear on tasks?"

"I'll keep digging into the robbery," Fuentes said.

"Rigo," Grey continued, "you focus on Cassius Turbierri and Tarquin Vern. Their proximity to the shooter is no coincidence."

Rigo's assignments were clear. He had just settled in at home, ready for a few hours of sleep, when a message from Grey buzzed in:

"FBI task-force head reports Turbierri and Vern flying to France tomorrow.

Your tickets are ready—commercial flight, early morning. Meet the FBI liaison at the U.S. Embassy in Paris."

He groaned aloud. Sleep could wait; he'd rest when he was dead.

By the time his flight touched down at Charles de Gaulle, exhaustion clung to him like a second coat. Agent Andrea Tatin, the FBI liaison in Paris, met him at the arrivals area.

"Welcome to Paris, Detective Rigo. The surveillance team is already in place. Turbierri landed an hour ago—he's under watch."

He nodded, fighting a yawn. "Good. Maybe after this I can get a decent beef bourguignon—or at least a baguette sandwich."

Tatin smiled faintly. "Maybe later. Right now, our intel says Turbierri's meeting with Tarquin Vern at the Tuilleries Gardens. We can grab a bench nearby."

A ring was heard within the vehicle, and Tatin pressed the button of her car device to answer it.

Tatin listened and nodded. *"Reçu. À tout de suite au Louvre,"* he answered.

"Any news," he asked.

"Turbierri is heading towards the Tuileries Gardens," Tatin reported. "We can still record Turbierri meeting with another person."

His captain's words came back to him—the ancient rivalries, the power struggle within the Church. Maybe everyone here was connected somehow, he thought. Maybe the bloodlines and betrayals reached all the way back to the time of Christ.

It was only a hunch—his gut talking again, but his gut had never been wrong.

Chapter 22

S imone

Outside the Louvre Museum, Paris

Saturday, October 21—12 p.m.

A bridal entourage brightened the midday crowd, their dresses and flowers adding splashes of color against the pale stone. Tourists drifted past, pausing for pictures near the I.M. Pei glass pyramid. The festive scene lifted her mood.

Xavier arrived a moment later, cheeks flushed, shirt damp with sweat as though he had run a marathon. Stray tendrils of hair clung to the nape of his neck. She had the impulse to brush them aside—but stopped herself. It was high noon, in the most public of places, and she needed to remember who she was.

This was the place where she had first met him.

Last year, the Harper Art Institute had been planning a major exhibition on artistic forgeries from the fifteenth to the twentieth century. Simone had flown to Paris to negotiate loans from several major museums and she'd stopped by the Louvre to meet her friend Julian, hoping to consult him about two Michelangelo works she wanted to borrow.

Walking toward the curators' wing, she felt a light tap on her shoulder.

"Julian asked me to meet you," the stranger said. "Xavier Jang, Vatican Museum. At your service."

Who in the art world didn't know the name? His credentials were impeccable—but it was his closeness to Pope Lucas that kept rumor mills humming.

"I've just finished my Sorbonne lecture," he said easily. "Thought I'd drop in on Julian before heading back to Rome. He mentioned you needed a Michelangelo expert."

"Let me call Julian, all right?" she replied, stepping aside to dial.

"Ma chérie, you've met your blind date?" Julian teased the instant he picked up. "He's single, Simone. I know him, I know his family—and the two of you can talk about art all day and all night."

"*Tu es coquin*—you're such a naughty man," she hissed into the phone, half laughing.

"You'll thank me tomorrow," Julian said before hanging up, his laughter echoing in her ear.

She turned and walked back toward the man her mischievous friend had sent to meet her.

"Call me Simone, Mr. Jang," she said, extending her hand.

"Xavier," he corrected gently. "Please—call me Xavier."

His handshake surprised her—firm but rough-hewn.

"A sculptor?" she asked, raising a brow.

His smile deepened, a mix of surprise and amusement. "How did you know?"

"My mother is one," she replied. "It's your hands. They give you away. What medium do you use?"

"Wood," he said, his face lighting up, eyes crinkling at the corners.

"I'd love to see your work—if you'd allow it," she said, cautious not to intrude. She knew how protective artists could be of their creations.

"Of course," he said warmly. "I'd be honored."

"I'm guessing sculpting is your true passion," she teased, "and lecturing at the Sorbonne just pays the bills?"

He laughed. "The reverse, actually. Sculpting keeps me sane after the day job."

"*Touché*," she said, smiling.

"Now," Xavier said, his tone turning professional, "where is the Michelangelo painting in question?"

She led him up the grand staircase to the second floor, where two canvases hung in quiet majesty.

"Ah, very astute," Xavier murmured, stepping closer to the first painting. "Very few have ever concluded this isn't a Michelangelo."

He took three measured steps back, then forward again, studying the brushwork and framing. "Of his forty-eight known paintings, forty are housed in the Vatican Museum. The rest are scattered. This one came from Napoleon's private collection."

"Although the composition is superb and the colors luminous," Simone said, "it's too perfect—as if the artist knew the destination before he began."

"Which is not how artists work," Xavier agreed softly.

"I'd like to subject it to forensic analysis—to uncover the artist's original intent," she said. "If Julian approves my request."

"Once the layers are revealed, you'll see the artist's first thoughts, his hesitations," Xavier said. "Harper Art Institute has the equipment for it. Let me know what you find."

"I'm sure Julian will send it gladly," Simone said. "It would be a shame if it proves to be a forgery."

Xavier nodded, then smiled. "By the way, what are you doing tomorrow? It's my last day in Paris, and I've barely seen the city. It would be nice to explore it with a comrade-curator, art historian, museum head."

"So many titles," she said with a playful salute. "But I'm game, comrade."

She had been to Paris hundreds of times before—it was practically home, her family's base during summer tours of Europe—but something about this invitation felt different.

She had a very busy schedule but was intrigued that, although Xavier was the head of the Vatican Museum, in demeanor, she felt like she was talking to one of the many painters and sculptors she had known in her life. There was nothing pretentious about him.

They started their day by visiting the studios of Serge Kiloff and Anri Sonjay, painters who had not yet established themselves in the Parisian art world. Sonjay and Anri were neighbours in Les Sirhah, in the underbelly of Paris, a pocket of the city far from any tourist map.

Both artists were salt-of-the-earth people who lived an artist's life, not driven by money or status. Their styles were eclectic, humorous, and with a unique point of view. She purchased paintings from both and made them promise to visit Harper Institute in the future.

"Think their lives will change now that the great Simone Harper has chosen their work for a show?" Xavier asked, nudging her.

"I don't think so. I've met and seen many painters who stayed true to themselves even after fame hit." She grinned. "Of course, there were one or two assholes along the way."

"I'm guessing they were assholes even before they got famous," he said.

"Right you are," she said.

When they left Les Sirah, she hesitated at the curb. "I don't feel like getting back in the car yet. Mind walking a little more?"

"Not at all. Lead the way."

Les Sirhah shifted into a livelier neighborhood as they climbed towards Sacré-Cœur Basilica. Artists lined the sidewalks selling sketches, quick portraits, handmade trinkets, and postcards of the Paris scenery.

"Bonjour," Xavier greeted them warmly, shaking hands, studying canvases. He bought a couple of small pieces before moving on.

She watched him, amused. "You really have a soft spot for artists."

"We work with the paintings of artists hundreds of years ago," he said. "Most were poor individuals who didn't know where their next meal was coming from. But they kept on painting."

"*Coup de foudre*"—a bolt of lightning. Her mum always said she felt one on the day she met her father. The feeling of being struck by a flash of electricity in the middle of the day felt surreal. But everything had changed that moment. The sounds around her became muted, and the people around her were hazy. All she could see was Xavier—his face, his mouth, the curve of his lips she suddenly wanted to kiss.

The artist handed him a brown paper bag filled with sketches. Xavier reached out for it with his rough, calloused hands.

Simone reached out at the same time—her right hand taking the package, her left closing around his hand before she could think better of it.

"I'll get it," she murmured—and then softer, almost a whisper—"Let me hold your hand."

She lifted her gaze to meet his. Surprise flickered in his eyes, followed by a quiet, helpless laugh.

"I must have bought a masterpiece?" he asked.

"*Je prends aussi le chef-d'œuvre pour madame*—I'll take the masterpiece for the Mrs. too," the artist jested, and laughed.

"*Tout à fait!*—Absolutely," he said, a questioning look from his eyes. Was she sure?

She then placed Xavier's right hand on her cheek then reached out to kiss him.

"*Je prends vos tableaux aussi!*—I want those paintings too," the other artists hooted, and the rest clapped and cheered.

"*Oh là là… l'amour est dans l'air*—love is in the air," she heard other people say.

Simone laughed as she hugged Xavier, her hand brushing the back of his jacket, and he brought his arms around her.

"Can we take a walk back to the Louvre?" she asked Xavier.

"That's an hour's walk. Are you ok with that? I lived in this neighbourhood for two years for post-grad work, so I know a few shortcuts back," he said.

He guided her from Les Sirah to the side streets nearest the Sacré-Cœur Basilica, which was now teeming with tourists. He steered her through another road towards Rue du Cardinal Dubois and stopped for a while to view the panoramic view of the city.

"Be ready to go up and down a hundred steps, shall we?" Xavier said with a teasing smile, leading her toward the cobblestone steps along Rue Maurice Utrillo.

"But I could stay here forever," she said, stopping to admire the lush shrubs. "Look at that—it's like walking through a Monet painting."

"That's lilac and holly," Xavier said, steadying her hand as she descended the uneven steps. "And those are chestnut and apple trees lining the road. They bloom wild here."

They climbed together until the steps flattened at Place du Tertre, where artists painted quick portraits under striped umbrellas.

"Would you like to stop and drink some water?" Xavier asked.

"But I can already see Montmartre," she said, her voice bright with wonder.

Xavier took her hand then, his gaze lowering to her fingers. "This feels perfect," he murmured and pressed a gentle kiss against her knuckles.

The world seemed to dissolve around her. The noise of Paris softened to a hum; the crowd blurred into a wash of color.

In her mind, she was walking beside the Seine, its waters shifting between deep aquamarine and muted silver. The skies were powdered blue, the trees aflame with autumn reds and golds. It was a perfect day—too perfect.

Was it possible to fall in love at first sight?

She loved everything about him—his eyes, his voice, the sculptor's strength in his hands, the quiet intellect behind every word. For once, she could imagine her parents' approval. Xavier was a man her father could debate with for hours—a peer in passion and discipline, and someone who truly understood her world.

Everything between them felt effortless, inevitable.

That afternoon, back at the Hôtel Fougère, she invited him to her room without hesitation. The air between them was heavy with the unspoken, but their laughter carried through the space—soft, nervous, electric. When they finally touched, the world fell away.

His hands traced her shoulders, her skin warm beneath his palms. She felt as though she had come home—not to her parents' house, but to herself.

They slept tangled in each other's arms, the exhaustion of walking and wonder lulling them into dreamless sleep.

When she stirred awake, the room was washed in the pale gold of early evening. Xavier was already dressed, sitting by the window, watching her.

"My brother's in town," he said casually, his voice low. "He's inviting us to dinner. Would you like to meet him?"

Her heart lifted. "Oh, that's nice," she said, stretching lazily. "Is your brother visiting you?"

"He promised to see me before I left the Sorbonne," Xavier replied, fastening his watch.

"Then let me get dressed," she said, smiling.

It was early evening. The sun still shone brightly, casting long golden rays over Paris, and the air was crisp. She followed Xavier's lead past the Louvre and Tuileries, their footsteps echoing along the Quai des Tuileries, that elegant promenade between the river and the garden. They crossed the Pont Alexandre III, its gilded angels glimmering in the light, and paused to watch the river swirl beneath them.

The wind whipped around her, sending a chill through her coat. Xavier noticed and, without a word, slipped off his jacket and wrapped it around her shoulders.

She had never felt so peaceful—so alive.

"Where are we going?" she asked, curiosity laced with a thrill of uncertainty.

"You'll see," he said, eyes forward, the corners of his mouth hinting at a smile.

They followed the Seine until they turned onto Avenue George V, then onto Avenue du Président Wilson, where a row of black cars gleamed under the streetlights. Men in dark suits stood silently outside a grand building. Xavier slowed his pace, reaching inside his jacket.

"Here it is," he said.

They stopped in front of the ornate façade of the Apostolic Nunciature.

"We're here," Xavier laughed softly, sensing her surprise. "You didn't expect this, did you?"

"Pray tell," she said, half wary, half amused.

Security officers approached, requesting that they hand over their bags. Once cleared, Simone stepped into the marble foyer, her eyes adjusting to the grandeur of the interior.

Someone was watching. She felt it—a man near the staircase, his gaze fixed on Xavier. Then, from the landing above, another figure appeared: a tall man with distinctly Asian features, dressed in clerical robes. He was beckoning.

"Simone," Xavier said quietly, "this is His Eminence, Cardinal Mathew Jang, Titular of Sancti Giuseppe d'Arimatea al Monti. My brother—my adoptive brother."

The Cardinal descended the staircase, smiling warmly. He greeted her with kisses on both cheeks, the scent of incense and polished leather faint on his robes.

"Welcome, Simone," he said. "We'll be done in a few minutes, and then we'll dine together."

He motioned for them to sit in a grouping of russet-upholstered chairs beneath two national flags—Italy and France—crossed elegantly at the far end of the lobby.

Simone's eyes were immediately drawn to the paintings that lined the walls.

"Amazing," she whispered. "They have treasures just hanging here like it's nothing. Botticelli, right?"

"Right on the nose," Xavier said with quiet pride.

"His early work," she murmured, leaning closer. "Madonna and Child. I wonder who the model was."

"They used several," said a voice behind her.

She turned. Cardinal Mathew was back, smiling. "When Botticelli apprenticed under Fra Filippo Lippi, he often borrowed his master's models. A habit he never outgrew."

"Mathew, your supersonic ears again," Xavier teased. "You can't resist when the talk turns to Renaissance gossip."

"Guilty as charged," Mathew said. "Come, Simone—let's have some repast."

He offered his arm, and she took it, letting him lead her through double doors into an opulent dining hall. The ceiling was frescoed in soft pastels; crystal chandeliers shimmered above gilded moldings.

But what stopped her breath were the paintings—a trove of Botticellis, Raphaels, and unnamed masterpieces fit for a Vatican vault.

And then she saw them.

Men in black, standing at attention along the walls, their eyes following her every step. In the center of the room, one man sat. His hair was white, leonine, unmistakable.

Pope Lucas.

"Your Highness—" she caught herself, mortified. "I mean, Your Holiness."

Her voice faltered. She had seen the Pope on television countless times, but never this close. The air around him seemed to hum with authority, yet his expression was unexpectedly kind.

"*Caro Santo Padre, incontra la mia amica*—dear Holy Father, meet my friend," Xavier said softly.

"So glad to meet you, Simone," Pope Lucas replied, switching effortlessly to English. "Be at ease. I've known Mathew since Xavier was a tiny tot. Mathew was a novice, and I was a young chaplain at San Giorgio. Paris was on my list before Xavier finished his Sorbonne term, so here I am."

He gestured toward a small, round table where porcelain cups and a silver tea service were waiting.

"Let's have tea, shall we? Tell me, what brings you to Paris?"

"I'm curating a retrospective on art forgeries," Simone said, her hands clasped tightly in her lap.

"Forgeries?" The Pope's brows rose. "Fascinating. That must be a difficult subject."

"It is," she replied carefully. "It's a year-long project—choosing which works to include, studying provenance. But I get to see paintings I've never encountered before. Artists I didn't know existed."

"And what exactly are you looking for?"

Before she could answer, Xavier interjected, "She asked for my help with the Michelangelo paintings at the Louvre."

"Ah." The Pope's smile thinned slightly. "While you're there, you might also examine the Da Vinci studies. Many are not from the master's hand."

Her heartbeat quickened. That casual remark—too specific, too pointed.

Her father's voice echoed in her mind: Trust no one—especially Rome.

He had raised her without church or creed, believing that faith made them visible to enemies who had hunted their bloodline for centuries. Descendants of the Apostles, he'd said once. It's both a gift and a curse.

Now she understood.

How could she have been so blind? Was this meeting orchestrated? Were Xavier, his brother, even the Pope himself, part of something larger—something ancient?

Her chest tightened with shame. Only hours ago, she had given herself to Xavier, believing in something pure, something hers.

"I'm afraid I'm not feeling well," she said abruptly, rising from her seat.

Three faces turned toward her, startled. For a moment, no one spoke.

"Please—excuse me," she said, and before anyone could respond, she turned and strode out.

She heard Xavier call her name as she descended the grand staircase.

"Get an auto—now," she blinked twice, activating her neurolenses.

By the time she reached the entrance of the Papal Nunciature, an autonomous vehicle glided to a stop. She slipped inside just as Xavier appeared at the doorway, calling after her.

"Go," she told the car.

Within an hour, she was back at her hotel. Her hands shook as she packed. The silk dress she had worn that afternoon still carried Xavier's scent. She folded it carefully, her throat tight.

On her ArqPad, she booked her father's jet for a late-night departure from Paris–Le Bourget, the private terminal beyond Xavier's reach.

As the city lights flickered outside her window, she whispered to herself, "Amanda will tell me the truth."

But even as she said it, she already knew the answer.

That was the last time she had seen Xavier Jang—until a few days ago.

Chapter 23

Xavier

Le Café Marly, Paris

Saturday, October 21—1 p.m.

Tarquin. Who did he work for?

One of the Pope's enemies? Which one?

"Xavier, you look like you've seen a ghost." Simone tore a roll from the basket on the table. "Let's have a bite before going to Arles. Come, sit down."

His pulse raced, but he forced it to slow. Simone's eyes were on him—curious, searching. He needed to tell her about Tarquin, yet not alarm her.

"I heard Pope Lucas isn't well," she said gently. "How is he feeling?"

"I don't really know. I haven't had a casual chat with him in a year," Xavier replied.

"A year?" Simone's tone sharpened with surprise.

"Pope Lucas asked me for a favor a few days ago," he said, his voice flat. "I granted it."

Mathew and Lucas. Lucas and Mathew.

He was five again, small enough that his head barely reached his brother's hip when they visited the seminary.

"Lucas," Mathew had called across the hall, "come meet my brother, Xavier."

The young head priest appeared with curls that brushed his shoulders and a laugh that filled the room.

"Are you a Roman god?" Xavier had asked, wide-eyed. "You look like the statues in the Vatican."

Mathew and Lucas burst into laughter, clutching their sides.

"Padre Lucas is head of the seminary here," Mathew whispered. "He's the big boss."

"A Roman big boss, then," Xavier had said, stumbling over the words.

Lucas—his "Roman god"—lifted him onto his shoulders, carrying him through the Seminario Maggiore di Giuda, pointing toward the vineyards glimmering under the afternoon sun.

"A healthy body needs movement to stir the mind and the heart. I encourage all my priests to labour with their hands—to harvest, to press, to sweat. The fruit will reward them," Lucas had said.

Lucas had taken him to the seminary's vineyards—acres of green stretching to the horizon—where grapes were sorted, cleaned, pressed, and left to ferment for years. Padre Lucas and Mathew had chased him through the presses, and he could still hear his laughter echoing in the air—one of the most exhilarating moments of his young life.

"A glass of wine?" Simone's voice pulled him back. She handed him a glass, the crimson liquid catching the Paris light.

He blinked and returned to the present.

Le Café Marly's terrace overlooked the Louvre courtyard—slightly elevated, its marble balustrades framing the gleaming pyramid designed by I. M. Pei. The hum of tourists below was a faint undercurrent to their silence.

"I was thinking about the first day I met Lucas," he said quietly. "At Maggiore di Giuda."

"Pope Lucas really used you as bait to find the rest of Eliana's writings?" Simone asked.

"Yes," Xavier said. "Those two—Mathew and Lucas—are thick as thieves. That's why I broke off contact with them."

"But you brought the Da Vinci and Van Gogh studies to New York," she said, startled.

"A dying man's wish. A poor one, in hindsight. We exposed you to people hunting for Eliana's papyri."

"Xavier, what did you get us into?" Simone's anger flared. "You could have asked me outright about my father's collection. Pope Lucas could have asked if I'd heard of the Eliana document."

A vein throbbed at her neck. She set her glass down sharply.

"Would you have told us?" Xavier asked softly. He pushed his plate away. Lunch was ruined.

"I trusted you," Simone said. "I would have told you if you'd asked. What I won't forgive is being cornered by three men, interrogated as if I had no mind of my own. As if I'd just blurt everything out because one of them was the Pontiff."

"I'm sorry, Simone," he said. "Pope Lucas can be a brute. I was used too. After you left, I had to question everything—my loyalty, my past."

"Like what?" she asked, her tone quieter now.

"The feeling of betrayal you felt— I shared it. It made me wonder: was I, too, merely a pawn? Why was I brought into their circle so young?"

"And?" Simone pressed.

"I had to question my adoption. Did they choose me for a reason? Did Mathew and Lucas already know who I was?" He hesitated. "I returned to Korea to trace my lineage."

"You're a descendant of Yosef of Arimathea," Simone said slowly. "The disciple who buried Yeshua in his family's tomb. Legend says he fled—taking his own copies of the papyri—and his descendants scattered through Europe, eventually reaching Korea through marriage."

Xavier stared at her. "How do you know that? My brother Mathew and Pope Lucas told me a few days ago, same time as he requested to bring the two studies to you in New York."

"My ancestors were hunted too," Simone replied. "For two thousand years. My father built Amanda 2, a DNA-verification machine. After Paris, your DNA was tested. So were Lucas's and Mathew's. But the DNA taken was too faint. It didn't survive the Paris trip. I wasn't sure then if you were a friend or an enemy."

"Friend, Simone," he said softly. "Lucas is a descendant of Mary Magdalene. He confessed a few days ago. Mortality forces confession. He wanted someone to carry on the work."

Simone's face paled. "Did he think I was descended from one of the Apostles too?"

"He wasn't certain," Xavier said. "But the rumours persisted—your great-grandparents fleeing from Lund, Sweden, that mysterious art collection built from a butcher's fortune. Rumours that your bloodline was as guarded as mine."

"I'm not surprised your ancestors ended up in Korea centuries ago to escape the wrath of the Apostles' enemies," Simone said, her eyes misting as she spoke.

Did she finally see that he had never been part of Lucas and Mathew's plan?

She rose and stepped toward him.

"I'm sorry I didn't trust you," she said, and embraced him.

"We only had two days together, Simone," he whispered, kissing the top of her head. "Thank you for those two days."

She tightened her arms around him, then lifted her face and kissed him softly on the lips.

"Let's try not to keep secrets from each other?"

"Hmmm. I'll try," she teased, then her eyes grew serious. "Did you find any more papyrus copies of Eliana while you were in Korea?"

"I was more focused on finding my ancestry—and why I was adopted," he said, taking both of her hands in his. "I remember being hungry as a small child before I was taken in. That's what stays with me."

"Come," Simone said gently. "Tell me everything."

He nodded, and the noise of the café faded away.

His father had been a teacher once, until the school shut down. For months, there was no work. They lived on kimchi and rice, barely enough to survive. One day, a priest came to speak to his mother. Mathew Jang.

The conversation had been long and serious. Afterward, his parents sat him down and said they were in danger—that they would go live with the priest's family in Italy, where he could study safely. He hadn't understood why they had to leave Seoul so suddenly, but he didn't question it.

"Always remember your name, Ri Jyeon Heok, and your home," his mother had told him. "We'll see it again one day."

He hadn't understood everything she said, but he memorized his name—and where he came from.

It was seared in his memory that day he met his adoptive family for the first time. The Jangs had a long line of diplomats and ambassadors in their family. They'd been based in Rome for a decade, because the patriarch, William Jang, served as Ambassador-at-Large. Mathew, after university, had chosen the priesthood.

By some mystery he couldn't fully grasp, he became part of theirs.

"Hey, what do I call you?" Mathew had asked him once.

"Ri Jyeon Heok," he'd answered, hesitant.

"That's quite a mouthful for the locals here in Rome," Mathew said, chuckling. "How about another name?"

"A superhero? Steven? Like Captain America?"

"Too many Stefanos here in Rome, Ri Jyeon Heok," Mathew said, laughing.

"Then how about Xavier? Like Professor X!"

"Hmm... the locals will call you Javier, and that's all right," Mathew replied. "Xavier, it is."

He smiled faintly at the memory.

"So you were targeted since childhood," Simone said, pulling him back to the present.

"In hindsight, yes," he said quietly. "But perhaps it saved my life. I don't know what the enemies of Eliana would have done if they'd found my family back then."

He paused. "Kill me, perhaps."

Then Xavier reached for her hand.

"Your life is in danger," he said quietly. "I followed Tarquin to the Tuileries. He stole your DNA—when we were dancing at Ade Lane. He's discovered your true heritage. I still haven't identified the group he works for, but he's out to kill us."

"Tarquin?" Simone's eyes narrowed. "I have a good head for people, Xavier. Running an institute means I deal with thousands every year. I don't believe Tarquin would harm me. We survived a shooting together. Trust me on this."

"I'll protect you," he said. "I failed you once—last year, with the Pope and Mathew—but give me another chance. Please forgive me."

"I believe you," she said softly. "And I forgive you." She brushed her fingers against his cheek, a tender gesture that undid him. He moved closer, meaning to kiss her, but she stopped him with a hand to his chest.

"Xavier," she said, her voice steady, "I have a secret of my own. Pope Lucas tried to pry it from me last year. Yes, I am a descendant of one of the Twelve Apostles."

His breath caught. "Which one?"

"Simon Peter," she said. "My family has been in hiding since the burial of Christ. My father made me promise—on his deathbed—to guard our identity and to keep searching for other writings of Eliana. You're the first person, aside from Gabby, that I've ever told."

"Thank you," he whispered. He drew Simone into his arms. "Thank you for trusting me."

He didn't care who was watching. He kissed her forehead, her closed eyes, and finally her lips.

The kiss lingered—longer than it should have.

How scandalous they must have seemed.

When they finally parted, they heard applause. A crowd had gathered on the steps below the restaurant, some clapping, others smiling through tears.

Simone, ever composed, blew a kiss toward them, then bowed with theatrical grace. The applause swelled, echoing across the Louvre courtyard—laughter, delight, and a warm, bright wave of humanity rising into the Paris air.

Chapter 24

Xavier

Nîmes–Arles Airport, France

Saturday, October 21—4 p.m.

The Flying Vault touched down at Nîmes–Alès–Camargue–Cévennes Airport without a hitch.

"No representative from Harper Art Institute to greet us this time? Awwww," Tarquin said in a faux-sad tone. "It's best to drive in this town."

"You're a real ball of light, Tarquin," Gabby muttered, her voice weary.

"Anything to wake you up, ma chérie," Tarquin teased.

"Kids, I'm afraid we're on our own for this one," Simone said.

"I'll rent a car," Xavier offered.

They ended up with a Peugeot 308—compact, nimble enough for the cobbled Roman roads that crisscrossed the town, roads first laid by soldiers two thousand years ago.

Tarquin swung his bag over his shoulder. "I'll skip this one and wander on my own. See you before Paris. Just message me, okay?" He walked off without waiting for an answer.

"He really gives off a strange vibe sometimes," Gabby said as she climbed into the car.

"Like all of us?" Simone replied, a knowing smile softening her words.

Xavier started the engine. A strong gust swept through the open window, tangling Simone's hair, but she didn't care. The Camargue plain unfolded before them—flat, silver-lit stretches of salt, lagoons where orange-pink flamingos dipped their beaks into the water, and black bulls grazed under tamarisk trees heavy with wind.

Arles shimmered ahead—a city of painters and ghosts. Gauguin, Picasso, and Van Gogh had all chased its southern light. But beneath that light lay the bones of Rome: arches, columns, and stone streets still breathing empire. Founded in 46 BC by Julius Caesar, Arles had once been called the Little Rome of Gaul.

Xavier slowed the car as they reached rows of cafés at Place du Pont. The air smelled of espresso and citrus, the murmur of early cocktails and laughter rising through the gold-tinted afternoon. Shadows lengthened on the sun-dappled roofs, turning chairs and tables into glints of amber and rose.

He glanced at the stone columns near the square—remnants of a city that had outlived conquerors. The ochre walls seemed to hold light itself.

They stopped near Le Café La Nuit, where Van Gogh had painted Café Terrace at Night. Xavier parked, scanning the street.

Where was Tarquin? He wanted to follow him, but instinct told him to stay close to Simone.

"Looks like every table is occupied," Simone said. "The waiters can barely keep up."

"It's like Van Gogh just stepped out," Gabby whispered. "Almost everything's the same."

"Even the doorway where the hovering figure once stood," Xavier added. "No crosses now, no numbers hidden in the ceiling scrollwork. He left his codes elsewhere."

"I don't think we'll find anything here," Gabby said. "It's packed."

"Let's walk," Simone suggested. She led them away from the crowd. Their path wound past small gardens and shuttered homes, the sounds of the square fading into a hush.

"A piece of bread, anyone?" Simone said, producing a small bag. "And wine. I saved these from the plane—for emergencies like this."

"You're an angel," Gabby said, laughing. "Are we even allowed to walk around drinking wine?"

"*Mais oui*, of course," Xavier said. "Just don't get drunk and sing," he teased.

"Then cheers—to Arles," Simone said.

They stopped beneath a grove of plane trees, their leaves rustling gently like whispers. Their toast was quiet and reverent, as if a loud celebration would break the spell.

For a while, they walked in silence, each lost in their own thoughts.

"What's the connection between the study and this place?" Simone asked softly. "How could Eliana's work be hidden here?"

"Look at it through Van Gogh's eyes," Xavier said. "Even grief becomes light."

She smiled faintly—then froze. A tap-tap-tap sounded on her shoulder. The staccato rhythm of her com device. Nic. He was supposed to call only in emergencies.

"Excuse me," she said, stepping a few feet away. The breeze carried her voice back to them—low, urgent, and uncertain.

Xavier's hand tightened on the small bottle of wine. Whatever peace Arles offered was gone.

"Hmmm, how are we? *Comme ci, comme ça*—so-so," Simone said in a tentative tone. She listened, then added softly, "All right. I'll set it up."

She opened her ArqPad, and Nic's face appeared on the hovering screen.

"Maybe this will help," Nic said. "Lisa Gherardini, the model of the Mona Lisa, and Van Gogh, both suffered from breakdowns. Dr. Gachet, Van Gogh's physician, has a house nearby, in Place du Fortun. I'm sending you the coordinates. His descendants might hold some clues."

"Isn't that the doctor with the foxgloves and the yellow book?" Simone asked.

"Right again, Professor Harper. Happy hunting."

Nic's image dissolved, replaced by scanned letters in front of them.

"Nic sent copies of Van Gogh's letters about Dr. Gachet," Simone said, reading aloud.

"I think we must not count on Dr. Gachet at all. First of all, I think he is sicker than I am—or shall we say, just as much. Now, when one blind man leads another blind man, don't they both fall into the ditch?"

"Very observant, Monsieur Van Gogh," Xavier murmured. "*C'est l'hôpital qui se moque de la charité.*"

"The hospital mocking charity," Simone translated with a grin.

"Simone—look." Gabby pointed. "Foxgloves. In the hedges!"

At the edge of the path, pink-violet foxgloves rose nearly two feet high, nodding gently in the breeze.

"Let's go, if everyone's up to it," Xavier said.

The small gate creaked open. Behind the hedge was a field—an ocean of foxgloves swaying under the pale sun. White wooden crosses dotted the grass.

"A cemetery?" Xavier whispered.

"Gives me the shivers," Gabby said. "Foxgloves are poisonous. They can raise the dead—or kill the living."

"And how do you know this?" Simone teased.

"Medieval medicine," Gabby said. "They call it digitalis. Dr. Gachet used it on patients. In the nineteenth century, it was brewed into tea to lift depression. There's documentation on it—even among medieval painters in the Vatican archives."

"That's solid," Simone said, nodding. "You've probably read more on those medieval treatments than any of us." She bent down to read the names on the nearest crosses. "Madeline Blanc. Gabrielle Fournier. Arielle Denis."

She frowned. "They sound like local personages. Let's have Nic run an analysis on these names later."

"Why are there no men here?" Gabby asked.

A couple passed by on the road beyond the fence, and Xavier stepped forward.

"*Excusez-moi, monsieur*—excuse me, sir," he began.

The man turned, smiling. "Oh, I speak English."

"Is this a private cemetery?" Xavier asked. "Are we allowed to enter?"

"Of course," the man said, beckoning them closer. "I'm Louis Bernard. I live five minutes away."

"Xavier," he introduced himself. "And these are my colleagues, Simone and Gabby."

"The women buried here," Simone said. "Were they leaders of the town? There seems to be no men."

Louis chuckled. "Many of them served their Order. Not all are women—you'll find family mausoleums along the side. Some have men's names."

"Order?" Gabby asked. "You mean, a religious one?"

"Yes, the Church of St. Hannah of Kerioth." He glanced at his watch. "My wife's waiting for her baguettes. If you follow this path, you'll find the church. Bonne journée—have a good day!"

He hurried off down the lane.

Simone stood still, brows drawn. "There's no church here," she said.

Gabby was already scrolling on her phone. "Wait—look." She turned the screen to show a magnified view of Café Terrace at Night. "There's a spire in the background. The Kröller-Müller Museum version shows it—like a cathedral tower."

Simone took the phone, squinted, then turned slightly.

"If you imagine the painting as a clock face, the spire sits around two o'clock." She pointed down a narrow gravel path through the cemetery. "That way."

Xavier nodded. The three of them walked on. More tombs. More women's names.

The wind picked up, stirring leaves and whispering through the foxgloves, like a voice that almost wanted to speak.

"Is this place peaceful because no men are buried here?" Gabby asked, then laughed.

"I believe so. Men make everything complicated. Kapow," Xavier said, miming an explosion with his hands.

Simone smiled but didn't answer. The path narrowed, hemmed in by hedges and foxgloves swaying in the wind. At its end, two dark spires rose beyond the treetops.

"There," she whispered.

They stopped in silence. The spires—familiar, impossible—were the very ones from Van Gogh's Café Terrace at Night.

A weathered sign was nailed to the old wooden door:

SAINT HANNAH OF KERIOTH.

Chapter 25

Eliana

Wadi Sirhan, Northeastern Arabia

In the third year of Gaius Claudius (AD 43)

In the vast expanse of Wadi Sirhan, the spice caravans travelled by night to escape the burning heat of the day. Guides—men whose eyes could read the moon and the stars—were indispensable to the journey's progress.

Caravan guards always rode ahead to mark the next place of rest. Before the sun reached its zenith, the travelers would halt beneath groves of giant tamarisk trees. When the heat began to wane, just before sunset, the caravan would move again.

For days she had seen nothing but ochre and red sands, broken only by outcrops of black volcanic rock. The landscape reminded her of the long wandering of Moses—endless, uncertain, shadowed by thirst and the fear of unseen enemies.

Eliana shifted to the edge of her howdah and lifted the curtain to peer outside. Hired soldiers walked beside the camels, their swords glinting at their sides. Enormous Molossian dogs loped along in rhythm with the march; sometimes they barked, sometimes howled in chorus—a strange, wild music that unnerved her at night yet made her feel protected.

Nicanor's sudden reappearance in the Hejaz Desert had unsettled her. Now, alone in the vast wilderness, she had nothing but time to think.

She longed for the sea.

The sea—every memory of her father, of Yeshua, of Yudah and Nicanor—was bound to it.

A week after their journey to Caesarea, where they had watched Terence's play Adelphoe, Yudah and Nicanor had come to their village in Kfar Nahum.

Her father and Yeshua had been overjoyed, taking them straight to the Sea of Galilee to meet the other fishermen. That night they went out to fish, and by dawn they returned, their laughter echoing across the water as they hauled the nets to shore.

She could still hear it—their voices, their joy—as they gathered at her family's house. Even if her savta worried about feeding so many unexpected guests, she said nothing and smiled at all of them.

Eliana had not been allowed to join the men at sea, but when they returned, she was permitted to eat with them. Yudah and Nicanor were the youngest, so Yeshua asked that she sit beside them. Her father had objected, but Yeshua waved it off.

"Let her enjoy their company," he had said. "They will not be children forever, Shimon."

It was the first time she had seen the two men up close. Both had jet-black hair falling past their elbows, tied neatly with thin leather cords—a style unfamiliar in Galilee. The men of Kfar Nahum wore coarse wool from the fleece of the sheep they tended at home, but these two wore robes of Egyptian linen, a fabric her savta treasured.

They studied her with quiet amusement. She decided to test them. Pretending to cast a fishing line into the invisible waves, she broke the silence.

"So, how old are you two?" she asked.

Their serious expressions gave way to laughter.

"Seventeen," Yudah said. "And you?"

"Eleven," she answered proudly. "We're closer in age than I thought! What brings you here to Kfar Nahum?"

The two exchanged a look and laughed.

"Anti ziburita ḥaviva!—you're a delightful busy bee, Eliana, is it?" said Nicanor.

"Lā anā ziburita dīlakh!—I'm not your little bee!" she retorted, indignant.

She stood, gathered her food, and marched away—leaving their laughter trailing behind her like ripples across the water.

Her father noticed the commotion and was about to stand, but Yeshua placed a calming hand on his arm, silently urging him not to interfere.

Eliana looked around for her savta, her father's mother, and sat beside her to finish her meal. Nearby, Maryam, Yeshua's mother, and Maryam of Magdala had also paused when she joined them.

"Here, have some of my bread, Biti Eliana," said Maryam of Magdala kindly.

The word ziburita, little one, might once have made her smile, but not today. Why did everyone still see her as a child? She frowned and tore her bread in silence.

Her eyes wandered toward Yeshua. He felt her gaze and turned. His smile reached her across the courtyard, and she returned it. He was the only one who truly understood her—the only one who encouraged her to learn new tongues, to travel beyond familiar paths, to speak with strangers older and wiser than herself.

When the meal ended, she excused herself, claiming she needed to wash the dishes.

Behind the house, she gathered the earthenware plates. From a jar, she scooped out ash and mixed it with water, scrubbing until the clay gleamed dull in the fading light.

Yudah sidled up beside her, holding something sticky before her eyes—a fig split open, its flesh glistening with a drizzle of honey.

"T'enā! Divsha!—Fig, honey!" she gasped, delighted.

Her hands were grey with ash, so she rinsed them quickly in the water jar before taking the fruit. She bit into it—the taut skin giving way to sweetness.

Yudah smiled, then glanced toward Nicanor, who stood watching from a distance.

"Think you can forgive him for calling you ziburita—little bee?" Yudah asked. "He meant no harm."

Eliana nodded, then hesitated, her curiosity overtaking her temper.

"Stop! Why are you here in Kfar Nahum? Why aren't you back in the theatre at Caesarea? I loved the play—Adelphoe—and you were perfect as the two brothers. You have the face for it, Yudah. But him—" she pointed at Nicanor "—not so much."

"Min pum d-yalda!—straight from the child's mouth!" Nicanor exclaimed, falling to the ground, clutching his stomach in laughter.

"You deserved that," Yudah said, chuckling. "Now come, help with the dishes."

"Ḥas li, barti. Lā 'emar lakh ziburita.—Forgive me, child. I won't call you little bee again," Nicanor said, his tone soft with apology.

Eliana approached him and offered the other half of her fig with honey. He accepted it with a sheepish smile.

At that moment, her savta, and the two Maryams appeared at the doorway, carrying more plates to be washed. They lingered, watching the reconciliation unfold.

"Will you two stay and come with us to Cana tomorrow?" her grandmother asked. "Yeshua's cousin Hananiah of Cana is to wed Mara, our neighbor from Kfar Nahum. We'll escort the bride there—it's a day's walk."

"We'll be there," Nicanor said, grinning. "Like bees following the honey!"

He dashed away, laughing, as Eliana chased after him.

At dawn the next day, about fifty villagers gathered at the village well, their voices mingling with the bray of donkeys and the rustle of woven baskets. Together, they began the long road to Cana.

Mara, her beloved neighbour—whom she had known since infancy—was radiant in a linen robe embroidered with flowers by the village women. She was lifted onto a donkey, and the procession began with the bright sound of tambourines and the laughter of friends rising in the cool morning air.

Her father, Shimon, brought out their own donkey, Hivra, named for the pale grey of her hide. He hoisted Eliana onto the beast's back and walked beside her as they joined the train of singers and well-wishers.

At first, the chatter centred on the bride and her family—anxious yet excited about the day ahead. The mood was joyful, the air alive with promise, for everyone rejoiced that their Mara would be wed into the family of Maryam and Yeshua.

One of the elderly neighbours lifted his voice in a familiar psalm:

"Behold, how good and pleasant it is…"

Voices answered, weaving melody and rhythm into their steps:

"…when beloved brothers dwell together in unity!"

The men sang:

"How great, how beautiful!"

And the women replied:

"Together, in unity!"

Eliana turned once to look behind her. The Sea of Galilee shimmered white and silver in the early light. Nets lay spread upon the shore where children darted and shouted, careful not to touch the slippery glint of the morning's catch.

The air smelled of fish and pitch—the tar drawn from the Dead Sea to seal boats. But once the sea disappeared, the wind shifted, and the fragrance of wild herbs—thyme, sage, and rosemary—rose from the hillsides.

She called out to her father that she wished to walk. Smiling, he offered Hivra's seat to Yeshua, who accepted and mounted, while Eliana walked beside her father.

Soon, Yudah and Nicanor fell into step beside her, keeping her company.

By midday, the songs had faded; the sun was fierce, and the steep road toward Magdala tired the travellers. Then Yudah began to sing softly, his voice low as thunder over the Galilee:

"For everything there is a season,

and a time for every matter under heaven.

A time to plant,

and a time to pluck what is planted."

Then Yudah and Nicanor's voices rose, deep and clear.

"A time to kill,

and a time to heal."

The two voices blended in harmony, strong and solemn. To Eliana, it sounded as heaven might be—where prayer and song were the same breath, and angels sang in chorus, radiant and full of light.

When the song ended, the villagers burst into applause, stamping their feet and shaking their tambourines.

"Od, od!—More, more!" they cried.

Yudah answered with another hymn, one that every heart knew:

"Hodu l'Adonai ki tov, ki le'olam ḥasdo!—Give thanks to the Lord, for He is good, His mercy endures forever."

As they climbed higher along the slopes of Mount Arbel, the air changed again. The scent of thyme and rosemary gave way to dust and sunbaked stone. But as they descended toward Nasrath, the land softened—flat and generous, with rows of almond and pomegranate trees flanking the road.

At last, they rested beneath the shade of a great pomegranate tree. Families rolled out woven rugs and unpacked their meals—round flatbreads, olives cured in salt, and hard goat's cheese wrapped in linen.

Goatskin flasks were passed among the elders, filled with water and wine. Mothers poured smaller portions for their children. The laughter dulled as the noon heat thickened; many lay down beneath their cloaks, drifting into brief sleep.

Eliana noticed that Yeshua did not rest. He had wandered to another tree farther away. From her seat, she could not see his face, only the outline of his figure against the burning light.

She rose quietly.

Through the branches, she saw him lift his hands to the heavens.

He was praying again.

She watched him for a long moment.

What were his prayers this time? She wondered.

Someone tapped her on the back. When she turned, it was Nicanor and Yudah; they too were peeking at Yeshua, who stood apart, praying in silence.

They stayed hidden behind the low pomegranate trees until drowsiness overcame her, and she drifted into sleep.

"Eliana, time to wake up."

A gentle nudge, a voice soft as wind through reeds. It was Yeshua, his kind eyes filled with concern.

"Is it time to go?" she asked.

"It is—if we want to make it to the wedding," he said with a laugh, glancing at Yudah and Nicanor, who were sprawled in different stages of sleep.

"Qūmū, banayya!—Wake up, my beloved children," Yeshua said, nudging them with a smile.

Eliana leaned close to Nicanor's ear and made a buzzing sound. "Bzzz, bzzz..."

It was Yudah who stirred first, sitting up in surprise before reaching over to shake Nicanor awake.

"Let's go to Cana?" Yeshua said.

Rested and revived, the villagers broke into chatter once more. The final leg of the journey began with renewed energy; tambourines rattled, songs rose bright and jubilant, and laughter rippled through the air.

Soon, the vineyards of Cana came into view. Townsfolk lined the road, awaiting the arrival of the bride.

"It's as if all Galilee is here, Abba," she said, nudging her father, who now walked beside her.

"Yes," Shimon replied, shading his eyes. "Looks like Cana and Nasrath both. Hananiah's mother is from Nasrath."

She reached for his hand. The crowd pressed close, and she felt small and uneasy, the noise and heat overwhelming.

"Come," her father said gently. "Let me lift you onto Hivra so you can see."

From her perch, she had a bird's-eye view of the celebration. Her shoulders loosened. The world felt right again.

A cheer rose from the crowd. People began clapping and stepping aside to make room for one another.

It was Hananiah, the groom, making his way forward. Mara smiled as he approached. Hands reached up to help her dismount from the donkey. When she stood, the two clasped hands, their faces glowing with shy joy, and began walking uphill toward the groom's family home.

Palm fronds, olive branches, and sprays of myrtle lined the court-yard path leading to the house. From her vantage, Eliana could see lilies and roses adorning the doorway, but the crowd was too thick for her to glimpse the fathers of Hananiah and Mara reciting the marriage blessings.

Then she noticed a man weaving through the crowd with an anxious expression on his face.

It was Mattithiah, Hananiah's brother.

"Have you seen Yeshua? Or Dodta Maryam?" he asked the neighbours from Kfar Nahum, his voice tight with worry.

One of the villagers pointed Yeshua out to him, and Mattithiah hurried toward them.

"Go down from the donkey, Biti Eliana. We need to help Yeshua and Maryam," her Abba said in a brisk tone.

She slid off Hivra's back, brushing the dust from her robe. Ahead, Mattithiah was speaking in urgent tones with Yeshua and Maryam. What was happening? Then, without another word, Mattithiah turned and hurried away, Yeshua and his mother following close behind.

Her father and Maryam of Magdala joined them, their steps quick and anxious. Yudah and Nicanor joined her, and they all followed the group as they moved through the narrow corridor.

Mattithiah led them to the back of the house, where the air turned cool and sweet with the scent of crushed grapes. She realized where they were—the family's wine cellar, where harvested grapes were gathered, pressed, and left to ferment in great clay jars.

"Dodta Maryam, Yeshua, my father got carried away, and the festivities have gone on since yesterday, from morning until night. The wedding feast has only just begun, and I have only two jars left," Mattithiah said, his face ashen, as if he were about to faint.

"I don't know what to do. Please, help me, Yeshua," he said, his voice breaking.

"Hush," Maryam said softly. "Go back to the festivities, and let us see what can be done."

When he had gone, she turned to her son and spoke in a low voice. Eliana strained to hear, and Yeshua's reply was clear in the silence of the cellar.

"Ti emoi kai soi, gynai? oupō hēkei hē hōra mou," he said.

"Lady, what does this have to do with us? My hour has not yet come."

The look on Maryam's face was tender but pleading. Yeshua sighed.

"Shimon, Yudah, Nicanor, find which jars are filled with wine and which with water," Yeshua said.

The three men hurried to obey, climbing the makeshift ladders to peer inside the giant jars.

"Water here," Nicanor called.

"Water here too," Yudah said.

"The remaining ones are water jars, Yeshua," her father added.

Eliana frowned. What was he going to do with the water jars?

Yeshua turned away from them. He closed his eyes, hands lifting toward the low ceiling. He stood in silence for a long moment.

Then he lowered his hands and faced them again.

"You are not to speak of this to anyone," Yeshua said and walked out.

Yudah leaned over the nearest jar, then jerked back. "It's wine now!" he shouted.

A ripple of gasps filled the cellar.

"It's a miracle," her father said, awe breaking into his face. "He has turned the water into wine. Nicanor, find Mattithiah and show him. I will look for Yeshua."

Mattithiah arrived at a run. One glance at the stunned faces, and the deep red gleam inside the jars, and he fell to his knees, weeping like a child.

Above them, laughter and music swelled once more. The wedding feast had been saved—and Eliana knew it was because of Yeshua.

Chapter 26

Eliana

Aila, Nabataean Region

Year 4 of King Malichus (AD 43)

The sea.

After longing to see the sea for endless days, the colours of sand in ochre and red, interspersed with black volcanic rock formations, changed. Even the air began to change. It carried a different scent, faint but certain. They were emerging from the desert and approaching the open sea!

Palm groves lined the side of the road, replacing the lonely acacia trees lining the desert in their journey.

And then, she saw it—the shimmer of water.

She heard cries of joy, hooting, and clapping from the camel howdahs around her. They had reached Mare Rubrum—The Red Sea.

The world seemed drenched in blue—the sky, the sea, and even the distant mountains mirrored one another in a vast horizon.

The signs in Latin of Mare Rubrum were all over the road. Some brave, or perhaps naughty, Egyptians had defaced another sign. The words "The Great Green" were written instead. Ah, yes, it was the name the Egyptians called this vast body of water that linked the land trade routes to one another. Although the sea shifts its colours from white to blue, depending on the sun's angle, the Egyptians called it the Sea of Green—for green symbolized life and fertility, and this vital waterway gave them a means to sustain themselves.

Some travellers had changed the cover of their howdahs to a sturdier leather base to withstand the salt spray that now misted the camels' hair and the woven shells of the caravan.

The procession slowed. Then came three loud, piercing sounds from a shofar. The caravan guards shouted in unison:

"To the springs of Aila!"

The date palms and tamarisk trees she had glimpsed from afar were signs of a natural spring or a nearby shallow well.

"Are you going down?" Nabil asked, sidling his camel close to hers.

"I'll stay nearby," she answered.

"I can accompany you if you would like to look around the market-place," he offered. "We must stop at Aila to gather fresh supplies before we proceed to Petra. Some merchants from our caravan will unload the frankincense and myrrh we carried from Egypt. They'll reload grain and wine for the return journey. This stop may take a while."

"Thank you, *Akhi*—older brother," she said softly. Nabil's cold disposition toward her had warmed over the past thirty days. She followed his instructions, and never gave him trouble. She treated him with utmost respect as a follower of Yeshua, and as a trusted helper of Apostle Thaddeus.

The thirty-day journey along the Incense Road had been compli-cated and tortuous. Thousands of miles of dunes became a tedious sight after a few days. A glimpse of the market—voices, colors, human faces—would be a welcome change.

Just then, a sentry of Nabataean soldiers in military formation marched along the roadway, their uniforms distinctly different from those of their Roman counterparts. It was not the metallic tunics or deep reds or deep green colours that soldiers had been wearing since she was a young child. Their garments were lighter, layered tunics in sand and coral, adapted to the desert landscape.

The soldiers continued their march. She did not realize she was holding her breath until they passed by. It reminded her that she had to be on her toes all the time. Even if they were not the fierce-looking Roman soldiers, the Nabataean soldiers were carrying weapons and were alert to any trouble.

From her pocket, she drew a length of cloth to cover her hair. Slipping her feet into sandals, she was eager to visit the open-air marketplace.

Down by the shoreline, Roman cargo vessels, Arabian dhows with their distinct triangular sails, and other smaller boats dotted the shore of Mare Rubrum. The air was heavy with salt spray, and the distinct pungent smell of fish drying in the sun—a smell that seemed to cling to her skin.

A chorus of voices was heard as Nabataean, Greek, Aramaic, and Arabic traders were selling their textiles, pottery, and food in open-air tents. She was drawn to the wooden figurines in one stall, and suddenly thought of Yeshua.

She stopped where she stood. Ten years had passed, yet the memories were as sharp as sunlight. Is this what grieving is? A never-ending cycle of despair and happiness, at the most inopportune time.

Yeshua had once carved small wooden figures by hand—one for each of the Apostles, and one for her. She reached inside her robe and brought out the one she had kept: a tiny carving of Hivra, the family donkey. Yeshua shaped it from sycamore wood, lighter and more flexible than olive wood.

She brushed her thumb across its smooth surface and thought of him in his tool shed. When she was very young, his routine was as regular as the dawn peeking in the morning. After her chores in her own home were done in the morning, she would walk to Yeshua's home. Dodta Maryam was around the house starting preparations for the midday meal, and she would help her chop cucumbers and onions, roast freshly caught fish wrapped in vine leaves, or help salt olives in a jar.

When those tasks were done, Maryam would smile. "Go help Yeshua," she would say.

He was always at work, pounding a nail into a stool or shaping wood for a neighbour who needed a chair. The fishermen slept after their long nights at sea, but Yeshua never seemed to tire. When there were no other tasks, he carved little wooden figurines instead.

One morning, she had asked if she might touch his tools.

"Would you like to learn how to carve, Biti Eliana?" Without waiting for her answer, he gave her an olive twig, and she accepted it.

"It's hard wood, but a good way to begin. Keep this—it's yours. This is an iron chisel, my father Yusef gave this to me when I was a boy. It reminds me of him every day."

"Dod Yeshua, it's beautiful," she said, tracing the handle. "One day, I'll carve your face in wood."

Yeshua laughed, and said, "Then I'll wait for that day, Biti Eliana."

After that, they worked in companionable silence—Yeshua shaping his little figurines, she scraping bark from her twig. When the sun rose higher, he straightened and called. "Time to go to the shore."

She followed him outside towards the shore. He mended fishing nets, while she played in the sand with the other children. Mothers gutted and cleaned the morning's catch to sell them fresh in the market.

By then, her father had woken from his nap and joined his brother, Dod Andraos, repairing the nets beside the waves.

Those were simpler times, she thought. A thousand years away.

"Eliana."

She froze. That voice—one she had not heard in ten years. Nicanor.

"What are you doing here?" she asked, her voice low, but shaking.

"Visiting Petra. Visiting Yudah's family," Nicanor said, his tone casual, almost taunting.

"Have you no shame?" she said. "You know I'll tell the truth, don't you?"

"You know I can stop you anytime," he spat. "It depends whose story holds up."

"You are the devil." She reached into her robe, drew out a silver coin, and slammed it onto a stall. "Here—find someone else to betray and fill your purse."

The metallic clang cut through the market's noise. Women balancing baskets on their heads stopped mid-stride. Children froze, clutching their mother's robes. Fishmongers and merchants turned, eyes wide, as silence spread like a wave.

"*Lā shāwē 'ant lə-ṭelālī dən-'eḇar b-'ūrḫā*," she said through clenched teeth. "You are not worthy of even my shadow passing on the road."

Then she turned and walked away.

Her steps quickened. She pulled her shawl tighter over her head, searching for a way out of the market before the Nabataean guards—now moving between stalls with their spears and round shields—noticed the disturbance. Relief washed through her when she saw no Roman insignia. The Nabataean Kingdom, ruled by its own kings, was still free from Roman control.

She stopped for breath, scanning the rows of tents for the caravan. Camels rested in the shade, their flanks rising and falling slowly in the midday heat.

"There you are, Biti Eliana," Nabil said, catching up. "I heard the commotion with Nicanor. Serves him right that you lashed out. Shall we return to the caravan?"

She nodded. Words would not come.

They walked in silence. Traders haggled over spices and cloth; women balanced bolts of linen on their heads, and children darted through the crowd, selling ripened fruit. It was an ordinary day in the market—except for her. Her hands still trembled. She touched her cheek, trying to steady herself.

Nabil slowed his pace, falling slightly behind as if to give her space. Their first stop was the camel enclosure. The beasts knelt in neat rows, freed from their howdahs, eyes half-closed in rest.

"It's good to see them resting," she said quietly. "Tomorrow they'll carry heavy loads again. I'll be glad when we're on our way."

"We rest here tonight and leave at dawn for Petra," Nabil said. "I bought carrots and dates for your Samuel."

She smiled faintly. She had never grown used to camels—their gait so different from the donkeys of her youth—but Samuel had proven gentle and sure-footed, steady even on narrow ledges.

Nabil reached inside his basket and fed Samuel, then reached under the camel's chin and patted his neck. "Five more days to go, Samuel," he said.

"Five more days to go and I won't see him anymore," she said in a mournful tone, as she patted the camel in between the ears. "Habibi, I will miss you, huh."

"*Tūn, 'akulū*—Come and eat, Master Nabil, my Lady Eliana," someone beckoned from afar.

They both turned at the voices calling them. It was the servant serving Eleazar's family tent. As valued members under his care, they were provided with their own tents at night and were included in the meals cooked for the family.

Another servant and his helper were preparing supper: lentil soup, preserved cheeses, fermented olives, and bread. A fire pit burned in the center of the camp, its glow casting warmth and a small sense of safety in the vastness of the desert.

After dinner, Eleazar brought out a triangular harp, while Nabil brought out his flute to sing the 'Song of Songs.' that ancient book of love poetry often turned into song. The melody drifted through the tents until the night wind grew too fierce to remain outside.

When the cold descended, everyone withdrew.

"Good night, Eliana," Nabil said. "Try to rest. I bought you some figs and honey. Some oranges too. You can eat it inside your tent."

"Good night, Akhi Nabil," she said in a formal tone.

The scent of juniper wood and pine needles hung in the air, sharp and citrusy. Now and then, a berry popped in the fire, releasing a peppery note that mingled with the acacia smoke, lulling her toward sleep.

But sleep would not come.

Her mind wandered to that night in Cana when Yeshua turned water into wine. The celebration had been rapturous—laughter, song, and the heady sweetness of the wine, the finest Cana had ever known.

After that, people began to whisper who He was. Yet for her, the mystery only deepened.

In the days that followed, she had spoken to her father, to her Savta, to Habibti Maryam—and to Yeshua Himself.

"I could not tie the knots together," she remembered telling them. "*Lā meḥabber qishrei.* I could not understand what had happened."

When Yeshua was baptized by Yohanan, his cousin, and the famed prophet at the River Jordan, Yohanan cried out to the people that Yeshua was the Son of God.

Did he mean Yeshua was not of this world? Was He divine—of the stars, of heaven itself?

Her understanding of God, and that of her ancestors, had always been of One apart from man: unseen, unutterable, a righteous judge who punished sin in every form.

When Yeshua performed the miracle at Cana, it slowly dawned on her—He was the same man who had taught her to carve figurines, helped her gather wood for the hearth, swam with her and her father in the Yam Kinneret, urged her to learn new tongues, and laugh at all her jokes.

Was Yeshua from the heavens? A Son of God?

How could that be?

What was Yeshua trying to say? That His love for us was personal—yet endless and unconditional? If He was the Son, then God, His Father, must be love itself. For Yeshua showed us what love meant. He preached forgiveness, urged us to turn the other cheek, and even in anger, there was compassion in His eyes.

Day after day, He performed wonders—healing the sick, raising the dead, feeding thousands with a loaf and two fish, walking on the waters. A single miracle was beyond understanding; how could a mind like hers contain them all?

In those days, Yeshua was a man aflame. He moved with urgency, as though time itself were closing in. He turned night into day and day into night. From the moment the dove descended upon Him at the Jordan, life around Him became like the spinning wheels of Roman chariots—rushing faster and faster until they vanished in a blur.

During those extraordinary days, Yudah and Nicanor were her closest companions. The youngest among the followers, they often talked together, trying to make sense of what they had witnessed.

When the day's work was done, Yeshua would turn to the three of them and ask what they had seen. He listened—truly listened—as though our youthful eyes perceived something others did not.

Yudah and Nicanor never returned to Tiberias to resume their lives in the theater, though she often asked why.

"It's because we want to follow Yeshua's path," Yudah would answer. "I want to learn from Him. He is unlike any teacher I've known."

Yudah and Nicanor were like two spotted sheep among the flock—different, vivid, impossible to mistake.

Yudah's father had been born in Kerioth, but Yudah himself was born in Athens, where his father served as a Judean envoy to the Herodian court. His duty was to oversee Rome's Greek provinces and ensure their harmony.

"Did you go to private academies, or were you taught at home?" she asked one evening.

"And where did you learn that, Biti Eliana?" Nicanor teased.

"From Dod Yusef of Arimathea," she replied. "He said he studied at a private academy in Corinth."

"I went to a rhetor," Yudah said, closing his eyes as if remembering. "That was brutal—but fun. My life was never the same. We studied Homer, Demosthenes, and Isocrates under the guidance of an orator. That's where I first fell in love with acting."

"We did enjoy the bacchanalia," Nicanor added with a grin. "Wild times." He winked at her, and she couldn't help but laugh.

"Maybe to you," Yudah said with a grimace. "*Misteh rava*—Drunken feasts not for me. I was just too happy when my father returned to Tiberias."

"Ahh, you're too serious, Yudah," Nicanor said with reproach.

She had always been aware of the special bond between Yudah and Nicanor—both born in Athens, both raised in privilege, sharing the same tutors, games, and confidences whispered between lessons.

They looked different from the rest of them, moved differently, their ease born of wealth and entitlement.

When she turned twelve, Yudah formally requested Eliana's hand in marriage to Nicanor.

She recalled that day vividly.

They had welcomed Shabbat the evening before; tools were set aside, even the fishermen drew in their nets for the night. The world had gone still, a hush of peace settling over the village as lamps were lit and prayers were uttered. Everyone was in a relaxed mood for the sacred days.

At dawn, the villagers gathered at the synagogue. She always loved that place, with its walls made from dark basalt stones, stones that were carried to the Galila landscape by the lava flows of nearby Mt. Peres, when it was an active volcano thousands of years ago.

Oil lamps flickered along the walls, casting a bright glow throughout the room. The men and women sat on woven reed mats scattered on the floor. Her father, as an elder in the community, unrolled the Torah and began to chant the Shema, the prayer every Judean knew by heart.

"Hear, O Israel, the Lord our God, the Lord is One."

After her father's recitation, Yeshua or Dod Andraos would rise to receive the Torah and read other passages, such as Psalms and Proverbs, and afterward explain their meaning.

Crowds had begun to gather whenever Yeshua spoke. People from neighboring villages walked miles to hear him teach at dawn. His words carried a quiet power that stilled the restlessness of the heart; for a time, the worries of the week seemed to vanish.

When prayers ended, the families returned to their homes and laid out the midday meal in their courtyards. No cooking was done—it was forbidden on Shabbat.

Her family often joined Yeshua's household. Low tables were set in the courtyard; mats and pillows scattered for kin and guests.

Stewed mutton, chickpea and barley stews, and warm bread were passed around the table. Wine from the Galila vineyards filled their cups, accompanied by dried cheeses. After the hurried morning tasks, everyone slowed down—content, laughing softly as they ate ripened grapes, figs, dates, and pomegranates.

It was then that Yudah rose, faced her father, and said,

"On behalf of Nicanor's parents in Athens, and as his family's friend, I am here to formally request Eliana's hand in marriage to Nicanor."

Conversation stopped. A few polite claps broke the silence.

Marriage proposals were usually made in private, among kin, not before guests. A daughter's opinion was always sought—but now every eye turned to her.

Her father cleared his throat. "We can speak in private—Nicanor, Yudah. Yeshua, Andraos, Maryam of Magdala, Eliana and Maryam of Nasrath—come. Let us sit under the fig tree." He pointed toward the tree at the edge of their property.

"May I bring Savta too?" she asked. She wanted her grandmother's wisdom close by.

"Bring my Emma to the fig tree," her father said.

Yudah and Nicanor brought extra reed mats, and soon they were seated in the cool shade.

"Well then, you heard what Nicanor had to say, Biti Eli," her father began.

"I heard," Eliana said, glancing at the faces around her—the ones she loved and those who loved her. The two Maryams leaned forward, smiling. Her Savta already had tears in her eyes. Yeshua caught her gaze and smiled gently, as if to say, Speak what is in your heart.

"Go on," her father urged.

"I don't want to marry at this time," she said to her father. "I want to follow you—and Yeshua. I don't even understand a fingernail of what He speaks about, but I want to learn."

Nicanor's face stiffened. "But women are meant to bear children and keep the household. Why would you wander the world with Yeshua?"

"What if I'm not ready for that life?" she said. "And besides, you don't love me, Nicanor. You love Yudah."

The words fell into the air like a struck chord. Gasps rippled through the circle.

"What in God's name, Eliana?" her father exclaimed, rising to his feet.

"It's true," she said, meeting Yudah's and Nicanor's eyes. "I hear you talk together. Among the wealthy in Athens, such bonds are accepted—a mark of status and education. But it is not our way. Isn't it true that you were companions of the bed?"

"Eliana, stop," her Savta pleaded. "Give Nicanor respect. Speak to him privately—please, child, let this end."

But she could not be silenced.

"It is true, Eliana—but it is not part of my life anymore," Yudah said.

"Can you truly say that, Nicanor?" she asked, turning to him. "Why not admit you love this man? No one here will judge you. But why must you marry me?"

Nicanor's face flushed deep red, caught between shame and fury. He rose abruptly, turned, and fled.

"Oh, Biti Eliana, you didn't have to say it that way," her father said softly.

Eliana's chest constricted. She ran after Nicanor, calling his name, but he was already gone.

Yudah darted in the opposite direction, searching the alleys. His footsteps echoed through the narrow streets, where lanterns flickered in low doorways. Eliana searched too, asking the merchants and neighbors if they had seen him, but no one had.

For months afterward, they searched—through markets, ports, and caravan stops—but Nicanor had vanished like smoke in the wind. Sometimes, at dusk, Eliana thought she heard his laughter. She would turn toward the sound, heart lifting, but there was only emptiness.

Meanwhile, the crowds around Yeshua grew larger each day. People brought their sick, their dying, their broken-hearted to Him.

"*Ayk nura b-husha*—fire among the thorns," her Savta said, describing how news of Him spread.

Before dawn, Yeshua now retreated to the hills near Kfar Nahum, seeking silence before prayer. Eliana and Yudah often accompanied Him.

One morning, as He descended from the hillside, a great crowd had gathered near the synagogue.

"Roman centurions," Yudah whispered. It was the first time they had seen soldiers watching the assemblies. Sensing danger, Yeshua quickened His pace.

When He reached the synagogue, He raised His arms in prayer, and the crowd grew silent.

"We cannot gather here anymore and disturb the neighborhood of Kfar Nahum," he said. "I will come to your villages instead. *Hēnōn 'innūn shlīḥai d-məsayʿūn lī*—these are my Apostles who will help me."

"Did He say *shlīḥai*? Helpers?" someone whispered.

"Yes, in Aramaic, it's helpers—envoys," another man replied. "In Greek—apostolos."

Then one of the elders, rising with reverence, lifted the phrase into Hebrew—"*Êlleh shelūḥai asher yaʿazrūni*—these are my apostles who will help me."

The crowd pressed closer, trembling with anticipation.

"Who will He name?" a woman cried out.

"Shimʿōn Kēfā."—"Simon Peter," Yeshua said, and applause broke out.

"Andraos."—"Andrew," someone shouted, "Shimon's brother!"

"Yaʿaqōv bar Zavdai."—"James, son of Zebedee."

"Yōḥanan bar Zavdai."—"John, son of Zebedee."

"Philipos."—"Philip."

"Bar-Tolmay."—"Bartholomew."

"Mattai."—"Matthew."

"T'ōmā."—"Thomas."

"Yaʿaqōv bar Ḥalfai."—"James, son of Alphaeus."

"Shimʿōn ha-Qannāy."—"Simon the Zealous."

"Yehuda bar Yaʿaqōv."—"Thaddeus, son of James."

"Yehuda Ish-Qeriyyot."—"Judas, man of Kerioth."

"Maryam d'Magdala."—"Mary of Magdala."

The crowd stirred at the sound of her name.

"The world must be ending," someone muttered. "I'll chew my own sandal before following a woman's word. I'm out of here."

"Son of a dog! Why include a tax collector?" one man shouted. "He bleeds us poor fishermen to fill Rome's coffers!"

Another spat on the ground and stormed away.

"I'd sooner eat the basalt stones than take orders from a woman," a younger man near Eliana muttered.

Almost half the crowd dispersed, cursing as they went.

Eliana's gaze moved over the faces that remained, searching for steadiness—and then she saw him.

Nicanor.

His expression was a storm: rage, disbelief, and something wounded flickering beneath it.

He turned sharply, disappearing into the retreating crowd.

It was the last time she saw him for three years.

————◆————

Wadi Musa—Nabataean Highlands
Year 4 of King Malichus (43 AD)

Mare Rubrum had become a distant speck behind them. For three days, they had crossed the Arabian desert once more, riding through miles of harsh and unyielding terrain.

By day, Eliana and Nabil spoke little, conserving strength in the fierce heat. At noon, the caravan halted so the camels could rest, continuing again after nightfall when the wind turned cool.

At dawn, they set out again. The endless dunes gave way to color—patches of green and yellow, streaks of orange across the rising slopes. The air grew lighter as they climbed, and the stillness of the desert gave way to sound: the whir of insects, the distant cry of birds.

Before long, they entered a dense, wooded region scented with the ripe aroma of figs and pomegranates. The caravan quickened its pace. A wide valley unfolded ahead, bright with vineyards stretching to the horizon.

"Wadi Musa! Wadi Musa!" the caravan leaders cried out.

The Valley of Moses—a name she had read in the writings of historians. Her heart swelled. Petra was only a day away.

Because of the milder air, they did not pause at noon. When the sun finally sank, the caravan stopped at the outer station for the night. Campfires blazed, and the travelers' talk was filled with anticipation: tomorrow, they would reach the heart of the Nabataean kingdom.

Eliana lay awake long after the others had slept. It would be her first sight of Petra, and her thoughts were full of its fabled red cliffs and carved temples.

At dawn, the shofar sounded outside her tent. Time to move again. Servants hurried to strike the tents, fastening ropes, checking supplies. There was no morning meal; everyone was intent on the final day's journey.

Soon the sun rose, and from a distance the red canyon walls glowed like fire. The road widened, allowing other caravans to pass. From behind her came a sharp whistle—Nabil's signal. She drew back the curtains of her howdah.

To her right, another procession of camels moved alongside them. It was not a spice caravan but one meant for travelers. The animals were richly adorned—saddles draped in Judean textiles dyed blue from murex shells of Shikmona and scarlet from the kermes insects of Negev oak and terebinth trees. On several of the covers gleamed the mark of the Lion of Judah, the royal emblem of her homeland.

"Judea!" Nabil shouted from his perch.

At his call, the people in the other caravan stirred; curtains lifted, curious faces peering out.

Only one howdah remained closed. Inside, she caught a glimpse of the faint silhouette of a woman.

Eliana's curiosity quickened. Who could she be—a noble traveler, a priestess, a scholar? Whoever she was, the stillness of that unopened curtain drew Eliana's eyes again and again as the two caravans moved side by side toward Petra.

Chapter 27

S imone

St. Hannah of Kerioth Church, Arles

Saturday, October 21—5:15 p.m.

Simone reached the front steps first.

"What denomination is this chapel?" Gabby asked. "It doesn't have the tall spires of a Lutheran church—or the wide awnings of the Protestants."

A woman was tending the flower beds near the entrance. Simone called out softly. The woman straightened, garden tools still in hand. Her posture was regal, her face calm—a person accustomed to peace.

"Madame, excusez-moi—excuse me, I'm Simone Harper, from New York. I have a gallery there and would like to ask about your church," Simone said in French.

"I studied in the States. No need for French," the woman said, smiling faintly. "I'm Yvette Raglan, head of this church. Fire away."

"What religious affiliation is St. Hannah's?" Gabby asked.

Yvette's smile deepened. "Legend says Mary of Magdala founded this church for pilgrims passing through Arles. It's been burned to the ground more times than I can count—believers persecuted, relics destroyed. The Merovingians rebuilt it under papal authority. Later, it was refashioned in the Medieval and, finally, Romanesque style."

"But which denomination now?" Gabby pressed. "Catholic? Presbyterian? Baptist?"

"We belong to none," Yvette said simply. "We belong to ourselves."

"I take it you have women priests—and different scriptures?" Xavier asked.

"Yes, all of that," Yvette replied. "We read both Catholic and Protestant texts. But our guiding writings—those others call apocryphal—have been preserved by women across generations."

Simone leaned forward. "May we see them? Have you ever heard of the writings of Eliana?"

"*Mon Dieu*—my God!" Yvette whispered, startled. "My great-grandmother Helene was treated by Dr. Gachet when she fell ill. He mentioned writings that troubled him, but we never saw them. Still..." She hesitated. "Come in. You may look around."

"Controversies like witch-hunts and burnings?" Gabby muttered.

Yvette sighed. "Exactly. I don't usually invite strangers in, but I trust my instincts. Follow me."

She led them up the worn stone steps and opened a pair of heavy carved doors. The interior was dim, the air scented with the fragrance of beeswax and age.

"This way." Yvette guided them through a narrow corridor and stopped before a cabinet. Inside, a box overflowed with old books and loose parchment.

"A trove," Xavier murmured, sifting through the pile. "But no writings of Eliana."

"Rumor says Dr. Gachet was a descendant of Saint Hannah," Yvette said quietly. "Whatever copies he kept disappeared long ago."

"No oral tradition? Nothing passed down?" Gabby asked.

"I'm afraid not. You may browse what we have. I'll be in the sanctuary."

Simone wandered through the nave, admiring the rounded arches and barrel-vaulted ceilings. Small windows let in thin slants of light, softening the gloom. The church felt ancient, resilient. Yvette lingered by the altar, both watchful and welcoming.

"It's beautiful," Simone said.

"Thrice burned, countless times ransacked," Yvette replied. "Rebuilt in the twelfth century. Van Gogh even painted its silhouette. But our spire—our spire has always survived."

On the walls hung frescoes of Christ's life, from His birth to His death. Yet most depicted the women who followed Him—faces of devotion and endurance. Simone stopped before one: Mary of Magdala at the empty tomb.

A faint wisp of smoke drifted across her vision.

"Is something burning?" Gabby shouted, running toward the altar.

Yvette darted up a side landing. She returned moments later, breathless. "Follow me! The fire's upstairs—some of our papers are there. Don't stop for anything." She pulled a key from her pocket. "The originals are secured elsewhere, but we keep copies here. Quickly!"

They ran after her as she unlocked a heavy door leading down a narrow, dark passage.

The air was cold, the stone walls slick beneath Simone's fingers.

"The builders chose stone that could survive fire," Yvette said with a nervous laugh. "Our forefathers had a morbid sense of humor."

Xavier pushed open a door ahead. Light poured in. "This way—an exit!" He reached for Simone's hand. "Run!"

"I'll stay and meet the fire trucks," Yvette said, voice steady though her eyes glistened. "We're used to this. Au revoir. Prayers that we meet again!"

They stumbled out into the smoke-filled cemetery. Tombstones blurred in the haze.

"Your scarf," Xavier said. He tore it in half, handing one piece to Simone and one to Gabby. "Cover your nose and mouth." He pulled his jacket over his head, eyes squinting against the soot.

The air was thick, acrid. Shapes loomed in the smoke—trees, stone markers, shadows. Then Xavier vanished from view.

"Xavier?" Simone called.

"Oh shit!" his voice rang out, followed by a thud.

She froze, afraid to move.

"What the—!" another voice groaned from the ground.

"Son of a bitch!" Xavier hissed.

And then she recognized the other voice—sharp, incredulous.

Tarquin.

Chapter 28

Tarquin

Nîmes–Arles Airport, Arles

Saturday, October 21—5:00 p.m.

The sights and sounds of the airport felt strangely familiar. Tarquin had been here before. As a child, his parents had brought him to Arles every summer. Then suddenly, the visits stopped. He had never known why.

After Simone, Gabby, and Xavier waved him off, he booked a ride into town. At Place du Pont, he stopped before L'Escargot, where a long line of people waited outside the boulangerie.

The scent of butter and caramelized sugar tugged him backward in time—to those summers as a boy, waiting in that same line while his mother bought Kouign-amann. The thought of its eighteen delicate layers made his mouth water even now. Maybe that small joy had been the start of his lifelong love for food, for craft, for creation itself.

He turned away from the main street and wandered toward a leafy avenue where mothers pushed prams and children skipped alongside them. The city sounds softened as he walked toward the cemetery.

A patch of purple caught his eye by the roadside. Foxgloves. Still growing in the same place after all these years. His mother had always warned him never to touch them—poisonous blooms, deceptively beautiful.

He looked around, searching for a familiar landmark. The path was unchanged. He remembered how his mother had once held his small hand as they walked here to visit the graves of his ancestors.

Ah, his parents.

Could he ever forgive them for giving away Van Gogh's Night Café thirty years ago? It looked similar to Café by the Terrace, but the study was an interior scene, with one lady drinking wine. They had claimed it was a "donation," but he had never understood to whom or why. The painting had been his earliest memory of wonder, the first artwork that made him feel the pulse of eternity in color.

His childhood had been a blur of constant relocation—never staying in the same school for more than two years, never finding a sense of belonging. By nine, he could already speak four languages. By twelve, he had learned how to disappear into any culture.

Years later, one ordinary afternoon in Ruislip, everything changed. He had been walking with his parents when a group of men cornered them, shouting, "Son of Judas!"

The words stung like stones. He turned to his father afterward, shaken.

"That," his father said, weary and quiet, "is why we've moved from country to country. There are people—organizations—who believe we descend from Judas Iscariot. They seek the bloodline, and they hunt it."

Not long after, his parents sat him down. His mother's voice was gentle, resigned. "There are stories you deserve to know, Tarquin. It's time."

"Why did we visit Arles every year?" he asked.

"Because Dr. Gachet was our ancestor," his father replied.

"The same Gachet who treated Van Gogh?"

"Yes. A direct descendant."

"Direct—from the Judas line?" Tarquin asked, incredulous.

"Yes," his mother said softly. "From one of Judas Iscariot's brothers. The family practiced the healing arts—physicians who treated those afflicted in mind and spirit. We descend from Yaakov."

"I thought our bloodline came from the priests of Benjamin," he said, confused.

"There were many who held high office," his mother explained. "Even Yudah and Yaakov studied in Greece while their father served as a diplomat. Our true ancestry was hidden for survival."

He hesitated. "Did Judas truly betray Christ?"

His father exhaled. "According to an apocryphal text—the Gospel of Saul—Jesus knew of the betrayal. He was God. He foresaw His death. Judas was chosen to fulfill it."

His mother reached for his hand. "There was another writer," she said. "A woman named Eliana—Simon Peter's daughter. Her writings were lost to time. Our family spent generations searching for them."

"Why?"

His father's eyes grew distant. "Because Dr. Gachet once possessed her manuscripts. When Van Gogh was in the asylum, the doctor entrusted some of them to him—perhaps as a form of therapy, perhaps because he recognized in the artist the same divine madness. But we never learned if he gave him all of them."

Tarquin frowned. "But why Van Gogh?"

"Artists were chosen to hide the works," his father had explained. "They had powerful patrons—people who could protect them. Through symbols and hidden details in their paintings, they left clues to Eliana's writings, meant for those seeking truth—and to mislead those who hunted her words for the wrong reasons."

His mother's voice had softened. "We've kept running because men who still preach that Judas betrayed Christ have tried to erase every trace of what really happened that night."

The memory of that conversation lingered as he walked. He stumbled, cursing under his breath. "Merde." He constantly cursed in French.

The rock that jutted between the tombstones—his childhood landmark—was still there. He smiled faintly and counted the rows. On the fifth, he turned left.

There it was.

The Gachet Family Mausoleum.

The door was locked, but he remembered the code—Dr. Gachet's birthday. His parents had made him memorize it without ever explaining why. He keyed it in; the light flickered green. Inside, the air was cool and dry, heavy with the scent of marble and candle wax.

He knelt and touched the tombstone, tracing the carved letters before bowing his head in reverence.

"We therefore commit this body to the ground,
Earth to earth, ashes to ashes, dust to dust;
In sure hope of the Resurrection to eternal life."

Van Gogh had been Dr. Gachet's patient, but they had become friends. If Gachet truly descended from Yudah, had he shown the papyrus pages written by Eliana to Van Gogh? Had the families of the

Apostles kept in contact through the centuries? How had his father known who to give the drawing to?

When his parents died in that senseless accident, all records vanished—no letters, no diaries, no one left to ask.

Only this place remained to give him a sense of belonging to any family.

He touched the tombstone. Did Van Gogh know the secrets, hiding them in paint and color?

And had the Gachet line hidden the papyrus here, in stone and silence?

He looked around the mausoleum, his pulse quickening. The safest place... could it be this very tomb?

"Holy shit," he whispered. "No way—but maybe..."

He stood, scanning the walls. His parents had brought him here every year without explanation. Maybe his father hadn't been praying—he'd been checking on something.

He ran his fingers along the wall etched with the family names until he found two: Emmanuel and Olive Vern.

His throat tightened. He missed them fiercely. It had been during his first internship in New York when the call came—an accident, both gone.

After settling their estate, all he inherited was a townhouse and a silence that made no sense.

He remembered his father cleaning the tomb, always circling to the back, disappearing for minutes at a time. Why there?

Tarquin knelt, feeling along the base of the marble, fingertips brushing dust and stone. No ridges. No hinges. He flattened his palm over the center of the slab and pressed.

A faint vibration hummed under his hand. Then—numbers lit up in dim amber light.

His heart jumped. He entered the same code as the door. A muted click. A panel rose silently, revealing another lock—this one marked with a narrow groove beside it.

A fingerprint reader.

He pressed his thumb against it. A sharp sting. "Ow! What the—"

A tiny pinprick. Blood scan?

Before he could curse, gears whirred. A small vestibule lifted open from the floor.

"Bingo." He grinned, adrenaline surging. "Merci, Papa et Maman."

A black pouch glimmered inside the hidden compartment. Tarquin reached in and drew out a long, thin metal box—about the width of his palm. The metal was uneven to the touch, hand-forged, its surface faintly patterned like fish scales.

He turned it over in his hands, feeling its weight. Whatever was inside had been sealed for generations. He slipped the box back into the pouch, tucked it into his backpack—too bulky—and finally slung the pouch across his shoulder. One last glance. Nothing seemed disturbed. He switched off the lights and moved toward the exit.

Then came voices.

He froze.

Outside, two men in dark clothes stumbled into view, gasoline cans clattering at their feet. Their masks caught the light for an instant.

"What the fuck..." Tarquin whispered. Arsonists? Here?

He didn't think—he charged. Swinging the metal pouch, he slammed it against one man's thigh. The man yelped and fell, gasoline spilling across the ground. Tarquin followed with a punch square to the jaw.

"*Putain!*" he hissed, ducking as the second man lunged. Hands clawed for his hair. The smell of gasoline and smoke filled the air.

"*Qu'avez-vous fait?* What have you done?" Tarquin shouted.

"*Ce n'est pas ton affaire, idiot!*" the man spat back.

Tarquin's fist met his mouth before the sentence finished. The attacker went down, motionless—then kicked out suddenly, catching Tarquin's shoulder. Pain shot through him.

"Oh shit..." He staggered, wincing, as the man vanished into the smoke, dragging the cans away.

The haze thickened, the acrid scent burning his lungs. He turned to pursue—when something heavy crashed into him. Then another. Then another.

"What the hell—?"

He started swinging instinctively. "Back off! Fuck you!"

"Tarquin, is that you, you son of a bitch?" a familiar voice shouted.

He froze. "Xavier?"

"God, it's so dark in here," Simone gasped.

"Simone, please—let's get out before this place burns!" Gabby cried.

Tarquin caught his breath, lowering his fists. "Easy, easy! I'm fine." He couldn't hide the excitement in his voice. "But you won't believe this—I found a metal box. It could be part of the Gospel of Eliana!"

"A convenient find," Xavier said bitterly. "Aren't you with the Obscurati—ordered to silence Simone?"

"What?" Gabby lunged at him. "You traitor—!"

"Hey! Stop—listen!" Tarquin held up both hands as Xavier pulled Gabby back. "I'm not your enemy. I'm here for the same reason—to find Eliana's writings. To understand my lineage."

Simone's voice was cautious. "Your lineage?"

"Dr. Gachet was my ancestor," Tarquin said. "Direct line... to Judas Iscariot."

Xavier made the sign of the cross. "Santa madre di Dio."

"Oh my God," Simone whispered.

Gabby stared at him. "Is that true?"

Tarquin nodded once. "And I think the rest of the documents are in this duffel."

"What?" they all said at once.

The distant wail of sirens grew louder—ambulances, fire trucks, police.

"We can't stay here," Simone said. "They'll seal off the area."

"No time," Xavier answered. "We have to move now."

"Where is safe?" Simone asked.

"Rome," Xavier said.

The flashing lights were getting closer.

"Then Rome it is," Simone said, determined. "After you, Professor."

Gabby moved beside Tarquin. "You're hurt—take my shoulder."

"I tried to stop the bastards who set the fire," he said through clenched teeth. "Got one of them—but he escaped."

"If we don't hurry, we'll be explaining this to the Arles police," Xavier muttered.

Tarquin managed a grin despite the pain. "Can't wait to collapse on the Flying Vault's plush seats—and maybe grab first-class food for the road."

Chapter 29

R odrigo

St. Hannah of Kerioth Church

Saturday, October 21—6:30 p.m.

"Holy Mother of God, what kind of shitshow have we walked into, Detective Rigo?" Andrea Tatin, FBI attaché to Paris, muttered as they stood before the smoldering church.

"Too late to the party," Rigo said dryly. "What I need now is a jet to shadow our jet-set POIs."

He pulled a photo of Tarquin Vern from his notebook. "Let's talk to the Commissariat. Maybe they saw him."

"I'll go first," Tatin said, adjusting her discreet FBI pin on her lapel. "The locals like to speak French to the French."

While she approached the officers, Rigo surveyed the scene. The fire was mostly contained; the stone façade of St. Hannah's still stood intact. Smoke curled through the air, mingling with the faint, chemical sweetness of accelerant. Gasoline, most likely.

What the hell were Simone Harper, Xavier Jang, Gabrielle Henry, and Tarquin Vern doing here?

Just hours earlier, he'd been having lunch at Café Marly when word came in: Simone's next stop was Arles. With Tatin's help, the FBI had commandeered a helicopter to shadow her team. The French pilot had grumbled, but the operation moved fast.

The Police Judiciaire hadn't been thrilled about American oversight, but eventually a local officer, Gerard Arneux, agreed to assist. By the time they reached Arles, Arneux reported a fire near Place du Pont. A group matching their suspects had been seen heading that way.

On the flight, Rigo had studied his notes, scrolling through images of Van Gogh's Café Terrace at Night. He compared the Kröller-Müller Museum's oil painting to the charcoal drawing owned by Pope Lucas.

"Holy shit," he'd whispered then, and the same thought returned now. The discrepancies were obvious: the oil painting showed a building with a spire—the very silhouette of this church. But the drawing? No spire, no trace of St. Hannah's.

He counted the figures in the oil: twelve seated, one standing waiter—thirteen in all. And behind them, a shadowed cross motif barely visible on the café wall. Scholars had speculated for decades that Van Gogh intended it as a re-imagining of the Last Supper.

Thirteen apostles, Rigo thought. Not twelve.

A movement caught his eye—Tatin returning with three people: a woman in clerical robes, a man in plainclothes, and a police officer.

"Detective Rigo," Tatin said. "This is Commissaire Étienne Bernard and the Abbess of St. Hannah's."

"A pleasure, even under these circumstances," Rigo said, shaking hands.

"Were these four individuals seen here?" He showed the photos of Simone, Xavier, Gabby, and Tarquin.

The Abbess leaned forward. "I saw three of them," she said. "But not this man." She pointed to Tarquin's picture. "Perhaps he was in the cemetery."

"Merci, Madame l'Abbesse, Monsieur le Commissaire," Rigo said, nodding. "That's all I needed."

"I hope you find them soon," Bernard said. "Au revoir." It was apparent the Commissaire had other questions to ask the Abbess, and he turned towards her, speaking in rapid French.

"God bless you," the Abbess added with a calm smile.

As they turned away, Rigo began circling the perimeter, noting scorch marks near the vestry.

"Where was Tarquin Vern during all this?" Tatin asked beside him. "Did he even set foot in France?"

Before he could answer, his jacket buzzed with a vibrating tap-tap. He adjusted his lens—an encrypted call from his NYPD captain.

"The main suspect's heading to Rome, Rigo," the captain said. "We've got an FBI jet grounded at Nîmes. You can hitch a ride—no need to wait for commercial."

"Perfecto," Rigo said, pressing three fingers to his lips.

"One more thing," the captain added. "We just secured a no-knock warrant for Tarquin Vern's townhouse and for Cassius Turbierri's headquarters at St. Anthony the Divine Church. We'll send updates."

"Copy that, Captain."

"Bring Vern back for questioning, Rigo. And move fast."

"Yes, sir. I'm on it."

He turned to Tatin. "Back to the airport. Our POIs are heading to Rome."

Tatin grinned. "Ooh, FBI jet? Now you're cookin', good-lookin'."

He laughed—short, hollow, all business. "Let's just hope we find that Turbierri and Vern in Rome, so I can finally go home to New York."

Chapter 30

S imone

Above the skies of Rome

Saturday, October 21—8 p.m.

"Is it possible to open this box?" Simone asked Tarquin.

The long metal case lay across his lap, slung like an extra satchel. Miraculously, it showed no trace of rust. French customs hadn't even blinked when they boarded the private jet.

They gathered around it, the hum of the engines underscoring their curiosity.

"No thumb-scan here," Gabby said, tapping the surface. "This thing predates DNA locks by a century."

"It looks hand-forged," Xavier noted, studying a square plate etched with numbers. "We'll need the right combination."

"Try Gachet's birthday," Simone suggested. "Tarquin, do the honors."

"June 25, 1850... let's see... six-two-five-one-eight-five."

Nothing.

"How about 185006?" Xavier tried.

No click.

"Maybe 185000?" Simone offered.

Still nothing.

Gabby scrolled through her old phone. "His wife—Hermione Gachet—was born October 2, 1851. One-zero-zero-two-five-one?"

Silence.

Tarquin frowned. "Then perhaps his most famous patient—Vincent van Gogh. March 30, 1853." He keyed in 185333.

Click.

The lid lifted with a soft sigh of metal.

"Oooh..." Tarquin exhaled, reverent.

"What's inside?" Gabby leaned forward.

A sheaf of brittle brown pages, rolled tight as an ancient scroll.

"Copies, maybe," Simone murmured, awed. "My God, I wish Nic was here with his gadgetry."

"We can test them at the Vatican Museum," Xavier said. "Their lab can run baseline dating."

Simone hesitated, eyeing the fragile paper. "Let's not touch more than we must. If the teardrop emblem's on these pages, it's too important to risk contamination."

"I'll call ahead," Xavier said, already reaching for his phone. "The Vatican may lack Harper Institute tech, but their conservators are second to none."

"The Vatican Museum," Tarquin repeated slowly, as if tasting the words.

"Yes," Xavier said matter-of-factly. "The Pope is expecting us."

Tarquin's eyes widened; Gabby's face lit up with childlike excitement.

Over the intercom, the pilot's voice broke in:

"Signori, we'll be landing in Rome in fifteen minutes. Benvenuti a Roma."

"Kismet," Gabby whispered. "Perfect timing."

They turned toward the windows. Below them, the Tiber shimmered like a molten ribbon; the domes and spires of the Eternal City glowed in the night. Even from here, the Vatican lights blazed like stars.

Tarquin's expression softened—wonder, disbelief, and something older stirring beneath. Simone had a dozen questions about the metal box, the scroll, the lineage of secrets—but all of that would have to wait until they touched the Roman ground.

Chapter 31

Eliana

The Shadowed Siq, Nabataean Kingdom

Year 4 of King Malichus (AD 43)

A hundred million years ago, the land beneath Samuel's hooves lay under the sea—waters teeming with sharks preying on smaller sharks, squids, and drifting crustaceans. When the Arabian plate rose, the sea vanished, leaving a deep gorge—a narrow valley whose walls of iron and quartz soared a hundred feet.

They had finally reached Petra.

Only forty to fifty camels out of four hundred were allowed to pass through this narrow valley, and they were part of Eleazar's aguda—a smaller group of camels wearing the murex blues and kermes reds of Judea on their backs.

The passage opened suddenly, and light spilled onto a vision so magnificent that Eliana forgot to breathe. Before them stood the Treasury—its tall Corinthian columns carved directly into the red sandstone, its façade glowing like fire under the afternoon sun. It was said to hold the remains of King Aretas, Petra's most powerful ruler.

They paused in reverent silence, bowing their heads before moving deeper into the living heart of the city.

Petra, crossroads of the known world: caravans from Egypt, merchants from Syria, and Arab traders from the southern deserts all converged here. The men's tunics mirrored the desert itself—sand, clay, and crimson—while the women dazzled in linen gowns of fiery red, azure blue, and sunlit yellow. Silver and gold adorned their necks and ears; kohl lined their eyes in graceful arcs.

As the caravan wound farther inward, a neighborhood emerged—a cluster of homes facing the Treasury. Some were simple one-story dwellings, others carved into the cliffs themselves, the homes of the fortunate.

"We are here now, Biti Eliana," Nabil said.

He led her to the side of the neighborhood where their camels could rest. A boy of around ten approached them to tether and feed the animals.

They stepped down from their howdahs and continued on foot. Every courtyard they had passed faced the Treasury, and from within came the comforting scents of juniper smoke and bread baking on stone. She glimpsed dried meats, figs, and dates hanging by the ledges of the courtyard.

When it turned into a narrow lane climbing upward, Nabil halted.

"It is here," he said quietly. "The home of Yaakov and Hannah, mother of Yudah of Kerioth," Nabil said.

A long line of people stood in front of the house. The hum of conversation rose and fell like the tide.

Suddenly, someone called to her from across the courtyard.

"Eliana! We met when we visited you in Kfar Nahum—it's me, Yaakov."

She turned and studied the young man's face.

"Yaakov? You were only a boy then," she said, astonished.

"Ten years is a long time," he replied with a shy grin. "A boy grows into a man eventually. Nabil, good to see you. Apostle Thaddeus has been waiting for you nearly a week. How was your journey?"

"Very well, Yaakov," Nabil said warmly. "And how are you and Dodta Hannah?"

Eliana interrupted before she could stop herself. "Where's Yohan?" The words came sharper than she intended. Yaakov and Yohan—twins, inseparable since childhood. If one was near, the other could never be far.

Yaakov's smile faded. "You haven't heard, have you? After Yudah—whom some call Judas—took his own life, Yohan was never the same. He shut himself away, stopped eating... until one day, he tried to end his life too."

"Poor Yohan," she whispered, her voice breaking.

"My mother saved him," Yaakov said softly. "She nursed him back little by little. She was a diplomat's wife in Athens once, but she left it all behind—to heal others, to heal us. Since then, we've vowed to become healers ourselves. Come, she'll be overjoyed to see you."

He led them through another lane, where two sandstone buildings stood apart from the rest. A line of patients waited outside beneath an arch marked with a curious emblem: two serpents entwined around a staff, topped with wings.

"Isn't that a physician's mark?" Eliana asked.

Yaakov nodded. "We use it for those who come seeking healing."

Inside, the air was dim and fragrant—thick with the scent of oils and herbs. Curtains divided rows of mats where the sick lay resting. The smell was unlike anything she had known—warm, earthy, divine.

"My mother and I traveled to India to learn Ayurveda," Yaakov explained. "Four months from Gaza to Kerala. A pilgrimage of healing and of grief, after the deaths of Yudah and Yeshua. We learned to blend Indian oils—turmeric, sesame, black pepper—with the balsam, myrrh, and frankincense of Judea and Egypt."

By one of the mats, a man knelt in prayer, anointing a patient's hand with oil. Eliana recognized him at once—Apostle Thaddeus.

She bowed her head and whispered a prayer of her own.

"Eliana—is it truly you, my dearest girl?" came a voice, soft and melodic, from a nearby bed.

"Dodta Hannah," she breathed. "Peace be with you. My father sends his love."

The woman rose, her presence radiant even in age, and gathered Eliana into a warm embrace. She smelled of cinnamon and rose.

"How is your father, Shimon? And your Savta? Apostle Thaddeus has spoken of your writings," Hannah said, eyes shining.

Eliana could not speak. The tears came unbidden as Hannah held her close. There was no bitterness, no shadow of the past between them—only the joy of reunion, and the strange, holy peace that always seemed to follow those who had known Yeshua.

"I want to give you what I've written," she said softly. "About the time we spent with Yeshua. There is much about Yudah in it."

Hannah's eyes filled at once. "I am deeply touched, my dearest Eliana." Tears spilled down her cheeks. "We will treasure it. We remember Yudah every day. We honor his life by doing what he would have wanted—by loving others as he loved the Father."

Yaakov stepped closer. "We host a gathering here every Sunday. Would you allow us to read some of your writings to the people gathered tonight?"

"But of course," she said.

"We would love to hear you speak as well," Hannah added.

"Anytime I speak of Yeshua, my heart feels lighter," Eliana said. "And please, let me help you with your patients. It will ease the lines—and give you rest."

"God bless you, my dearest Eliana," Hannah whispered.

"God bless you too, Dodta Hannah. It feels just like when Yeshua was alive and people waited hours to be healed."

The line stretched far down the street, faces weary yet filled with hope. Eliana thought of Yeshua standing at the end of a line like this—touching the blind, blessing the dying, restoring the broken. But now, they were the healers. His beloved followers had not forgotten. They continued His work—healing the sick, comforting the poor, bringing light where others brought fear.

She rolled up her sleeves, baring her forearms. "Where can I wash my hands, Dodta Hannah?"

Hannah led her to an enclosed courtyard at the back, its stone cool beneath her palms. The air was fragrant with rose oil and myrrh. Eliana poured water over her hands and face, the chill reviving her spirit.

When she returned to the clinic, raised voices and movement drew her toward the entrance. People were kneeling, their heads bowed before a woman in a dark robe.

"Maryam of Nasrath," she whispered—and tears blurred her vision.

"Biti Eliana," Maryam said. They met in the center of the room and embraced each other.

"It's been so long," Eliana said.

"Too long," Maryam replied. "I came with the others—Philipos and Mattai. We can help Hannah for now, and talk later."

And so they worked—side by side, hands anointing the sick with oil, murmuring prayers into the quiet air. Many who came were dying, others already half-departed. Yet none were turned away.

By midday, their garments were soaked with sweat and oil, their bodies aching—but the line had dwindled. All who came were seen, comforted, touched. And as they gathered for a simple meal, the scent of frankincense rose above them like a blessing.

Chapter 32

Xavier

Ciampino Airport, Rome

Saturday, October 21—9 p.m.

It was as if an invisible hand had arranged everything—Customs, Immigration, even the waiting vehicle.

As they stepped off the plane, a man in black sprinted across the tarmac and pulled Xavier into a tight embrace.

"Father Sebastian. Come stai—how are you?" Xavier said, his voice softening.

Sebastian's hair had gone noticeably greyer since Xavier had last seen him barely two weeks ago. Something had changed.

"Meet my friends," Xavier said, motioning Simone, Gabby, and Tarquin forward.

"I'm Gabby, Father. *Roma è bella di notte*—Rome is beautiful at night," Gabby said with a tired smile.

"Simone," Simone said simply, extending her hand.

"Tarquin," Tarquin said, his tone clipped.

Father Sebastian greeted each of them warmly before turning back to Xavier. "Your brother is waiting at the Courtyard."

"The Courtyard?" Xavier asked, startled. "Why such a public place?"

"Visitors are gone. It's as private as private gets," Sebastian said.

"Then Courtyard it is."

A black van rolled up beside them. Two more men in dark suits stepped forward, escorting them into the vehicle.

Night had settled over Rome—that ancient city of ruins and relics, its walls still whispering the language of centuries.

The van crawled through traffic. Xavier leaned back, his muscles unclenching for the first time since Arles. He turned to Simone, but she was gazing out the window, lost in thought. Tarquin, however, was watching him.

"Is Rome home for you?" Tarquin asked.

The question caught him off guard. "Yes," Xavier said slowly. "Rome has been home since I was a boy. I came from Seoul—my adoptive father was the Korean ambassador during my brother, Mathew's, teenage years. My real parents joined the family later and retired here."

He studied Tarquin's face—olive-skinned, dark-eyed. North African? Perhaps Moroccan blood.

"And you? Was Arles your home?" Xavier asked.

"Arles was my father's childhood home," Tarquin said. "We visited Dr. Gachet's grave every other year. I grew up there until I was nine years old. Then London."

"Childhood memories," Xavier mused. "I still remember the road up the hill to my mother's house in Guryong Village. The walls were so thin she stuffed newspapers in our clothes to keep me warm."

Tarquin gave a small laugh. "My mother stuffed newspaper in my ears once—after someone called me Judas."

Xavier frowned. "How would they have known? Even as a child?" Then his tone hardened. "I still wonder how the Obscurati allowed you inside their enclave."

Tarquin held his gaze. "I worked with them to find the lost writings of Eliana—to understand Yudah. Not to kill anyone. I'm not a murderer."

Xavier reached over and clasped Tarquin's hand. "I heard them, Tarquin. I heard them say you would harm the descendants of the Apostles."

The silence between them was heavy, pulsing. Could Tarquin be trusted?

Then Tarquin spoke again, voice low. "How sure are you that the blood I gave the Obscurati was really Simone's? I could have switched the samples."

Before Xavier could respond, Simone reached across the space between them and took both their hands.

"I could hear you," she said softly. "Let it go, Xavier. I believe Tarquin."

He let go.

He thought of how Tarquin had shielded them during the Whitney attack, and how he had brought the Gachet document safely to Rome.

Maybe he isn't the bad guy after all.

As the illuminated façade of St. Peter's Basilica appeared through the van's window, conversation stilled.

Consecrated by Pope Urban VIII in 1612, the magnificent Church—designed by Bramante, Michelangelo, and Maderno—rose in solemn majesty above the square. The largest Church in the world, it fused Renaissance grandeur with Italian Baroque splendor. From her seat, Simone could see the perfect geometry of its dome against the indigo night.

"Thaddeus, Mathew, Philip, Thomas, John," Gabby murmured, counting the statues crowning the façade. "Part of my studies in medieval art."

"Andrew, John the Evangelist, Bartholomew, Simon, Matthias," Tarquin added quickly. "They were my childhood rhymes."

Xavier smiled faintly. "My brother will be pleased to hear that. There he is—waiting by the entrance."

The spires of St. Peter's shimmered under the floodlights as the van circled the driveway and came to a stop beneath the arched portico. Five men in black surrounded the vehicle.

When the door opened, a man—an older version of Xavier—stood waiting.

"Xavier."

It was Mathew. He stepped forward and embraced him tightly.

"Welcome to Rome," he said, turning to the others. "Simone—it's good to see you again."

Simone's smile didn't reach her eyes. The old hurt between them lingered, invisible but alive. Mathew didn't seem to notice; his gaze had already moved to Tarquin.

Simone drifted a few steps away, pausing near a row of veiled statues as Cardinal Mathew led them inside.

Xavier caught up to her.

"Why are these sculptures covered?" she asked quietly. "Not just this one—all along the hall. Are they being lent to other museums?"

"They're being sold," he said, voice flat.

"Sold? Why?"

"Because of the scandals—the child-abuse cases, the legal settlements. Pope Lucas has done all he can, but the coffers are nearly empty. The Church teeters at the brink."

Simone's eyes lingered on the draped marble figures. "The loss is monumental."

"There will be treasures again," Xavier said. "But Lucas—his health fades. His enemies multiply. You've seen how calculating he can be. He's thinking of eternity now, not just his earthly legacy."

He wanted to say more, but Mathew and Gabby were approaching.

"Can we pass through the Sistine Chapel?" Gabby asked eagerly.

"Of course," Mathew replied, his tone buoyant.

He led them on with a sprightly gait. Two peas in a pod, people often said of the Jang brothers, though Xavier doubted that was still true.

"Michelangelo!" Gabby gasped as they entered.

Xavier's mind flickered back to his youth—when Pope Lucas and Mathew had invited him to the grand unveiling after restoration. He'd been thirteen, bewildered by the grown men weeping beneath a ceiling. But when he looked up, he'd understood.

The colors—acid green, orange-red, chrome yellow—were a hymn to creation itself. The figures, massive and godlike, seemed carved from light. The fresco told the story of humankind—its agonies, triumphs, and faith.

"The seven prophets of the Old Testament and the five pagan Sibyls all foretold the coming of the Savior," Mathew said softly.

"The colors are still incredible," Simone whispered.

"That was Michelangelo's genius," Mathew said. "He painted hues the Church had never dared to imagine—vivid, almost violent. They shocked Rome for decades."

"Can we take pictures? Some areas could use a touch of restoration," Gabby said.

"Fire away," Mathew said indulgently. "Take as many as you like."

Suddenly, movement stirred at the far end of the chapel. A phalanx of Swiss Guards marched in, crisp and silent.

"What's happening?" Gabby whispered.

And then a ripple passed through the room.

"It seems the Pope has made an appearance," Xavier said.

Like stagehands changing a set, attendants appeared with quiet precision. A simple chair was placed near the altar.

Then he entered.

The man whose visage was known across the world—Pope Lucas—strolled into the chapel. His leonine hair gleamed beneath the frescoed vault, his broad shoulders still proud despite illness. His gait, once brisk and commanding, was now measured, but the presence was unmistakable.

It was the Pope, in the flesh.

Chapter 33

S imone

The Sistine Chapel, Rome

Saturday, October 21—10 p.m.

"Greetings. Welcome to the Vatican," Pope Lucas said with warm enthusiasm. Xavier knelt, kissed his ring, and whispered something in his ear. The Pope murmured a brief prayer—then turned to Simone.

"Xavier relayed the message to Mathew while you were flying in. I heard you've recovered some documents from Arles. The staff from the Vatican Museum are here, even at this late hour, to assist in authentication." He gestured toward the corridor. "Let's walk to the Belvedere Courtyard, where you can sit and relax a little."

They crossed a narrow hallway lined with frescoes. A faint breeze met them as a door opened onto the courtyard. Under the portico, a small table for six had been laid. Silver platters and tea arrived; the papal staff withdrew discreetly once the guests were served.

Pope Lucas exchanged a glance with Mathew, who nodded to the guards. They stepped quietly into the hallway.

"Before anything else," the Pontiff said, "I must ask forgiveness from you both. Yes—the Cardinal and I arranged the meeting at the Apostolic Nunciature in Paris so we could meet you. We had hoped you'd take an interest in Xavier, so he could find the writings of Eliana."

"Machiavellian," Xavier muttered, unable to hide his anger.

"Unbelievable," Gabby said. "Why not just call them? Why all the subterfuge?"

"Through the centuries, the Shimon line has proven elusive," Pope Lucas explained. "They fled Sweden in the 1800s, like Christopher Harper, with only a few dollars in their pockets. They kept their identity secret for generations."

Xavier fell silent.

"I believe I'll be punished for this one day," the Pontiff said quietly. "But I acted to protect the descendants of the Apostles. Xavier was a child when we traced his bloodline to Yosef of Arimathea."

A gasp escaped Tarquin.

"From great wealth to destitution in Seoul—your ancestors hid well."

He looked toward Simone. "I tried to reach you through Xavier. Many of the Twelve Apostles were entrusted with sacred works of art—paintings that became both currency and repository for Eliana's writings. Am I right, Simone?"

"Yes," she said. "You are correct, Pope Lucas. I am the descendant of Simon Peter—the Rock."

"I am descended from Apostle Thaddeus," Gabby added. "The Pope contacted me recently."

"Your Holiness," a priest interrupted, entering the room. "The Vatican Museum has the results from the Gachet box."

All conversation ceased.

"Let them in," Pope Lucas said.

A man stepped forward. Xavier rose to meet him. "Pope Lucas, this is Michael Salvatorre from the Vatican Museum—my colleague. Any news?"

"Your Holiness," Salvatorre began, bowing. "Your Eminence, Cardinal Mathew. Signor Xavier."

"Speak, quickly," the Pope said.

"Looks like we've struck gold. The documents need further verification at the Harper Art Institute, but they appear to be Eliana's writings."

A cheer rose around the room.

"There are twenty pages, Your Excellency," Salvatorre continued. "One in particular may interest you."

The Pope took the parchment, read it silently, then handed it to Tarquin. "Please, read—it concerns your ancestor Yudah."

Tarquin accepted the pages and read aloud:

"Yeshua proclaimed the Apostles. There were thirteen of them: Shim'ōn Kēfā, Andraos, Ya'aqōv bar Zavdai, Yōḥanan bar Zavdai, Philipos, Bar-Tolmay, Mattai, T'ōmā, Ya'aqōv bar Ḥalfai, Shim'ōn ha-Qannāy, Yehuda bar Ya'aqōv, Yehuda Ish-Qeriyyot, Maryam d'Magdala."

"Including Maryam angered Yeshua's followers. Nicanor, not among the thirteen, grew enraged. He left the group and plotted betrayal, with help from the Sanhedrin."

"There were thirteen," Xavier exclaimed. Voices erupted around the table.

"Quiet," the Pontiff ordered. "Let Tarquin finish."

"My God," Pope Lucas whispered. "After two thousand years—was it Nicanor who betrayed Jesus?"

"No wonder they tried to silence us," Xavier said. "It wasn't Yudah at all."

"We must find the rest of Eliana's account," Simone said. "The truth about Nicanor."

Salvatorre handed over duplicates. "Here are the same copies I gave Mr. Vern."

"Thank you, Signor Salvatorre," Pope Lucas said. "Perhaps the next pages will surface soon."

He turned to the group. "Great balls of fire—the five descendants who hid Eliana's writings are all here. Gabby, Thaddeus; Tarquin, Judas; I, Mary Magdalene; Xavier, Yosef of Arimathea; and Simone, Simon Peter. I've spent my life trying to protect you—and the works themselves. Now that I am dying of cancer, I can finally see the end in sight."

Simone's throat tightened. "There are things Eliana says that no other writer of her time dared say."

"It is her truth," Pope Lucas said.

"Even if it changes everything," Gabby added.

"My time is ending," the Pope said softly. "This gathering—five living descendants of the Apostles—is a miracle."

Applause broke the tension.

"Even if it upends the world," the Pope said, "you must publish Eliana's writings. The Church is crumbling. Her words might be our redemption."

"Dinner is ready," Mathew announced. "Let's enjoy a meal while we await further findings from the Gachet box."

"I'd be honored if you all stay the night," Pope Lucas added. "But first, let us eat."

⸻ ◆ ⸻

After a dinner of ravioli, roast chicken, and the freshest vegetables from across Italy, the Pope invited the young chefs who prepared their meals. They entered shyly, then rushed toward Tarquin, phones out.

"There's a bigger celebrity than me here," Pope Lucas laughed.

"He's the famous chef from Battling Chefs on Geoflex, *Santo Papa*!" one exclaimed.

"They don't usually ask visiting chefs for photos," the Pope said kindly. "You must have captured their hearts, Tarquin."

"How about coffee and dessert in the Uffizi Room?" Mathew suggested.

The room glowed softly, its walls alive with early Leonardo sketches. Simone took it in—the light made everyone gentler. Xavier's anger had eased; Tarquin was laughing with Gabby.

"Promise me," Pope Lucas said, "that you'll publish Eliana's writings once they're authenticated."

"The soonest possible," Simone promised. "If we reveal her truth, maybe it'll take the targets off our backs."

Was it only that morning they had been in New York? The fire in Arles felt a lifetime ago.

"So—are you still flying back tonight?" Mathew asked.

"Not in a million years," Gabby said. "We're not leaving until we find the next document."

"Then let's compile everything," Xavier said. "The pages given to Mary Magdalene, Judas, Yosef of Arimathea, Simon Peter, and Thaddeus."

"Twenty from Mary Magdalene," the Pope said.

"Twenty or more from Judas," Tarquin added.

"Twenty from Eliana herself," Simone said.

"Five from Thaddeus," Gabby added.

"None from Yosef of Arimathea," Xavier admitted. "Nothing survived in Korea."

"There's one page Eliana gave to Nicanor," Simone said. "My father kept it. I don't know how it fits with the rest."

Tarquin activated his ArqPad; a holographic map shimmered. "The numbers 56 and 72 appear in the Mona Lisa. Edinburgh lies at latitude 56—right on the mark. Of the five recipients, only Yosef of Arimathea is said to have traveled to Europe."

"The same coordinates mark Lund, Sweden," Simone said. "My grandparents searched its church for years."

"Maybe a false trail," Xavier said. "They fled Lund in the 1800s and settled in New York."

"Legend says Jesus traveled with Yosef of Arimathea," Pope Lucas murmured.

Tarquin dimmed the map; the room fell into Leonardo's golden glow.

"Thirty-five cities lie along latitude fifty-six," Gabby sighed. "One lifetime isn't enough to search them all."

"Then we'll start there," Tarquin said.

"Edinburgh interests me," the Pope added. "Its abbey once claimed relics from the Cross.

"But why Edinburgh?" Simone asked.

"It was Queen Helen, mother of Constantine," Mathew said.

"Her name even echoes Eliana," Tarquin added.

"So many possibilities," Simone sighed. "So little time. But I vote for Edinburgh."

"Then we'll meet in the morning," Mathew said.

"It was such a lovely evening, but I'd rather leave tonight," Simone replied. "We have a jet."

"Lucky you," Mathew smiled. "We have the Popemobile—and the Pope flies commercial."

Laughter broke the tension. Coffee was served as they studied the Gachet pages.

Simone approached the Pontiff. "Thank you, Pope Lucas, for trusting me with the Da Vinci and Van Gogh studies. They've opened a new path to the truth of Christ's final days."

She hugged him lightly. "And I'm sorry—for my anger. For everything."

"I'm sorry I deceived you," he said. "Many have died to protect Eliana's words. Now, perhaps, we can end that cycle."

"The perfect crime—hidden for two thousand years," Simone whispered.

"Many enemies have tried to silence those who tried to speak the truth about Eliana's writings," the Pope said. "But not this time. Good luck in Edinburgh. Keep me informed."

"I will. Thank you, Pope Lucas."

"One day, visit your ancestor's tomb," he said.

"I promise I will."

"Xavier," the Pope called. "A word?"

He motioned to his guards. "*Per favore, mettete due sedie un po' più in fondo*—two chairs further back, please."

The Pope and Xavier sat together, heads bent—like priest and penitent, though this time it was the Pope confessing.

When they rose, Xavier's face was ashen; whatever he'd heard weighed heavily.

"One last picture?" Mathew asked the group, while a security man offered to take their picture.

The flash caught them mid-laughter.

"*Vi rivedrò, figli miei*—I will see you again, my children," Pope Lucas said.

As they walked toward the Sistine Chapel, Simone looked back.

The Pontiff still stood there, hands raised in farewell, the light of Leonardo's paintings forming a halo around him.

Chapter 34

R odrigo
St. Peter's Basilica
Saturday, October 21—11 p.m.

"Alfeo Gonzalez, thanks for the cappuccino. I knew you were looking forward to seeing me—and eating at your favorite restaurant," Rigo said as they stood outside Romeo's, a coffee shop directly across from St. Peter's Basilica. "Not too bad for such touristy prices."

"Oh, give me a break, Rigo," Alfeo replied. "We missed today's special—fried baby octopus with pesto and potatoes, or tripe with tomatoes and pecorino—but there'll be a next time. And you did keep your promise: you said you'd call me, even if it's just for coffee."

"Admit it," Rigo said, smiling. "I miss your grandmother's cooking back in Astoria. You must miss it too, now that you're a priest. How's Vatican life treating you?"

He and Alfeo had gone to the same Catholic high school in Astoria, Queens. Their careers had taken different paths, but the bond had survived. Whenever Rigo had work in Rome, they met without fail.

"A lot of infighting inside the Vatican walls," Alfeo said quietly. "Pope Lucas keeps pushing for inclusion—women, the marginalized. That doesn't sit well with some here. But enough gossip. Let me drive you back to your hotel? Rome isn't the safest city to walk around in at night."

"I'm not a wide-eyed kid from St. Francis High anymore, Alfeo."

"Maybe you're just offended by my little Fiat. Not American enough?"

"I love your Fiat. Can we trade? Mine comes with sirens that go off if I so much as breathe on it."

"Always the comedian," Alfeo said, laughing. "Take care, Rigo—and stay away from shadowy corridors."

"I know you're a certified exorcist, Father Gonzalez, but I'm not afraid."

"Try to catch tomorrow's Mass, you heathen. I'm presiding."

"See you at dawn. I'll be the one with the tail and two horns."

"Very funny. See you tomorrow—before you fly back to New York, I hope."

They hugged, and Alfeo drove off into the Roman night.

Rigo lingered, circling the Basilica, thoughts heavy.

The Harper case still made no sense.

The shooting at the Whitney had produced a suspect—an unhinged man whose online rants touched every corner of the ideological spectrum. He had confessed that someone inside the museum had ordered him to shoot. Madness, perhaps—but his story carried the smell of truth.

Yet the handler who gave that order had vanished. Who had manipulated the unstable man's mind?

Paolo's instincts turned toward those who had subdued the shooter.

Nothing about Tarquin added up. The celebrated head chef of Nazzarín NYC, a social-media darling—yet an absentee boss for months, jetting from Morocco to Istanbul to Rome. He had been in Rome a week before the shooting. Why?

Tarquin's face had also shown up on a security feed at the High Line, the night Simone was there. Coincidence?

Then came the robbery at the Harper Art Institute—Da Vinci and Van Gogh studies lent for research, vanished within hours.

The few surviving pages of The Gospel of Eliana in Rigo's possession had shaken his entire precinct. They'd called in an ancient-manuscript specialist. Thanks to new technology, translations took minutes—but authentication still demanded experts from multiple institutions.

Each clue was like smoke—visible, but impossible to hold.

That was why he was in Rome. To dig deeper. To lean on his contacts. To reach out to his old allies in the FBI's Rome office.

"I thought that coffee talk would never end," a voice said from the shadows, followed by a firm clap on Paolo's shoulder.

"Andrei Russo," Rigo said. "My FBI liaison in Rome. I was waiting for you at the café—why didn't you join us? Father Gonzalez would've loved to see another Catholic mug from home."

"I can't risk being seen around here," Russo muttered. "Too many bridges burned."

"You mean the priests from the U.S. now reassigned to Rome—for various crimes and misdemeanors," Rigo said.

Russo didn't answer, only adjusted his coat. Rigo studied him. They'd first met back in New York, chasing diplomatic scandals that rattled the U.N.—the kind of cases that left scars on both sides of the law.

"I've been working my contacts for this case," Russo said. "It's a mess. Interpol chatter says they're looking into Tarquin Vern—inside the Vatican. What's going on, man?"

"Why don't we walk a bit—through St. Peter's Courtyard?" Rigo suggested.

"I haven't walked there in years," Russo replied.

"Alfeo will kill us both," Rigo said with a grin. "You're inside the Vatican, and half the priests you've investigated ended up in jail. Maybe a few streaks of fire will strike us for skipping Mass all these years."

"All right, all right, Detective Rigo. Geez, you've turned into an old man," Russo teased.

"Guess what?" Rigo said. "I tracked Tarquin's whereabouts. He was in Rome a few days ago. And he's here again—inside the Vatican. With Simone Harper."

"The survivor from the Whitney Museum?" Russo asked, his voice suddenly alert.

They turned toward the vast open space of St. Peter's Courtyard—the heart of the Basilica, where millions gathered to glimpse the Pope on the balcony. The marble expanse shimmered under the floodlights.

Built in 1506 under Pope Julius II and completed in 1615 by Paul V, the Basilica stood on the very ground of St. Peter's tomb, a monument to his martyrdom and the faith that rose from it.

As they neared the line of apostolic statues, Rigo stopped short. Several black SUVs were idling near the colonnade. Then, one by one, they pulled away—silent, deliberate, vanishing into the night.

"Oh no," he muttered. "They're on the move again."

"Then let's follow them," Russo said, already heading for the street.

Chapter 35

Eliana

The Healing Center, Nabataean Kingdom

Year 4 of King Malichus (AD 43)

Maryam of Nasrath met Hannah of Kerioth at the healing center, and all conversation stopped.

They embraced, tears glimmering in their eyes.

"You haven't aged a day, Maryam," Hannah said softly.

"I draw strength from the memory of Yeshua—and from ensuring His work is never forgotten," Maryam replied. "Show me what you're doing, Hannah. Please, don't stop what you've begun here."

As they moved among the rows of beds, Eliana watched them closely. Maryam had not aged since that terrible year—ten years past—when her son was crucified.

Instead of collapsing in grief, she had grown stronger, her will transfigured by loss.

Four helpers now assisted Hannah, and the center was full that day.

"It's time for a pause," Hannah said. "Let's return home for *Se'udat ḥubbān*—a meal of love."

They walked back together through the narrow streets. Inside the house, a low table stretched across the floor. Loaves of barley bread, wheels of fermented goat cheese, and small clay pots of herbed olive oil surrounded a rack of roasted lamb. A great earthen jug of wine stood in the center.

"Come, be seated," Hannah beckoned toward the reed mats. She and Maryam took their places in the middle of the table.

When all were settled, Hannah raised her hands.

"We gather here in memory of Yeshua. In the name of the Father and His Son, Jesus. The Lord be with you."

"And with you," Maryam answered.

"Let us reflect on the days behind us, and our transgressions, as we prepare for this meal," Hannah said.

"Have mercy on us, Lord," Eliana murmured.

"Grant us Your peace, Yeshua," Maryam said.

"Amen," Eliana whispered.

"Let us partake of the food prepared for you," Hannah continued. "Who will recite a passage from the Old Books?"

"I will," said Apostle Thaddeus. "This is Isaiah."

He straightened, his voice resonant but weary, and spoke from memory:

"Coasts and islands, listen to me; pay attention, distant peoples.

Yahweh called me from the womb; He pronounced my name before my birth.

He made my mouth like a sharp sword; He hid me in the shadow of His hand.

He made me a polished arrow and concealed me in His quiver.

He said to me, Israel, you are my servant, through whom I shall manifest My glory.

I said, My toil has been in vain; I have exhausted myself for nothing.

Yet my cause is with Yahweh, my reward with my God.

And now Yahweh has spoken—He who formed me in the womb to be His servant,

to bring Jacob back to Him and reunite Israel to Him.

He said, It is not enough for you to be My servant to restore the tribes of Jacob.

I shall make you a light to the nations, that My salvation may reach the ends of the earth."

"The Word of God," Thaddeus concluded, lowering his head.

"Thanks be to God," Eliana replied.

"What is your favorite teaching from Yeshua?" Hannah asked.

Maryam smiled faintly. "I remember when someone asked Him, 'How many times must I forgive my brother or sister who sins against me?'

And Yeshua answered, 'Not seven times,'" she said.

"'But seventy-seven times,'" Maryam said, then turned to her. "Tell me, child—have you ever forgiven someone not once, but more times than you can count?"

Eliana hesitated. The room became quiet around her.

"You've heard this story," she began. "On the night Yeshua was taken by the chief priests and elders—for proclaiming He was the Son of God—it was Nicanor who led the Sanhedrin guards to Him.

"After vanishing for three years, Nicanor sought his cousin Yudah when he heard that he was in Yerushalayim. Yudah, trusting him, invited Nicanor to dine with Yeshua. At the end of the meal, we all walked across to Kidron Valley, to the Mount of Olives. Yeshua asked to be left alone while He prayed. My father and I, with Dod Andraos and Dod Thaddeus didn't listen to Him, but went with Him to pray.

"We stopped at another spot while Yeshua continued, so He could have space to pray alone.

"But I hid and went nearer. I saw Him fall to the ground and pray. I've watched Him many times before, but this time, He was in agony, praying to the heavens and not finding calm. One moment, He rubbed his sweat away, and instead of sweat, there were drops of blood in His sleeve. But despite being in pain, He would check on the other Apostles, telling them to keep their eyes open. Was He expecting something to happen? We all tried, but one by one, everyone fell asleep, including me.

"In the deepest part of the night, a group of men entered with lanterns and torches, armed with swords and clubs. Nicanor stood up to greet them, and pointed Yeshua to the Sanhedrin mob.

"And when Yeshua was dragged away, it was Apostles Yudah, Thaddeus, and Mattai who tried to prevent Him from being taken. Thaddeus and Mattai were knocked unconscious by the mob, and they dragged Yudah along with them. Yudah begged Nicanor to spare Yeshua's life, but soon the mob focused their ire on Yudah, whose head fell on a rock, and became unconscious. He died that moment. Panicked, Nicanor carried his body to Akeldama by foot, and with the help of other people in the mob, hanged Yudah to make it appear like he took his own life. Nicanor then placed silver coins in his pocket to infer that the coins were his payment to betray Yeshua.

"I saw it with my own eyes. Tell me—how does one forgive such a thing?"

Silence fell. Men and women wept openly. And Eliana, realizing what she had spoken aloud, sat motionless. What had she done?

Maryam spoke softly, her voice steady yet full of sorrow.

"My son said those words. However, forgiveness is never easy—especially when a crime has been committed, as it was in Yeshua and Yudah's case. Yeshua was human and yet divine. Forgiveness is a human act reaching toward the divine. Only by communing with the divine through prayer can we truly move on. And forgiveness... is the first step."

The air grew heavy with grief; the food lay untouched.

In her graceful way, Hannah rose and walked to the end of the table. She took the loaf of bread and the jug of wine, then returned to her place.

"This is the bread of the Lord, who gave Himself for us," Hannah said. She broke the bread into many pieces.

Apostle Thaddeus stood and received them from her hands. One by one, he distributed the pieces to the guests, who had risen to receive them.

"Amen," many whispered as they took the bread.

When all were seated again, Hannah reached for the jug of wine and poured it into a clay cup.

"This is the cup of mercy," she said, "sealed in His blood and written upon our hearts. Let us drink in memory of Yeshua's death and resurrection."

The cup was passed from hand to hand, each person drinking reverently. When it returned empty, Maryam lifted her hands in blessing.

"Go now in peace," she said.

"Peace be with you, Dodta Maryam and Dodta Hannah," the guests replied.

The gathering slowly softened into conversation. Stories flowed—memories of the days when Yeshua still walked among them. Grief gave way to laughter, and joy flickered again like oil in a lamp.

That night, beneath the Nabataean stars, the courtyard was alive with remembrance. The conversations around the table continued until nighttime. The grief had lifted. In time, there was a lot of laughter around the courtyard as they recalled many significant events that happened in Judea when Yeshua and Yudah were with them.

Those precious memories would endure—through the people who had loved them.

Chapter 36

S imone

Above the Skies in Rome

Sunday, October 22 – 2 a.m.

Pope Lucas had pressed a small gift into her hands as she left, and it took all of Simone's discipline not to open it at once.

Now, inside The Flying Vault, she finally unwrapped it.

It was a simple wooden cross, the grain rough beneath her fingers. A small tag beside it read, "Olive wood."

There was a note from the Pope:

"To my newfound friend,
May you be the voice of your generation.
From wood once meant to be thrown away—resurrected."

She could still hear his voice as he'd said it, smiling.

"My, that looks beautiful," a soft voice crooned.

"Oh, hi Jill. Stacy off for the night?"

"Yes, ma'am. As are the pilot and co-pilot. Can I get you anything from the pantry, Ms. Harper?"

"Just sparkling water, please."

Xavier and Tarquin were fast asleep in their lounge chairs. The cabin lights were dim. Then a faint beeping broke the silence—one tone, then another, escalating into a cascade of alarms.

"What's happening?" Tarquin asked, jerking upright.

"Oh my God," Gabby said, staring at her phone. "Pope Lucas was found unconscious in bed."

Xavier rose immediately, calling someone as he moved toward the window.

"Is he dead?" Simone whispered, reaching for the remote. The wall screen came alive with breaking news: Pope Lucas found unconscious in his private residence.

"I just called the Vatican," Xavier said. "He's alive—thank God. It's good we left when we did. The police are already there, and our presence would have raised questions. The announcement came only after we departed."

"Jill, please pull up the live feed," Simone said.

The flight attendant tapped the controls. News anchors' voices filled the cabin:

"Reports from Vatican sources confirm the Pontiff remains in critical condition."

"Speculation grows over possible successors, including Cardinal Iñaki Turbierri, a staunch conservative and frequent critic of Pope Lucas—particularly on the question of women's roles in the Church," the newscaster said on the live broadcast.

"This makes it even more urgent," Simone said quietly. "We have to find the rest of Eliana's writings."

"But where do we start? Everything's in chaos," Gabby replied.

"I don't want to go back to New York yet," Simone said, gripping the armrest. "We're too close. Edinburgh is the logical next step."

"There aren't any paintings to guide us this time," Tarquin muttered.

"But there are the references to Helena, mother of Constantine the Great," Simone said. "She was rumored to be the daughter of King Coel of Britain."

"She journeyed to the Holy Land," Xavier added, "building churches to mark the great events of Yeshua's life. And legend says she recovered the very cross of the crucifixion—distributing fragments of it across Christendom."

"So," Tarquin said, bringing up a 3-D map on the cabin screen, "do we search both Edinburgh Castle and Holyrood Palace?"

He traced a glowing line across the display. "See this path between the two? A perfect straight line. Now overlay the main roads..."

"It forms a cross," Simone whispered. "Unbelievable."

"Exactly. The Mona Lisa's coordinates—latitude fifty-six—align right here," Xavier said. "We start at the center point of that cross."

"There's only one way to know if Eliana's writings are hidden there," Simone said. "We have to go there ourselves and look if there are other clues to find more Eliana writings."

She glanced down. The olive-wood cross was still in her hands—she'd been holding it since the moment they left the Vatican.

What did Pope Lucas mean by "May you be the voice of your generation"?

Would The Gospel of Eliana rewrite the story of faith itself? Would it open the Church to the forgotten voices of its past?

She didn't know.

But she did know this: finding Eliana's writings were now the most important mission of her life.

Chapter 37

E liana

Mare Nostrum

Year 4 of King Malichus (AD 43)

She had always longed to heal. Dodta Hannah, noticing her quiet fascination, began teaching her the ancient art of massage and its path toward restoration. The healing brought by the Eastern remedies and the fragrant local oils filled Eliana's heart with joy.

That peace ended the day she saw Nicanor near the healing center.

It was time to move again. She wanted Dodta Hannah and Yaakov free from the strife Nicanor's presence brought, and leaving Petra would grant them peace.

When would she ever be free of that man?

Nabil had remained with her in Petra, and at Dodta Hannah's request, he often led the *Se'udat ḥubbān*—the meals of love shared with the growing community eager to hear about Yeshua.

One afternoon, a trader from the Red Sea route arrived at Dodta Hannah's home. He handed a leather pouch to Yaakov, who quietly passed it to Eliana.

Inside lay a small map and a folded note in her father's hand:

"Come to Aili.
Seek the House with the Slanting Roof.
Further instructions await you there.
Look for Demetrios, son of Mattathias."

She showed the message to Dodta Hannah and Yaakov. Together with Nabil, they planned her departure, joining a spice caravan bound for Aili.

At every stop along the way, followers of Yeshua welcomed them—offering water, food, and quiet blessings for their journey.

In Aili, she found the House with the Slanting Roof exactly as described.

Demetrios, son of Mattathias, greeted her and led her to the *Kybernētēs*, the captain of a merchant dhow. He agreed to take them across the Mare Nostrum to Myos Hormos.

The voyage lasted ten days, the desert winds swelling their lateen sails. The oarsmen—fifty strong, weathered men called the *kōpēlatai*—welcomed her with laughter and curiosity. Each evening, she and Nabil sat among them, telling stories of Yeshua and His compassion for the poor and the broken.

When they finally reached Coptos, on the east bank of the Nile, she saw her father waiting for her.

From that moment on, she never left his side.

The communities of believers were growing now.

Homes were opened, lamps were lit, and wherever they went, they were met not with fear but with warmth and joy.

They had traveled westward to Gaul to visit Maryam of Magdala, but word reached them that she and David had already gone north to Din Eidyn, where Yusef of Arimathea lay gravely ill.

Her father decided at once to follow—to pay his respects to the man who had believed in Yeshua from the very beginning.

Horses had replaced camels in these lands, making the journey swifter. They went north, crossing the Via Agrippa toward Gesoriacum—territory beyond Rome's full grasp, where local chieftains demanded tribute. They traded Nabataean and Egyptian oils for hides as the weather turned colder.

Their passage grew easier once they spoke Maryam of Magdala's name. The tribes knew her, and lowered their tributes, even offering safe conduct through their valleys.

Word came that a vessel owned by Yusef of Arimathea awaited them at Gesoriacum. When they reached the coast, four plank-built boats stood ready, laden with cargo and guarded by armed attendants. Each boat carried ten guards to ward off pirates, thirty rowers, a skilled helmsman, a steward to record the gifts and tributes exchanged along the route, and two servants to prepare the meals.

As days slipped into weeks, and weeks into a month, her father and Nabil would sit by the fires each night on the beaches where they camped. The pilots, stewards, and oarsmen slept in separate tents, but before resting, they would gather around the flames to listen as her father and Nabil told stories of Yeshua.

They spoke in whatever tongues the men understood, and soon the stories flowed as if Yeshua Himself were among them.

"Fifty days after His death," Shimon said one night, "Yeshua sent the Holy Spirit to all the Apostles as wind and fire. We were given many gifts—to heal, to prophesy, to speak in every language. Yet even with all these gifts, how can one explain who He truly is?

"God is the sun, Yeshua the sunbeam, and the Holy Spirit the warmth that remains when the light touches you."

The men listened in wonder.

The next day brought a surprise. As they entered the lands of the Brigantes, nearing Din Eidyn, Apostle Thaddeus joined their party.

"Never a dull day in *Yamma d-Britannia*—the Sea of Britain," her father greeted him, embracing him warmly.

"Mercurial winds, fierce storms, high waves—what have we not seen, Ahi Shimon?" Thaddeus laughed. "We've faced it all. Biti Eliana, how are you?"

"Not your Biti anymore," she teased. "But turning green from the cold."

"We traded our last amphorae of Galilean wine for these wool cloaks," her father said. "All this, just to see Yusef of Arimathea."

"You could have refused the invitation," Thaddeus said with a grin. "But you'd never turn down Yusef's offer of a free voyage."

"It's his ship—who am I to say no?" Shimon replied, laughing.

"We're under Yusef's protection," said the captain. "His prayers keep us safe. I've not had an accident in ten years."

"How does Dod Yusef do this every year?" Eliana asked. "The sea is too perilous."

"Says the woman who crossed the deserts from Egypt to Trans-Jordania," Thaddeus chuckled.

"Well, I saw Maryam, mother of Yeshua and Hannah of Kerioth," she said. "That was worth every hardship."

"And so is this journey," Thaddeus answered.

"Nothing fazes you, The One," she teased.

At that, both men burst into laughter.

"And what am I called, little one?" her father asked playfully.

"Kepha—The Rock," she said, smiling. "Yeshua called you that, the first time you met him."

A bronze buccina sounded—a long, resonant blast announcing landfall ahead. The coastline emerged through mist. Watchfires burned on the cliffs, and warriors in cloaks dyed yellow and red stood sentinel.

Soon, the horns onshore answered with a mournful note, a warning: strangers approaching Din Eidyn.

"Yusef of Arimathea commanded me to bring you north of Britannia," said the captain. "It's a wild land, but they know his ship. No one will harm you."

"North of Britannia?" Nabil asked. "What kind of place is this?"

Everything about the voyage felt strange—the seascape shifting from Mediterranean blue to cold northern stone. The chill pierced her bones; even wrapped in animal skins, she could not get warm.

Why would she hide her writings in such a faraway land?

She heard laughter near the stern—her father, Thaddeus, and Nabil talking in the fading light. She trusted them with her life.

"Yusef has carried Yeshua's word to these distant shores," said the captain quietly beside her. "And here, in this land of volcanoes, he made his home."

Chapter 38

S imone

Edinburgh, Scotland

Sunday, October 22—8:00 a.m.

"Me bonny boss!" a man with a thick, guttural Scottish accent called as the group stepped out of the hangar at Edinburgh International Airport.

"Charlie, you're a sight for sore eyes," Simone said, grinning. "Sorry for the short notice. Meet my friends—Xavier, Gabby, and Tarquin. Everyone, this is Charlie McLaren, head of the Harper Art Institute in Edinburgh."

"Xavier! Good to see you again. Thanks for that advice on the Caravaggio exhibit—you saved us a load of trouble," Charlie said. "And Gabby—ye'll hae me blushin', lass. Tarquin, now that's a braw name if I ever heard one."

"Charlie, my lad, I'd give anything for a blood sausage and a Guinness," Xavier said.

"We can have that after our reconnaissance," Simone replied. "Charlie, you can be another set of eyes. We're untangling a few clues we've uncovered."

"Och, I'll be the chauffeur and ye be the spies," Charlie laughed, jingling his keys.

He led them to the parking lot and unlocked a Citroën SpaceTourer. "Brought the tank around for ye, hope ye're a happy lass, Simone."

"Perfect," she said, settling into the front seat.

As the van rolled out, Simone gazed through the misted window. Edinburgh always felt alive beneath her feet—an ancient creature dreaming under the city's cobblestones. Three extinct volcanoes lay sleeping beneath: Castle Rock beneath the fortress, the mound of Calton Hill, and the great dragon's curve of Arthur's Seat.

Every time she returned to Edinburgh, the air felt older than Rome, she thought.

"Charlie," Xavier said, unfolding a map of the city, "if Holyrood Castle and Edinburgh Castle form the staff of a cross, then the North and South Bridges would be the crosspieces—the shoulders of the crucifix. It aligns with the cruciform geometry."

"Bang on the money, my lad," Charlie said with a grin.

"Let's trace it," Simone suggested. "Castle, Holyrood, and then the bridge at the center."

"Aff we trot then," Charlie said, steering through the fog.

They circled Edinburgh Castle, the fortress rising out of black volcanic rock like a ship made of shadow.

"What madman builds atop a volcano?" Tarquin muttered.

"A madman who knew his defenses," Gabby said.

Charlie chuckled. "A fortress on a cliff, m'lads. The core of an ancient volcano, eighty meters high—nature's own rampart."

"I wish we could stay here and take in the views. But we can go back here later. Now we go off to the opposite end—Holyrood Castle," Simone said.

"Aye, aye, ma'am, Off tae Holyrood Palace we go!"

Just one mile away, Holyrood Castle, the monarch's residence, was resting at the foot of Arthur's Seat. The castle, stately yet intimate, seemed cradled by the hill behind it.

"To your right is the famous Arthur's Seat," Simone said. "They say it has the shape of a sleeping dragon."

"Is the King in residence today?" Xavier asked. "Will we be able to explore the grounds?"

"Naaah," Charlie said. "But his ancestors' ghosts roam the halls, mind ye. This house began as an abbey for the Augustinians. Holy Rood means Holy Cross."

"Of course it does," Simone murmured, her eyes gleaming.

"There you go!" Gabby said. "Our clues are all over the place. Holy Guacamole, we might as well start digging here."

"Without the King's permission, ye can't. There's priceless art in the King's Gallery," Charlie warned. "Right then—aff we trot tae the bridges."

Traffic was light, the fog thick. Pedestrians moved like shadows, collars up against the chill.

"We're turning onto North Bridge," Charlie said. "I'll slow down—ye spot anything, I'll stamp on the brakes."

"Nothing yet," Xavier said.

For a moment, tufts of fog lifted, revealing the city's bones—medieval spires and modern glass coexisting on volcanic stone.

"Now onwards to the South Bridge," Charlie said.

"Stop! Stop, stop!" Simone exclaimed.

Charlie braked hard. "What is it?"

"Let's get out. I'll show you something."

They climbed out. Tarquin stretched, then sprinted fifty meters down the empty road and jogged back, restless energy radiating off him. Simone, Xavier, and Gabby stood near the ledge.

"That man can't stay still," Gabby shook her head.

To the west, Edinburgh Castle jutted from the cliff like a landlocked battleship. Below them, trains slipped in and out of Waverley Station. To the east, the Balmoral Hotel's clock tower kept its eternal vigil, and beyond that rose Arthur's Seat—an ancient mound, veiled in mist.

"Think of the Mona Lisa," Simone said quietly. "Remember the number seventy-two beneath the bridge. When Da Vinci painted it, this bridge didn't even exist. The Old North Bridge in the 1600s was..." She turned to the map, tracing a finger.

"At wee Waverley Station," Charlie supplied.

"Let's move the line further till Waverly Station," Simone said. "If we stood on the exact spot of the old bridge and faced seventy-two degrees north, the Eliana trove could be beneath Arthur's Seat."

"Very possible," Xavier said. "A dormant volcano, riddled with crags and bogs. Perfect for secrets."

"If we faced south, seventy-two degrees points toward the National Gallery," Gabby said.

"Interesting choice," Xavier mused. "Their vaults are climate-controlled—ideal for preservation."

"If we faced east or west, there'd be communities now," Simone said. "My vote's for Arthur's Seat."

"I second that," Gabby said.

"I prefer the Gallery," Xavier countered. "How about you, Tarquin?"

"I also vote for the Gallery," Tarquin said.

"Charlie?" Simone asked, smiling.

"Arthur's Seat, lass. She's kept her mysteries longer than any gallery," he said firmly.

"Well then," Simone said, eyes brightening, "majority wins. To Arthur's Seat."

"Let's go a-hunting," Tarquin said, grinning.

———◆———

Charlie drove them back toward Holyrood Palace and eased the van into a public parking bay. The fog had finally lifted, and the pale light revealed Arthur's Seat in full view—its slopes dark and glistening from the earlier mist.

When they had all alighted, Simone turned toward the great hill.

"Look," she said quietly. "They say it looks like a sleeping dragon... but does this scene feel familiar to any of you?"

The others followed her gaze. Along the western edge of the park, the Salisbury Crags rose like the flank of a giant beast—sheer volcanic cliffs, scarred by old quarrying. The cuts were still visible, ancient wounds in the rock.

"Joseph of Arimathea was a wealthy trader of Judean goods," Xavier said thoughtfully, "and it's rumoured he reached these shores. If Eliana ever visited him, she would have seen this same cliff. It would've reminded them of Golgotha, the place of the Skull—where Jesus was crucified."

"Wait," Gabby said. "Wasn't Golgotha a hill?"

"Not exactly," Xavier replied. "It was a disused limestone quarry outside Jerusalem. My ancestor, Joseph of Arimathea, was the one who requested Jesus's body from Pontius Pilate. He wrapped it in linen and laid it in his own tomb."

Tarquin folded his arms, frowning. "But Golgotha looks like a hill now. It's inside the Church of the Holy Sepulchre."

"Aye, and that's because of the architecture, laddie," Charlie said with a chuckle. "Centuries of building have covered the old quarry face. But there's a hollow down the slope here, same as the ones back home. See there?" He pointed toward a dark cleft beneath the Crags. "That's a quarry-lookin' cut, right enough."

Simone turned to the map spread on the bonnet of the van. "The seventy-two-degree line doesn't point to the summit of Arthur's Seat," she murmured. "It aligns slightly off—to those dark basalt cliffs of Salisbury Crags."

"Then that's where we'll search," Tarquin said. "Though it's like finding a needle in a mountain."

Gabby exhaled, eyes wide as she took in the scale of the rock face. "How in heaven's name can we find anything where Joseph of Arimathea's descendants buried Eliana's writings?"

Chapter 39

R odrigo
Edinburgh, Scotland
Saturday, October 22—9 a.m.

Word had reached Interpol that Tarquin Vern and Cassius Turbierri were on two separate flights to Edinburgh, and the NYPD had
coordinated with the FBI liaison in Scotland that their Persons of
Interest were expected to touch down in Edinburgh by 8:00 a.m.

He left the bureaucratic maze of arranging his flight to the bosses,
and by midnight, he was able to board a commercial flight to London.

Agent Daniel James, the FBI liaison from the London office, met
him with a warm handshake as they boarded a chartered Cessna Ci-
tation for a one-hour flight to Edinburgh.

"Great to see you again," he said. They worked for six months in a
joint FBI–NYPD Cybercrime task force dealing with dark web fraud
and money laundering.

"How's London? You've been here a year?" he asked.

"I'm FBI, but can't arrest anyone. Everything goes through Home Office, MI5, Scotland Yard—everything," James said. "But this case got the bosses jumpy, with the trifecta of the shootout at the Whitney, the robbery at the Harper Institute, and persons of interest somehow tied to the brother of Cardinal Iñaki Turbierri, possibly the next Pope."

"Whoa, you've been up to date," Rigo said in surprise.

"I was reading the case while waiting for you," James said. "I've coordinated with the Detective Chief Inspector at Police Scotland HQ. Messages have come non-stop about Tarquin Vern and Cassius Turbierri, secret head of Obscurati. Now with the Pope being unconscious, all eyes are on those two, if they appear here."

"There is still no link that the activities of Cassius relate to his brother, Iñaki Turbierri, leading contender for the next Pontiff. But what are the odds that they're not related in some way," he said.

Messages started flashing on his phone during the flight.

"They just got a 'no-knock warrant' on Tarquin Vern and Cassius Turbierri's residences," Rigo said. "They'll update us once it's done."

He fell sound asleep, exhausted from the past twenty-four hours of travel from New York to Paris, to Arles, to Rome, and now to Edinburgh.

He woke up as the plane landed at Edinburgh Airport.

"Just an update. Detective Constable Shane McPhee of Police Scotland HQ tailed Tarquin and party from the airport. They're just driving around the city as we speak. Cassius Turbierri slipped through their watch. Unbelievable," James said.

"We can tail them all day. But judging by how they hopped from country to country, I'd bet they'll be in Edinburgh for a few hours, then go to another country. The rich are different from you and me, my friend," he said in a sarcastic tone.

They were waiting at the airport curb when a car stopped, the driver rolling its window, and shouted.

"Agent James and Detective Rodrigo, hop in. Detective McPhee told me tae lift ye at the airport. I'm DC Rory Brown. Let's trail the punter into Edinburgh," Brown said.

As they climbed into the vehicle, a message pinged into his phone. They heard the pinging of messages on the phones of Agent James and DC Brown.

"Successful entry into St. Anthony's the Divine Church and Vern's Residence under a no-knock warrant. Evidence recovered sufficient to support an arrest. FBI and Police Scotland HQ notified."

"Right, we can collar Tarquin Vern now. Wi' a bit o' luck, we'll find Turbierri too," Brown said.

"What a clusterfuck," Agent James said.

"A definite shit-show. Let's arrest those motherfuckers," he said. DC Brown turned on the siren in his car, and they were off to arrest Tarquin Vern.

Chapter 40

Eliana

Din Eidyn

The Last Year Before Rome Crossed the Sea (AD 43)

A flotilla of boats sailed beside them as they neared the shores of Eidyn. Voices rose from the water's edge—

"Bring the boats tae Eidyn's firth!"

"Row awa for the waters o' Eidyn!"

Men in colourful woollen cloaks of green and yellow checks greeted them, their garments woven in vivid patterns unlike anything Eliana had ever seen. Their long hair, stiffened with chalk and powdered white, caught the light. Some bore blue-dyed markings upon their faces—symbols of rank or ritual—that lent them the fierce grace of warriors from another age.

When their boat had entered the Oceanus Britannicus days earlier, she had seen men on distant shores dressed in undyed wool, their heads bowed, their movements weary. But here, in Din Eidyn, life seemed to pulse with colour. Men carried fish traps slung over their shoulders; women balanced shallow baskets brimming with the night's catch. The scene reminded her of the fishermen of her Galilean village—only here the garments gleamed with hues and patterns she had never known.

From the hills, the roll of drums drifted down to the shore. A cavalcade of horsemen descended from the crest, their woollen jackets a pageant of red, gold, and deep blue—the dyes themselves a testament to the land's hidden riches.

In her younger years, Eliana might have felt ashamed of her simple robes. Yet she thought of Yeshua, who had worn the humblest garments with the quiet majesty of one clothed in light—the Son of God, robed in the colours of soil and sand.

As their vessel drew closer to the strand, she recognised the familiar bearing of Dod Yosef, standing before the horsemen who awaited them. Once a senior member of the Sanhedrin, his wealth and influence had allowed him to claim Yeshua's body after the crucifixion at Golgotha. In the years since, he had vanished from Judea and built his trade across lands untouched by Rome.

Her father had told her that Yosef had prospered in these faraway isles, trading Celtic gold, iron, and copper for the olives, wine, and fine pottery of the Mediterranean. His ships, he said, bridged worlds.

When the boat grounded upon the shore, Yosef stepped forward, his face lighting with recognition.

"Welcome, Shimon Kepha and Thaddeus. I am old now, but grateful to see you before I die," he said, embracing them both.

Her father placed a hand upon Nabil's shoulder. "This is Nabil—one of the most loyal followers of Yeshua."

Yosef turned then to Eliana. A furrow deepened between his brows.

"Are you Eliana? It has been ten years since I last saw you."

"Yes, Dod Yosef," she answered softly.

"I have prepared a feast for you," he said. "My home away from home awaits."

Servants brought horses for each of them, and as Eliana mounted, she looked back to see their belongings loaded onto a cart drawn by sturdy northern horses. Yosef's dwelling stood at the edge of the village—a dome-shaped hall with a hearth glowing at its centre, its thatched roof heavy with smoke and warmth.

At the doorway stood a lady dressed in saffron yellow, a deep cloak of woad blue draped across her shoulders. Two young boys stood beside her.

"My wife, Lady Taranisca of Caesarea, and our sons, Cynon and Talor," Yosef said.

"Welcome to our home," Lady Taranisca said with a gentle smile. "We have prepared something for our honoured guests. Your home is our home."

Her voice carried both the cadence of distant Caesarea and the calm assurance of a woman who had long made peace with foreign shores. Eliana watched as she took the boys' hands—shy, curious eyes peering at the travellers—while the warmth of the hearth reached out to meet them.

Wines in tall amphorae lined the side table, and before them lay a profusion of dishes one might find in any Judean home—flat loaves beside preserved olives and hummus, with roasted meat set proudly at the centre.

"Sit, everyone, and partake of the food. This moment here is a time to rest," Yosef said, patting Shimon's cheek before taking his place at the middle of the table.

"Habibi Shimon, Habibi Thaddeus—envoys of Yeshua—sit beside me. And you, Nabil, beside Habibi Thaddeus. Eliana, sit next to your father," Yosef of Arimathea said warmly.

Eliana obeyed, aware of the honour her seat implied—privilege accorded only to family and trusted guests in any Judean household.

"Yeshua loved to eat together," Yosef said as they settled. "Meals were sacred to him."

"And he loved to listen to us after a day of healing or teaching," Shimon Kepha recalled.

"Oh, you only loved hearing the sound of your own voice, Shimon," Thaddeus teased, and laughter softened the evening's solemn air.

"He never judged what I said," Shimon replied. "Nor did he speak harshly of those we met or healed."

"But when Yeshua spoke, you listened," Yosef added.

Thaddeus nodded. "I remember his deeds more than his words. There was never a day he did not feed a beggar, comfort the sick, or listen to a weary soul. Beyond the miracles, what I cherished most was his humanity—even as he was God."

From the hearth came the scent of baked fruit; rhubarb pies appeared, a northern delicacy marking the hour's lateness as the sun faded beyond the hills.

After the laughter quieted and the wine was poured again, Yosef leaned forward. "Tell me, Shimon—what brings you to this far shore?"

Shimon's voice grew soft. "We came to see you. We heard you were bedridden, yet you came yourself to meet us. My daughter carries scrolls that must be kept safe. She wrote an account of what she witnessed during the last three years of Yeshua's life, and there are many who would silence such words."

"I helped recover parts of it in Egypt—hidden in the pyramids of Giza," Thaddeus said.

Yosef's brows rose. "I can hardly believe it."

"Eliana was with me," Thaddeus continued. "We travelled together to reclaim her writings."

"Nicanor," Yosef muttered darkly. "*Ben beliyya'al*—son of a scoundrel! I heard what he did to Yudah of Kerioth."

"She was the only witness, Dod Yosef," Shimon said gravely. "Her life will always be in danger. It is better that her writings be hidden, perhaps for a time when they will serve a purpose."

A shadow crossed Yosef's face. "After Yeshua's death, I fled Judea. I could no longer face the Sanhedrin without rage. Had I stayed, I would have killed them—or they me."

"It was not Yudah who killed Yeshua," he went on. "It was a cabal of priests and council members who plotted his arrest. I was in that chamber. They controlled the Temple's wealth—its taxes, its currency, the trade of animals for sacrifice. When Yeshua taught that forgiveness did not come from coin or offering but from repentance and faith, his fate was sealed. Nicanor was entangled with them, and on that dark day, he lured Yudah to take the blame."

Shimon's jaw tightened. "Nicanor never forgave Eliana for refusing his proposal. His bitterness deepened when Yudah was chosen among the Twelve, and when Maryam of Magdala was called to stand beside them."

Eliana lifted her gaze. "I gave another set of writings to Maryam of Magdala, Dod Yosef—when I met her in Egypt on her way to Gaul. And another to Hannah, Yudah's mother."

Thaddeus nodded. "Maryam of Magdala told us her name should be kept hidden. It stirred too much resentment. Many were not ready to accept that Yeshua had named her."

"That is not our burden," Yosef said quietly. "Let others judge and quarrel. We concern ourselves only with what Yeshua taught. Yet few will believe that a woman could chronicle his life. Did you write of the others who walked with him—Maryam, Maryam of Magdala, Marta, Maryam of Beit-Anya, Yohanah?"

"Yes, Dod Yosef," she said. She was touched that he remembered the women who helped Yeshua during those days.

"They are well, I hope," Yosef murmured, his eyes dimming with memory. "Before I die, I would like to see them once more, especially Maryam of Nasrath—if the Lord wills it."

Shimon reached across the table. "Can you keep some of these pages for her, Dod Yosef?"

"Of course," Yosef said. "I know a place where they may rest unseen. But let us speak of it tomorrow. Tonight, we rest."

Everyone nodded in quiet agreement. The long journey—one hundred and twenty days across sand, sea, and storm—was ending. Eliana saw peace settle upon her father's face. To see Yosef of Arimathea again, the man who had stood beside Yeshua at His final hour, was to close a circle that had begun on Golgotha.

———···◆···———

At dawn, the servants brought a generous breakfast: smoked fish from the Forth estuary, broiled eggs from wild hens, and cured meats whose savour filled the hall. Ale was poured even at morning, alongside steaming bowls of mint and heather infusions. To end the meal, bilberries and blackberries drizzled with honey lent their dark sweetness to the table.

When they had eaten, Dod Yosef rose and beckoned to her. He led her to a corner where long grey cylinders lay stacked.

"I have used these lead casings to hide coins, jewels, and pigments," he said, resting a hand on the cool metal. "They appear too ordinary to tempt a thief, yet preserve whatever is placed within. Your writings will remain safe if wrapped first in oiled cloth, then sealed beneath tar."

"Thank you for thinking of such protection, Dod Yosef," her father said.

"The Romans mined lead in Spain and in Gaul," Yosef replied. "They fashion pipes and vessels for their treasures. It seems fitting that the same metal will now guard the words of Biti Eliana." He smiled, then turned toward the door. "Come. Bring your writings. Let us go to the site."

Horses waited in the pale light. The morning sky hung low and grey, and the wind cut to the bone. The sun wavered behind clouds, uncertain whether to show itself. No one spoke. The horses moved through wild gorse and heather, releasing scents of cinnamon and honey that sharpened the senses. The lead stallion snorted and quickened its pace.

They climbed until Yosef halted on a rise.

"Here it is," he said. "The Crag of Eidyn."

"It looks like a black tooth rising from the plain," Shimon exclaimed. "The same basalt stone as in Galila?"

"Yes," Yosef answered. "But this one seals an ancient volcano, long asleep."

They descended the slope until the dark mass towered above them. Yosef drew rein and pointed ahead.

"Tell me what this place stirs in you."

Shimon's voice broke. "Good God."

Eliana's stomach tightened. The hill before them mirrored Golgotha—the same harsh ridges, the same hollows where wind gathered its voice. Even the shadows fell in familiar shapes. The memory of cries and hammer blows rushed back with the gusts that swept the ridge.

"It reminds me each day of Yeshua," Yosef said quietly. "Not an hour passes that I do not think of what He gave, for us."

Her father traced the sign of the cross upon his forehead, his lips, and his breast. Thaddeus did the same.

"Since the beginning," Yosef said, "men have cut stone from such hills. Golgotha itself was a quarry once, the place of execution beyond Yerushalayim's walls. We shall do the same here. Who would imagine that a quarry would guard a woman's testament?"

The road was slick with morning rain, the horses' hooves slipping on patches of clay. Then, through the wind, came the thunder of hooves—many of them.

"Yosef, stop!" a voice shouted, cutting through the gale.

A young man rode up, wrapped in thick animal hides, the glint of fine jewelry at his throat.

"Brigo!" Yosef called. "What in heaven's name are you doing here?"

Brigo's grin was sharp as flint. "Aithar Yosef, see what the hounds dragged to the fire." He gestured to a rider behind him—a man bound in ropes, his eyes blindfolded, his mouth gagged.

Thaddeus stiffened. "I know this man. He's Nicanor, from Judea. Untie him."

"Untie him?" Brigo scoffed. "Loose that rope and he'll bite like a wolf."

"Drag him down and cut his bonds," Shimon ordered. "Unbind his mouth—let him spit his poison if he must."

Brigo pulled the gag free. Nicanor's first words were a snarl.

"Give me your writings, Eliana! Her words are false—blasphemy against Yeshua!"

"Kin to the dark ones," Shimon said, his face taut with fury. "Yudah's blood stains your hands, and still you stand proud."

"Brigo," Yosef commanded, "bind him fast and throw him into the pit."

Brigo retied the man's wrists, looping a longer rope about his waist. "He'll walk in the dust beside the horse," he muttered. "Then down he goes." With a gesture to his men, he turned away, dragging the captive behind.

Shimon watched them disappear into the mist. "How did he find us?"

"I swear there is only one true reading of Yeshua's words," Nicanor spat, "and it is not yours."

Yosef's gaze hardened. "Who betrayed our place to him?"

"The world crawls with foes, as Yeshua warned," said Thaddeus.

When the hoofbeats faded, silence returned. Yosef shivered once and said, "My flesh rebels, yet Yeshua taught us to turn the other cheek. He will not see the sun for many seasons. Let him live with the taste of his shame." He turned to Eliana. "Do not fear, Biti Eliana. I will keep your work safe until my last breath."

Eliana could not move. The hatred she had seen in Nicanor's eyes left her trembling. Only when he was gone did she feel air in her lungs again.

"Come, let us hide your words," her father said.

"It is a heavy burden, Dod Yosef," she whispered.

"Do not tremble, Biti Eliana," Shimon said. "You are Yeshua's witness. The truth stands—no man or woman can tear it down."

She met his gaze and nodded. "Indeed. The truth will open the door to us."

Yosef gestured toward the dark hill. "Men are waiting in the quarries. They are melting the pitch now, so we can seal everything quickly."

Four men crouched near the fire, busy with their tasks. The sharp smell of burning tar drifted through the air. Others were preparing lead casings and strips of oil cloth.

They stopped and dismounted. Her father reached for her hand as they walked towards the workers.

"You may decide how you would want it to be hidden," her father said gently.

Eliana drew out the papyri from her two *peras*, and divided the scrolls into five bundles.

"Ready?" her father asked. She nodded.

"The quarries await," Yosef of Arimathea said. "We will set the lead boxes between the broken crags—perhaps in the very teeth of the stone."

The skilled workers of Yosef of Arimathea were sure-footed and deft with their hands. Eliana passed the scrolls to them, and the workers accepted them with quiet respect. The papyrus pages were rolled in oil cloth, placed inside the lead casings and closed with a fitted cap. A sharp hiss rose as the boiling pitch touched the cold metal, sealing the container instantly.

Two other men were already hanging along the face of the Crags, having marked out the best hiding places, listening for a hollow sound, searching for pockets deep enough to conceal the scrolls.

Once all the casings were sealed, the workers carried the lead cylinders up to the waiting climbers. Eliana watched as the men slid each container into the fissures. Then, with practiced movements, they sealed the openings with stone and earth until no sign of the hiding place remained.

"Well done, beautifully done, Dod Yosef. Can we offer a *Se'udat ḥubbān*—a meal of love, for the workers later? Eliana would be glad to cook for them, to thank them for their hard labour."

"But of course, Shimon Kepha," Dod Yosef clapped him warmly on the back. "Eliana, if you choose to remain here in Din Eidyn, you could fill those crags with your writings, eh?,"

They all laughed.

A sigh of relief escaped from her. At last, her testimony was safe and hidden in the Crags. If Nicanor cannot bear the truth, she thought, let these words endure until the time is right for them to be uncovered. Then the truth shall set all free.

That evening, Nabil asked for her father's blessings—and for Yosef's. Both men agreed, and Yosef ordered that a feast be prepared in their honour.

Eliana had wished for something simple—a breaking of bread in remembrance of Yeshua. But the generosity of Yosef of Arimathea could not be restrained. For three days the people of Din Eidyn gathered: chieftains and clansfolk alike. Venison, mutton, and wild boar filled the tables. Salmon, trout, and eel smoked over open fires, and wheels of cheese and amphorae of wine seemed never-ending.

She sat among them, watching faces illuminated by firelight and laughter. It had been so long since she had seen such joy. Since Yeshua's death, sorrow had hung like a pall over every heart she loved. But here, at last, there was light again.

Eliana felt a deep, unspoken peace settle over her.

Chapter 41

X avier

St. Arthur's Seat

Monday, October 23—9 a.m.

Their destination was not the summit of Arthur's Seat but the natural cliff line descending toward Salisbury Crag—a black basalt wave frozen in motion, heaved up from the earth and arrested mid-surge. It loomed before them like a titanic force turned to stone, poised forever to devour the land beneath their feet.

Xavier measured the height with his eyes — roughly that of a mid-sized building in central Edinburgh. Yet in 40 AD, when Eliana had entrusted her writings to Yosef of Arimathea, this Crag had ruled the landscape of Din Eidyn. Centuries of quarrying — with picks, hammers, and chisels biting at the rock — had honed its walls into angular scars, a testament to human persistence against the passage of geologic time.

"The Crags rise about a hundred and fifty feet," Simone said, consulting her tablet. "They stretch for almost one point six kilometres. We could split into four teams and search each section for traces of Eliana's writings."

Xavier gazed at the cliff face, dark and forbidding. "In the Vatican Museum," he said, "many early altars were carved from this same basalt. But no sculpture could be shaped from it — too hard, too brittle."

"Then perhaps it was used to conceal, not to create," Simone mused. "Hidden like the Dead Sea Scrolls — so many fissures and hollows where something could lie unseen."

Tarquin crouched near a broken ledge, tracing a vein of mineral with his finger. "The Vatican exhibit on the Scrolls was one of my favourites," he said. "Imagine hiding copies of every book of the Old Testament in a handful of desert caves."

"There were limestone cliffs in Qumran too," Xavier added.

"Every book in the Bible, plus a few that never made it into the canon," Tarquin continued.

"You really do know your scriptures, Tarquin," Gabby said, smiling.

"I wanted to understand Judas," he replied softly. "What he might have read, what he might have believed."

Simone glanced toward the Crag's shadow. "The Dead Sea Scrolls were sealed in clay jars, stored in narrow caves and hidden under stones," she said thoughtfully. "I wonder what containers they would have used here, in this damp, northern climate."

"Clay wouldn't last long under Scottish rain," Gabby said. "I'd wager bronze."

"How about lead?" Xavier asked, his voice low as he studied the dark fissures along the rock face. "The Romans used it for their viaducts—and for containers to hold jewellery, perfumes, and precious documents."

Simone nodded slowly. "If the coordinates to Eliana's writings were discovered in the sixteenth century, during Da Vinci's time, they might have stored them in cave-like hollows. The closest equivalent here would be the fissures within the Crags, spaces where a container could be pushed inside, then sealed beneath basalt stones."

"Meaning," Tarquin said, rubbing his hands together, "we look for loose rock, places where something could have been shoved in and covered."

"Exactly," Xavier replied. "Cracks created by quarrying, half-open cavities, would be perfect. Once sealed with stone, no one would suspect what lies beneath. I'll team up with you, Tarquin."

Gabby laughed, already scanning the uneven slope. "Men versus women, then? Let's see who finds something first." Her eyes sparkled. "My Ethan would love this kind of treasure hunt."

But Simone, still staring up at the Crags, suddenly froze. "Wait," she said. "I have an idea."

Everyone turned toward her.

"If we look at Van Gogh's Café Terrace at Night, the stars too bright for the hour—what if the stars aren't random at all?" Simone said slowly. "What if it's a map? A code for where the containers were hidden?"

Gabby already had her phone out. "There it is," she said, zooming in on the glowing constellations above the café awning.

"Let's grid these," Tarquin said. He pulled out the Arqpad, snapped a photo, and tapped a few keys. A grid overlay appeared. "Sending now."

"Let me see. Still no image," Gabby said, impatience rising. "Alright, I got it! Simone and I can explore A to C, the western edge."

"Then Tarquin and I will cover D to F , the eastern side of the Crags," Xavier grinned. "Ready for our great adventure, Monsieur Tarquin?"

"But of course, Professor Jang," Tarquin replied with theatrical flair.

As they walked, Tarquin asked, "By the way, did you finish reading the Eliana writings from the Gachet box?"

"I did."

"How did they make you feel?"

Tarquin gave a low whistle. "Not surprised that Judas was described as the most handsome and the most educated of the Apostles. Why do you think that never appeared in any of the canonical Gospels?"

"Or that he was Yeshua's favourite," Xavier said quietly. "Always by His side." He paused. "Those who were different—those were the ones Yeshua loved."

"Maybe that's why Judas loved Mary Magdalene and Matthew the most," Tarquin said. "Three souls out of step with the others."

The eastern Crags loomed before them, their sheer walls rising like a serrated fortress. Tarquin let out another whistle. "Look at those scars. Imagine how many temples and altars were hewn from this rock."

They approached the cliff. Vertical columns cut deep into the hill, their edges sharp; broad horizontal ledges jutted out like primitive steps. The chiselled faces and flattened platforms gave the Crags their strange geometric beauty—half natural, half wrought by centuries of human hands.

"God, these rocks are intimidating," Tarquin murmured. "If Yosef of Arimathea hid something here, it would have to look like part of the landscape." He tested the ledges with his hands. "I wouldn't stash it below, too visible. Higher up, maybe—around grid C2."

"Tarquin, be careful," Xavier warned. "You don't have—"

"I borrowed this from one of the pilots," Tarquin said, producing a screwdriver from his back pocket. "Never hurts to be prepared."

Two hikers passing on the path stopped to shout up at Tarquin.

"Climbin' the Crags is banned, laddie—only eejits dae it," one of the men called.

"Aye," another called, with a bark of laughter. "It's yer funeral!"

Tarquin ignored them. Xavier stepped closer, ready to catch him if he slipped. Tarquin wedged the screwdriver into a fissure, prying loose a cluster of stones. Pebbles tumbled down the slope with a sharp clatter.

"Another container, maybe?" Xavier asked, his voice rising with the echo. "Like Dr. Gachet's box?"

"Something like this?" Tarquin called back, his tone half-teasing. He reached into the crevice and pulled out a dark bundle wrapped in a blackened cloth. "I'll let it roll down, okay?"

A heavy thud struck the ground beside Xavier. He crouched and lifted the object—an ancient pouch, its linen or wool stiffened with pitch until it hardened to a waterproof shell. The surface was fissured with mineral crusts, the outline molded to whatever it had protected for centuries.

He bent closer, raising his phone to take a photo—when a cold, unfamiliar voice rang out behind him.

"Don't touch that," the man said. "Hand it over. Now."

Xavier froze.

"Tarquin!" the voice barked again, sharper now. "Get down—and help me out."

He knew that voice.

Turbierri.

The same man who had shadowed Tarquin through the Tuileries Gardens.

Two others flanked him, both with guns drawn.

Before Xavier could react, a blur of motion exploded behind the assailants—Tarquin. A man flew backward, bones cracking with a sickening snap. In one seamless movement, Tarquin's left foot connected with another man's temple, his right hand slammed into the second's ear, and his left fist drove deep into the attacker's solar plexus. The man folded soundlessly, crumpling into the grass.

"Not a chance we're handing anything to you, scum," Tarquin hissed.

Turbierri lunged for a fallen gun, but Xavier was faster, tackling him hard and pinning him by the shoulders. He drew back his fist, ready to strike—

"Freeze! All of you!"

The shout cut through the wind.

Six figures closed in around them: two in plain clothes, lanyards flashing warrant cards; two in navy uniforms with POLICE SCOTLAND emblazoned across their chests, and behind them, Detective Rigo from the NYPD—alongside a man in a dark jacket marked by a small circular blue pin.

"I'm Detective Constable Shane McPhee of Police Scotland," the lead officer announced. "By authority of Police Scotland, you are under arrest—Cassius Turbierri—on a United States extradition warrant requested by the New York Police Department. The charges include multiple counts of murder and the theft of major artworks and ancient manuscripts. You do not have to say anything, but it may harm your defence if you fail to mention something you later rely on in court. Anything you do say may be given in evidence."

A crowd had gathered, phones raised, voices whispering.

"Detective Rigo—what's happening?" Simone's voice broke through. Her hair whipped wildly in the wind, as she pushed to the front beside Gabby.

Another officer stepped forward. "I'm DC Rory Brown. By authority of Police Scotland, you're under arrest, Tarquin Vern—for the theft of major artworks and ancient manuscripts. You do not have to say anything, but it may harm your defence if you fail to mention something you later rely on in court. Anything you do say may be given in evidence."

The man with the blue pin stepped forward. "Daniel James, FBI. Mr Vern, you're facing federal charges under Title 18, Section 668—major art theft—and racketeering conspiracy under RICO."

"Major art theft and manuscripts?" Gabby whispered, stunned.

"You'll be taken to St Leonard's Station and held pending extradition," DC Brown continued. "Do you understand the charges?"

Uniformed officers moved in, cuffing Turbierri, Tarquin, and the two disarmed gunmen.

"Tarquin—wait!" Simone pushed through the tightening ring of officers. He turned at the sound of her voice, met her eyes, and managed a faint smile.

"We'll get you the help you need at the station," she promised.

Xavier hurried forward. "Detective Rigo—hold on!"

Rigo stopped and walked back to meet them halfway down the misted path. "Xavier. Simone. Gabby. I'm relieved all of you are safe."

"Detective, Tarquin's been helping us," Xavier said quickly. "He was working with us to locate the remaining Eliana writings—"

"I know," Rigo said gently, though his tone stayed neutral. "But this is an active, multi-agency investigation. The process has to play out. Stay nearby, I'll personally handle Mr Vern's paperwork and make sure his transfer to New York is expedited."

"The object he found," Simone said urgently. "It could belong to Eliana's writings."

"It'll be handled by Police Scotland," Rigo assured her. "This entire area is now a crime scene. Their forensics team will search the Crags for additional artifacts. Tarquin will appear before the Sheriff's Court within the hour; extradition between the UK and the US is typically straightforward. I promise I'll keep you updated."

Without waiting for further questions, he turned and jogged after the arresting officers.

Behind them, Gabby began to cry, and Simone wrapped her in a tight embrace.

Xavier stood frozen for a moment. When the guns had been aimed at him, only one thought had seized him – Simone. Was she safe? Where had she been standing? He replayed the moment, his pulse still uneven.

Their bond was still fragile, yet no longer tentative. They had finally cleared the air in Paris only yesterday. Yesterday? It felt like a lifetime ago.

Yet, one truth crystallized in him with absolute certainty: he would do everything in his power to lift her burden, to stand beside her. He had loved Simone from the moment he saw her—perhaps even before he understood what love required.

"Are you all right?" Her voice broke his thoughts as she ran to him. Before he could answer, she was in his arms.

"I'm fine," he said, pressing a kiss to the crown of her head.

A soft cough reminded them they were not alone.

"Uh, guys?" Gabby said, glancing toward Charlie, whose jaw hung open at the open display of affection between his boss and the head of the Vatican Museum. "Shouldn't we go to Tarquin now?"

"Aww, Charlie, you can close your mouth, lad," Simone teased. Then her expression shifted. "Yes, let's follow him to the station. I'll call Legal in New York and find out how we can support his case."

Chapter 42

S imone
St. Leonard's Station, Edinburgh
Monday, October 23—1 p.m.

The glass door to the holding area slammed shut behind Xavier, leaving Simone and Gabby alone in the narrow corridor. The fluorescent lights hummed overhead, too bright, too cold. Somewhere beyond the hallway, Tarquin was being processed—fingerprinted, photographed, interrogated like a common criminal.

Detective Rigo came out from the holding cell, and the three of them stood up and pummelled him with many questions. "They'll transfer him upstairs for questioning any minute," he said. "The extradition request from New York complicates everything. Scotland wants to keep him until the Vatican weighs in."

"The Vatican?" Simone repeated, tense. "Why would the Vatican be involved?"

Rigo opened his mouth—then froze.

A door at the far end of the corridor clicked open.

A man stepped through.

Tall. Stoic. Dressed in a tailored black suit with a silver lapel pin—a miniature cross within a shield. Eyes sharp enough to cut glass.

Simone had seen men like him before. Once in Rome. Standing behind the Pope. Silent, watchful.

Swiss Guard Intelligence.

The man approached them with the quiet authority of someone used to entering locked rooms.

"Detective Rigo?" he asked.

"Yes, that's correct," he answered tentatively.

"Professor Jang," the man bowed slightly to Xavier. "May I have a word with both of you?"

The three men walked to the far end, but Simone stood up and stepped to the water cooler near the group. They spoke in whispers, but she could hear their conversation slightly.

"I'm Commander Rafael Benatti of the Pontifical Swiss Guard. I came as fast as I could from Rome." His voice was deep, steady. "I've come regarding the detainment of Officer Tarquin Vern."

Detective Rigo repeated the last few words of the Commander, "Officer Tarquin Vern?"

Xavier's expression shifted between shock and dread. "Commander Benatti? What—how—?"

Rigo stepped in. "Commander, with respect, Mr. Vern was arrested under Scottish jurisdiction—on U.S. charges. Until the paperwork is cleared, he's—"

Benatti lifted a folder—thick, heavy, Vatican-sealed.

"This is a diplomatic request for immediate custody," he said calmly. "Tarquin Vern is an active member of the Pontifical Swiss Guard,

Special Operations Division. He is a commissioned officer acting under direct authorization from His Holiness Pope Lucas."

Rigo swallowed hard. "Swiss Guard?"

Benatti didn't waver. "Officer Vern has been embedded for months on a classified security assignment. His presence in Edinburgh is not coincidental. His actions today were part of an ongoing investigation regarding threats to the Apostolic bloodlines."

Gabby went near Simone, and listened as well. "He never said a word," Gabby said.

"He was under oath," Benatti said. "Only two men knew the full extent of his mission—myself, and the Pope."

Xavier looked shattered—equal parts relief, guilt, and awe. "So, he wasn't working for Turbierri? He wasn't part of anything criminal?"

"Tarquin Vern," Benatti said, "has risked his life repeatedly to protect all of you."

The room tilted for Simone.

A guard pushed open the holding room door. "Commander? He's ready."

Benatti nodded. "I'll speak with him first."

Simone stepped forward. "Please—Commander—can we see him?"

Benatti studied her for a heartbeat, assessing, weighing, understanding more than she said aloud.

He didn't say anything, but instead turned and entered the holding room.

It explained everything about Tarquin's mysterious aura, his guardedness.

Gabby touched her arm gently. "Simone... he didn't betray us. He was protecting us."

She swallowed hard.

Her heart hurt with sudden clarity.

"No," she whispered. "We never even knew. Poor Tarquin, I've misjudged him."

Xavier went near her and gave her a side embrace. "Look, I'll stay here and be with Tarquin. Why don't you and Gabby return to New York. I doubt they'll allow us to see him yet, though if all goes well, he might be released soon," Xavier said quietly.

"What about the Pontiff?" Simone asked gently. "He's still unconscious. Shouldn't you be with Mathew?"

"I'll go back when there's definite news," Xavier replied. "I'll coordinate with Mathew—and with the Vatican—so Tarquin can be released. Pope Lucas must have arranged contingencies in case the Obscurati intervened. I also want to review the analysis of the Gachet box. Send it once you have it."

Simone hesitated.

Part of her had expected him to fly back to New York with her. But the conversation with the Pope in Rome had changed something in Xavier—drawn him inward, sharpened his focus. He seemed quieter now, more deliberate, as if carrying a weight he hadn't fully named aloud. Would that distance widen between them? There was no time to dwell on it.

"All right, no time to waste," she said briskly. "Actually, I need your jacket."

"My jacket?" he asked, startled.

"Yes—now." She was already digging through her bag until she produced a folded plastic sheath. She slid the jacket inside and sealed it.

"You can have my jacket," Simone said. "We'll be flying in the Falcon soon, and I have a jacket there. I need to verify something about Cassius Turbierri." Then, catching Gabby's eye, she added with a small smile. "Ready to see your cute Ethan?"

Gabby laughed through the remnants of tears. "Yes, Ethan. I almost forgot I had a son today." The last twenty-four hours had been a storm; perhaps any of them might have forgotten who they were, swept up in events no one could have predicted.

"I'll drive you both to the airport," Xavier offered.

"There's no need. We'll get one for ourselves." She touched his arm lightly. "I'll see you soon in New York?"

"Yes, I'll be there soon," he answered, his voice distant. He pulled her into a brief, warm embrace.

"Give hugs and kisses to Tarquin, Xavier," Gabby said.

"One special kiss from you, Gabby," Xavier replied, teasing lightly.

At that moment, Commander Benatti stepped out of the holding cell. Xavier crossed to speak with him again. Simone watched the exchange from a distance—the furrow in Xavier's brow, the tightened jaw, the controlled, measured intensity settling over him like armor.

Simone had never seen that expression before. His gaze was sharp, unyielding—dangerous to anyone who dared stand in their way.

An enemy, she thought, would swerve from that gaze.

Chapter 43

S imone
Teterboro, New Jersey
Monday, October 23—3 p.m.

The frantic calls began the moment the Flying Vault touched down in Teterboro.

A dozen messages flashed across her phone—most of them from Nic, the last reading: *Call me. Urgent.*

"Nic, what's happening?" she asked, breathless.

"I called the police," Nic said, his voice trembling. "The Da Vinci and Van Gogh paintings—they were found in your office, Simone."

Her pulse skipped. "Which part of my office? I haven't been there since the Whitney shooting four days ago." Then realization struck. "Oh God—the storage alcove wasn't part of the crime-scene perimeter."

"We're not allowed to touch anything," Nic said. "The police are photographing and tagging every piece of evidence. I'm sorry, boss—I panicked. The Art—Theft Specialists from the NYPD Major Case are en route. They'll transport the works under police control."

"Tell them to wait for me," Simone said. "Do they look authentic?"

"As far as I can tell, yes. Unless someone forged masterpieces for fun. But if they're fakes, why return them to your desk?" Nic sounded lost. "None of it makes sense."

Half an hour later, Simone's car pulled up to the Harper Art Institute. Police lights washed across the façade.

"When will this ever end?" she muttered as she walked through the lobby.

She rode the elevator straight to the twentieth floor. This time, Simone noticed everything—the measured steps of uniformed officers, the faint hum of radios, the subdued awe that filled the corridor. The mood was reverent, almost ecclesiastical. Perhaps it was because the real paintings—the Da Vinci and the Van Gogh—were there in plain sight. Detectives and technicians would pause mid-stride, gaze at them, whisper something low, and move on.

A tall man approached as she entered her office. "Dr. Harper, I'm Detective Aidan Wyles, interim lead while we await Detective Rigo. It's the same case, so I'm just maintaining continuity. He's landing at JFK shortly."

"So soon? I thought he'd remain in Edinburgh until the extradition began."

"The Scots guard their jurisdiction closely," Wyles said with a faint smile. "Detective Rigo left as soon as he delivered Mr. Turbierri and Mr. Vern to St. Leonard's Station. I believe Mr. Vern has been released. The U.S. Marshals are escorting Mr. Turbierri back. For now, the NYPD and the District Attorney's Office have a temporary custody agreement with the Met Museum. The works will be housed in the Met's conservation wing under police control. GPS tracking, armed escort, climate-controlled transport—the full protocol. A representative from the Met is en route."

"Thank you, Detective Wyles," Simone said. "Pope Lucas will be relieved that the studies are safe."

Relief flickered through her, tempered by unease. The paintings were back—but how? If they had been hidden inside her own office, was the theft an inside job?

Gabby, standing by the window, spoke softly. "Any news about the Pope? He'll be glad to hear this."

"At least we know the works aren't lost," Simone said. "He can recover them in time."

Gabby turned toward her. "Simone, you know I'm not taking over the Gianni collection, right? I only did it so the studies can be couriered by Xavier and brought to you."

"You're really not taking it?" Simone asked, eyes shining.

"How could I leave New York?" Gabby smiled.

"Thank God," Simone said, exhaling. "I'm not sure what Xavier's plans are now. He's been distant. But he'll move heaven and earth to help Tarquin."

Gabby nodded. Simone reached out and squeezed her hand. "Go home, be with Ethan. You've earned the rest."

"And you?"

"I'll wait for Detective Rigo. Maybe, finally, this will bring clarity—and a little peace."

Chapter 44

X avier
The Maignon, New York City
Sunday, October 23—5 p.m.

He had taken a later flight to New York, unwilling to leave Edinburgh until he knew Tarquin would be released.

Now, as the car wound through Lower Manhattan, the glass-and-steel lines of The Maignon rose ahead of him—Simone's home, suspended in the skyline like light caught inside architecture.

A place that felt more like her aura, than an address.

His thoughts drifted to the strange, unpredictable fortunes of the Apostles' descendants.

Yosef of Arimathea had once been one of the wealthiest traders of the ancient world; his ships had crossed every sea worth naming. Yet centuries later, Yosef's own bloodline—his bloodline—had nearly vanished into obscurity. In Seoul, Xavier's family had lived meal to meal, scraping by, invisible in a city that never slowed down. If Mathew and Pope Lucas hadn't found him as a child, he would have remained forgotten—one more broken link in an unending chain of faith, loss, and memory.

Pope Lucas had asked him to be the head of an organization protecting the descendants of the twelve Apostles—"*Custodes Luminis Antiqui*"—"Guardians of the Light." The role weighed heavier than he expected. There were too many enemies—Obscurati and others that Pope Lucas could not yet name. Could he truly protect Simone? Were any of the descendants safe?

He had another fear—what if he turned out to be as manipulative as Pope Lucas, using his power to achieve his ends? He had seen how Pope Lucas, a man of deep faith, had to rely on his own wits, trusting other people in their flawed ways to achieve his goals. He did not rely solely on prayer.

A quiet dread threaded through him.

Maybe Mathew would wear the title better.

Maybe even Tarquin. Tarquin was reckless, yes—but courageous in ways Xavier admired and feared.

And beneath all of it lay another fear he rarely allowed himself to confront.

What if he relished the power like Pope Lucas?

What if power twisted him into someone who justified manipulation for the sake of a holy cause? He had seen the Pope's deft pragmatism—his reliance not only on faith, but on calculation, on people whose goals did not always align with righteousness. Lucas was a man of deep belief, yes... but also a man who trusted imperfect allies to achieve necessary ends.

And Xavier could not shake the thought:

If the Pontiff had been more honest with him—completely honest—would that have changed everything?

Would Xavier have felt more certain?

Would he feel less alone in carrying a lineage he never asked for and a destiny he wasn't sure he deserved?

The Maignon drew closer, gleaming in the afternoon light.

He exhaled, bracing himself for whatever came next.

Chapter 45

S imone

The Maignon Building, New York City

Monday, October 23—6 p.m.

The elevator doors opened, and Simone met him at the threshold. Her hair was swept up, her face drawn but radiant with exhaustion. She kissed him lightly.

"Home at last," she whispered. "Gabby went home to Ethan."

"It's the first time I've seen your place," he said, stepping inside. A luminous glass sculpture of a mother and child caught his eye. "Your mother's work—Amara Nair Lim?"

Simone smiled faintly. "Many knew her art, few knew she was Gordon Harper's wife. To most of the world, she was Amara Harper."

"Not just a sculptor—she painted too," Xavier said. "I have one of her canvases in my flat in Rome."

Her mother's pieces lined the penthouse walls, giving warmth to the vast space. Floor-to-ceiling windows opened to a terrace garden that shimmered with evening light.

The doorbell rang. Detective Rigo stood there, rumpled and irritable as ever, Mr. Filigree behind him.

"I heard about the Da Vinci and Van Gogh turning up in your office," Rigo said, stepping inside. "The plot keeps getting thicker." He nodded at Xavier. "Professor Jang."

Simone gestured for them to follow. "Then this will interest you both. My father's work might finally explain how all of this connects."

She led them to a quiet alcove lined with books. Behind the shelves, a hidden steel door gleamed. Simone pressed her palm against a biometric pad, and the lock released with a low hiss.

"Meet Amanda 2," she said. "A machine that reads DNA traces. My father built it to protect us. I didn't have it in Paris when I met you and the Pope—but when I got home today, and ran my clothes through A2, the results were staggering."

She turned to Xavier. "Your DNA showed descent from Yosef of Arimathea. Pope Lucas's sample—taken from where he brushed my sleeve—matched the line of Mary Magdalene. My father spent decades mapping the bloodlines of the Apostles and those who surrounded Yeshua during his last years—followers, accusers, executioners alike."

Xavier's expression softened. "So that's why you bagged my coat yesterday. You wanted Turbierri's DNA."

Simone nodded. "I've never seen the genetic code of our enemies. We've heard legends about the killings of the Apostles' descendants for centuries, but no one has ever profiled them. Until now."

"The results?" Rigo asked.

"They'll be ready in an hour," Simone said. "After that, I'm donating the machine to the NYPD. My lawyer's already drafting the transfer."

Rigo gave a low whistle. "That'll change how we work, Professor Harper. And maybe how history remembers this case."

"I have something to show you," Simone said. "Come—it's in another room."

She led them down a quiet corridor to a small alcove lined with books. Pressing against one of the shelves, she revealed a hidden mechanism; the case swung open to expose a steel vault door. Simone placed her palm on the biometric pad, and a soft hiss escaped as the lock released.

The air inside was cooler, almost like being inside a church. Row after row of tall steel panels stood on rolling carriages—archival shelving like those in major museums, but here, it was inside a private home.

"My father's and great-grandfather's collections," Simone said. "Gabby Henry's family archive is here too, including Eliana's writings. I've been thinking of opening it as a permanent exhibit. Something that explains the legacy of the Apostles' descendants. Let people see, study, and decide for themselves."

Xavier pulled one of the panels forward. Paintings from the Baroque world slid into view—Rembrandts, Caravaggios, even a Vermeer.

"I'm speechless," he said quietly.

Detective Rigo cleared his throat. "Speaking of discoveries—Police Scotland completed their preliminary analysis of the resin-coated cloth pulled by Tarquin, from the Crags. Seventeenth-century script. It turns out that the Crags were used for centuries as a hiding place, containing political essays, banned writings, and testimonies from the 1800s. The site's now under protection. And good news—they uncovered three lead containers. From your sketches, there could be as many as ten, possibly dating back to around 40 AD."

"Three lead containers!" Simone clasped her hands, her eyes shining. "Add that to the Gachet discovery from Tarquin's family crypt in Arles, now secured at the Vatican Museum, and the pieces are finally coming together."

Rigo smiled. "A good day's work, Dr. Harper."

"Tea or coffee while we wait for the Amanda 2 results?" she offered.

"I'd love to, but I have to run. Rain check?"

Before Xavier could reply, the printer in the next room whirred to life.

"The results are in," Simone said, hurrying back to the DNA lab. A single sheet waited in the tray, white against the machine's steel housing.

"Here it goes."

Lines of genetic notation filled the page. Simone's eyes moved across them—then stopped.

"It's the patriarchal line of Zadok," she said softly. "One of the ancient priestly families of the Sanhedrin. If Cardinal Iñaki becomes the next Pope, he might try to erase every trace of the Eliana documents."

A sharp trill broke the silence. Xavier's phone.

"I have to take this," he murmured, stepping aside. He listened, then his shoulders relaxed, a slow smile forming on his face.

"The Pope has recovered," he said. "He's speaking to reporters right now."

Rigo let out a jubilant shout, startling the still air. Simone laughed and threw her arms around them both. For one brief, shining moment, centuries of loss and secrecy dissolved—and they were simply three people, rejoicing like children in the echoing vault of history.

—————◆—————

After the festivities, Detective Rigo finally went home, and Xavier—too exhausted to pretend otherwise—borrowed one of her loose shirts, collapsed onto her bed, and fell asleep almost instantly. Two days of travel, danger, and crisis had drained him to the bone.

Simone stayed awake.

She sat at her desk, the soft hum of the penthouse quiet around her, and studied the printout of Cassius Turbierri's DNA.

The priestly Zadok sequence glowed unmistakably on the chart.

Absent from Xavier's genome.

But present in hers—glinting like a hidden thread woven through the line of Shimon Kepha.

She traced the lines with her finger, wondering at what point in history those distant currents had converged.

When faith, betrayal, and survival had entangled themselves so tightly that their stories lived on not just in parchment, but in blood.

So much remained unknown.

Would the permanent exhibit she dreamed of—her father's legacy finally brought into the light—one day reveal what became of Eliana? Of her writings? Of the ones who had lived and died to safeguard the truth?

Simone leaned back, the page trembling slightly between her fingers.

Did it even matter whose bloodline rested in their veins?

Surely what mattered more were the choices they made—the good they carried forward, the deeds they offered the world.

Legacy, she thought, was not written solely in DNA.

It was written in courage.

And tomorrow, there was still so much to protect.

Chapter 46

Eliana

The Concordia, Grain Ship of Rome—At Sea
Year 10 of Caesar Nero (AD 63)

They held each other's hands in the darkness. Elisa, her ten-year-old daughter, would tap her inner hand, a signal that she was awake. It was time to go out of the women's quarters, reach for the ladder that would take her to the roof deck.

She would find Nabil on the deck too.

"Papa," Elisa would run to him and cry.

The sea was their companion the whole night, and the three of them would wait until the sunbeams slowly appeared in the early morning, a respite from another restless night on the deck.

The burning images of Circus Maximus filled their every wakeful moment, and chased them in their dreams.

They were not allowed to be seen by the crew during the day, and they used the time to sleep. The women's and men's quarters were filled with passengers who had escaped Rome as it burned.

After her marriage in Din Eidyn, she and Nabil decided to help her father in the growing communities in Rome. They settled in Trastevere, across the Tiber River, with a view toward the Circus Maximus.

It was a bustling neighbourhood, heavy with the scent of garlic, fresh fish, olive oil, and lemons, a few steps away from the Tiber, where ships bearing Egyptian grain and spices made their way upstream.

A community where families from Judea, sailors, dockworkers, and former soldiers of the Roman Empire congregated to listen to Via Christi, the movement to live according to the teachings of Yeshua.

There across the water from the Circus Maximus, they lived in harmony with the citizens of Rome. At night, the roar of the crowds reached their windows, thousands cheering during chariot racing games and gladiatorial combats in Circus Maximus, an open-air hippodrome.

She remembered when her father, Shimon, and Nabil had begun their little gatherings, no more than a handful of neighbors at first, breaking bread and sharing wine as Yeshua had done. Word spread, and soon, soldiers, dockworkers, and the widows of centurions came as well. They were the leaders of the underground Church in this neighbourhood. People from all walks of life would visit them to share bread and wine during meals. They called their fellowship Via Lucis—the way of Light—for they believed Yeshua's words were the bright flame that would never die.

Rumors reached them that Emperor Claudius knew of the existence of the movement. Some said he was suspicious of the strange rite of bread and wine. Whatever his feelings, he left them in peace.

But peace never lasts in Rome. The winds shifted when Claudius died, and Nero, barely sixteen, took the throne.

She remembered the first time she saw his likeness on a coin, passed from a fishmonger to her own hands—the eyes too young, the mouth cruel. Soon, soldiers were patrolling the streets. One night, they dragged a neighbor for questioning. Another morning, there were crude words on the walls for everyone to see: Leave this quarter, followers of the Galilean!

Then came stranger stories—that Augusta Poppaea herself had visited Trastevere in disguise to hear her father speak about Yeshua.

And finally the fire. Neighbors said it started in the shops and storerooms underneath the stands at Circus Maximus, and by nightfall, the flames had spread from roof to roof, destroying everything in its path. From their windows, she had seen the sky turn orange-red, heard the shrill trumpets calling citizens to form chains of water to help extinguish the fire. For six days, the city burned. When the winds turned, Trastevere too caught fire.

Afterward, Rome was a city of ash. The Senate steps were a mile away from her home, across the Tiber, up through the market streets. But the shouts she heard from the protesters passing through sounded as if they were at her door.

That was when the purges happened, waves of arrest that swept through the followers of Via Lucis. Her father decided it was no longer safe. It was time for Nabil, Elisa, and her to leave Rome.

They had both been adamant about staying with her father, unwilling to abandon him. But one night, Roman legionnaires pounded on their door, demanding her husband. She had hidden with Elisa and several neighbours in another house. By the next morning, Nabil was moving from house to house, calling her name until at last they found each other again.

There was no time to say farewell to her father. Soldiers surrounded their house since dusk. Borrowing a few garments from neighbours, they left for Ostia, the port at the mouth of the Tiber. There, they boarded a merchant vessel bound for Massilia in Gaul.

"Your father is safe," Nabil had told her as they left the harbour. "They're hiding him safely. His last request was that we board the grain ship owned by Yosef of Arimathea. It will carry us out of Rome."

She heard the words but could not yet accept that she had left her father behind. In the days that followed, she slowly had to face the truth that she might never see her father again. She promised herself to honour her father's wish: to live and keep Elisa safe.

By the fifteenth day, the ship neared Tarraco, where it would rest two days before sailing on to Massilla. Dozens of ships docked there, and rumours from Rome travelled from deck to deck. She and Nabil searched the quays for anyone with news of her father. They had gone from ship to ship trying to find news from Rome.

Then Nabil clutched his chest, and fell on his knees. A sailor from another ship had told him what she feared to hear—that her father, Apostle Shimon, was dead.

Nabil recovered after a time, but he was pale when he returned to the ship. That night, as the Concordia prepared to leave for its next destination, he told her what he had learned: her father had asked to be crucified upside down on the Cross, since he was unworthy to die as Yeshua did.

Nabil tried to appear strong for her and Elisa, but his guilt and sorrow gnawed on him. His appetite vanished and his face was ashen.

"Try to eat, Nabil," she pleaded softly. "Father would want you safe and well. You know him."

"I left Apostle Shimon with the mob," he whispered.

That night, grief took him.

At dawn, she and Elisa went up to the deck, following their usual routine, needing air after another sleepless night. They found Nabil in his usual place near the railing, sitting as though in thought, but he was motionless. Eliana screamed. Elisa threw herself on her father and wailed like a lost animal.

They were now on the high seas; the captain said they could not keep the body. The captain of the ship said that tradition dictated he be buried at sea. That day, Nabil's body was wrapped in sailcloth and tightly bound in rope.

Eliana knelt beside the body.

"May Yeshua receive you with a thousand angels in heaven," she whispered. "Tell my father Shimon, I will see him again." She made the sign of the Cross.

Four sailors lifted the shrouded body to the rail. At a signal, they tipped the body forward, and with one heavy beat of silence, Nabil was gone—swallowed by the sea.

The rest of the day, she and Elisa sat on the deck, gazing out to sea. The calm waves offered a fragile comfort against the storm of sorrow that raged within them—the grief of losing both patriarchs in their family.

Eliana spoke the prayer that Yeshua had taught to her and the Apostles—

"Our father, above the heavens,

Hallowed be Your name,

Let Your kingdom rise,

Your will be done, on earth, as it is in heaven,

Give us this day our daily bread,

And pardon our failings,

As we pardon those who wrong us.

And lead us not into the trial,

But deliver us from darkness."

That day, Elisa learned the prayer by heart, and Eliana knew her husband and her father would have been pleased.

As evening drew in, one question remained. Where would she go next? Rome still burned, and Nero's vengeance against the followers of Yeshua showed no mercy. It was not safe to go back.

She longed for Judea, yet the captain warned her that the voyage would take forty-five days. He suggested instead that they continue to Din Eidyn, another fifteen days' sail. She could decide later on whether to return to Judea.

"And you have kin there," the captain reminded them. "Better to have kin, for the little one," he said, nodding toward Elisa.

She looked at her daughter and felt a small glimmer of hope. She accepted the captain's counsel. They would sail for Din Eidyn.

Chapter 47

E lisa

The Navicula

Coaster Ship from Dubris—At Sea

Year 10 of Caesar Nero (AD 63)

Day 10 of our journey to Din Eidyn. Today, we transferred to a small coaster ship called Navicula. It was the smallest of all the ships we had sailed on, for the great grain vessels could not survive the rough waters of Mare Germanicum.

Through the days of travel, my mother began to cry less and to write more. We would climb up to the narrow deck together, finding a space where we would not be in the crew's way. Two men standing shoulder to shoulder were the width of the berth, and it was kind of the captain to give passage aboard Navicula. The deck planks were wet from the ocean spray, and every space was filled with sacks of barley and wheat, amphorae of wine, and baskets of dried and salted fish.

My Emma wandered among them, lifting the lids of clay jars filled with nuts, dried figs, and olives, closing her eyes to breathe the scent.

During the first days, she could not tell whether she would retch over the rail or roll about on the resin-stained floor.

The sailors were a rowdy lot, singing songs my mother would frown upon.

I tried to imagine what my father would have done if he were still alive. I knew he would be among them—hauling ropes to raise or lower the sail, and bailing water when we encountered rough seas, securing cargo, tending to goats and animals when they were carried aboard.

At night, he would sing the psalms and tell stories about Yeshua. The crew would fall silent, listening as he brought the tales to life—his voice deep and warm.

I missed him deeply. But the thought of the sacrifice he had made to ensure that my Emma could flee the dangers of Rome. He had risked everything. The best way to honor him was not to mourn, but to live.

My Emma began to help the cook with her duties, and soon they were speaking like old neighbours. The crew was always hungry, and meals were needed all day. In a way, this was good to keep her occupied. It kept her hands busy, and by night, she was so weary that I was happy she could rest from her sorrows for a few hours.

To keep me occupied, my Emma gave me pieces of papyrus to write or draw upon. This touched my heart. Since I was a child, she had given me only wax tablets. But this time, she offered her precious papyrus leaves, which she had bought in Alexandria. She also gave me a pen made from sharpened reeds.

I thought long and hard about what I should write, and this was the best way to begin, recounting the start of our journey to Din Eidyn.

Goodnight, my sweet papyrus and reed. I shall keep you now beneath my pillow.

Chapter 48

E liana
      Din Eidyn
Twenty Years After the Roman Crossing,
With Rome Still to the South (AD 63)

Word had spread that we were nearing Din Eidyn, and by the time we arrived, the shore was ablaze with torches and bonfires.

From afar, we heard the stomping of feet, some twenty men lining the shore. Drums that sounded like thunder rolled from the mountains to the sea, while deep blasts from the trumpeting horns echoed across the water, welcoming our ship.

"*Mama, ecce quam magna salutato*—are we important guests?" Elisa asked, pushing a stray lock of hair from her eyes.

"They know Sabba Shimon and your Abba," Eliana said, smiling at the thought of what her father would have said about such a welcome. "I visited here twenty years ago, so they remember me."

Her father had told her, not too long ago, that word had reached him of Yosef of Arimathea and his wife, Lady Taranisca having passed on. She wondered who would be waiting now at the shore.

As the coaster vessel neared land, she saw two young men waving with great enthusiasm. Behind them stood women and children, their smiles gleaming in the torchlight.

"Are those Cynon and Talor?" she murmured. "My, they've become grown men!"

Their striking physical appearance stirred a memory of Lady Taranisca's Caesarian roots—her Levantine clan had once mingled with the northern folk, her sons' hair marked by the deep brownish-red color of the earth, their eyes as gray as the sea.

"Mama, *quam bella vestimenta*!—what beautiful clothes!" Elisa said, her eyes wide.

Cynon and Talor broke from the group and ran to meet them at the dock.

"*Shlama*, Dodta Eliana—welcome to Din Eidyn," they said, with a slight bow, kissing her on both cheeks. "And who is this young lass? She looks just as you did twenty years ago."

"Oh, you boys," Eliana laughed. "This is my daughter, Elisa. Tell me, are you two now married?"

Two women and two small boys in colourful woollen tunics came forward, and Elisa watched every movement with quiet curiosity.

"Here stands my wife Boudina, and our lads Artos and Maeloc," Cynon said.

"And this is Senara," Talor said, beaming. "She is my promised one. In days soon to come, she will be my woman, and it gladdens me that you'll share the day with us."

"Looks like we just arrived on time for a big feast," Elisa said, and laughter rippled through the crowd, mingling with the sea wind and the crackling of the fires.

"You have a beautiful family, Cynon. And a lovely bride-to-be, Talor. Your father, Yosef and mother, Lady Taranisca, are smiling in heaven, seeing you live with such joy," she said.

"We have a surprise for you, Dodta Eliana," the two men replied with wide grins.

The drums and trumpets followed them as they climbed the hill toward the home of the patriarch, Yosef of Arimathea. Yet Cynon and Talor led her and Elisa farther inland, to a separate dwelling—a roundhouse with a conical thatch roof woven from reeds and straw.

Inside, much like the old home of Yosef, a central hearth burned bright. The floor was laid with stones, plentiful in Din Eidyn, and the walls were plastered with mud and straw, warm from the fire's glow.

"Dod Shimon and Dod Nabil never treated us as bothersome little ones when you all visited twenty winters ago," Cynon said. "We love them dearly."

"We heard from the captains of the ships that carried you. You are part of our kin now," Talor said.

"You are our family. Do not worry about a thing," Boudina said, smiling as her two boys began to run in circles with Elisa, their laughter filling the roundhouse.

"The meal is ready in our home," Cynon said. "The villagers have prepared it for many days. Come, the table waits for you, with food and fire," Cynon said.

Eliana paused and took a deep breath. She and Elisa were finally safe from the terrors of the past few weeks. In this haven, she prayed, there would be no more visions of Rome burning in flames, no more cries from Circus Maximus haunting her nights.

Then the tears came—a deep, wailing cry that she could not express in the past weeks.

"Mama, *ne plora*—don't cry," Elisa whispered, holding her hand.

"Thank you, Cynon, Talor, and Boudina," Eliana said softly. "I will be forever grateful. And now I am ready for the feast you have prepared with great care."

————⬥————

The next day, they rose early. A servant knocked softly on their door and brought breakfast—ale to drink with bread and cheeses, porridge sweetened with honey, and smoked fish to complete the meal.

After an hour, Cynon and Boudina came by and offered to walk her around the property. They brought along Artos and Maeloc, which pleased Elisa; though older, she was still a child, and could run freely with the two boys while the adults discussed serious matters.

The estate of Yosef of Arimathea had grown since she last saw it. There were more houses now, and watchmen stood guard along the outer borders of the land.

"Father always reckoned he'd stay in Din Eidyn only a few years," Cynon said. "He wished to rest from the strife he knew in Judea. It began with one house, but much has changed since then—we plough the field for grain, and we've built a granary to feed us all."

"Yes, it's beautiful," Eliana replied. "It was good that Dod Yosef stayed here. You know what happened to my father..." Her voice fell to a whisper.

"It grieves us deeply, the loss of your husband, and of your father," Cynon said, his tone heavy with sorrow.

They walked in silence until the path opened toward the crags, glowing under the pale early morning light.

"I miss my Abba every day," Cynon said quietly.

"I feel the same way, Cynon. Sometimes sorrow hits me in the most unexpected way," Eliana said softly. "My, it hasn't changed at all," she said, gazing at the cliffs. "Every bit as magnificent now as it was twenty years ago."

At the far edge of the property, they came upon a small hut, standing apart from the cluster of houses near the main hall. Cynon pointed toward it.

"Do you remember the prisoner the chieftains caught during your visit?" he asked.

"You mean, Nicanor?" she said, puzzled at first. "I thought Dod Yosef was going to imprison him."

"There are no prisons here, not as in Judea or Rome," Cynon replied, a trace of amusement in his voice. "Dod Nicanor was shut in that hut for a time, but when the day came for his execution, my father begged that his life be spared. He gave silver, cattle and grain to the chieftains in exchange. And since Dod Yudah, the injured man, had died in Judea, they heeded my father's words. Nicanor lived here in peace. He and my Abba became friends. In a way, my father's longing for Judea was eased by his presence."

"*Esrīn shnīn*—twenty years," she murmured. " Nicanor has been here all this time."

Boudina spoke softly. "Since Abba passed, Dod Nicanor's strength has withered. He hardly eats. And he speaks to no one."

"Like a filthy dog," said Artos, who had been listening. Before anyone could scold him, he ran off toward the field.

Cynon gave a weary smile. "Aye, wisdom from the bairn's mouth, is it?"

"May I see him?" Eliana asked. "In Rome, I worked for the sick and the imprisoned. Let me try."

"I'll bring Boudina and the lads home. Elisa can stay with them," Cynon said. "We two shall go together."

After bringing Boudina and the children back to the main house, they found Talor finishing his breakfast, and he joined them.

The three walked in silence toward the hut. Smoke rose faintly from the hearth, but the bowl beside it lay untouched.

"Dod Nicanor," Cynon called softly. "Cynon and Talor here. We've brought a visitor from Judea."

They stepped inside. The hut was dim, lit only by the fire at its center.

A figure sat hunched in the shadows. Eliana gasped. It was a man caked in grime, his hair long and matted. He did not answer Cynon's greeting.

"Nicanor, *ana hu, Eliana* – it is me, Eliana," she said softly.

There was no movement, no sound in reply.

"No need to say anything now, Nicanor," she murmured. "But I will come back."

She touched Cynon's and Talor's arms – a quiet sign that it was time to leave.

"I'll return tomorrow," she said, as they stepped outside. "May I request two helpers? We'll give him a bath and cut his hair, if that is alright with you."

Cynon nodded. "It shall be done."

The next day, Cynon accompanied her again, bringing two women servants. At the hut, a wooden tub awaited them, filled halfway with water carried from the well. Eliana took a cauldron and ladled water from the tub, setting it upon the hearth until it began to boil.

The hiss of water and iron drew Nicanor's attention. Slowly, he turned toward them, his eyes dulled but alive with faint curiosity.

"Nicanor min Qaryot," she addressed him in a formal tone, the way a healer might summon back a soul. "*Ana asya* – I am a physician. You must wash with water and oil. I will help bathe you. We do not need to remove your garments yet. Take my hand, and we will walk to the tub together. Rest when you wish before stepping inside."

Cynon, astonished, said, "I did not know you were a physician, Dodta Eliana. It will be a blessing to have one among us."

"I studied in Rome," she replied. "I worked with Dod Shimon and Dod Nabil tending the sick."

With care, the two servants guided Nicanor toward the tub and helped him into the warm water. They removed his clothes and began to brush his skin until the grime lifted away.

She reached into her satchel and drew out a small bar of hard wax. The servants gasped as she dipped it into the water and rubbed it into Nicanor's hair. The hut was filled with fragrance. She added more water, pressing the wax again until white bubbles rose and shimmered in the firelight.

"What is that?" Cynon asked in wonder. "We have something like this, but this scent seems to come from the heavens."

"I learned how to make this from Dodta Hannah-min-Kerioth in Petra," she said. "She added herbs and oils for healing. I can teach the women how to prepare it."

The two servants raised Nicanor's arms and helped him stand. They wrapped his body in soft wool to dry. Eliana bent to lift his knee gently while another servant steadied him, then she flexed his leg outward so he would know how to move the other in turn.

When he was steady, they seated him on a three-legged stool in front of the hearth.

"Nicanor min Qaryot," she called again in a formal tone. "*Ana asya* – I am a physician. You must cut your hair."

She drew out a pair of scissors and a comb to begin trimming his long, matted locks. She paused for a moment, aware that in many lands, touching another's hair was forbidden except for barbers or healers. She glanced at those around her, but the Din Eidyn folk watched silently, without objection. She cut six inches from his hair, and, instead of discarding it, wrapped the strands in a small linen cloth.

"You have everything prepared for this visit, Dodta Eliana," Cynon said with approval.

"I have done this often for soldiers returning from war," she replied. "Their wounds of the flesh were not the hardest to heal. It was what died inside them—the things they could not speak of."

When Nicanor's hair and body were dry, she took a vial of light oil and poured a few drops onto her palms, rubbing them together to warm it.

"Is that frankincense and myrrh? From Judea?" Cynon asked, his voice filled with wonder.

"Yes, I brought many oils for healing." She opened her satchel, revealing bottles filled with liquids of different hues. The familiar scents of home, the resins and oils, calmed her spirit during this difficult time.

As she rubbed the oil into his neck and shoulders, his body suddenly sagged forward. Everyone rushed forward to steady him, fearing he had fainted.

But Nicanor had not lost consciousness. He was sobbing.

They propped Nicanor back on the stool, and she continued massaging his neck and shoulders until he fell asleep.

"I think that's a good start," she said. "I can now help with Elisa cooking our mid-day meal."

"Dodta Eliana, you are our treasured guest. This is enough," said Cynon, nodding toward Nicanor, who slept soundly.

"*La milta, la milta* – oh nonsense," she said. And from that day forward, the mid-day meal became her and Elisa's task.

They cooked laganum, strips of barley dough boiled with shredded beef and wild thyme – a simple dish they often made in Trastevere. In the following days, she taught the women how to make simple Roman flour dumplings with fillings, lentil dishes, handmade sausages from sheep casings, and roasted meats.

Nicanor's health improved visibly. With the help of two servants, he found the strength to walk a few steps, and when she asked for a cane, Cynon brought his father's. She placed it in Nicanor's hands, and he used it to steady himself along the rocky paths.

For a month, she kept a routine with him, bathing him weekly, trimming his hair as needed, and healing massages every other day. Yet, he had not spoken a word to her or to the helpers.

She began singing songs she had known since childhood, hoping to awaken a memory, but he remained silent.

Then she thought of the wedding in Cana—when Yeshua's cousin Hananiah wed Mara of Kfar Nahum. What songs had they sung on the road to Cana?

She began to sing the Psalms, and for the first time she saw a smile on Nicanor's face.

"Behold, how good and pleasant it is when beloved brothers live in unity!" she sang.

"How great, how beautiful!" Nicanor answered.

"Together, in unity!" she sang back.

It was as if the song opened a door within him, and from that moment, Nicanor began to listen to her.

She held his hand as they both walked, and he turned to her.

"Biti Eliana, is it really you? I thought I heard your voice from a dream," he said.

"Yes, it's me, Nicanor," she replied.

"But how?" he asked, his words faltering.

"It doesn't matter," she said softly. "I'm here. Take your time—we're in no hurry."

She did not want to rush his healing, afraid that he was going to return to the condition she found him in on her first day in Din Eidyn.

The next day, Nicanor could not rise from bed. The servants said that he wept through the night. She sent for Cynon and Talor, and both came, calm and understanding.

"Each year, my father falls into his sorrow," Cynon said quietly. "He calls it—*libbēḥ mitqar' gowaeḥ*—as if his heart was torn inside him. Remembering what Yeshua endured in Judea, there were days my Da could not stand."

It was as if Nicanor's mind had wandered away again, and she resumed massaging his hands and arms.

"Biti Eliana, I can't go on living," he said at last. "I can't forget what I did to Yeshua, and to Yudah." He wept again, and she paused, feeling the weight of the torment he had carried for thirty years.

"I forgive you, Nicanor," she said gently. "Yeshua and Yudah would forgive you too."

The reality of the loss of her husband and father has not yet settled fully within her. But she knew this truth: it had never been one man alone who killed Yeshua in Yurishalayim or her father in Rome. Empires, rulers, and followers alike bore that burden.

Hearing her words stilled his cries. Forgiveness spoken aloud began his healing. Yet the more arduous journey—the forgiveness of himself—would take longer.

"Do you think there's still time to ask forgiveness from those I have hurt?" he asked. "I'd like to see them again, wherever they are... to return to Judea."

"Let's make you physically strong first," she said. "We can think about that in the days ahead."

"I've always loved you, Biti Eliana. But you never believed me," he said through tears.

"I know now," she answered, turning toward him. She took his hands and drew him into an embrace.

There were no words that she could say that would ease his pain for now. But she would help him heal. And when his strength returned, she would help him seek those he had wronged and ask their forgiveness, face to face. It was never too late.

Chapter 49

E lisa
Din Eidyn
The Last Year Before
Rome Turned North (AD 76)

When did I realize that my Emma Eliana was falling in love with Dod Nicanor?

When Dod Nicanor began to heal, they would take their daily walks along the Crags, and my mother would smile and laugh at whatever he said. He had been her childhood friend, and they had shared many extraordinary moments together when Yeshua was still among them.

I had never seen her smile or laugh this way before, and my heart softened toward Dod Nicanor. My Emma had always been formal with my Abba—tender and loving in private, protective of his well-being, and a steady anchor as he served my Sabba Shimon as his trusted *Bar Yemini*, his right hand.

We lived in peace in Din Eidyn for five years. Then, like lightning from a clear sky, Apostle Thaddeus appeared on our shore. He always seemed to arrive precisely when my Emma needed him most.

Apostle Thaddeus was tall and walked like a lion at rest—calm, yet his strength showed in every word and action. He reminded me of my Sabba Shimon, and of my Abba Nabil. He had travelled far, visiting communities that believed in Yeshua, reaching even the farthest corners of the world.

He embraced Dod Nicanor like a lost son, and spent much time talking with him—often without my Emma. Through those conversations, it became clear what Dod Nicanor wanted to do: to aid the Apostle in his ministry, and to ask once more for my Emma's hand in marriage.

Yosef of Arimathea was gone, and now, as the elder of the family, Apostle Thaddeus gave his blessing to the union. He had been present the first time Dod Nicanor sought her hand, when she was only twelve. It had taken thirty years for their lives to circle back to one another.

There was a simple, quiet celebration for this union, a meal my Emma wanted to share only with our closest kin. Of course, the household would not agree to such modesty and laid out a feast for the happy occasion, though this time without the other tribal chiefs from neighboring villages.

Apostle Thaddeus presided over the festivities, and in the end, he broke the bread and raised the wine in memory of Yeshua.

There's a saying in Din Eidyn: When the clouds break, they empty their bellies. After the turmoil of Rome, the long journey north, and the slow healing of Dod Nicanor, joy came to us like the storm.

By this time, preparations for my own wedding were underway. Cadwallon, son of the chieftain of Castle Rock, had asked for my hand, and the celebrations were to be held there, my new home among the Voltadiri clan. Apostle Thaddeus, my Emma, Dod Nicanor, and the entire Yosef of Arimathea family were present, and the festivities lasted three days.

When it was time to part, my Emma and Dod Nicanor prepared to return to Judea and see Maryam of Nasrath with Apostle Thaddeus. Along the way, they would visit Dod Ya'qub in Hispania, Dodta Mary of Magdala, and Dod David in Gaul. All had felt the wound of Sabba Shimon's death, but his brother Dod Andraos had been the most stricken, and my Emma wished to see him in Macedonia.

It was Dod Thaddeus who suggested that Nicanor take a new name—Timotheos—to mark his new life. From that day, Dod Nicanor's path changed. Timotheos became known among the early faithful as one of the fiercest leaders for Yeshua's name, preaching and writing across distant lands.

Was it my Emma's fate to be surrounded by those who shaped the very ground we walked upon—Yeshua, Shimon, Thaddeus, Nabil, and Timotheos? She would always say—*Marya sevyaneh*—This is what the Lord desired.

And so it is.

Now, I prepare for a thirty-day journey to Massilia, bringing my children Lili and Anna, now 12 and 10 years old, to meet my Emma and Dod Nicanor at last.

Word has reached me that I have a little sister, Mara, who is five years old! They have made their home in Massilia in Gaul, where a growing community of believers gather. Rome is still unsafe. many who believed in Yeshua were being hunted down, and Judea was a chaotic place since the Temple was destroyed in 70 AD.

There's a saying in Din Eidyn—Drink the mead while it is sweet, for winter comes soon enough.

I will take these sweet, cherished moments and visit my family. And if the hearth burns alive because of love, then let the harsh, winter moments stay forever at the door.

Chapter 50

Simone

Harper Art Institute, New York City

Saturday, April 23—6:00 p.m.(Six months later)

The air outside the Harper Art Institute pulsed with anticipation. Xavier, Tarquin, Gabby, and Simone stood by the entrance, awaiting the arrival of Pope Lucas. Thousands had gathered along the barricaded streets of Lower Manhattan, now closed to traffic. Reporters jostled behind the press lines, cameras fixed on the Institute's arched entrance, transmitting live to millions.

Above them, the low thrum of helicopters mingled with the rhythmic clop of NYPD horses. The atmosphere crackled—half electric, half reverent—the unmistakable charge of a Papal visit.

"Even a private visit by the Pope draws half the city," Simone murmured, exhaling.

Xavier touched her hand lightly. "He's the reason all this exists. Let's grin and bear it."

"I love it," Tarquin quipped. "All that publicity. I'd trade places with him for a day."

Gabby smirked. "You're joking, right?"

"Mostly," Tarquin winked, earning a laugh from the group.

Moments later, the Popemobile drew to a stop. Pope Lucas emerged to a roar of "Viva, Pope Lucas!" The crowd erupted in applause, cameras from devices rising like a forest of tiny lights. Six Swiss Guards and members of the Vatican Gendarmerie formed a tight ring around him, their Glock sidearms discreet but visible. A second ring of eight Secret Service agents from the Presidential Protective Detail shadowed them, faces impassive and alert.

Xavier tapped one of the aides. *"Ci penso io a Papa Luca. D'accordo—I'll take care of Pope Lucas, all right?"*

The aide nodded immediately, recognizing him.

"How are you holding up, Tarquin?" the Pope greeted warmly. "Quite the ordeal with the Edinburgh police, I hear."

"Innocent and free, thanks to your intervention," Tarquin said with a grin.

"Have they caught the thief?"

"Not yet," Simone replied. "There are suspects, but no arrests. The police suspect an inside job."

The Pope paused, gazing up at the massive banner unfurled across the Institute façade:

"The Hidden Gospel of Eliana: From Discovery to Revelation."

He read the smaller print aloud. "The modern journey of five descendants of the Apostles in search of the lost Gospel of Eliana."

Pope Lucas smiled. "What a journey it's been."

"Goodbye, anonymity," Tarquin murmured.

The Pope chuckled and crooked a finger at him. "You're far too handsome for anonymity," he teased, patting Tarquin's cheek.

Gabby shivered slightly. "Every time I see that banner, I still get chills."

"You've curated it for six months," Tarquin teased. "No butterflies left, surely."

"Some," she admitted. "Simone's kept parts of it secret—even from me."

"Come," Simone said, smiling at the Pope. "The exhibit officially opens with your visit tonight. It opens to the public tomorrow. We've even invited a lucky class from St. Luke's High School—your namesake."

Inside, the lobby opened to a soaring Great Hall—an 80-foot ceiling supported by steel and timber, giving the space the feel of a grand European market hall. The building's past as a neighborhood butcher shop inspired its industrial motif, with steel beams and wooden panels evoking knives and cutting blocks. At the center, a circular information desk served as a hub leading to the various galleries.

"I love this," Pope Lucas said, looking up. "Industrial, yet warm—like Trajan's market halls in Rome. My mother took me there as a boy."

Xavier led him through the first archway.

"The Maryam of Magdala Gallery," the Pope read, his voice soft with awe.

The gallery walls were lined with masterpieces—Da Vinci's study, a Van Gogh sketch—all from the Pope's own ancestral collection. Nearby, the writings of Eliana, once hidden behind secret panels, were now displayed in full view. A digital screen allowed visitors to toggle translations of the ancient papyri.

"Amazing," the Pope said. "I could spend a whole day here just reading her words."

Projected on a nearby wall were magnified images of the Mona Lisa, focusing on the faint letters and numbers hidden in the left eye.

"All secrets surface eventually," the Pope murmured. "A lesson worth remembering."

They continued to the next gallery—The Shimon Kepha Gallery.

"My God," the Pope breathed, "a treasure trove of Medieval and Renaissance paintings rivaling the Vatican."

"All from a penniless Swedish immigrant named Harper," Tarquin said. "Hard to believe your ancestor owned all this, Simone."

She laughed. "One of my staffers is researching the Harper saga. It's stranger than fiction."

"You can circle back here later. But I'd suggest we move to the next gallery," she said, leading them into the Yudah Kerioth Gallery. "Some of these pieces, Your Holiness, you've already seen in the Vatican."

The exhibit room darkened, simulating the Gachet family crypt where Tarquin had first found the metal box containing Eliana's writings. A hush fell over the visitors as dim light revealed the stone textures of the replica tomb. Beneath the simulated grave was a digital keypad where guests could attempt to unlock the hidden writings.

"How many tries does one get?" the Pope asked, his eyes twinkling.

"Three," Simone replied with a laugh.

Pope Lucas leaned forward, typing in two combinations—both incorrect. "Ah, stubborn thing," he muttered. Then, after a pause: "How about... Van Gogh's birthday?"

A chime sounded, and the vault panel slid open. "Bingo!" he exclaimed, clapping his hands together like a delighted child.

The facsimile of the papyrus documents emerged, softly illuminated under glass.

"Oh, you're brilliant, Pope Lucas," Gabby said, shaking her head.

Tarquin crossed his arms. "Maybe this will finally lift the stigma around Judas."

"The Catholic Church doesn't recognize these writings," Pope Lucas said gently. "Yet I cannot deny Eliana's hand in them. Remember—Maryam of Magdala was called a prostitute by Pope Gregory. And in 2016, Pope Francis restored her name, referring to her as the Apostle to the Apostles. Belief evolves. Slowly, painfully—but it does."

"In this case," Xavier said, "Eliana speaks of the thirteenth Apostle—an idea that didn't sit well two millennia ago."

"Nor does it now, if you ask most people," Tarquin said. "But who knows what they'll think in another thousand years?"

Gabby clapped her hands lightly. "Enough theology for now! I've been dying to see the Crag findings. Simone wouldn't even let me peek."

Simone smiled, her eyes glinting. "You'll see why."

The lights dimmed again as they entered the Yosef of Arimathea Gallery.

It was the largest hall in the exhibition. Three walls bore a panoramic projection of Salisbury Crags—immense, breathtaking, almost alive. The stone face changed colors with the passing hours, following the real-time light of Edinburgh. Visitors could approach and touch the walls, where faint fissures pulsed with subtle illumination.

"Tap the cracks," Simone instructed. "Find the one that hides the cloth."

A group of students from St. Luke's High School eagerly obeyed, giggling and squealing as they tapped random spots. When someone found the correct fissure, the wall panel clicked—and a replica of the lead box sprang out, accompanied by a faint metallic echo.

"I'd love to visit Salisbury Crags myself one day," Pope Lucas said, gazing at the projection. His voice softened. "You must congratulate the team that extracted those writings."

"They'll be here tomorrow," Simone said proudly. "All fifteen of them—flown in from Edinburgh as our guests."

"Splendid," the Pope said. "Now—how many boxes were found in total?"

"Twenty-one," Xavier answered.

The Pope pointed to a nearby display — a smaller resin-coated cloth molded in the shape of a small box. "And this one? Elisa? Her writings were found in the Crags?"

"Yes," Simone nodded. "Eliana's daughter."

Pope Lucas exhaled. "So many secrets kept for two thousand years... and now they emerge. It will take decades of scholarship to grasp their meaning for the modern Church."

Xavier led him toward the adjoining room. "You might like this next section—the stolen gospels recovered from Cassius Turbierri's collection. Returned by their rightful owners, who've kindly lent them for the exhibition."

Detective Rigo stood inside the gallery, quietly observing the display.

"Detective Rigo," Simone called out, beckoning him closer. "Your Holiness, this is the man who led the investigation into the theft of your Da Vinci and Van Gogh studies—and pursued Cassius Turbierri, head of the secretive Obscurati."

The Pope smiled wryly. "Ah, Cassius. I heard he quite literally locked himself to his own cell."

They shared a chuckle.

"Some of the stolen gospels were thousands of years old," Rigo said. "Many belonged to the descendants of the Apostles who were hunted down during the persecutions. The Turbierris had even kept writings of Eliana—ones suggesting that the Sanhedrin, not Judas, orchestrated the betrayal."

The Pope turned slowly, taking in the gallery. Fifty gospels gleamed under soft light, arranged in three rows—The Gospel of Nicodemus. The Gospel of Thaddeus. The Gospel of Simon the Zealot. The Gospel of Yosef of Arimathea. Visitors stood silently, reading each inscription as if before relics.

"The Gospel of Nicodemus—that one's new to me," the Pope murmured.

"As are Thaddeus, Simon the Zealot, and Yosef of Arimathea," Xavier added.

Gabby's eyes shimmered. "Imagine if more are still hidden somewhere. The scholars will go mad with joy."

From the next room came the sound of youthful laughter—shouts, then a sudden squeal of surprise.

Pope Lucas turned sharply. "What's happening?"

The final gallery was unlike any other.

There were no paintings, no manuscripts—only a single object standing in the center like an altar of light.

It was a sleek, metallic structure marked AMANDA II—a machine designed to read a person's DNA and trace their genetic lineage back to the Apostolic era.

"Ohhh, I can't wait to see if my genealogy got mixed with another Apostle," Gabby said, eyes gleaming. "There must have been intermarriages we never knew about."

Beside the Amanda II was an enormous wall projection showing portraits of the central figures in the life of Jesus. As each visitor placed a hand on the scanner, faint threads of light rippled across the display, connecting names and bloodlines—Simon Peter, Maryam of Magdala, Nicanor, Thaddeus, Eliana.

The Amanda II was Simone's idea. If people knew which lineage flowed in their veins, would it shape the choices they made tomorrow? Would it burden or liberate them?

She had traced her own results weeks ago.

The bloodline of Shimon Kepha—and Nicanor.

It had startled her at first, the convergence of two streams that were once thought to be separate. But she would never hide it. Truth, however ancient, had to be faced—not feared.

———◆———

When Pope Lucas had departed and the Institute finally closed for the night, the group gathered at a pop-up bistro near the entrance—a tongue-in-cheek eatery called Blood Sausage, created specially for the opening.

Xavier and Tarquin had loosened their jackets; Simone and Gabby had slipped off their shoes, the marble floor cool beneath their feet.

"Hey, Tarquin," Xavier said, pointing at the food stall. "New restaurant?"

Tarquin grinned. "Inspired by my Edinburgh prison meals. I call it haute incarceration." He winked. "Kidding—the pubs were great. I just borrowed a few ideas and refined them. And honestly, I owe Pope Lucas, Cardinal Mathew, and you, Xavier. Without your intervention, I'd still be dining in a cell."

"After he regained consciousness, the Pope was deeply worried," Xavier said. "He followed your case every day. He's pleased with the exhibit, too. I think he's considering retirement—like Benedict. He wants to devote his remaining years to finding the rest of Eliana's writings."

Gabby leaned in, curious. "Then we'll start with his family's homes. You just know there's more tucked away in his archives."

"I'll remind him," Xavier said with a grin. Then he turned to Simone and brushed a strand of hair from her cheek. "*Un pensiero per me?*—a thought for me?"

Gabby smiled knowingly. "You're awfully quiet, Simone."

"I'm just relieved the Secret Service are gone," she said. "We can finally breathe."

She hesitated, then smiled faintly. "Actually... there's something I want to show you."

Gabby's eyes widened. "What? Did you two break up already?"

"We're *smielato*," Xavier teased, laughing. "Lovey-dovey to the point of nausea."

"Oh God, I'm about to vomit," Tarquin said dramatically. "Haven't heard lovey-dovey since middle school."

"Then follow me," Simone said, standing.

They crossed the dimly lit hallway and re-entered the Gospel of Eliana exhibit, entering a smaller, private gallery.

"Before I show you," Simone began, "I've always wondered why my father had only one page of Eliana's writings hidden behind a Warhol painting we've owned since the 1970s, the one marked with three teardrops and the letter N equivalent—

⁓

Maybe Eliana meant to give it just to Nicanor. The page contained just one word—'Arise'.

"So I consulted Natalie, our archival expert. She manages all our documentation. I asked if she'd ever come across anything kept in the Institute—letters, artworks, objects—connected to that word."

Gabby's hands pressed together in anticipation. "And?"

"She found a photograph of my parents with Andy Warhol and Jean-Michel Basquiat. Both artists had written 'Arise' on the back—a wink, a code perhaps. My father must have known something—but never told me."

Xavier's expression deepened. "The shooting at the Whitney... the Last Supper exhibit. You think Cassius Turbierri orchestrated that as a message?"

"Exactly," Simone said. "Warhol created more than a hundred Last Supper pieces. What if Arise was a cipher pointing to specific ones?"

"Each letter could correspond to a Last Supper version," Tarquin said, eyes widening. "A for the first, R for the eighteenth, I for the ninth..."

Gabby caught on. "S for the nineteenth, E for the fifth. Five works—A-R-I-S-E."

"Precisely." Simone pushed the door open.

The others gasped as they entered.

Five Last Supper works by Andy Warhol filled the space, each one unique—from small silkscreens to vast multi-panel compositions. Some echoed Da Vinci's solemn geometry; others were irreverent parodies—Christ flanked by detergent logos and potato chip brands, sacred imagery colliding with consumer culture.

"Oh my God," Gabby whispered, hands to her mouth. "I've never seen this selection—not all together."

The faint light shimmered over the paintings, the colors muted yet alive—a final dialogue between art, faith, and time itself.

Simone stood before them quietly.

Arise.

The word pulsed in her mind—not as a command, but as an invitation.

Across from the ARISE display stood a darker, more provocative installation:

"Ten Punching Bags (Last Supper)," a collaboration between Andy Warhol and Jean-Michel Basquiat—ten white punching bags suspended from the ceiling, each printed with the face of Christ and stamped with the word JUDGE.

"It was meant to be exhibited in Milan, directly opposite Da Vinci's Last Supper," Xavier explained. "But the Church found the imagery offensive—too irreverent, too physical. The parishioners protested, and the show was pulled in 1985."

"Even now it would stir outrage," Gabby said softly. "Now I understand why you didn't let Pope Lucas see this room."

"He's aware," Simone replied. "I'll brief him later. He can handle the truth."

Tarquin stepped closer to one of the punching bags, brushing it lightly so that it swayed. "Christ was judged in a sham trial and crucified. Yet in the end, He returns as the Judge. The irony is divine."

Gabby laughed, her tone playful. "Tarquin, you're brilliant. I think I'm falling in love with you."

Simone squealed.

"Relax," Gabby added, kissing Tarquin on the cheek. "Like a brother, of course."

"Ooooh, to be in love," Xavier teased, pressing his hands together to form a heart.

Gabby and Tarquin exchanged amused glances.

"Alright," Simone said, reclaiming the floor. "Xavier worked hard to secure this loan. The Director of the Warhol Estate is an old friend of Pope Lucas. Warhol was a devout Catholic—he attended Mass daily, wherever he was. He even visited the Vatican before he died, and St Patrick's Cathedral held his memorial."

Gabby tilted her head. "So if Warhol somehow possessed a fragment of Eliana's writings, how would two geniuses like Warhol and Basquiat have hidden it?"

"You're changing the subject," Simone teased. "But fine—love can wait."

Simone then crossed her arms thoughtfully. "I had the artworks analysed — UV, near-infrared, multispectral, even X-ray reflectance. All we found were fabric fibres and faint water stains. No text."

Gabby frowned. "Eliana once wrote about the gift of tongues after the descent of the Holy Spirit. The Apostles were also granted prophecy. What if she foresaw Judgement Day — like John's Revelation?"

Tarquin nodded slowly. "Or maybe she encoded it. When my family—descendants of Judas—were persecuted in France, my father wrote in lemon ink. The letters appeared only when heated."

"Heat lamps!" Xavier and Gabby said in unison.

"I'll call Nic in Conservation!" Simone said in excitement.

"Basquiat's canvas is linen," Tarquin said. "It can handle moderate heat."

Within minutes, Nic arrived with two technicians—along with Natalie, the Institute's archivist, camera slung around her neck.

"Everyone," Simone said, "this is Eric Blackridge from Conservation, and you know Natalie from Archives. They'll document every step."

"Congratulations on finding Eliana's writings," Eric said to Tarquin. "Your story's inspired half the staff."

Tarquin bowed slightly, acknowledging the remark.

"Let's begin," Simone instructed. "Start with The Last Supper, Series I—the small 40-inch piece that was displayed during the Whitney shooting. Set the heat at eighty degrees. Left-hand corner first."

The articulated lamp arm hummed to life, its bulb glowing orange. They watched as the technician directed the beam toward the top of the canvas.

Nothing happened.

"Raise it to ninety-five," Simone said.

Still nothing.

"One-ten?" Xavier suggested.

"If you smell caramelized sugar, you're close," Tarquin said, grinning.

"Ms Harper," Eric said, glancing at the gauge. "May I increase to one-twenty?"

She nodded.

A faint scent of burnt sugar wafted through the room. Then, as if from the paint itself, faint brown strokes began to surface—curling, thickening, joining.

"Jesus Christ," Tarquin whispered.

Across the white background of The Last Supper, letters materialized—ancient, elegant, unmistakable.

The scroll of Eliana's signature appeared: three teardrops, the mark of Nun.

"Eliana's sign," Xavier breathed. "Given to someone whose name begins with N."

He leaned closer, reading aloud the words that glowed faintly under the lamp:

"Hezoy d' Eliana—Visions of Eliana."

"Like the Book of the Apocalypse written by John of Patmos," Tarquin murmured.

The room fell silent. Even the hum of the lamp seemed to bow to the weight of the discovery.

The letters were now visible, shimmering faintly under the heat lamp. Everyone stood motionless, drawn toward the canvas as if before a living oracle.

The text was written in Syriac Estrangela—the same flowing hand as all of Eliana's surviving works.

"The First Mirror appeared.

In the year two thousand sixty and thirteen, a beast with many eyes roamed the earth.

Its tongue of fire burned letters and numbers, every breath devouring the secrets of men, women, and children.

They worshipped this beast until the stars vanished, cities crumbled within an hour, and the sea hurled its heavenly weight upon the land.

And then there was silence—

a silence more terrifying than all the wars combined."

"Apocalyptic," Tarquin murmured.

Simone now understood why her father had kept the original papyrus and given only a copy to a Catholic writer. The truth had been too dangerous for its time.

On the far side of the gallery, a second team adjusted another lamp onto a Basquiat canvas. Within moments, faint brown letters bloomed across the linen.

"The Second Mirror.

And the number is seen as two thousand and seventy-two.

Men built their thrones of power upon towers of stone higher than mountains.

But when the Sun appeared and never left, the city of steel below melted away."

"She even wrote the year," Gabby whispered. *"Eliana was fearless."*

A gentle tap on Simone's shoulder—Xavier. His arm slipped around her waist. She leaned into him, eyes closing briefly as the weight of the words settled on her heart. Could Eliana truly have seen the end of the world?

For a moment, the chaos of discovery faded. Simone's head rested against Xavier's chest, and peace washed through her like a prayer. Then she exhaled, steadied herself, and raised her voice.

"Everyone—stop the process. That's enough for tonight."

The chatter died instantly.

"We'll transfer all works to Conservation. I'll request clearance before proceeding further. And double the security on this gallery, please."

She wanted to continue, to uncover every secret here and now, but the works were too precious. The next phase had to happen under controlled, scientific supervision.

Nic began directing the careful dismantling of the Warhol pieces. One by one, they were lifted from the walls and carried upstairs under watchful eyes.

When the room emptied, Simone sank to the floor, her gown pooling around her like spilled light. She stretched her legs and let out a long sigh.

"I'm glad you suggested the lemon ink, Tarquin," she said.

The others joined her, forming a small circle in the center of the gallery—exhausted but glowing from the discovery.

"Your ancestors survived centuries of persecution," Xavier said. "No wonder you knew how to send secret messages."

"Who could have imagined Eliana wrote so much—and hid it so well?" Gabby whispered.

"She chronicled her time," Simone said softly. "And warned of ours."

Tarquin nodded. "This find is so important. Let me help any way I can! "

Simone laughed. "Quitting your day job, Tarquin?"

He grinned. "Still with the Swiss Guards. And still keeping my cover as a chef in Nakharin. Not yet sure where I'll be in the future. My relatives are coming tomorrow to see the Yudah Kerioth Gallery. They're... proud, I think. For once."

"Speaking of resignations," Xavier said, taking her hand, "I'm working with Pope Lucas in *Custodes Luminis Antiqui*. But I'm giving up my post at the Vatican Museum."

Gabby's eyes widened. "Are you transferring to New York? No way—"

A spark of light caught Simone's hand. The diamond flashed.

"An engagement ring?" Gabby squealed. "You're impossible, Simone Harper! When were you going to tell us?"

"I'm telling you now," Simone laughed. "Looks like we'll all be close by—uncovering Eliana's legacy together."

"And close by for the wedding?" Gabby jumped up, doing a cheerleader's spin. "Can Ethan be the page boy?"

"He can be anything he wants," Simone said, still laughing.

Gabby turned mischievous. "Speaking of discoveries—Eliana's apocalyptic mirrors weren't all in the Warhols. Maybe we should check Pope Lucas's other residences. Spill it, Xavier—where are they?"

"Oh, just the usual," he teased. "Venice. Paris. A castle in Germany, perhaps."

"Perfect honeymoon itinerary," Gabby said. "After the wedding, we chase prophecies."

The laughter rose again—warm, unguarded, echoing through the gallery like music.

Simone leaned back, watching her friends beneath the soft glow of the emptied walls. For the first time in years, she felt all the weight she carried had been eased. The secrets of millennia were surfacing at last.

In her heart, she sensed the presence of another—Eliana, daughter of Simon Peter, smiling from across time.

Her struggle to preserve truth had not been in vain.

The words she hid in paint, papyrus, and faith had finally been found.

Was her purpose to warn the world? To heal it? Or simply to speak the truth before the silence returned?

Whatever the answer, Simone knew the path was open now—a road stretching through centuries, waiting to be answered.

And she was ready.

-— ▢ — THE END —▢ —

Appendixes

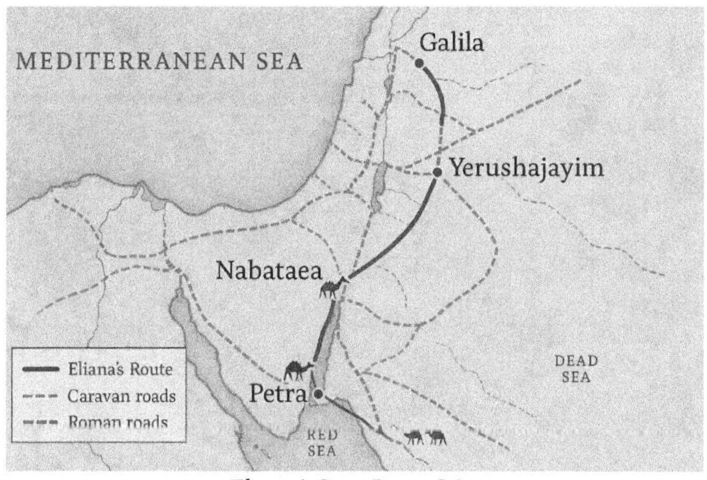

Eliana's Spice Route Map

Eliana's Sea Route Map

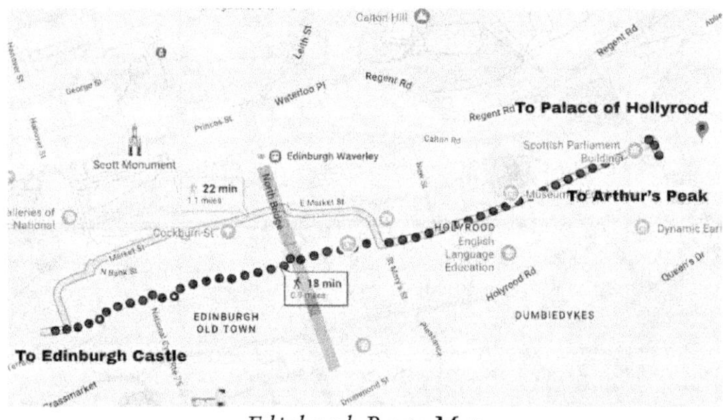

Edinburgh Route Map

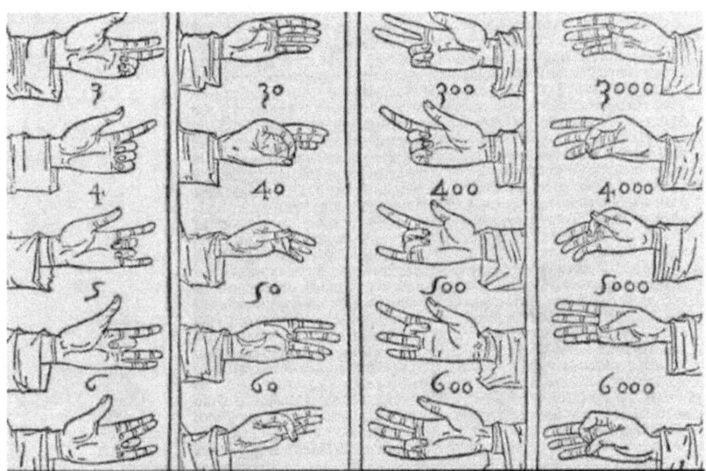

Hand gestures illustrating a Renaissance finger-counting system attributed to Luca Pacioli.

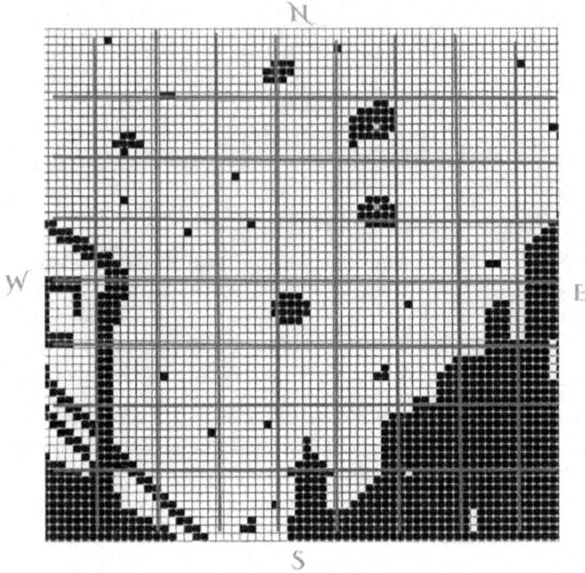

Dot-grid coordinate map based on Café Terrace at Night, Vincent van Gogh, 1888.

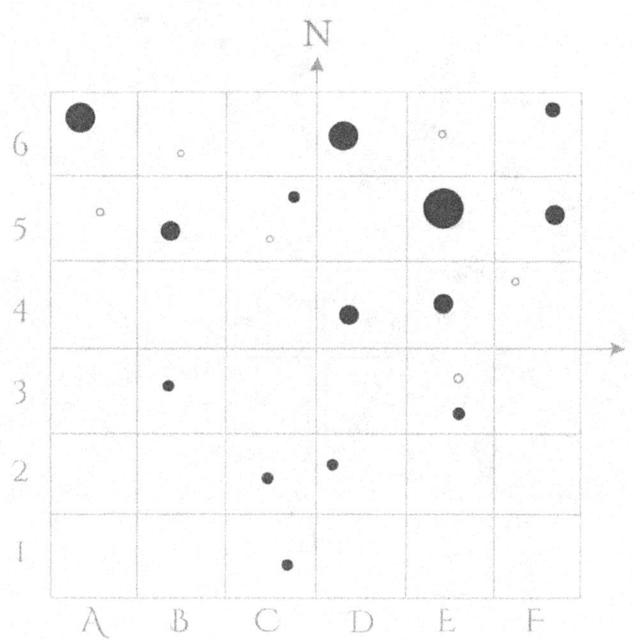

Pixel star map based on Café Terrace at Night, Vincent van Gogh, 1888.

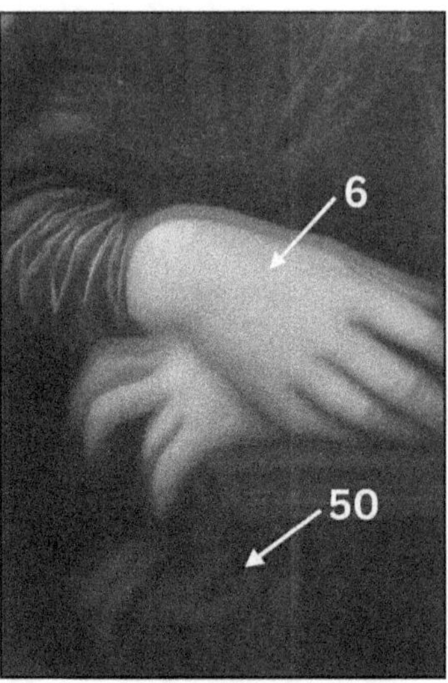

(Left) Mona Lisa,Leonardo da Vinci,c.1503-1506, Musée du Louvre, Paris. (Right) Mona Lisa study, private collection,(Pope Lucas).

(Left) Cafe Terrace at Night, Vincent Van Gogh,c. 1888, Kröller-Müller Museum Otterlo, Netherlands (Right) Cafe Terrace at Night study, private collection,(Pope Lucas).

Reading Group Guide

This Reading Group Guide for The Gospel of Eliana includes discussion questions, thematic prompts, and contemplative angles designed to enrich your book club experience.

The questions invite readers to explore the novel's unique fusion of ancient history and modern intrigue, and to reflect on how memory, faith, legacy, and truth shape identity.

We hope this guide deepens your enjoyment of the story and encourages meaningful conversation long after the final page.

This Reading Group Guide contains spoilers. Readers are advised to complete the novel before engaging with the discussion questions.

Topics and Questions for Discussion
Before Reading / First Impressions

Before reading this novel, what did you know about the Apostle Simon Peter? How does the very idea of an unknown gospel challenge or expand your perception of early Christian history?

The novel moves between ancient Judea and modern-day New York. What were your expectations for how these two worlds might connect?

Eliana's Journey (40 AD Timeline)

How does picturing Eliana as a child—curious, observant, and spiritually attuned—shape your sympathy for her adult choices? Does seeing her lineage change how you regard Simon Peter?

Eliana's voice often combines faith, trauma, and longing. What aspects of her character did you empathize with most: her obedience, her rebellion, or her yearning for truth?

The novel intersects with real historical places, including Kfar Nahum, Petra, Wadi Sirhan, and Din Eidyn. How did the geographical movement contribute to your understanding of ancient diaspora, exile, or pilgrimage?

Eliana inherits a dangerous secret. What does the novel suggest about the cost of bearing sacred knowledge?

Is truth something to reveal, to guard, or simply to survive?

Modern Timeline: Simone Harper

Simone's world is shaped by technology, museums, academic rivalries, and digital surveillance. What parallels did you notice between Simone's struggles and Eliana's?

Simone's relationships—with Xavier, Tarquin, Gabby, and the art world—are fraught with hidden motives. Which relationships did you trust most? Which unsettled you?

As the puzzle grows darker, Simone wrestles with her own identity. How does her journey redefine what it means to inherit a legacy?

Faith, History, and Interpretation

The novel complicates familiar biblical narratives through marginalized voices, particularly those of women. Did this shift alter your understanding of authority or early Christianity?

If an ancient manuscript surfaced today proving that an alternate gospel existed, how do you think governments, churches, and the public would respond? Would truth unify—or fracture?

The Custodes Luminis Antiqui and the Obscurati represent opposing approaches to truth: protection versus suppression Do you believe secrets are ever justified for the greater good?

Themes of Memory, Legacy, and Identity

The novel connects personal memory with collective history. How do memories—both private and shared—shape destiny in the story?

Eliana's and Simone's lives echo across time. What does the novel suggest about which voices history preserves—and which it erases?

Is faith portrayed primarily as certainty, struggle, inheritance, or transformation? Did the novel shift any of your own perspectives on belief?

Final Reflections

Do you believe Simone's discovery will change the world, or only those who dare to believe it? What does truth ultimately cost her?

If Eliana could speak directly to readers today, what message do you think she intended history to hear? What lingering questions or curiosities did the novel awaken in you—historical, spiritual, or personal?

Optional Enrichment Prompts for Book Clubs

The following activities may enhance group discussion:

— Listen to ancient Aramaic hymns or psalms while discussing the Judean chapters.

— Explore maps tracing Eliana's journey across the ancient world.

— Examine artworks referenced in the novel and consider how visual storytelling parallels sacred texts.

— Debate the question: Is truth a burden, a weapon, or a gift—and who decides?

Acknowledgements

I have often wondered why I write stories. There are many memories so vivid, so powerful, that I yearn to recapture them, seeking to understand the meaning they continue to hold in my life,

How does one explain seeing the splendor of sunsets along the sands of Subic and Boracay, or find words worthy of the wonder I felt as young teenager traveling by ship with my family through the islands of the Philippines, the exhilaration of weekends spent with an adventurous uncle, Nick, who drove through the Midwestern cornfields, along the rivers in the Ozarks, exploring the cities of Chicago, St. Louis, St. Paul as though each city was an archeological dig —my mother and I willing captives to his restless spirit. Then there was another uncle, Ramy, once a professional race-car driver, who barreled through the rough roads of Luzon with such breathtaking speed and precision, I felt utterly safe in the thrill of it all.

Memories also dwell in smaller, more intimate rooms: my father at the piano, playing like a concert artist, despite not being able to read a single note; my mother's chortling laughter when something truly amuses her; my husband's twinkling smile; my children's delightfully funny remarks. These moments carve indelible marks upon the heart – marks that a thousand words cannot really capture. Memories shape me, and in turn, shape how I move through the world, how I see others, and how I love.

Memories are the threads that bind the million jagged pieces of living into something that resembles a life.

And so, the journey of Eliana mirrors my own—hers set in the ancient landscapes of Judea, the vast expanse of desert, the formidable seas of the Atlantic, and the rugged frontiers of forgotten worlds. The memory of places I have travelled over the years have marked me deeply as well, and I have tried to honor them in these pages—the austere magnificence of Egypt and Petra, the lush landscape of Israel, the electric pulse of New York, the luminescence of Paris, and the mist-shrouded mystery of Edinburgh.

But more than places, it is the memories of people who have, with their presence, attention and love shaped me. Their voices, and even their absences become my compass.

To my parents, Leo and Cording
Thank you for the bloodline, the genes, and your gift of presence and laughter. I think of you often.

To my family—Bons, Bodi, Eric, Mathew, David, Lily, Nat, Anna, and Paolo

Memories of you are a constant source of delight and inspiration. Your presence in this world challenges me to become a better person and writer.

To my extended family and friends-

The memory of your love and friendship is a balm that eases life's many whirlwinds, and I thank you with all my heart - Ninang Dora, Gil, Raul, Rodney, Lorna, Arlene, Frances, Bing, Lilibeth, Ali, Dick, Kate, Rocky, Irene, Alice,Bembem, Boots, Freddie, Bobby, Miriam, Elen, Simonette, Dimples, Karl, Kaye, Kay, Karla, Mark, Pat, Rico, Chit, Mela, Chichi, Ditas, Gina, Liz, Yam, Jody, Hermeeh, Tes R., Joel, Dindin, Emma, Kleng, Monina, Felina, Abbie, Mary Anne T., Cecilia, Leah M, Therese, Anai, Cecille C, Nancy, Rachelle, Anzelle, Mel S, Mau, Bolen, Mel, Annie, Sol, Med, Gerone, Jo, Anilou, Bunny, Maridol, MaryAnne M, Maribelle, Linda, Mardie, Grace, Niña, Alex, Bamba, Veronica G., Tintin, Pinky C., Vince, Hazel, Gio, Leah E, Yoly, Cathy G, Lolet, Mario, Marie, Odie, Gloria, Ene, Rafa, Maurice, Carol and Dan.

To my daily prayer group, memories of that quiet harbor we shared and those moments when we communed with the heavens, continues to be a profound comfort, made richer by your presence. Thank you Javo, Cecile CJ, Leah, Finesse, Tonet, Susan, Titoy, Meg, Pocholo, Mae, JP, Yvette, Ruben, Gil, Ji, Chinky, Ondoy, Doris, Boyet, Mon, Cecille S, and Bryan.

To my teachers and mentors

Your wisdom is a treasure I carry into every line I write—Allison, Tosca, Hank, David, and the authors whose brilliance marked my imagination: Diana Gabaldon, George R. R. Martin, Walter Mosley, Charlaine Harris, and other writers too many to mention. To the master artists who taught me to translate vision into form : Daniel Greene, Gregg Kreutz, Fernando Sena, Molong Galicao, Dante Silverio – the memory of your voices, your wisdom given generously to other artists, echo through these pages in ways you may never fully know.

To the musicians whose work sustained me

Your words and music comforted, consoled and lifted me through the highs and lows of finishing this novel. Special thanks to Pio, David, and Ray for the songs in the first Lola Amour concert album, and to Raye, Olivia Dean, and the APO Hiking Society whose voices and artistry pulled me through midnight to dawn writing times.

To my editor, Susan Krawitz

You saw this novel in its earliest gleam, and urged me to go deeper, always deeper. You were my North Star in moments when the path blurred, when I would otherwise have been lost.

To my husband, Bons

Thank you for holding space for me in my silences, for letting me drift into other worlds while you kept our own steady. Through every late-night scribbles, you anchored home and hearth with limitless cheer, patience and profound love. This book would not have been possible without you.

And to my God,

Memories of that unconditional love, encountered in prayer, sowed the first seed of this book. Capturing those experiences on paper was near impossible, yet I attempted it, refracted through the fragile prism of Eliana's gaze.

About the Author

Born in the Philippines, and based in Singapore with her husband, Mayet weaves history, faith, and forbidden memory into stories that blur the line between what is recorded and what is forgotten. A novelist with an enduring fascination for history, lost cities, and the silenced voices of women in scripture, she combines meticulous research with a lyrical narrative style that reimagines the past with startling immediacy.

Her work explores the hidden corridors of power—religious, political, and personal—and the enduring question of who gets to write history. The Gospel of Eliana is her most ambitious novel to date: a journey across millennia, where fragments of truth survive in manuscripts, bloodlines, and those bold enough to seek them

She divides her time between Manila and Singapore where her children are based.

More from the Author

Fourteen Days

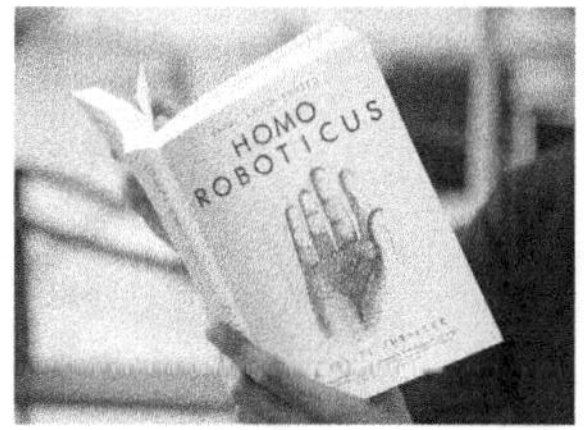

Homo Roboticus

www.mayetligadyuhico.com

www.ingramcontent.com/pod-product-compliance
Lightning Source LLC
Chambersburg PA
CBHW051001180726
48291CB00006B/1924